W9-AHA-327

Behind Every Lie

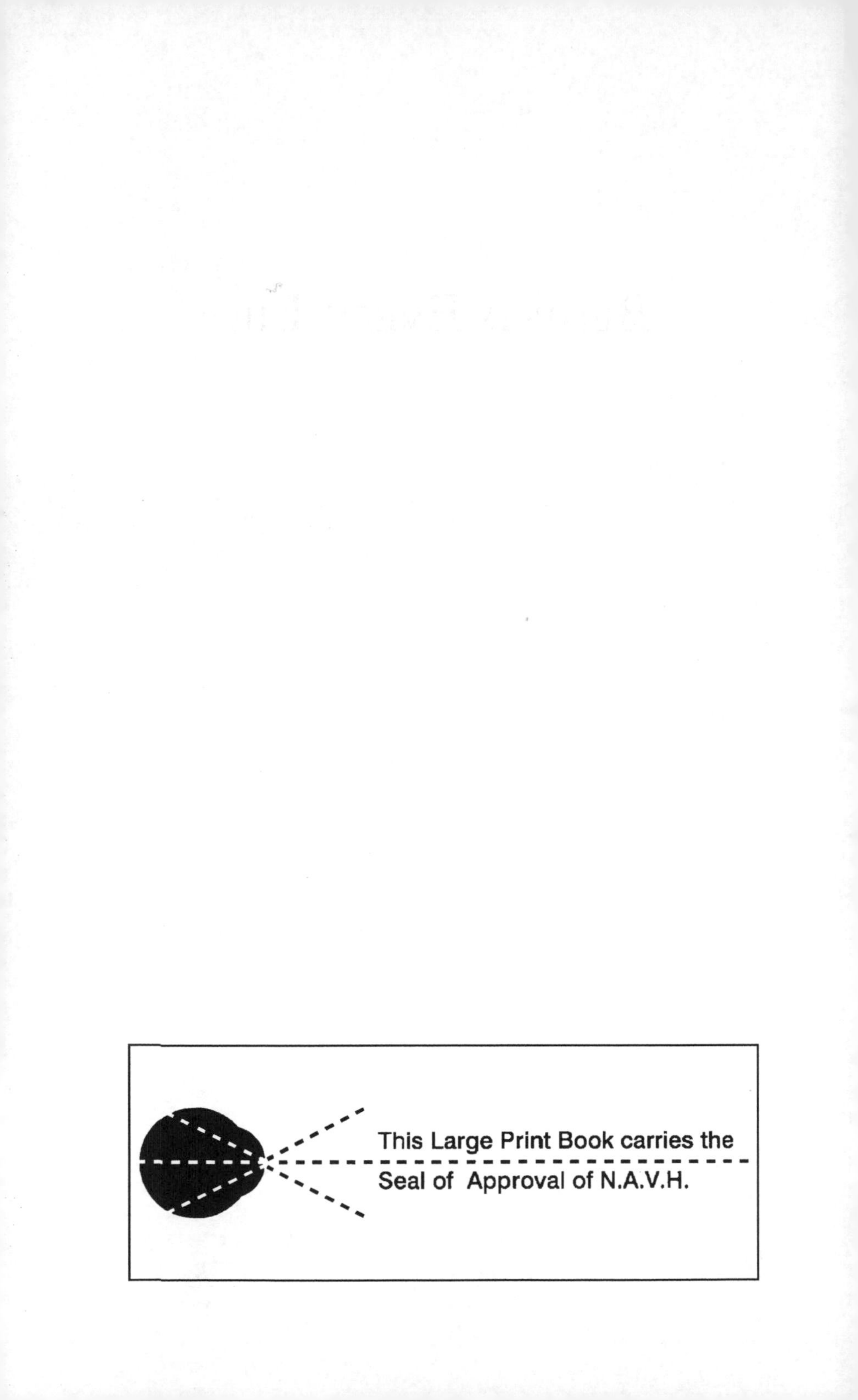
This Large Print Book carries the
Seal of Approval of N.A.V.H.

BEHIND EVERY LIE

CHRISTINA McDONALD

THORNDIKE PRESS
A part of Gale, a Cengage Company

Thorndike Press, a part of Gale, a Cengage Company

Thorndike Press® Large Print Core.
The text of this Large Print edition is unabridged.
Other aspects of the book may vary from the original edition.
Set in 16 pt. Plantin.

LIBRARY OF CONGRESS CIP DATA ON FILE.
CATALOGUING IN PUBLICATION FOR THIS BOOK
IS AVAILABLE FROM THE LIBRARY OF CONGRESS

ISBN-13: 978-1-4328-7633-3 (hardcover alk. paper)

Published in 2020 by arrangement with Gallery Books, an imprint of Simon & Schuster, Inc.

Printed in Mexico
Print Number: 01 Print Year: 2020

For Carly. For taking a chance and believing in me.

Also for Emily Doe, and every Emily Doe who's had their worth, their confidence, and their voice stolen. You are the warriors.

The world breaks everyone and afterward
many are strong at the broken places.

— Ernest Hemingway,
A Farewell to Arms

Prologue

What have I done?

The thought charged at me, stark and unrelenting. Blood was everywhere. Under my fingernails. In my mouth. In my hair. It was streaked across my shirt. On the floor, it blackened and congealed, filling the air with its metallic breath. The sickly sweet scent clung to the back of my throat.

My mother was slumped on the floor in the living room, mouth gaping, brown eyes staring at nothing. A dark pool of blood seeped from a gaping wound at the base of her neck. The urgent beat of her pulse had faded to an unrelenting nothingness.

Both my hands were clamped around her throat. An emotion thudded so viciously in my chest it was painful, like searing.

"Mom!" I tried to scream.

But only a choked sob came out.

Hail clattered against the windowpanes. The wind thrashed against the house. The living room lights flickered and darkened. Fear, salty on my tongue, shot through me like an electric pulse.

Suddenly I was outside, the night sky pressing on my skin.

The burning scent of ozone scorched the fine hairs of my nostrils, mingling with the pungent scent of wet earth. Black and purple clouds roiled in the night sky. Thunder rumbled ominously. The air crackled with electricity, static lifting the fine hairs along my bare arms. Rain skidded into my scalp, licking at my face.

Tears mingled with the rain on my cheeks as I ran. I was crying so hard I could barely breathe. I skirted the perimeter of the elementary school and pounded toward the park, passing cars parked neatly along the curb. In the distance, a metal statue, the Seattle skyline just beyond.

There was a massive *boom,* an explosion as I drew level with the statue. Then only light was all around me, inside me, crashing against my retinas, hissing along my nerves, an explosion inside my organs.

I fell to the ground spasming, crippled with pain. Fire engulfed me from the inside, every nerve ending flayed open. I was no longer in control of my brain or body. They had cracked into a million pieces.

And then there was nothing.
Blackness swallowed me whole.

ONE:
EVA

Liam parallel-parked on Langley's main street like it was the easiest thing in the world. Three movements: stop, reverse, straighten. Done. I'd never mastered the skill.

In the distance, a chilly morning wind whipped off the waters of Saratoga Passage, kicking the waves into frothy tips. The snow-capped Cascade Mountains rose in the distance. Scarlet and gold leaves licked the coastline along Whidbey Island. There were no rain clouds yet today, the promise of a crisp fall day held out like a gift.

"My hero," I teased. "I just need to get you a little black hat and you can be my chauffeur."

Liam reached into the backseat and grabbed one of the black baseball hats his builders wore. He put it on and grinned. "Your wish is my command, my lady."

He brushed his lips against mine, pulling

me tight against him so I smelled the expensive sandalwood-and-citrus cologne he wore.

"I'm only going to work." I smiled against his lips.

"I know, but I want more of you, Eva Elizabeth Hansen." His blue eyes danced as he slid his hands lower down my back.

I laughed and pulled the baseball hat off, running a hand through his hair. It was still thick and sandy blond, not a strand of gray, even though he was more than ten years older than me. "Are you working in Seattle today?"

Liam was a successful property developer with offices in Seattle and here on Whidbey Island. He spent most days in meetings, elbow-deep in profit and loss reports and zoning ordinances, or driving to and from property sites.

"No, I'm here. I have a meeting in an hour, but I'll be at our new site over in Greenbank after that. My builders got the structure up for the new strip mall so I need to take a look at it before the inspector comes by later this week."

I raised my eyebrows. "That was fast. I thought you said you didn't have the building permit yet?"

Liam shrugged. "It's just a technicality. I

know they'll approve it. Just sometimes the bureaucracy takes time to wade through." He straightened his navy tie and glanced at his watch. "Don't worry. I'll be here to pick you up after work."

"I have that dinner with my mom and brother tonight, remember?"

"I thought we were going to that Thai place you love over in Coupeville." Liam said it in that way he had: a statement, not a question.

"No, that's tomorrow." I hesitated, unsure of myself. "Right?"

Liam showed me the calendar on his phone. "It's today."

"Oh God, I'm so sorry!" I clapped a hand over my mouth. "I totally messed up! Remember I told you my mom won the Seattle Medal of Courage? Andrew organized this dinner to celebrate. . . ." I bit my lip. "Should I cancel? Maybe I should cancel."

"No, you should go. You wouldn't want to disappoint them."

"I'm sorry!"

"Why don't I go with you?" His face was expectant, hopeful.

I froze. "It'll be boring," I said carefully. "Besides, my family is weird."

He laughed. "Aren't all families weird?"

Liam knew better than most how weird

families could be. He'd grown up so poor his dad kicked him out at sixteen, telling him he needed to fend for himself. I was sure that sort of rejection would have laid me flat on my face, but it didn't seem to bother Liam. He said it had just made him strive harder to succeed.

"I'll introduce you soon. I promise." I looked at the time on my phone. "I'll see you at home later, okay?"

I loved saying that. *Home.* After dating for a year and a half, I'd finally moved into Liam's house. My princess-cut diamond ring winked in the morning light. Slowly but surely my life was coming back together. A large part of that was thanks to Liam.

I leaned across the console and kissed him good-bye. "Love you!"

"Love you most!"

I headed up Langley's main street, a charming combination of antique shops, independent bookstores, eclectic boutiques, and art galleries. Town was quiet, the tourists gone now that fall was here. I hunched in my favorite green corduroy coat, a dreamy vintage style with a belted waist and buttoned front. I shoved my hands into its wide flap pockets, my boots clicking sharply against the pavement.

My neck suddenly prickled, the feeling of

someone's eyes on me heavy and hot. Something moved in my peripheral vision. I swung around to look, but there was nobody there. The American flag above the door of the tavern at the end of the road flapped in the wind. Across the road, an elderly couple walked hand in hand along the sidewalk.

I scanned the road, the familiar feeling crawling over my body. I closed my eyes and breathed in. Nobody was there. Nobody was ever there.

I scuttled down the quiet lane to the Crafted Artisan, the art gallery where I rented space to paint and sell the clay pottery I made. Mostly dishware, pots, and vases. My favorites were the special requests from customers who stopped by the gallery with a piece in mind.

The bell over the door chimed as I entered. The gallery was small but brightly lit, with glossy white paint, black tiled floors, and varnished redwood accents. A wall of floor-to-ceiling metal shelves holding colorful ceramics lined one wall; another featured a collection of glass mosaic works.

The owner, Melissa, was standing in the middle of the gallery. She held a dark-green vase with a crackle glaze that looked like it had been broken. An intricate web of gold beads filled the cracks. Her blue-black curls were wild around her round face, dark eyes winged with black eyeliner and coated in mascara, a slash of red lipstick on her mouth.

"What's that?" I asked, slipping my coat off and stuffing it under the cash register desk.

"I met a woman on the beach in San Diego this summer and we got to talking. Turns out she's an artist. She makes the most beautiful pieces, so I offered to display her work."

I smiled. Melissa was one of those über-friendly types, like a hairdresser or one of those women in the makeup department at Macy's, someone people told their secrets to without meaning to. She liked people, and they liked her. She'd become a good friend since I'd moved to the island, even if I still couldn't bring myself to tell her the whole truth about my past.

"Look at the detail! She wrapped each broken piece in fabric, then used these beads to patchwork the pieces together. It's based on kintsugi."

"What's that?"

"It's a Japanese art. The artist fixes broken pottery by filling the cracks with gold. Usually they use epoxy to glue the pieces together. It's supposed to highlight the damage instead of hiding it."

I lifted the vase from her hands and examined it. "It's beautiful."

"Oh, by the way." She reached behind the cash register and handed me a flyer for an art exhibit in Seattle in the spring. "You got mail."

"Thanks." I glanced at the flyer and dropped it in the garbage.

Melissa shook her head, one hand on her hip. "Why do you do that? You could totally get your work shown there!"

"Melissa, these are trained artists. They've been doing it their whole lives. I only bought my kiln and wheel a few years ago. My little homemade pottery can't compete."

"What is it going to take for you to just trust in yourself a little?"

She plucked the flyer from the trash and thrust it at me so I had no choice but to take it.

But I knew the truth: I couldn't trust myself at all.

Two: Eva

The first rumble of thunder came as I turned in to the parking garage in downtown Seattle. Despite morning sunshine, clouds had rushed to fill the afternoon with rain, and it looked like we were in for a storm.

I took my ticket from the machine and slowly nosed the car into a tiny space, wincing when my bumper scraped against a metal pole. I sucked at driving. I'd already stalled the engine an embarrassing number of times driving off the ferry. This was why I always let Liam drive.

I shook my umbrella open, hard drops of rain thumping against it like handfuls of gravel. I walked up the street's steep incline, my thighs and shoulders still burning from my lunchtime yoga class with Melissa.

Another low rumble of thunder. I ducked my head and tilted the umbrella over my forehead, keeping my eyes fixed on my phone. It was, I'd learned, the best way to disappear. Instagram told me one college friend had been promoted at work, another had just had her second kid. I had forty likes and six comments on my picture of my engagement ring.

As I arrived at the restaurant, I slid my umbrella closed and reached for the door, noticing as I did an elderly homeless man sitting under the restaurant's awning. Matted gray beard. Sad, rheumy eyes. Ancient, weathered face. He was drenched. No coat. A crumpled umbrella lay on the soggy cardboard box under him, its frame bent and broken. My heart crunched with sadness.

"Here, take this," I said gently. I pressed my umbrella in his hand.

His eyes lit up and he smiled, revealing a row of missing teeth. "Have a blessed day, miss!"

The restaurant was crowded. Mom was already sitting at a table in the middle of the room, her beige khakis, shapeless V-neck sweater-vest, and no-nonsense brown shoes clashing with the linen-draped tables and elegant Renaissance-style murals.

"You're late," Mom said, her crisp British accent disapproving.

"Sorry, Mom." I knew she hated it when I called her Mom instead of Mum, which was probably why I did it, some stupid, knee-jerk reaction left over from my teenage years. "Traffic was pretty bad for a Sunday."

I expected her to scorch me with a critical comment as I gave her a quick side hug, but she stayed silent. She smelled of pine trees and cotton body lotion, a bizarre bouquet of nostalgia that launched me back to happy family camping trips and sulky adolescent silences. I wondered if all mother-daughter relationships were as complicated as ours.

"Congratulations on the award!" I said. "You're an actual, real-life hero!"

"Don't be daft." She waved a hand in the air.

I squeezed into a chair across from her, the only place I could comfortably eat as a lefty. My fingers fluttered to my mouth and I nibbled a fingernail.

Mom gave me the Look, her makeup-less eyes tiny behind thick, black-rimmed glasses. "I'd rather hoped you'd grown out of that."

I dropped my hands and twisted my engagement ring instead. I wanted to tell her I was usually better, but she broke into a coughing fit. Her face reddened as she clutched her chest. She pulled a Kleenex from her bag and blew her nose.

"Are you okay?"

"Oh, just this bloody cold. Can't seem to shake it." She touched a hand to her head and winced. Was her skin tinted yellow, or was it just the restaurant's lighting?

"I saw Jacob yesterday," she said. "He's moved back home to take care of his dad. Apparently Bill has cancer."

Jacob Hardmann had lived across the road from us when I was a teenager. We'd met at the school bus stop when we were twelve. He was my best friend, and once, briefly, something more. But his work as a photographer took him out of the country a lot, and it had been years now since I'd seen him, or really even thought of him.

"Really?" I couldn't hide my surprise. "Bill was pretty violent. I didn't think they got along."

"Well, since Barbara died there isn't anyone else to care for him. Jacob's a good boy. He always does the right thing."

Not always, I thought.

"So, tell me. How are wedding plans coming along?" she asked. "When's the big day?"

"Oh, I don't know," I said vaguely. "We haven't really planned anything yet. We're in no rush."

That wasn't exactly true. Liam was already

pushing to set a date, calling around for venues, organizing a meeting with the priest in Coupeville.

Mom adjusted her glasses, her brown eyes suddenly sharp. "Have you told Liam about what happened?"

I looked at my hands. Shame slid down my spine, cold and sticky, like tapioca pudding.

"I can't," I whispered. This was exactly why I didn't want them to meet. Liam couldn't know about my past. What if he didn't believe me? Worse, what if he rejected me? It was easier to pretend it had never happened. "He'll think I'm broken or something."

When I looked at Mom, her face was uncharacteristically soft. "Darling, I'm not entirely certain one can ever become unbroken, but I do know we can be strong and brave and broken and whole all at the same time. It's called being human."

"Can we please not talk about it?"

Mom's forehead creased, her eyes puzzled. She was a stern, stoic physics teacher. She dealt in hard facts and cold truths. She didn't understand how I could pretend nothing had happened. But I'd learned that if you didn't let yourself feel too much, you could tuck the trauma into a box, seal it up, and get on with your life.

"I rather think telling the truth would be a better way to start a marriage," she said.

Aunt Lily swept in then, saving me from answering. She was wearing navy stilettos and a drapey linen pantsuit, her silver-platinum bob wrapped in a navy scarf that trailed over one shoulder.

"Hello, my lovely!" She kissed me on both cheeks. "Look at you! So pretty. And I love your hair that way!" She patted my cropped hair, recently streaked with toffee and bronze highlights.

Aunt Lily wasn't my real aunt, but she'd been Mom's best friend since she'd moved into our neighborhood when I was twelve. They'd both grown up in England, Mom in the north, Lily in the south, and bonded over a love of pinochle and old musicals. Mom was rules and discipline while Lily was laughter and fun. She gave us cake for breakfast, let us watch scary movies before bed, and even took me to get my belly button pierced when I was sixteen, much to Mom's horror.

"Where's Andrew?" She kissed Mom on the cheek.

"He's been held up at court. He'll be here shortly," Mom replied.

"Well, this is lovely! It's been ages since

we've done anything together."

"Too long," Mom agreed. She turned to me. "Andrew mentioned you've moved in with Liam?"

I bit my lip. Mom had a fantastic poker face, but I still sensed her disapproval. It was there in the lift of her eyebrows, the purse of her lips, like when I dropped out of college to be a dog walker, or when I was fired from my job as a barista because I could never wake up in time, or when I decided to be an artist rather than studying thermodynamics or quantum theory.

"We've been together a year and a half and we're getting married. . . ." I trailed off, realizing I sounded defensive.

"Well, I'm sure he's lovely. We'll meet him when you're ready for us to." Lily reached for a piece of bread from the basket the waitress had left and slathered a chunk of butter on it. It was too cold, the bread tearing as she stabbed at it.

I tossed her a grateful smile.

The waitress arrived, and Lily ordered a glass of champagne, Mom a pint of Post Alley Porter.

"I, um . . ." I scanned the drinks menu, my heart kicking into gear.

"Good Lord, it's just a drink, Eva! Not a

life-or-death decision." Mom sounded irritated.

I felt like a deer in the headlights. I knew I was being stupid, but even choosing a drink seemed impossible.

"How about a vodka cranberry?" Lily suggested kindly.

"Yes!" I turned to the waitress. "Only no vodka. Just cranberry."

I smiled at Lily, relieved she'd made the decision for me. Mom scowled at her. I almost rolled my eyes. They were best friends, but sometimes they were more like an old married couple, right down to the arguments and nagging.

"Tell us how you've been, Eva," Mom said, putting her hand on mine. "We hear from you so rarely these days."

I threw her a surprised look. Mom wasn't one for physical displays of affection. She had helped me with my homework, made sure I behaved and was polite and didn't skip school, but hand-holding? Not so much.

"I'm good. Busy. Lots of work coming up to Christmas, plus I've been packing and moving into Liam's. You should see his house! It's gorgeous! Here. . . ." I swiped through the pictures on my phone and held one out to them. "Here's a picture."

"It's stunning!" Lily exclaimed. Mom nodded her agreement. I smiled, warmed by their approval.

The waitress returned with our drinks, and Lily raised hers to Mom. I quickly followed suit. "I believe congratulations are in order. To you, Kat, for saving a little girl's life. We're so —"

An elderly lady pushed past my chair, her elbow jabbing into my back. I lurched forward, my glass slipping out of my hand. Ruby-red liquid splashed across the white linen, onto Mom's lap.

Mom and Lily both jumped up. An embarrassing red splotch was spreading across Mom's pants.

"I'm so sorry!" I grabbed a linen napkin and tried to wipe Mom's pants clean.

"Eva, stop! You're making it worse!" she exclaimed.

I plopped, impotent, into my seat, cheeks burning.

The waitress whisked the stained linen away and brought a glass of soda water, which Mom used to dab at her pants, then bustled about relaying the table. A few minutes later we were settled again, fresh drinks in front of us.

"I'm sorry," I said again.

Mom reached for her beer, her eyes filling

with something I couldn't identify. Resignation? Worry? "Honestly, darling, it's fine. It wasn't your fault."

But it didn't matter whose fault it was when you blamed yourself.

Mom smiled at me, and a jumble of emotions filled my chest. Uncertainty. Love. Hope. But just then, my brother rushed in, bursting the moment like a soap bubble. Andrew's cheeks were bristly with a neatly trimmed beard, glasses glinting in the candlelight. He'd inherited our mother's shitty eyesight; I'd gotten her pale English skin.

Mom's gaze peeled away from mine, brightening at the sight of him. Andrew murmured something to the waitress, and she returned a second later with a short glass of amber-colored liquid.

He shed his coat and sat next to me, lifting his glass in a toast and smiling. "To Mom. The Messiah."

I looked down at my cranberry juice, wishing I'd gotten the vodka after all.

THREE: EVA

I couldn't move.

Consciousness was a fickle thing, fading in and out. Everything in me hurt, a pain so deep it felt like I'd been cooked in a microwave.

Time passed. Sounds returned. A low thunking. A rhythmic beeping. Squeaking wheels. A periodic buzzing, material swishing, soft murmuring voices.

I propelled myself through a viscous darkness, bursting through the oily film of consciousness. My head hurt, hot, jabbing pain bolting around my temples and ricocheting through my body. A phosphorescent glow clung to the edges of my vision. The scent of burning hair lingered in my nostrils; under that, disinfectant and cold, recycled air.

What happened?

I tried to sweep through the cobwebs clouding my brain and figure out why the hell I hurt so much. The last thing I remembered was spilling cranberry juice all over my mom.

Something scratched at the surface of my mind, a fingernail against glass. Muffled voices came from very far away. A low ringing echoed in my ears, punctuated by an exasperated female voice.

Unconscious.

Murder.

Lightning.

A flash of memory bore down on me like an image emerging from a Polaroid.

My mom crumpled on the floor. An overturned chair. Light. Then shadows. Then the image disappeared and I was running. And then nothing — the memory was gone.

I struggled against the weight of my eyelids and moaned. I was in a hospital. A doctor in a white lab coat with a stethoscope draped around her neck approached. She was tall, midforties. Ruler-straight body. She had blond hair pulled into a tight ponytail, almond-shaped blue eyes, and cheekbones rising sharply under freckled skin.

I tried to speak, but my throat was too dry, my tongue glued to the roof of my mouth. She popped a straw in a plastic cup of water and held it to my lips. I slurped greedily.

"Hello, Eva." Her voice was soft and comforting. "I'm Dr. Patricia Simm. Your fiancé's just gone to get a coffee, but he'll be back shortly."

Liam. I exhaled, weak with relief.

"How are you feeling?" Her voice sounded muffled, as if she were speaking into a ball of cotton.

"I hurt," I croaked. I tried to sit up, but the room slithered around me. Pain seared along my skull.

Dr. Simm helped me sit, then pressed her stethoscope to my chest and listened. "Can you squeeze my fingers?"

She placed two of her fingers in my palms, and I squeezed, my fingers thick and awkward. She then probed my arms, lifted and bent them at the elbows.

"Do you feel this?"

"Yes."

"Good. There's a little weakness on your left side but nothing to be concerned about."

As she lowered my left arm, I caught sight of a strange pattern on my skin spreading up from a gauze bandage wrapped around my forearm. I pushed the hospital gown sleeve up higher. The visible skin on my arm was covered in pink, fernlike markings, feathery branches stippled with angry red blisters.

"Wha . . . ?"

"Those are called Lichtenberg figures. I know they look psychedelic, but they're harmless. They trace the path of the electricity that went through your body when you were struck by lightning."

Struck by lightning?

She straightened, flipping the stethoscope back around her neck and smiling wryly. "They'll disappear in a few weeks. Right now they're a testament that you survived something extraordinary."

I stared at her blankly.

"Don't worry if it's all still a blur — that's completely normal after getting struck by lightning. You've been unconscious since they brought you in early this morning. Your left eardrum burst, so you're likely experiencing some temporary hearing problems —"

Liam burst in, crossing the room in two long strides.

"Eva! Thank God you're all right!" His hair was standing on end, as if he'd just rolled out of bed. His jaw was thick with morning growth, and his eyes were red-rimmed and shadowed. He wrapped his arms around me. "I got the first ferry I could when the police called."

I laid my head against his shoulder, feeling safe for the first time since I'd woken. He was wearing one of the tight, Lycra T-shirts he wore for rowing, the slippery material cool against my throbbing ear. I touched my head and winced. A thick bandage covered a tender lump just above my left temple.

Dr. Simm noticed. "You got a pretty fierce bump to the head, so I've scheduled a CAT scan. The burns on your ears are from where your jewelry melted, and we had to cut your shirt off. We have some antibiotics in your IV to make sure those blisters on your arm don't get infected. We'll keep you in for observation for a few days, and I want to run a few more tests now that you're awake, but physically speaking, you're a remarkably lucky woman."

She went on to list the physical afflictions I might experience: Parkinson's-like muscle twitches, severe headaches, scar tissue from the thermal burns, temporary or partial paralysis in my weak left hand.

"What we really need to look out for," she continued, "are psychological issues: paranoia, personality changes, mood swings, memory loss. Even trouble concentrating. All of these we'll watch for and deal with if they arise. You'll need to take it easy at first, okay? Lots of rest to help your mind and body heal. And I'll prescribe you some meds to help."

Dr. Simm glanced over her shoulder. I followed her gaze. A man I didn't recognize approached from the corridor and paused in the doorway. He was of average height and build with a thin mouth and short-cropped, dark hair that showcased tiny ears. His eyes were deep-set in a long, wolfish face, an intense, piercing blue against his pale skin. He radiated a sort of feral aggression that instantly set me on edge.

"Hello, Miss Hansen. I'm Detective Kent Jackson. I'm part of a task force with the Seattle Police Department."

His accent was East Coast, the flattened consonants and distended vowels of Boston. He stepped into the room, his brown leather jacket creaking over a collared blue shirt and dark jeans.

I squeezed my eyes shut and I knew. Somehow I knew what he was going to say.

"I'm so sorry to tell you this. Your mother has unfortunately died. We believe she was murdered and we're investigating it as a homicide."

When I opened my eyes, tears blurred the room like a watercolor. Liam's face crumpled, raw with disbelief. He pulled me tight against his chest, and for a minute the only sound in the room was me sobbing.

"Miss Hansen, can you tell me what you were doing late last night?" Detective Jackson asked.

I looked from Liam to Dr. Simm to the detective, trying to conjure my last concrete memory after dinner with my mom. I closed my eyes. Flashes of silvery images danced just beyond my grasp. Mom's face. A knife. A sharp, white light. Slashes of blood. I pressed my fingers to my forehead, trying to catch one.

"I can't remember," I whispered.

Four: Eva

"Let's get you to your CAT scan," Dr. Simm said.

The detective looked like he wanted to argue, but she silenced him with a glare. She waved to a passing nurse who entered the room. They unlocked the wheels and pushed me into the corridor, Liam following. The detective stared after us, his brow furrowed as his sharp eyes skewered me, and I turned my head away.

"Why can't I remember?" I tasted fear in my mouth, acrid and bitter.

"Getting struck by lightning can injure the nervous system, causing short-term memory loss," Dr. Simm explained as she rolled my bed down the hall. "Our brains encode new memories so they can be stored and recalled later, but if you were struck by lightning before your brain had time to encode a memory and put it into storage, you might have problems recalling it later."

I closed my eyes, blocking out the overhead lights. The hospital bed turned left, the wheels humming against the floor as it glided down the hall.

"When will I remember?"

"It's difficult to say, and everybody's different. Those memories might not come back at all. Just rest, give it time. The good news is you weren't directly hit by the lightning. I would expect your memories that had a chance to be encoded will return slowly, like pieces of a puzzle slotting into place."

After the CAT scan, Dr. Simm wheeled me back to my room. Detective Jackson stood when we entered, his thin lips pulling into an approximation of a smile. His hard, pale eyes glinted in the jaundiced light.

I stiffened. Liam glowered at him, his hand warm on my back, anchoring me. Dr. Simm ignored both of them. She checked my reflexes and helped me stand to make sure I could walk unassisted, then examined my left arm again. The dead feeling in my fingers was being replaced by a prickly pins-and-needles sensation; the marked skin drummed a fiery beat.

"I need to check on some other patients," Dr. Simm said, jotting notes in my chart. "You okay here?" Her gaze was direct, and I knew if I wanted, she'd get rid of the detective. But I needed answers only he could provide, so I nodded.

"Hello again, Miss Hansen," the detective began. He rummaged in his coat pocket, pulling out a black pen and a small spiral notebook. He clicked the pen, in and out. *Click, click.* "Eva, can I call you Eva?"

I nodded, but Liam shook his head. He pulled himself to his full height. He was a head taller than the detective — bigger and broader too, his chest solid from mornings rowing in the misty lake at the bottom of our yard.

"This isn't a good time, Detective," Liam said. He was using the boomy, authoritative voice he usually reserved for his building sites, low and loud for maximum effect.

"I understand, but I do need to ask Eva a few questions. Who are you?"

"I'm Eva's fiancé. Liam Sullivan." He extended his hand and the detective shook it.

"Detective Kent Jackson."

"Well, Detective, as you're aware, Eva was struck by lightning last night. I'm afraid you'll need to wait to question her any further."

Detective Jackson smiled thinly, ignoring Liam and turning to me. Liam's eyes flashed with anger. He was not a man people usually ignored.

"We've been able to track down your brother. He was en route to L.A. for work but he's on his way back now."

"What happened to my mom?" I tried to sit up straighter, wincing in pain. The hospital room tilted dizzyingly around me. Liam put his hand in mine, and I gripped it, anxious for something to hold on to.

Jackson's eyes were like lumps of hot coal on mine.

"We had a call from a neighbor who heard shouts from your mom's house. Officers on the scene found the front door open. There were signs of a struggle. Her body was on the floor in the living room. She'd been stabbed."

He told me all of this as if he were reading a report on stocks and bonds, his voice cold and dispassionate.

I was glad I was in bed. My legs were rubbery. My arm buzzed. I felt like someone had scooped my insides out, leaving just a raw, pulsing hole. This must be a nightmare.

"Someone killed her," I whispered.

The detective studied me, as if the shape of my face would reveal what my brain could not.

"Yes."

"Who?"

"We're pursuing a number of leads." He clicked his pen again. *Click, click.* "Now, I have a few questions for you."

Liam puffed his chest up like an angry peacock and glared at the detective. "Absolutely not. We'll call and make an appointment once Eva's been released from the hospital."

"It's fine," I murmured.

"No. You need to rest. You can't even remember last night! You need time for your memories to piece together."

I snatched my hand away. "I *need* to find out what happened to my mom!"

Liam looked surprised, then hurt. "Eva —"

"Please. . . ." I cut him off, my voice cracking.

Indecision played out across his face. Finally he relented, moving to sit on a chair against the wall. But his body remained coiled tight as he watched the detective.

Detective Jackson shifted his weight and addressed me. "Did your mom ever tell you she was in danger in any way?"

I shook my head, flinching as starbursts of pain exploded inside my skull. My heartbeat pounded in my damaged ear. "No, never."

"When was the last time you spoke?"

"Sunday."

"Yesterday?"

"Yes. We had dinner. We were celebrating."

He nodded, appearing attentive, focused, with none of the indifference I remembered from the last time I spoke to the police. But his presence sucked the air from the room, making me feel claustrophobic and tense. I didn't trust him.

"I saw she won the Seattle Medal of Courage last month."

"Yes, that's why we were celebrating."

"She saved that little girl's life. What was she, three? She'd fallen on the light rail tracks in Pioneer Square. Your mom climbed onto the tracks when the train was approaching and grabbed her."

"Yes."

"Do you know of anyone who had a grudge against her?"

"A grudge?"

"Yes. Any enemies, bad blood, people who were angry with her? Family feuds, maybe?"

Why is he asking me that?

I swallowed hard. "No. I don't think so."

"It's odd that someone would be murdered so soon after being in the public eye."

Click, click.

"Is it?"

"Don't you think?" He let the question sit between us for a moment. "What time was your dinner?"

"Our reservation was for five p.m."

"And what about after? Where did you go?"

I hesitated, trying to remember. "I got the ferry home to Whidbey Island. Why are you asking me these things?"

He ignored my question. "What's the last thing you remember?"

I closed my eyes, allowing myself to shuttle back, to track the path of last night. Images flitted through my mind, clicking into place. "I was in the garage. I'd fired a set of bowls in the kiln."

I looked at Liam for confirmation. He nodded, his face gray with worry.

"The timer went off. . . ." The sharp ring of earthenware hitting concrete rang out in my mind. My eyes flew open. "I took the pieces out of the kiln, but I tripped and dropped the tray and they smashed on the floor. I was cleaning it up when Liam came in. He told me he was going to make something to eat."

I paused, reaching for the memory, but that was where it stopped. I tried to swallow past a dusty throat. "I can't remember anything else."

"So you remember other things, earlier in the day, for instance, just not past when the pottery broke?"

"No. Nothing," I whispered.

Detective Jackson looked doubtful. My spit went thick in my mouth. He didn't believe me.

"I want to remember!" I exclaimed, my voice too loud.

Liam looked alarmed by my outburst. What was wrong with me? But it was true. I wanted to remember, but the harder I tried to hold on to my memories, the further they sank beneath the waters of my subconscious.

"Eva, you shouldn't be talking right now." Liam came and stood by me. "Remember what the doctor said. You need to rest."

Detective Jackson looked up from jotting notes and addressed Liam. "Do you know what time Eva came back from dinner, Mr. Sullivan?"

"Maybe eight or so."

"And what time did she leave in the night?"

Liam's jaw worked and he shook his head. "I'm sorry, I sleep like the —" His eyes darted to mine, apologizing for being tactless. Once Liam was asleep, there was no waking him. He was an early-to-bed, early-to-rise kind of guy, the good angel on my shoulder. He'd convinced me to exercise more, give up gluten, start an IRA, keep my calendar organized. He'd been a good influence on my more free-wheeling ways.

"What'd you do after you ate?"

"Eva had a migraine, so I got her meds for her and she went to bed. I worked for a few hours and joined her. The next thing I knew, you guys were calling."

Jackson looked at me again, his expression guarded. I could see shades of something creeping into his face.

"How'd you hurt your hand?" he asked.

I looked down. A thick white bandage was taped to the inside of my left palm. Something flashed in my mind, not a memory exactly, but something more ethereal, a sensation.

In my mind I see a knife. I recognize it. It's one of the old-fashioned wooden-handled boning knives my mom keeps in her kitchen. It's covered in blood.

My skin prickled with sweat, first hot, then cold. I inhaled sharply.

"I cut it," I said. "Yesterday, when I was picking up the pottery."

Detective Jackson looked at me for a long moment. Liam stepped in front of me, blocking the detective's gaze with his body.

"I think that's enough now, Detective," he

said firmly. "Eva's told you everything she knows. You can direct any other questions to my lawyer."

Detective Jackson opened his mouth to argue, but snapped it shut. Liam had that effect on people. They just did what he wanted. Call it charm, charisma, whatever, people rarely questioned him. And if they did, he persisted until he got what he wanted. Liam's confidence, his certainty, were exactly why I fell in love with him.

Detective Jackson lifted his palms, like he was saying, *You win.* He pulled a card from his wallet, dropping it on my lap.

"Kat Hansen was murdered. I'm going to do whatever it takes to find out who's responsible for that."

He turned to go, then stopped and faced me. He held my gaze, direct, stony. "Again, I'm sorry for your loss."

FIVE: EVA

Once the detective had left, Liam turned to me. "All right, tell me what you really remember."

He'd crossed his arms over his chest and was frowning. Hurt corkscrewed through me. Didn't he believe me?

"I don't remember anything," I whispered.

"Babe, this is important!" Worry creased the skin between his eyebrows. "Your mom's been murdered, and that detective is trying to question you."

I put my hands over my face, tears pressing against my eyelids. "I don't know! I don't know what I remember! I can't do this, that cop . . . It doesn't matter what I say! He's only going to believe what he wants to anyway!"

Liam sat next to me, his weight dipping the bed as he put his arms around me. I turned my face into his chest and leaned against him, needing his reassurance.

"Don't worry. I won't ever let anything bad happen to you. I'll take care of this."

He stood and started pacing, his mind whirling three steps ahead, mentally making lists of things to do. Nobody was as good in a crisis as Liam. When he set his mind to achieving something, he put all his energy into making it happen. He'd found me when I was at my lowest, picked me up, and fixed the broken pieces.

"I know a guy at the SPD," he said. "I'll call him and find out what exactly they know. And then we'll call my lawyer. But first I need you to tell me what you really remember about last night. We're on the same team here — I just want to make sure I know everything so I can help."

I let my head drop back onto the pillow, wincing in pain. I ran a hand through my hair, my fingers gently kneading my aching skull. The IV tugged at the inside of my arm. I was profoundly tired. Like on a cellular level.

"I already told you," I said wearily. "I don't know."

"Anything can help. Do you remember getting home or going to bed? Or cutting your hand?"

"I don't remember anything!" I shouted.

We both froze. Liam's mouth fell open in

shock. I had never shouted at him, never lashed out, not even once. I could be sulky, maybe a little brooding, but never angry. Liam said it was the artist in me. In fact, it was one of the things he mentioned when he proposed. *I love that we never fight. I want to spend the rest of my life knowing I make you happy.*

Liam puffed his cheeks out and exhaled sharply. I knew exactly what he was thinking: *What the hell is wrong with her?* I was wondering the same thing.

"You believe me" — my voice hitched — "right?"

I needed Liam to believe me. I couldn't lose him — he was the only stable thing in my life.

Liam rubbed a hand over his jaw, the stubble making a harsh rasping sound. "Look, everything's going to be fine. I promise."

It was only after he'd left that I realized he hadn't answered my question.

I woke that afternoon to the sound of rain pattering against the dirty window next to my bed. Anemic light filtered through the blinds. Beyond that, the sky was sullen, a hard, uniform gray. The sleep had done wonders, and physically I already felt better.

I could move my arm, my ear didn't throb as much, and my headache had dimmed.

Outside, a small brown bird hopped onto the window ledge. It stared at me solemnly. I took a crumb from the uneaten sandwich that had been left for my lunch and unlatched the window. It only opened an inch, but I pushed the crumb through and watched as the bird grabbed it and flew away, leaving me vaguely lonely.

A shadow, sharp as a sword, appeared on the other side of the frosted-glass door. It hovered there, someone trying to peer inside. My palms went slick.

Somebody's there.

I shrank against the bed, heart throbbing, feeling trapped and terrified. Images tumbled over me, twisting and shifting. I was running in the dark. Black and purple clouds. The air crackling. Rain hitting my scalp. The sound of shoes hitting wet pavement.

"Eva! What's wrong?" Liam's voice came from very far away. His arms circled my hunched body, warm and solid, and I realized I was rocking back and forth. My face was damp with tears.

"Someone's there," I whispered.

Liam's footsteps faded as he walked down the hall, then a minute later returned. He shut the door with a soft click.

"It's only a doctor." He gently pressed me onto the bed. "Here, lie down."

I struggled against him. "No! I need to go home!"

Liam's eyebrows shot to his hairline as he sidestepped my flailing limbs. My heart and head were pounding in tandem. I felt like I was floating out of my body, looking at myself and wondering who the hell had replaced me.

I swung my legs around to the floor, tentatively putting weight on my feet.

"Didn't you hear the doctor?" Liam's clenched jaw gave away the worry he meant to mask. "You need to rest, let your brain recover. You're hooked to an IV, for God's sake!"

Our eyes locked, mine pulsing, a staccato flicker in my peripheral vision. Fear poured ice through my veins. I ripped the tape from my arm and the IV out in one smooth motion.

Liam gasped. "Eva! What are you — why'd you do that?"

We stared at the blood pumping from the inside of my arm. I hadn't thought it would bleed so much.

Liam grabbed a handful of cotton balls from a canister and pressed them to my arm. "That IV was in a vein! What is wrong with you?"

The blood was already clotting, oozing instead of pumping. "Where are my clothes?"

"Don't you remember? They had to cut your shirt off. There was no sign of your coat."

I groaned, frustrated I'd forgotten.

"Eva . . ." Liam's gaze was on the lightning marks that peeked out of the gauze bandaging on my arm. "Does it hurt?"

The marks looked like cracks embossed onto my skin, a mosaic of broken shards that climbed up my arm.

"No," I lied. I tapped the gauze back down. It hurt like hell, but I'd rather eat my arm than stay in the hospital another minute. I had to get out of there. A deep sense of urgency pressed down on me. "I'm fine. Can we go home?"

I hobbled to the cupboard on the far side of the room. My body throbbed. My equilibrium was totally off. Inside I found a plastic bag with my things. My leggings and shoes were fine, my cell phone unharmed. But my socks were singed, my shirt and green corduroy jacket missing.

I slid my leggings on, then rolled up the hem of my hospital gown, pulling the ends together and tying them in a knot at my waist, nineties-style.

Liam sighed. "You look ridiculous."

I ignored him and walked unsteadily to the open door.

"Eva, stop!" Liam's fair eyebrows scrunched into balls. "What is going on? This isn't like you!"

I knew I was behaving out of character, but I couldn't seem to find the words to explain how terrified I felt. An overwhelming sense that I wasn't safe here crashed over me.

Suddenly I was sobbing in giant, messy gulps, spluttering and gasping for air. I knew that something very bad had happened, worse than before. Something, or someone, threatened me still, but I couldn't remember what.

"Please! Someone . . . I was running. . . ." I wasn't making sense, the words coming out wrong. I couldn't convey what I was thinking because I couldn't rely on my brain to tell me the truth.

"Shhh . . ." Liam pulled me against him, so tight I could barely breathe. "It's okay. Remember, the doctor said this could happen. You just need to rest. Let's get you home. I'll get your meds later."

Downstairs, the chill of fall slid in through

reception's rotating doors; then suddenly we were outside and I tasted it on the breeze, saw it in the harsh slant of the shadows cast between clouds bloated with rain. The wind whispered ominously in the treetops as we crossed to the parking garage. The remnants of a storm were everywhere: broken boughs, torn leaves, standing water, pieces of garbage strewn over the road.

Liam kept his arm around me as he led me to the car. I caught sight of my reflection in the window as he unlocked the door. My short hair was more disheveled than usual, tufts sticking up in every direction. My eyes were charcoal-hued, circled by dark moons and sunken in my small, pale face. A massive bandage covered the lump on my temple.

I swiped at the water on the window, smearing my reflection into a swirl of distorted colors, someone completely unrecognizable from the person who'd stood there only seconds before.

The Mukilteo ferry terminal glowed in the fading light as we pulled up. Workers in high-vis vests shouted and waved their arms as we drove onto the boat. Soon it was chugging into the choppy waters of Puget Sound. The trip was only twenty minutes, so we didn't bother going upstairs. Instead, I left Liam checking his phone while I went to the back of the car deck.

I stared at the steel-gray waters churning behind the ferry. Tears filled my eyes as reality smacked me in the face. This time yesterday I was about to get this ferry into Seattle to see my mom.

The mist swirled up and combined with the moisture on my cheeks. My relationship with my mother had become prickly these last few years. Distant. I'd never forgiven her for her cruel words, the arguments we'd had.

And now she was dead.

My cell phone rang. I looked at the caller ID and saw it flashing *Andrew.*

"Eva!" my brother exclaimed. "What's going on? I'm at the hospital. Where are you?"

Andrew was the kind of person who waited a half hour after eating before going swimming; who stopped at a stop sign even in the middle of the night. If the sign said DON'T WALK ON THE GRASS, he didn't walk on the grass. There was no way he'd understand my need to run, to hide, to get away from this.

"I left," I said.

"You *left*?" He sounded incredulous. I could hear footsteps striking pavement, the brisk, efficient walk of a lawyer. "You can't just leave the hospital. It's against the rules!"

"I had to get out of there!"

"Eva, come back to the hospital. This isn't like you."

"I don't understand what's going on!"

"Neither do I, but the detective will figure out what happened to Mom." I heard just the hint of a tremor in my brother's voice.

"I can't. I need to go home!"

"Do you have any idea how bad that will look? The police are already suspicious of you. . . ."

"What?" The noose around my neck tightened. I desperately needed somebody to explain what the hell was happening.

"Don't you know?" Andrew asked. "The paramedics found you a few blocks away from Mom's house last night. That's where you were struck by lightning. Eva, the police think you might have been there when Mom was killed!"

Six: Kat

London
25 Years Before

The first time I met Laura, she bit me.

I had taken Eva to the playground at Hyde Park, which, in retrospect, was an utterly ridiculous decision, as she had a dreadful cold. But that day the sky had been washed a spectacular blue by the previous night's rain, golden light filtering through the trees. Daffodils were blooming along the footpath, dancing on the cusp of spring's breath. As Eva trotted over to the sandpit, I pulled a fresh handkerchief from my bag and wiped moisture from a green bench before sitting.

Eva walked her teddy bear, Barnaby, across the pockmarked sand, murmuring childish secrets to him. She sneezed, her wispy blond curls bouncing in the breeze, and I instantly regretted bringing her outside when she was ill. A good mother would have stayed home, cuddled up on the couch watching cartoons on the telly. But I was going mad after days trapped inside by torrential rain.

I lifted my glasses off my nose and polished them on my coat sleeve as I watched her play. Suddenly a searing pain sliced through my shin.

"Ow!" I jumped up, holding my leg. A little girl peered up at me from under the bench, her eyes glittering with cheeky delight.

She was a tiny thing, about the same age as Eva, nearly four. Her hair was an unusual shade of red, a cross between cinnamon and mahogany. It was long and wild, knotted with leaves and twigs. She had mud smudged across one cheek and was wearing a pink, gauzy ballerina outfit under her jacket.

I glared at the child, but she seemed immune to my fury. She grinned at me from her position on all fours.

"I'm a dog!" She stuck her tongue out and panted.

"Don't be daft!" I huffed, rubbing my sore shin. "I've certainly never seen a dog ballerina before."

The child's face fell, and I felt cruel in that way I often didn't understand. *Socially awkward,* my husband, Seb, always called me.

A woman with long, flame-red hair broke off from a group of yummy-mummys — black clothing, oversize designer prams, each with a takeaway coffee in one hand and a baby in the other. She was immaculately presented, full makeup on, gauzy, figure-skimming dress swirling, dangly earrings flashing. Her four-inch stacked heels sucked into the thick mud as she tottered toward us. I looked down at my practical, mud-splattered Wellington boots and couldn't help feeling ever so frumpy.

"Laura, what have you done!" She scooped the child up and kissed her forehead. She was beautiful, feminine in a way I would never be, with soft curves and the same delicate bone structure and milk-pale skin as the girl. The neckline of her dress had slipped to expose the white lace of her bra. I looked away to preserve her decency, but she seemed not to have noticed one bit.

"I'm being a dog, Mummy!" Laura exclaimed.

"I hope you aren't biting again, Laura-loo!" she scolded, looking mortified.

"It's fine," I said.

"Mummy, look!" Eva shouted from the sandpit. "I wrote my name!"

"Well done, darling!" I called.

Laura wriggled out of the woman's grasp and went over to examine what Eva was doing. Eva showed her the letters, then handed her a stick and told her to have a go.

"Wow!" the woman said. "How old is your daughter?"

"She'll be four in a few months."

"And already writing her name? That's astonishing! You must be chuffed to bits! Laura's four in August, but she isn't even close to writing her name yet."

"I was training to be a teacher before I fell pregnant." I couldn't help the curl of pride that rose in me. "I'm preparing her for school in September."

"Laura's starting as well."

I pushed my glasses up my nose, my face feeling stiff as I struggled to unstick my tongue from the roof of my mouth. She was so exquisitely beautiful, so alluring that it was quite intimidating.

"I'm Rose." She extended a hand and smiled. When I shook it, it was smooth and cool, her fingers long and tapering to nails that were perfect pink ovals.

"I apologize for Laura's behavior." She rolled her eyes. "The girl can be positively feral sometimes."

"Not a bother."

"Do let me take you out to coffee to make it up to you!" She clapped her hands like a child and grinned. "Look, there's a café just over there!"

"But, your friends —"

"I don't really know them." Rose waved a dismissive hand. "We were just chatting about children. Do say yes! It would make me feel so much better about Laura using you as a chew toy!"

"Very well, then."

Rose called Laura to her, and I had no choice but to follow with Eva. She led us to a wooden pavilion with gray cladding and white trim overlooking the park. She ordered hot chocolate with marshmallows for the children and coffees for us from a spotty teenage boy running the till. I watched her, marveling at how easy she found conversation. It was quite extraordinary. Her tongue did not trip; her gaze did not waver. I found socializing all quite beyond me, really.

The boy behind the cash register seemed a bit overwhelmed by Rose's attention, his gaze occasionally dropping to the triangle of creamy cleavage exposed where her neckline dipped a little too low. I itched to tug it higher or to scold the boy, but Rose did nothing to discourage him, giving him a five-fingered wave as we headed to an empty table at the back of the café to await our drinks.

As soon as we sat, Rose slipped her heels off, setting them on an empty chair, then stretching her legs out and wiggling her toes. I wrinkled my nose, glancing at the filthy floor.

"Goodness! What was I thinking, wearing heels to the park?" Rose exclaimed with a charmingly self-deprecating laugh. "But I was simply desperate to feel more myself! You know how it is caring for small children. You lose such a piece of yourself!"

The waitress brought our drinks, sloshing liquid onto the table in her hurry to leave.

"Mummy, I wanted marshmallows!" Laura thrust her lower lip out.

Rose looked annoyed, although I could not be certain if it was at Laura or the waitress. She beckoned the waitress back.

"I ordered marshmallows with these," she said.

The waitress narrowed her eyes. "They sank. You'll have to go purchase more."

"Certainly." Rose began rummaging in her handbag.

"What? No." The injustice of it upset me greatly, though perhaps it wasn't my business to intervene. "The air bubbles in marshmallows mean they are less dense than the cocoa. They will float unless you squeeze them into balls to make them more dense than liquid. Did you do that?"

The waitress scowled and stormed away, returning a moment later with a small handful of marshmallows. She dropped them into both mugs of hot chocolate. They bobbed once, twice, then floated to the top. The waitress shuffled away looking embarrassed.

Rose burst out laughing. "That was amazing!"

I smiled and looked down at my coffee. I liked the sound of her laughter and how it made me feel: as if I had just awoken, somehow. There was something about her. She was . . . magnetic. I was utterly drawn to her.

"Physical laws are infallible," I said. "It is one of the few certainties in life."

"Mummy, may I have your biscuit?" Eva asked.

"Certainly, my darling." I plucked the biscuit off my coffee saucer and handed it to her.

Laura looked expectantly at Rose, but Rose shook her head and laughed, giving a little shrug. "Sorry, I already ate mine!"

She shook three packets of sugar into her coffee, stirred, and took a massive gulp. "I really shouldn't have another coffee. This is my fourth today!"

Bored with the hot chocolate, Laura grabbed Barnaby from Eva, causing Eva to cry out in dismay. Her eyes, Seb's sapphire blue, welled with tears. I rummaged in my bag and extracted a pad of paper and some crayons, handing them to Laura whilst retrieving Barnaby for Eva. She was far too old for a security object, but I couldn't bring myself to take him away. The bear was becoming quite bedraggled these days, the yellow daffodils on his tie fading to a dirty gray. His hat, the trumpet-shape of a daffodil, had detached on one side.

"Oh, do stop being beastly!" Rose exclaimed crossly. She touched her fingertips to her temple and scowled at Laura. "I swear, some days I think about hiring a nanny!"

I tried to imagine the luxury of having someone else do all the dirty work.

"Why don't you, then?" I asked. "Hire a nanny, I mean."

She looked surprised. "Well, it . . . it isn't what mums do, is it?"

I didn't know how to respond. Who was I to say what a real mum would do? Mine certainly had been no example to live by.

She took a sip of coffee. "My mum fell ill

when I was young and she died a few years later. I suppose I always wanted to create the traditional home I didn't get." She looked away. "Hiring a nanny would mean I'd failed at that. That I was a bad mother."

My gaze leapt to Laura. Her long hair was tangled, her nose crusty with snot, her ballerina outfit streaked with mud. A piece of the gauze at the shoulder was torn. The child desperately needed a bath.

"I reckon it would make you a better mother." I bit my cheek, embarrassed. "Goodness, that sounded horrible! I do apologize. What I meant is, more hands make light work and all that!"

Rose threw her head back and laughed, exposing her slender neck. "I never thought of it that way. My husband agrees with you," she admitted. "He's recently rebranded his art gallery and he's away on business a lot, so he's no help whatsoever."

"Look! I drew a rocket!" Laura interrupted, holding her picture out to us.

"Well done," I said. I slid a blue crayon from the box and drew a rocket next to hers. "Did you know that rockets make it rain?" I drew a cloud under the rocket. "The smoke from the exhaust turns into clouds, and eventually, after the rocket has disappeared, the clouds start to rain!"

"Wow!" She picked up the crayon and drew clouds and rain in a frenzy of blue swirls.

Rose looked at me over the rim of her coffee mug. Her steady gray gaze made me feel itchy and hot all over, but also, strangely, like a cat being stroked. "This is a crazy thing to say, I know, but — would *you* want to be our nanny?"

I lifted my glasses off my nose to polish them, letting my eyes sweep over her face. She didn't appear to be joking. But Seb would never allow it. He liked me home with Eva, dinner on the table when he got home, laundry washed and neatly folded. It was our deal: he kept us financially secure; I took care of our daughter and made our house a home.

"I don't . . ."

"Of course." Rose smiled and shrugged. "That was too forward. I do apologize."

"No, it isn't that." I laughed, a surprised whoosh of air. "To be perfectly honest, I'm not certain we could afford to put Eva in nursery while I work."

"Why, bring her with you! The children would have each other to play with. And look how well they get on!"

We watched Laura and Eva coloring together.

"We wouldn't want to impose. . . ."

"Not at all. It would be lovely! I could start painting again, and Laura could learn so much from you before school starts!"

A gentle thrill buzzed through me. But I would have to ask Seb before I replied.

"I'll give you my number." Rose jotted her number on a crumpled receipt and handed it to me. "Do think about it. I'm afraid I must dash. We have a playdate organized soon."

We left the café, and Laura and Eva bounced over to a clutch of daffodils swaying in the soft breeze, their hands knitted together. Laura picked one and tucked it behind Eva's ear. Eva giggled.

"Thank you for the drinks," I said.

Rose leaned forward and hugged me, her lips brushing my cheek. A gentle shiver raced down my spine as her hair tickled my ear. A strange, heady flush climbed my throat and stained my cheeks. I pulled away abruptly.

"It was lovely to meet you." Rose's eyes twinkled. "Please do phone me. My offer is genuine."

I called Eva to me, and we said good-bye and headed in the opposite direction. As we walked, her gaze strained backward over her shoulder, at Laura and Rose.

Eva brought that daffodil home and put it on her bedside cabinet. It stayed there until it withered and shrank, eventually crumbling into tiny fragments that were cleared onto the floor and forgotten.

I am aware that the mind plays tricks. Brains are strange and capricious things, and we humans are deluded to purport to be in control of them. A memory is no more reliable than the weather, broken, warped by the teller's view. But I remember that daffodil. The incandescent yellow glow against Laura's skin as she inhaled its scent before she gave it to Eva. Perhaps that's why daffodils always remind me of her.

Of the beginning of the end.

Seven: Eva

"The police think I was at Mom's house?" I asked Andrew, stunned. I pressed my phone against my good ear, my palms slippery with sweat as I stared at the ferry dock looming closer. Fear and adrenaline made my fingers tingle. "What does that mean? They don't think I . . . ?" I couldn't even finish the sentence.

"Eva!" Liam called from the car as the ferry horn blared. I waved that I was coming.

"Don't worry, they aren't preparing an arrest warrant or anything yet," Andrew said. "They have to finish collecting evidence, do lab tests, interview witnesses. But I think they're suspicious of you. My buddy on the force said the fact you were near Mom's —"

"I wasn't there! I got the ferry home after we had dinner!"

"The paramedics picked you up right by

Mom's house." My brother's voice was flat.

I opened my mouth to deny it, to swear that I would never physically harm our mother.

But it wasn't the truth.

Because I had harmed her before.

Badly.

"Everything all right?" Liam asked when I slammed the car door.

"Apparently the paramedics found me right by Mom's house around the time she was killed. My brother thinks the police are suspicious of me!"

Liam scowled, fingers flexing on the steering wheel. "That's why the detective was trying to question you! I knew he was up to no good. Don't worry, I'll take care of it. I'll call my lawyer when we get home."

I chewed my thumbnail, ripping the nail to the quick. Blood oozed from it, tasting of salt and rusted metal.

"Won't I look guilty if I call a lawyer?"

"You have to defend yourself. Trust me, we can't just sit here and do nothing."

A thin sliver of my fingernail splintered into my mouth, making a sharp snapping sound.

"Gross." Liam pulled my hand out of my

mouth, reminding me, suddenly, of my mom.

The ferry docked with a low thud. Liam put the car in gear, maneuvering into the lane of disembarking traffic. Twenty minutes later we turned into our driveway, gravel crunching under the tires.

I looked up at the three-story Washington log and timber-frame house Liam had built before we met. The house was nestled in the belly of the island. Red Douglas fir timbers perfectly complemented the surrounding evergreen trees. The pitched roof, gabled dormers, wraparound porch, and leaded windows were illuminated by the last rays of light peeking through a smattering of clouds that chugged slowly across the sky.

Liam opened my door and helped me out of the car. Mr. Ayyad, our nearest neighbor, was jogging along the lake's edge with his Siberian husky. Mr. Ayyad couldn't have been a day younger than ninety-five, yet he moved smoothly and gracefully, with none of the stiffness you'd attribute to the elderly. He slowed as he caught sight of us and raised a hand, his long gray beard dancing in the wind. I waved back as Liam cupped his arm gently over my shoulders and led me up the porch stairs.

Inside, Liam turned all the lights on. The

polished hardwood floor and fir beams overhead gleamed in the light. On the far side of the living room, an aged stone fireplace bisected floor-to-ceiling walls of glass that overlooked our private slice of Hidden Lake, spread like a quilt at the bottom of the yard.

I kicked my tennis shoes off automatically, losing my balance and almost knocking over the red-and-yellow art nouveau lamp I'd put on the entry table. I'd bought it at a garage sale a few years ago and I adored it. It was the only decoration here that was mine.

I crossed the living room and went into the garage. The pavement was cold under my bare feet. I threw the side door open and my cat, Ginger, streaked inside. She stretched her claws up my jeans and meowed.

I'd found Ginger in a box on the side of the road shortly after I moved here. She was badly malnourished and had a broken hind leg. Liam had told me to leave her at a vet's, but I couldn't abandon her when she was so obviously traumatized. I knew too well what that felt like.

I scooped Ginger up and pressed my face to her neck. Her motor instantly turned on, comforting against my cheek. Putting her down, I filled a bowl with cat food and set it on the floor. When I returned to the living room, Liam had moved my shoes off the carpet to the shoe rack, a gentle reminder to clean up after myself.

"Sorry! I don't know where my head is."

Liam smiled. "It's all right. You were just struck by lightning, after all."

Our eyes met, and we both burst out laughing. It felt good, like I'd found an island of normalcy in this chaotic world I'd woken up in.

"Sit down. I'll make you a sandwich." Liam stroked his knuckles down my cheek. I winced as the raw skin scraped my face. Liam's eczema had flared up again. "I'll get you a glass of water."

"A cup of tea, maybe?"

"Won't it just keep you awake?"

"You're probably right. Just water then."

I went upstairs to change into a clean shirt and yoga pants. When I returned, Liam was in the kitchen, barking orders into his phone. "I don't care what it takes, get that building permit approved." He paused, then sighed. "Fine. Up our budget. I'm not losing this project just because some new building inspector doesn't know how this works."

A second later, he came out of the kitchen

with a glass of water and a cheese sandwich.

"Everything okay?" I asked.

He looked irritated. "There's a new building inspector in town and he's making noises about denying our building permit."

"But you already have the building up, right?"

Liam frowned. "It'll be fine. Just a little more negotiating than I thought, is all."

"I think I'll go outside," I said.

"Are you sure? Maybe you should just go to bed. The doctor said you need to rest. Heal. Your head got pretty banged up."

He reached out to touch the bandage on my temple but I ducked away from his fingers. "I don't know. I just feel too trapped inside right now."

"You know you need to —"

"Honestly, I'm fine." I cut him off before he went into overprotective mode.

"Okay, well, are you all right if I do a few things for work then?"

"Sure, of course."

Liam was a workaholic. Any project, any job, he persisted at until he saw it through. I knew his drive was an unspoken *fuck you* to the father who'd rejected him when he was a teenager. But at least he'd turned a negative into a positive.

"The best success stories begin with

failure," he'd told me once when we first met. He'd smiled then, and I knew. This was a man who wouldn't give up on me. And I was right. Liam never gave up on anything.

I went outside to the sheltered wrap-around porch and curled up on one of the wicker chairs, draping a blanket over my lap. The grand old trees swayed and creaked as the wind raked over them, shaking pine needles over the ground.

After a few minutes the automatic porch light clicked off, plunging the countryside into darkness. Finally, hidden by the velvety dark, I bowed my head, tears scorching my cheeks. The grief I'd been burying all day cracked and poured out of me.

Flashes of an alley slick with rain.

The outline of a man's profile.

Someone calling my name.

"Eva. Eva!"

I lurched awake, my body covered in a cold, sticky sweat. Liam was sitting next to me on our bed. He stroked a finger gently down my cheek, his forehead etched with concern.

"Morning, sleepyhead. How you feeling?" He was freshly showered, his hair still damp, his boy-next-door face smooth from his morning shave.

I touched my temple and winced. "A little sore," I admitted. "What time is it?"

"A little after ten. I went and got croissants from that bakery you like in town."

I bolted upright. Pain skewered my head and my heart simultaneously as I remembered.

Mom was dead.

I tried to stand. I needed to call Melissa.

"Relax." Liam gently pushed me back down.

His voice, I realized, was clear again. My hearing was better.

"I took care of it. I told Melissa you weren't feeling well. I moved a few meetings around so I could take care of you this morning. You know . . ." He ran a fingertip down my nose so gently I shivered. "You could set up your studio here at home. We could clear out more space in the garage next to your kiln. You could start selling your work online."

I blinked. My brain was too muddled to even process that idea.

"Just something to think about." Liam stood and held up a small, butter-stained paper bag. "Have a shower and come downstairs."

In the bathroom, I peeled the bandage off

my temple. I touched the tender lump and froze, my left hand suspended in midair. I wiggled my fingers. My engagement ring was gone. A million worries about losing it collided inside my head, finally exterminated by one rational thought: the hospital must've taken it off for my CAT scan. I made a mental note to call them later.

The lightning marks on my left forearm were still wrapped, so I hunted in the first aid kit for a small pair of scissors. The bandage frayed and slipped as I awkwardly hacked at it with my right hand.

"Damnit!" Why didn't they make tiny scissors for left-handed people?

Finally free of the bandages, I studied the marks feathering up my arm. The blisters had started crusting over, but the fernlike discolorations were still angry and red. In a way, I was glad for the marks, for the physical reminder of what had happened. It was more than I'd gotten last time, when all the wounds were hidden.

I synced my phone to my Moxie showerhead speaker — a birthday present from Liam — and turned the music up full blast, tapping out a dance beat on my leg as I closed my eyes and let the hot water slide over my body. Fragments of memories flashed like a lightbulb with a loose connection. I shook my head. I wanted the cold black-and-white facts of what had happened the other night, but I couldn't seem to gather the threads into any logical order.

Downstairs, the kitchen was warm and bright, the dishwasher humming quietly, the air smelling of antibacterial wipes. Liam had laid the dining table with a crisp white tablecloth, a carafe of orange juice, and ramekins of butter and jam. Everything was perfectly aligned. A vase of the black roses Liam grew in his greenhouse sat in the center, the velvet petals releasing a spicy clove scent.

Liam shook the flaky croissants from the bag onto two plates.

"Tea?" he asked.

"Yes, please."

He flicked the electric kettle on and bustled about getting plates and napkins on the table. When the kettle boiled, he poured hot water over my tea bag and set a timer to let it steep for exactly three-and-a-half minutes.

My eyes fell on the table, the newspaper Liam had been reading.

The body of a woman was found in her house in Queen Anne last night, just a few streets behind popular Kerry Park. Police say the woman had been brutally murdered and are asking —

"Let me take that." Liam scooped up the newspaper and deposited it on the counter. The stark words paraded across my mind anyway.

"I called a defense attorney," he said. "The only evidence the police have is circumstantial. But he advised us to go in for an interview with the detective sooner rather than later. You can give them your fingerprints and DNA; obviously they'll already be at the house from other times you've visited. You have no outstanding warrants, so they'll have no reason to hold you. And it could take weeks to get the initial crime scene tests back."

My throat went dry and gritty. Would they pull my file? Would they find out about my past? Liam might learn everything I'd worked so hard to hide.

I stared out the kitchen windows at the lake. The water was the color of clay, the wind rippling across its surface. Drizzle painted the landscape a dull gray. A movement just beyond the porch caught my eye. I jumped, a tremor dusting my arms, but then my eyes adjusted to the murky light. The lake was empty. It was just the shadows of the trees whipping in the wind.

Liam was watching me; I could feel his eyes even though he was trying to hide it. He thought I was being paranoid and irrational. Was he right? Or was I just grieving?

I shivered, feeling raw and exposed. Liam set my tea in front of me, and I sipped it, not caring that it was too hot.

"I made an appointment with the lawyer in Langley first thing tomorrow morning," he said. "We'll talk to him together, then he'll come with us to speak to Detective Jackson in Seattle."

I should've felt grateful, but instead the grit of irritation slid beneath my teeth. What was wrong with me? Why was I being such an ungrateful bitch?

I picked up the butter knife and jabbed it into my croissant, slopped strawberry jam in the slit. Suddenly a strange mist oozed around my eyes. Electric pulses oscillated along the damaged skin on my left arm.

I stare at the blood cooling on my hands. It is everywhere. The harsh iron scent clings to the back of my throat, making me feel like I will vomit.

And clutched in my left hand is a knife.

EIGHT: EVA

I jumped up, the chair legs scraping hard against the kitchen floor. Pain flooded my head, making me press my fingertips to my temples.

"What's wrong?" Liam was there instantly, clutching my good arm. Light slanted through the window, defining his prominent jaw, sharp nose, the scattering of freckles over his cheeks. Worry lines were carved like quotation marks around his mouth. "Do you remember something?"

"I was at my mom's house." My hands were shaking. "I was standing in her living room. Liam, I was holding a knife!"

I set the butter knife on the table and looked at the bandage on my palm. The wound was suddenly hot, pulsing. "It must be how I got this cut."

Liam's mouth buckled. "Babe, that isn't possible. You cut your hand on the broken pottery. When I came into the garage, you were already bleeding. I helped you bandage it up. Don't you remember?"

"No. I . . ." Muddled memories darted around.

I looked at Liam. He was frowning, his mouth pursed, brows scrunched, his eyes full of pity. I closed my eyes. I didn't know what I remembered, what was real and what wasn't. I felt the knife, heavy in my hand. But was it real? Was it my hand?

Once again, I couldn't trust myself.

"You've had a traumatic injury." Liam wrapped his arms around me. "Your brain just needs time to heal. It's completely understandable you're mixing your memories up."

I leaned into Liam. At least I could rely on him. It was Liam who'd found me staring at a bottle of wine at a local restaurant two years ago. I'd only been on the island a few months and was contemplating drinking it, then another, and another, on the verge of wanting it all to end.

Liam was sitting on the outdoor patio near me, clearly waiting for someone. After a while, it became obvious his date wasn't coming. It was an unseasonably cold evening, and I was shivering in my thin coat. He offered me his jacket, and I offered him a glass from my bottle.

I'd been thinking about what had happened, regretting my every decision, so when he asked if he could join me I had no defenses left. It was his face — so calm and caring. He had this amazing quality to the way he listened, like he was interested in everything I had to say.

A few months later I got a flat tire on the outskirts of town, and he'd been driving by. He pulled over and put the spare on, then called a tow truck to take my car to a nearby service station. It was a relief to let someone take care of everything for once.

It took a while before I felt strong enough to go out with him, but when I did, everything just clicked like it was meant to be. He was older than me, but he had all the confidence and maturity that came with it. He was funny and charming, and eventually I started to forget the night my life fell apart. I owed Liam all of that. Not just my safety, but my sanity too.

"I think I'll go in to work," I said. That's what Mom would do, I decided. She had that whole British stiff upper lip thing going on. I would just keep moving like she would have.

"But the doctor said you need to rest," Liam argued.

"I'm fine, I swear. Besides, I know you

need to work. I can tell that new building is stressing you out."

Liam looked surprised. "I'm sorry. I didn't know it was so obvious. There was one tiny code violation, and now the building inspector's being a pain in the ass."

"Will you have to take the building down?"

Liam laughed. "No, of course not! He'll come around. I know how to deal with these guys. I am *not* losing this project." He moved to get his coat. "Come on, I'll drive you to the gallery. Just promise you'll take it easy today."

"I can drive myself."

He gave me a look. "How? Your car isn't in the garage."

I hesitated, trying to sort through the fractured pieces of my brain. But there was no memory there. Andrew said the paramedics had found me near Mom's house. Had I driven there?

Liam gathered our plates and took them to the kitchen sink. "You really shouldn't be driving anyway."

He was probably right. Pain radiated around my head, and my arm was buzzing. I hurried upstairs and swallowed a few ibuprofen, then grabbed my purse and my quilted coat, since my green corduroy one was still missing.

In town, I kissed Liam good-bye and made my way toward the gallery, listening to my voice mail as I walked. The first one was from Andrew, his voice low and tight, the way it used to get when he was little and trying not to cry.

"Eva, have you talked to the detective yet?" There was a long pause. *"They've cleared Mom's house. I can't . . . I can't go there yet. The cops gave me a list of crime scene cleanup companies. We need to choose one, okay? Call me."*

The next message was from my dad. We hadn't spoken much since he'd remarried a few years ago, but the sound of his voice brought tears to my eyes.

"Hi, sweetie. I've just heard. . . ." His voice cracked. *"Is there anything I can do? Call me. I love you."*

Just as I hung up, the slate-gray sky unleashed a flurry of raindrops. I hurried down the alley to the gallery. Inside, Melissa was bent over the desk at the back poring over reports from the cash register. She looked up, surprised to see me.

"Holy shitballs!" She gawked at the lump on my forehead. "What the hell happened to you? Liam said you were sick!"

She pulled me in for a tight hug, smelling

of hairspray and chocolate chip cookies. I winced and she let go.

"Christ, you look horrible! Liam start hittin' you or somethin'?" She laughed at her own joke.

"I got struck by lightning."

She burst out laughing. "No way!"

"Seriously."

Her smile faded. "Seriously? Are you okay?"

I bit my lip. "I don't . . . actually know," I said slowly.

As soon as I told Melissa what had happened, she locked up the gallery and brought me to the café across the street. We were huddled at a corner table overlooking the harbor. A thick mist crept slowly across the water, fingers of pale gray shrouding Puget Sound in a dewy cloak.

"The police think you might have *murdered* your *mom*? Christ." Melissa sat back heavily in her chair. "Do they have any evidence?"

"I don't know. But my fingerprints and DNA would be at her house anyway, so I don't know how to explain that it wasn't me, especially because I can't remember."

Melissa stared at me, appalled, the same way she'd stared at me the first time we met.

We were both waiting to get our hair cut, and I'd told my stylist I wanted my hair chopped to my scalp. Melissa's gaze had jerked up from the magazine she was reading.

"Honey, you don't want to do that," she'd said. She flipped to a page in the magazine and held it out to me. "Look here." She tapped a manicured fingernail on a picture of a woman with a small, pointy face and a carefully mussed pixie cut.

A few days later I saw a NOW HIRING sign on the door of the Crafted Artisan gallery. Turned out Melissa was the owner. She'd hired me on the spot.

"You gotta find yourself a lawyer, hon." She shook her head, her dark curls dancing around her face.

"Liam set up an appointment with one tomorrow," I said. "He's going to come with me to be interviewed by the detective."

"That's good, right?" Melissa's phone rang, but she pressed End and ignored it. "Right?"

"I don't want Liam to come with me."

"Why?"

I didn't answer at first. I lifted my teaspoon and stirred my tea, watching the milky liquid swirl dizzyingly. I felt like I was looking down from a very great height, about to jump but not sure where I would land.

"A few years ago, before I moved here, I was raped. It was a . . . really difficult time for me. I never told Liam. I don't want him to find out."

"Oh, honey . . ."

I didn't want her pity. I didn't want her to think of me any differently. I just wanted to say it out loud, to have someone understand how I was feeling.

"The thing is, I can't really remember that either," I said. I pushed my fingertips into my sinuses to keep the tears away. "I mean, I know it happened, I *know* it. But the police . . . I don't know, they didn't really believe me."

"What? Why not?"

"I was just so stupid. I was out drinking with a friend, and we were taking shots, like idiots, and I was drunk, but then I was *soo* drunk and . . ."

"It was *not* your fault!"

"When I woke up the next day, I took a shower. I wasn't thinking about evidence, but I guess I washed all of it away, so I couldn't prove anything. When I reported it, the cops put the pieces together and they built this picture of me as a slut, not a victim. They didn't believe me. And I couldn't remember it, exactly, so how could I prove it? The police didn't believe me, why should Liam? Why should I, for that matter?"

"Look, those cops were asshats!" Melissa was practically spluttering with fury. "You can't listen to them! *You* know what happened and you have to trust that. You could've filed a complaint against them. What a fucking shitshow!"

I smiled. I wished I had just a sliver of her confidence.

"I know Liam. He'll believe you and love you no matter what."

Melissa's phone rang again, and I waved at her to answer it. She hesitated, but snatched it up and walked a few feet away, speaking in low, angry tones. I checked my phone, scrolling through a handful of texts and missed calls from Andrew, my dad, Aunt Lily.

Shit. Lily. Mom was her best friend. Her only real one that I knew of. Lily'd always seemed a little lonely to me, despite a constant parade of unsuitable younger men. Maybe she'd needed Mom's unflappable nature and unswerving loyalty to counteract her fun, sometimes manic ways. She must be devastated.

"Sorry." Melissa slid back into her seat.

"I've had to suspend Scott's weekend visits with Claire. She caught him looking at porn last time she was there! *Porn!* Poor kid's scarred for life. Plus he forgot to pay child support this month. He just sits in his basement jerking off and playing video games. Anyway." She slashed a hand through the air. "Enough about him. I was thinking, maybe you should go back there. To your mom's house."

"Why would I do that? It's —" I started to say it was a crime scene, then remembered that it wasn't anymore, not according to Andrew.

"You need to trigger your memories somehow, right? Maybe going back will help you remember. And if you remember, you'll get your answers."

"I don't know. . . ."

I wanted to open my head, to force the memories out. From the moment I'd woken in the hospital yesterday, I'd felt like I'd been snapped back to four years ago, the police shaking their heads, their dubious, sideways glances. But how do you feel guilty for something you don't even remember?

"Well, look," Melissa said. "It certainly can't hurt to try. Just be careful if you do. Whoever killed your mom might come back."

■ ■ ■ ■

Back in the gallery, Melissa handed me a brown padded envelope that had come through while we were gone. "More mail for you."

I took the package into my tiny studio at the back and set it on the desk where I painted. I rummaged around for a pair of scissors in the top drawer and carefully slit it open. Inside were broken pieces of ash-fired brown and pink pottery, which I slid carefully onto the desk.

"What is it?" Melissa asked. She was leaning against the doorway that separated the studio from the art gallery.

I read the accompanying note out loud:

> "Dear Eva, You made this urn for me when my daughter passed away and this weekend my cat knocked it over. I know I'm asking you to perform a miracle, but can you fix it?
>
> "Fiona Hudson."

I paused. "I remember her. Her daughter died in a car accident. She stopped in here last summer and asked me to make an urn." I tried to fit the pieces back together. "There's a huge chunk missing here. How am I supposed to fix this?"

The bell above the door chimed. Melissa went to greet the customer and I set the pieces of the urn down, trailing behind her. I stopped abruptly when I saw who'd entered.

Detective Jackson.

And he was smiling in a way that made me very uncomfortable.

NINE: KAT

25 Years Before

"Bloody police," Sebastian grumbled. The news story on the car radio had been detailing a crime squad convicted of fabricating evidence. "Always making shit up."

He flicked the radio off as he parked outside the Regency-style house in Mayfair, London's poshest neighborhood.

I did not reply — I knew when my husband required my input — but it was an extraordinary statement for Seb to make. Half the police in North London were in his back pocket. Seb's shady dealings were no longer a big secret in our house. Be that as it may, it was necessary that I pretend I didn't know.

I studied Rose's house. The white stucco façade gleamed in the clean spring sunshine. Fluted pillars, elegant wrought iron balconies, and bow windows decorated the exterior. Even the lacy strands of ivy climbing over the door looked posh. Butterflies shivered in my stomach.

"Cracking house, right, Katherine?"

I kissed Seb's cheek, which was already dark and rough despite having shaved only a few hours before. I didn't reply as I didn't know what he was playing at. Was he tricking me? At any rate, silence was usually safest these days. Seb's temper had been more volatile than usual of late, likely a result of his new restaurant not doing as well as expected. The restaurant he was in direct competition with had initiated a special buy-one-get-one-free promotion to ensure its customers did not visit Seb's. He was furious and had been simmering for days.

I unbuckled my seat belt and pushed my door open, but Seb reached across the console and roughly grabbed my left breast, eyes glittering. I froze, my skin itchy with a sudden fear. He did this sometimes, not in a sexual way, in a proprietary way.

"These people are inconsequential," I said smoothly. "They were born into their wealth. They have not earned it."

Seb dropped his hand and smiled. I breathed a silent sigh of relief. I knew my husband. He did not like to feel inferior.

I got out of the car and unbuckled Eva from the backseat. I tugged her out, but the seat belt had looped around her leg.

"Oww!" she howled.

"Christ, Katherine! Be careful!" Seb glared at me. He was not a large man, my husband, but he had this ability to seemingly inflate his body, like a peacock.

"Sorry," I muttered.

I finally managed to wrestle Eva's small body out of the car onto the pavement. We waved as Seb drove away. I dropped to my knees and smoothed Eva's blond hair behind her ears. "Today you will get to play with Laura, but you mustn't misbehave. Promise you'll be on your very best behavior?"

"I promise, Mummy!" She nodded, her blue eyes earnest as she clutched her teddy bear tightly to her chest. "And Barnaby does too."

I rang the doorbell, and after a minute Rose answered. She had made rather less of an effort today than she had at the park: no makeup, bare feet, jeans and T-shirt, but still lovely.

"Katherine! I'm so happy to see you!" she exclaimed. Her cheek was impossibly soft when she pressed it to mine.

She pulled me into a very grand entry. A glittering crystal chandelier hung two stories above the entry, an elegant stairway sweeping to the second floor. I caught sight of my reflection in a gilt mirror. A neat and sensible woman stared back: brown wool skirt, clunky-heeled shoes, dishwater-blond hair scraped into a bun, bloodless lips. And next to me was Rose, beautiful and enigmatic, with skin creamy as morning milk, wide-spaced gray eyes, a generous mouth. We could not have been more different if we had tried.

I unglued my tongue from my sandpaper throat. "Thank you. It's lovely to be here."

"Mummy, is this a castle?" Eva whispered.

"This is Mrs. Ashford's house."

Eva smiled shyly and held up Barnaby. Rose knelt in front of her, shaking first Barnaby's, then Eva's hand. I immediately liked her for it.

"Hello, Eva," she said. "You may call me Rose if you like."

"Like the flower?" Eva asked.

Rose laughed. "Exactly like that! Now!" She straightened and clapped her hands. "Let me show you around. Laura appears to be hiding. She thinks it's jolly good sport. But hopefully we'll find her as we go."

Rose walked quickly through the house, her movements fast, excited, her hands flapping around her face like small birds. We followed Rose through an arched doorway that framed a formal living room with a white-stone fireplace, white couches, silvery drapes, and a series of framed black-and-white photos. More sitting rooms with equally luxurious decor followed, then the bathrooms and the designer kitchen.

"Your home is truly stunning," I said.

"Thank you. I did nothing to deserve it, I'm afraid. It's been in my family for ages. When my father passed a few years back, we moved in and renovated rather than selling."

A small, thin man wearing a navy suit and round wire-framed glasses bustled into the entry.

"Darling." Rose held a hand out to him. "This is Katherine, our new nanny. Katherine, this is my husband, David."

"Ah, Katherine." David smiled politely and shook my hand. His hand was small for a man, the bones of his knuckles sharp under pale skin. "Lovely to meet you."

"Likewise."

He glanced at a flashy silver watch on his wrist. "I must dash, I'm afraid. I'm rather late. I have a client arriving at the gallery this morning."

He slipped a black overcoat on and quickly vanished outside. Rose sighed, seeming irritated. She smoothed her hair over one shoulder, but a flame-red lock escaped, brushing the skin of her neck.

She looked up and caught me staring. I flushed and dropped my gaze, feeling exposed, as if I had been caught naked.

"I shall paint this morning," she announced. She glanced over her slim shoulder. "Now, where is Laura? That cheeky little monkey should be around here somewhere."

The morning passed in a whirl of childish games: coloring, playing dress-up, and learning letters, numbers, and animal sounds. Laura and Eva got along splendidly, so it was a pleasant morning indeed. I made sandwiches for lunch, and when I found the girls they were lying next to each other on their stomachs in the playroom, their legs kicking in the air as they colored.

"What're you drawing?" Laura asked.

"A bear," Eva said shyly.

"You can't draw a bear inside a house, silly!" Laura giggled. She was rather more outgoing than Eva, the leader in their imaginative play.

I left their sandwiches and returned downstairs with a cup of tea and a sandwich for Rose. I found her at the back of the house in a glass conservatory that had been converted into a painting studio. Paint-splattered canvas throws covered the floor beneath a handful of oversize easels and a cluttered wooden desk with an array of half-empty acrylic paint tubes scattered across it. The room overlooked a vine-shaded terrace, beams of light falling directly onto the paintings.

Rose had changed into overalls and sat on a stool in front of a painting, her hair damp and sticking to her forehead. The painting was appalling, a truly pretentious mess of large, colorful blobs splattered in geometric patterns against a black background.

"I brought you a cuppa." I held the mug out to her. "And a sandwich, if you're hungry."

Rose accepted the tea but set the sandwich aside.

"Thank you, that's very kind. Look!" She gestured at the painting and moved to stand next to me. "What do you think?"

"Oh, I wouldn't claim to understand art. I'm rubbish at that sort of thing."

"Even better! I'll get an honest opinion."

I cleared my throat, pretending to study the canvas. "It's . . . transformative. The colors are alive and so . . . revelatory."

Rose was silent for a moment, then she giggled. Soon her giggles had turned into great belly laughs, so infectious that I too began laughing. Before I knew it, we were both howling, as if we'd known each other for ages.

"Oh, Katherine!" She wiped her eyes. "*Transformative.* You are entirely too much! I absolutely adore you!"

"In retrospect, I should have stuck with 'it's lovely,' " I said wryly. "Truly, I know nothing about art."

"Here, sit." She waved at the bench that circled the conservatory, and we sat next to each other. Without her makeup, she looked very young and also a little brittle, as if she would break if a fly landed on her. She was far too thin, her clavicles sharp, her cheekbones jutting out from her face like arrows. Honestly, she looked like she could use an extra sandwich and perhaps a rather good shag.

"How are the girls?" she asked.

"They've had lunch and are coloring."

"Lovely. Thank you. Where are you from, Katherine? I can't quite place your accent."

"North of here. A village near Birmingham."

"Do your parents visit often?"

"My mother left when I was a teenager. And my father passed away a number of years ago."

"Oh, I do apologize."

"There's no need. I have my own family now. That's what's important." I searched for something to say, to not appear so awkward. "Your husband, David, he must love his work."

"Yes, he does. I apologize he rushed out so fast earlier. He's expanding the gallery to focus on Asian art, so he's quite busy right now. He spends quite a bit of time traveling, looking for new pieces. What about you? What does your husband do?"

"He owns a chain of restaurants in North London. He's just opened a new one in Camden."

"Is that how you met?"

"Yes, I was waitressing there whilst studying."

"How romantic!" she exclaimed. "Was it love at first sight?"

I cast my mind back, trying to remember. It's funny, in school I easily memorized pages of French parts of speech, recalled chemical interactions with astonishing ease. I'd once trained myself to memorize one hundred digits of pi. But I could not remember if I had loved Seb. My memory of our early relationship was like a journal entry: selective, incomplete, subject to interpretation.

"Not wholly, no," I said slowly. "He was very . . . busy, of course. I was closing the restaurant one night, and he invited me to share a bottle of wine he was sampling. I was utterly swept away by him."

I gulped a mouthful of tea, trying to stop the memory from rolling across my face.

At first, I'd been thrilled at Seb's attention. I was square-shaped, shortsighted, not used to the attention of handsome, charismatic men. But that night, in the restaurant's back office, his attention became overwhelming. I wanted to tell him to stop, but I feared losing my job. And then it was too late. His hand was in my knickers, his breath hot on my neck. His penis bulged against my thigh, a damp splotch already appearing on the thin material of his trousers. And whilst it didn't disgust me, exactly, I couldn't say it was truly what I wanted.

In fairness, Seb was chuffed to bits when I told him about Eva. We married soon afterward, and he had been an absolutely brilliant father to Eva.

"My father was David's mentor. David took over the art gallery for him." Rose smiled, but it didn't quite reach her eyes. "Dad thought the world of David. I did — I do too." She looked at her painting, drying on the easel, and bit her lip. "You must think me daft. So spoiled and entitled! All this domestic perfection, and yet here I am longing to retreat into my painting."

"No, you're mistaken," I denied, although that was exactly what I had thought.

"It's kind of you to say. I do realize how ridiculous it is. I started out rushing to perform my domestic duties, laying the dinner table, stocking the fridge, changing nappies, not to mention the bloody laundry, earning my A-plus as a housewife. These are surely happy problems, but I didn't realize fulfilling these duties wouldn't insulate me from wanting other things — painting, friends, late nights walking along the Thames. To be perfectly honest, I thought by now I'd be a successful artist living in New York, maybe Paris, carefree, child-free. Perhaps I sound selfish." She sighed.

"Certainly not," I replied. "There's more to raising a family than baking cookies."

She laughed. "Thank you, Katherine. I suppose sometimes life just doesn't turn out how you expect."

I thought of the nights when Seb got home late, his skin smelling of the sickly scent of other women. Or the nights he slid into bed, running his thick fingers over my flesh, and I'd recoil with a loathing so thick and black it was like tar. I had no family, no money, no security, but sometimes the idea of escape dangled tantalizingly in my mind.

No, I thought. *Sometimes life doesn't turn out how you expect.*

"I understand," I said.

Rose smiled slowly, understanding coloring the smooth planes of her face.

"I rather think you do," she said. "Would you like another cuppa?"

TEN: EVA

Detective Jackson glanced around the gallery. He picked up a sculpture and raised his eyebrows at the lofty price tag. Melissa's dark eyes ping-ponged between us.

"I'll just go for a cigarette," she said, sidling toward the door.

Jackson gestured toward my head as I stepped out from behind the counter. "How are you feeling?"

I gingerly touched the lump on my temple. The lightning marks on my arm buzzed with that strange electric thrumming, as if I'd put my tongue to the end of a battery.

"I'm okay. I mean, I'm better. I don't remember anything, but physically I'm better." I flushed. My teeth found a tiny piece of skin on my thumbnail. I tore it off, blood oozing along the nail. "I thought our interview was tomorrow?"

Detective Jackson pulled a small notebook from an inner coat pocket and thumbed the pages. "Yes, your fiancé made an appointment, but I told him I'd head up this way. I've always wanted to see Whidbey Island. I only moved here last year from Boston, and I've heard it's beautiful."

Liam knew he was coming? Why didn't he warn me?

"I know you've been through a lot the last few days." He whistled low and shook his head. "Struck by lightning. You have to be incredibly unlucky to get struck. Or maybe just lucky not to die, right? I mean, what are the odds?"

"One in three thousand in your lifetime."

He lifted his eyebrows.

I shrugged. "I looked it up."

He nodded toward the studio behind me. "That where you work?" His face was relaxed, but his pale eyes were sharp, calculating, the way a wolf looks when it's stalking its prey.

"Yes. It's my studio. I rent it for painting my pottery."

He skirted past me and went inside. I followed him, watching as his eyes landed on the broken urn I'd left on the desk. He picked up one of the pieces.

"What happened to it?"

"A client's cat knocked it over. She sent it to me asking if I could fix it."

"Can you do that?"

"I'm not sure yet."

Jackson picked up another broken piece. He held both up to the light and tried to slot them together. "It won't ever be the same again, no matter what you do."

He set the pieces back on the desk and turned to me. "We found your car." He pronounced it *cah.* "Do you remember parking it by your mom's house?"

I shook my head, mind churning. So my car *was* at my mom's! "No. I'm sorry, I don't remember."

"Could someone else have driven it? Taken your keys?"

I grabbed my purse from where I'd set it on the corner of my desk. I shoved aside gum wrappers, loose change, sunglasses, a packet of menthol Halls before finding my keys and shaking them at the detective.

"No, they're here."

"Does anybody have a copy?"

"I keep a spare key in a magnetic box under the car."

"Have you remembered anything else?"

"No. Look, do I need a lawyer?"

"*Do* you?"

Everything was suddenly too bright, too loud, too overwhelming. I wanted him to go away. Jackson snapped his notebook shut and took a step closer to me. My back pressed against the studio wall, the space seeming smaller than ever. I had nowhere to go. I knew he was doing it to intimidate me, and it was working. Sweat had broken out under my arms and along my hairline.

His mouth twisted in a cruel approximation of a smile. "I pulled your file, Eva. I was really sorry to hear about what happened to you."

His words were light, but his eyes were menacing. "I would've done a more thorough investigation than Detective Anderson did. You know he retired last year? Moved to Alaska to fish. But me . . ." He shook his head, his blue eyes narrow. "I never would've stopped until I found the guy who did that to you."

I dug my fingertips into my armpits, *hard,* desperate to stay grounded.

"Did you ever remember who attacked you?"

"No." I looked away.

"Did you ever wonder why you can't remember?"

"I . . ." I swallowed, my throat desert-dry. "I think I was drugged."

"But they didn't find any drugs in your system?"

I didn't reply. If he'd pulled my file, he

already knew the answer to that.

Jackson snapped his notebook open again. "Tell me again about what you remember the night your mom was murdered."

"I already told you! I can't remember anything!"

"I'm just wondering if not remembering is a defense mechanism you fall back on often."

"I was struck by lightning! I didn't choose to not remember!"

"What was your relationship with your mother like?"

I searched his face, wondering what the right answer was. He had a fleck of spit gleaming on his lower lip. A tiny scab on his chin from a shaving cut.

"It was fine."

"Interesting, because I found a domestic violence incident filed against you two years ago." He rifled through his notebook and pulled out a piece of paper. "Here it is. Third-degree assault. Eva, you attacked your mom."

"That's not what happened!" Adrenaline zipped through me like a live wire, pulsing in my head. My voice clenched around the jagged knife in my throat. "The police dropped the charges."

"Yes, I know. Katherine didn't want them

to press charges."

"This is crazy." I put a hand on my desk to steady myself, my knees rubbery. It was happening again. "I did not hurt my mom! That other time, that was an accident!"

Jackson's expression remained indecipherable, but I knew. He didn't believe me. He folded his mouth into a thin line. When he spoke his voice was almost sympathetic.

"Do you think you did it again? Maybe you were visiting her. You had a panic attack, then suddenly the knife was in your hand. You didn't know what you were doing but you were scared, afraid the man who attacked you was back. You plunged it into her neck, then you ran, but the lightning got you before you could get away."

"No," I whispered. My rib cage felt like it was being crushed.

The images felt vivid. I could imagine what he described. But was it real? Memories could become distorted, twisted to suit the teller, or ignored and forgotten, pushed away. I should know. I'd been doing it for years.

"Eva!" The front door banged open, the bell ringing wildly. I pushed past Detective Jackson and rushed out to the gallery, Jackson right behind me. Liam strode across the gallery and shoved a finger in his face.

"You! You can't interview her without a lawyer present."

Melissa peered in the front door uncertainly.

Jackson shook his head, his lips twisted in the barest of smirks. "Not an interview." He glanced at me. "We were just talking, right, Eva? Although I could arrest you and bring you in for questioning . . . if that would suit you better?"

Liam thrust his jaw out. "If you had any evidence, you'd have arrested her already. Now, get out of here, or I'll report you for harassment."

Jackson shrugged and walked to the door. At the last second he turned, impaling me with his pale eyes.

He'd already made up his mind about me. I could see it. His suspicion was shaping my story.

"Don't go too far, Eva," he said. "We might need you for further questioning."

ELEVEN:
KAT

25 Years Before

I mentally ticked off the chores I'd completed now that Eva was asleep: toys tidied, floors mopped, counters gleaming, laundry washed and folded. Everything just the way Seb liked it when he arrived home after work. I half-listened to classical music murmuring quietly on the radio as I finished ironing Seb's shirts.

The music ended abruptly, and a reporter started speaking: *"A fire has broken out at a restaurant in Camden. Police believe the fire started just outside the kitchen of the Gardener. Two people are missing and fire engines are working to contain the blaze. No official cause has yet been released."*

Horror braided my stomach. The Gardener was very near Seb's restaurant. I wondered if he knew the people missing.

The front door slammed and Seb entered carrying a rather large, heavy-looking box. I set the iron down and followed him into the kitchen. He dropped the box on the counter while I filled a glass with water and handed it to him.

"Hello, love. Let me get your dinner heated," I said, squeezing past him to open the oven, where I'd kept the stew I'd made for dinner. I poured a large serving into a bowl and put it in the microwave.

"Here." Seb dug in his pocket and pulled out a twenty-pound note. "Get us a beef roast for Sunday."

I put the money in the jam jar I kept on top of the refrigerator, along with the rest of the weekly allowance Seb doled out for groceries. I looked around to ensure that everything was perfect, already trying to gauge his mood, to preempt his every need.

"I like your watch." I nodded at Seb's wrist.

Seb smiled. "Rolex. In this business, the face you put on becomes your identity. This watch says, *Don't fuck with me.*"

"Did you hear the Gardener caught fire tonight?" I asked. "Two people are missing."

"Bloody hell!" Seb's blue eyes widened. "That's tough luck, innit? Maybe I should head over and have a gander in a bit, eh?" He chuckled, as if watching his competition burn to the ground was funny. It made my stomach roil. "Bung my keys over, would ya, love?"

I plucked his keys from the key hook and handed them to him. He sawed at the box he'd set down, throwing a glance to me. "The paperwork came through for Eva's school today. She's been accepted at that Catholic one you liked."

"Seb, that's wonderful!" I exclaimed.

"I thought you'd be pleased."

"I am! Thank you!" I kissed Seb on the cheek.

It had taken a bit of convincing for Seb to agree to pay for private education, but ultimately he had caved. For all his flaws, he wanted the best for Eva too.

The microwave beeped, and I pulled out the bowl of stew with a cloth as Seb withdrew two large tins of cooking oil from the box, followed by a packet of shortbread biscuits.

Suddenly I froze. The unmistakable odor of smoke wafted in the air. Seb smelled it too, I could tell. He lifted his head, nostrils flaring.

"What's that smell?" he asked.

I shook my head, a sickening feeling churning in my stomach.

The fire alarm screamed to life. We raced

toward the source of the smell: the living room. The ironing board was billowing smoke, the iron facedown. Seb's shirt and the fabric ironing board cover were on fire. Orange and yellow flames licked at the air above the metal skeleton.

"Water!" Seb roared.

He dropped to the floor, beneath the smoke, and yanked out the iron's plug. He cursed as a flaming piece of fabric fell next to him. I hurried to the kitchen to fill a pot with water and rushed back to the living room, water sloshing over my feet. Seb was beating at the flame with a rug, ashes and sparks flying into the air. When I dumped the water over the remaining flames, it hissed, a quiet, dying whisper. I threw open the sliding glass door and hot, black smoke billowed outside.

Seb turned off the fire alarm, plunging us instantly into a thick silence cinched tight with his fury.

"Seb, I'm so sorry!" I breathed. "The iron — it must have tipped over. I didn't think —"

"No. You didn't think, did you, Katherine?" he snapped. "You never do."

He was right. What rational person walks away and leaves a hot iron unattended?

I waited, frozen, hoping if I didn't move,

didn't blink, didn't say a word, that perhaps Seb wouldn't punish me.

The first time Seb had hit me, Eva was just a baby. I had burned his dinner, so he punched me in the stomach. I almost left him, but of course there was Eva to consider. And it was my fault anyhow. I decided then to try harder, be a better wife, a better mother.

But *better* is such an idiosyncratic word. My definition of *better* certainly didn't match Seb's.

And it wasn't so bad, really. Nothing like my father, when he was drunk.

Seb grabbed me, yanking my arm nearly out of its socket. I flinched, even though I had been expecting it. I imagined the purple bruises that would appear, and the stories I would spin for Rose tomorrow flashed through my mind.

I tripped on the stairs.

I ran into the banister.

I caught my arm on the chain swings at the park.

Motherhood and marriage had made me a remarkable liar.

The distant wail of a fire engine reached my ears. Seb released me and rushed to the front door, opening it as a fire engine and a police car pulled onto the sidewalk in front of our house. Neighbors had clustered in the street, staring up at the smoke curling over our house like a cloud.

Seb jogged down the stairs to meet the firemen as I hovered in the doorway, gulping in great breaths of warm summer air. I glared at my neighbors, hating them for their nosiness. Seb spoke animatedly to the firemen, rolling his eyes and laughing. He didn't see the police officer circle the back of the fire engine and approach me.

The copper was a rather large man, with a bulky body, a double chin, and a graying handlebar mustache. His black-and-white captain's hat read METROPOLITAN POLICE.

"Everything all right, missus?"

I pushed my glasses up my nose, soot and ash thick in my throat. "Yes. We had a small fire, but not to worry. We've extinguished it."

He assessed me with dark, hooded eyes, then glanced toward Seb, who was still laughing with the firemen. "Sebastian Clarke's your husband?"

"Yes."

He cocked his head at me. "When did he arrive home tonight?"

"I suppose it was about twenty minutes ago."

"Interesting."

I frowned. "Why so?"

"Two fires associated with your husband in one night."

"You must be mistaken —"

"Katherine!" Seb called. "Can you check on Eva?"

"Yes, certainly." How on earth had she slept through this chaos? I turned to the policeman. "Apologies, Officer . . ."

"Hamilton."

"Apologies, Officer Hamilton. I must check on my daughter."

I turned and went inside, but not before I noticed Seb's eyes tracking my every move.

The next morning Seb was still odd with me, his responses abrupt and cool. The scent of smoke lingered in the air, bitter on my tongue. I prepared breakfast quickly, hoping Eva would keep her chatter to a minimum. He was clearly not in the mood.

I watched Seb out of the corner of my eye, my mind on what the police officer had said last night. Could Seb have set fire to the Gardener?

Once, when Eva was a baby, one of our neighbors had a raging house party. Cars blocked the road, and the sound of thumping music kept us up late into the night. Finally Seb took his keys and went outside, keying every one of the visitors' cars. Our neighbor and his friends came outside shouting. Shortly afterward, the police arrived, but the officer was on Seb's payroll, so he arrested our neighbor for breaching the peace.

When Seb returned, he'd seen me watching him with wide, baffled eyes. "They won't do it again," he said, his voice flat. "Trust me, it does no good to be seen as soft. I have a reputation to look after."

I knew he was thinking of his own childhood growing up on a council estate in East London. There, the only people who survived were those who established themselves as powerful, respected, and feared. Seb's reputation meant he'd gained those things. But would he go so far as to commit arson?

Personally, I'd always believed that while revenge might be sweet, it was also very like a medicine: a little could cure you, a lot could very well kill you. But I knew now more than ever that Seb did not feel the same way.

"Mummy, what's that?" Eva's voice brought me crashing back to the present. She was pointing up at the spot on the living room ceiling that had bubbled from the heat.

"Mummy was playing with fire," Seb

answered for me. He shoveled another bite of scrambled eggs into his mouth. "Wasn't that a bit stupid of her?"

Eva looked horrified. "Mummy! We don't play with fire!"

"No." I forced a laugh. "You are most certainly right, my love. We don't play with fire. I was very silly, but I'll clean it up today."

Seb dropped us off at Rose's and left without another word. The sticky August heat wave was already warming the air, the sun a hazy orb hanging over the skyline. I pushed my damp hair off my forehead, realizing for the first time that my hands were trembling.

I spent the day jumpy and on edge, with Rose constantly asking if I was okay. By the time we were waiting outside for Seb to collect us at the end of the day, I was a ball of nerves, dreading whatever punishment he'd dreamt up.

I squirmed as sweat trickled down my back into my knickers.

"Where's Daddy?" Eva whined.

"He'll be here soon."

I rubbed a smudge of dirt from her face. What sort of mother couldn't keep her own child clean?

Eva slapped at my hand. My eyes widened

in surprise.

"I'm hot!" she howled. "I want to go home!"

I gritted my teeth, suddenly furious at Seb.

We waited in the soupy afternoon heat for another half hour before I realized: Seb wasn't coming. *This* was my punishment. I was not dim enough to suppose that Seb would let me off lightly, but dragging Eva into my punishment was a new low.

I thought about asking Rose for a lift, but telling her the truth was far too humiliating. We would simply walk.

I clasped Eva's hand, our palms slippery with sweat. "Let's go trekking!" I exclaimed. "It will be brilliant! Like we're in the jungle!"

"Can we be tigers?"

"Absolutely, darling!"

It took us over an hour, walking along the quiet, dusty streets of Mayfair, through the cool green of Regent's Park, and over Primrose Hill. Eva's tears started about midway home.

We arrived at the same time Seb did, our clothes dripping with sweat and dust. A heat rash prickled between my thighs. My knickers were, quite literally, in a twist. Meanwhile, he looked fresh as a daisy, his tie still tight, blazer draped neatly over one arm.

Eva threw herself into Seb's arms, her face streaked with muddy tears.

"You're a bloody mess, Eva!" He peeled her off him, looking at me in disgust.

Furious, I shoved past him and stormed into the kitchen. The house still smelled of smoke, so I threw the window open, then pulled a pitcher of cool water from the refrigerator. I filled two cups and handed one to Eva.

"Why didn't you collect us?" I snapped at Seb.

"I was at work."

"We had to walk home! In this heat! You should've been there."

"You must be taking the piss! One of us has to make real money, not play with some bloody toff who's too spoiled to look after her own kid."

I slammed the pitcher back into the refrigerator. Behind me, Seb ordered Eva upstairs.

"I can't believe you, Seb! You could at least think about Eva! Don't you —"

Suddenly, something flashed in the corner of my eye. I tried to duck, but it was too late. The sound of metal crashing against the refrigerator filled my ears, and something slick and wet exploded all over me. And then Seb's fist smashed into my stomach. The air rushed out of me, and white flashes of fireworks detonated as I slid, boneless, to the floor.

I gasped for breath. On the floor next to me was one of the tins of cooking oil he'd brought home last night, the aluminum flayed open from the impact. Oil dripped from my hair, gummed my eyelashes, coated my clothes. It dribbled down the cupboards, the refrigerator, plopping onto the tile. The edges of my vision waved and blurred, rather like a mirage.

Seb was breathing heavily, his jaw clenched. I had pushed him too far. I'd failed to heed the warning signs.

Eva's sobs were a siren in my ears. I needed to comfort her. That's what a mother does: sacrifices herself to keep her child happy and safe.

I struggled to stand, pushing my oily hair out of my eyes and forcing a smile. "Eva, that's enough now! I've made a little mess, is all! What do I say about messes?"

Eva's sobs slowed. "We clean them up."

I lifted my gaze and met Seb's. "That's right. We'll just clean it up."

Twelve: Eva

"Eva, I told you not to talk to him!" Liam exclaimed after the detective had left.

"Why didn't you warn me he was coming?" I asked quietly.

Liam paused. "What are you talking about?"

I scrubbed my hands over my face. Melissa was still outside, hovering in the doorway. "Could I get a cigarette?" I asked her.

She held one out to me. I stepped outside, bending forward as she flicked the lighter. The nicotine hit my head so fast it made me dizzy, smoke threading into the cloudy sky.

"Eva, you don't smoke!" Liam's mouth then dropped open. I knew he was thinking about what the doctor had said: *paranoid, personality changes, mood swings, memory loss.*

Check, check, check, and check.

"I need to get out of here." Smoke hissed

through my teeth. I was shaking, trying to hold in all the unnamed things I felt. My mind whirled like a drunk ballerina. "Melissa, can I borrow your car?"

"Sure." She dug in her back pocket and tossed me the keys. "I have the pickup too, so take your time."

Liam lifted his hands, baffled, as I walked away. "Eva, come on!"

But for the first time in a long time, I ignored him.

By the time I got to Seattle I'd calmed down enough to realize I'd overreacted. I pulled up behind my old Honda down the street from Mom's. Night had fallen. The October air was crisp, the yellow, orange, and red foliage crunching under my feet. I did a cursory search of my car — a Snickers wrapper, a half-full bottle of water, a pair of flip-flops. Nothing that stood out.

That familiar feeling crawled over my neck, and the fine hairs on the backs of my arms stood on end. Someone was watching me. I felt their eyes hot on my body. I peered into the darkness, heart thumping. Nobody was there.

I grabbed a flashlight from the glove box and hurried across the road. The green shutters of Mom's Queen Anne–style house were pulled tight, the lights all off. From the outside, it just looked cold and lonely, not like the location of a horrible crime.

Going around to the back, I fumbled under the bottom step for the spare key and unlocked the back door. The arc of light from my flashlight swept across white kitchen countertops, a hulking black stove, silver pots hanging from a ceiling rack. A cluster of daffodils was drooping in a crystal vase on the island, crumpled petals just starting to fall. Drops from the kitchen faucet plinked against the bucket sink.

On the hallway walls were some of Jacob's best black-and-white shots: a Cuban man with smoke curling around his head; a painted woman stretching into the immensity of the Maasai Mara. In the living room, I swept the beam of the flashlight over the room.

Loose white powder dusted every surface. Vases and knickknacks were broken, knocked to the floor. I ran my fingers over the dusty fireplace mantel, picking up a photo of Mom, Andrew, and me playing in the sand at the beach. Next to it was a baby picture of Andrew. There were, I realized for the first time, no baby pictures of me.

Next to the fireplace, Mom's favorite armchair was missing. On the floor where it used to be, a large pool of blood had drenched the sand-colored carpet, the fibers glued together into a dark, crusting mass.

I stared at it, trying to remember, but there was nothing but whirling fog, like trying to catch the tail end of a dream. I held a couch cushion to my chest. Mom's smell gusted off it. Childhood memories buffeted me so relentlessly I literally felt homesick: Mom reading me *Little House on the Prairie* before bed; making lemonade together; her shouting for Andrew and me to *turn the bloody telly off* and get to the dinner table.

The other not-so-beautiful memories came too: how brusque and critical she could be; the irritated fold of her brow when we argued; her cruel words before I moved out: *Stop being a victim and start being a survivor.*

An unbearable sadness knuckled into my ribs. Tears filled my eyes. Was the detective right? Had I, in a moment of rage or fear or extreme anxiety, killed my mom?

I thumped my forehead with my palm. With the pain came a sudden memory. I was reading a book in bed, like I always did to help me get to sleep. Liam was asleep next to me, both arms thrown over his head like a child. My phone chimed with a text message.

Mom: Hello Eva. Can you come over? I realize it's late but it's urgent.

Me: Ok, but I'll have to wait for the ferry. Can prob get next one but will still be an hour or so.

Mom: I'll be waiting. Love you.

I snapped back to the present and pulled my phone from my purse. I scrolled through my texts, but there was nothing from Mom. Not since we'd met at the restaurant, a text saying she'd arrived.

I must have deleted the texts.

I must have.

Either that, or I was going completely fucking crazy.

I prowled the house, hoping to trigger another memory. In Mom's office upstairs, I rifled through science magazines and a stack of high school physics papers, shuffled through academic books on string theory and quantum mechanics and the history of time. The light from my flashlight bounced around the room. I flung down the book I was holding. It landed with a hard thud on the filing cabinet next to the desk.

I yanked the top drawer open. One of the hanging folders at the back was crooked, the metal claws dislodged. I pulled it out.

Inside was a small, brown teddy bear with a faded daffodil-spotted tie and a sealed, letter-size envelope marked with my name in Mom's familiar neat handwriting.

I turned the teddy bear over, trying to remember if it was mine as a child. I didn't recognize it. I set it down and slit the envelope open. Inside was an old British birth certificate for Eva Clarke. Mine, I supposed, before Mom and my adopted dad, Mike, got married. There was also a letter folded into a small square and a ripped piece of an envelope with an address in London for a David Ashford, written in unfamiliar block handwriting.

I smoothed the letter on the desk, my damp fingers smudging the ink.

Dear Eva,

I've written this letter a thousand times and thrown it away each time. The truth is you are not my daughter. I should have told you about your past — our past — many years ago, but I wanted to keep you safe. If anybody knew who we really are, we could all be in very grave danger. Perhaps it is not an excuse, but your safety has always been my priority.

I am so sorry.

Mum xx

I sank slowly into the leather chair, my legs like whipped cream. I felt like I'd been punched in the stomach, breathless and bewildered. A dark, wet horror rose in my mind.

She wasn't my mom.

We were in danger.

But why?

I set the flashlight on the desk and pulled my phone from my back pocket to google the address on the scrap. The results showed a website for Selwyn House Art Gallery, owned by David Ashford. Clearly he'd been writing to my mom. Who was he?

A door clicked shut somewhere in the house, loud as the crack of a gun. Then the low thud of boots on hardwood. My whole body tensed. Goose bumps rose on my arms, fear turning my stomach to liquid.

Someone was in the house.

I stood, heart hammering. I looked around for a weapon, remembering Melissa's words. *Whoever killed your mom might come back.*

Thump, thump, thump up the stairs. I froze. Fear crawled up my back like bugs. The silhouette of a masculine form appeared on the other side of the smoked-glass french doors. I snatched the flashlight from the desk and clicked it off, plunging the room into total darkness.

The doors swung open. Fear turned my fingers to rubber bands. The flashlight slipped from my sweaty grasp, clattering onto the floor.

"Eva?" The voice was familiar.

"Jacob?" I stared at my old friend. "Shit! I nearly killed you!"

Jake eased the dimmer switch up, glancing dubiously at the flashlight I'd dropped. "With a flashlight?"

"What are you doing in here?" I braced a hand on the desk to steady myself, weak from the jolt of adrenaline.

"I saw you go around back. I was calling for you but you didn't answer. The door was unlocked."

I stared at Jacob, feeling rattled, as if I'd been abruptly shaken. I couldn't understand why he'd come inside. It had been a long time since we were kids and could walk into each other's houses unannounced.

He squinted at me, seeing my expression. "Sorry, I shouldn't have —"

"No, it's fine," I cut him off. "It's good to see you."

I reached out to hug him just as he moved to kiss my cheek, and we ended up caught in a clumsy half-embrace, his mouth landing on my jaw. We pulled apart and laughed awkwardly.

The last time we'd seen each other, we'd been naked.

Jacob's face was lean, brown from the foreign sun. He was still skinny, still not much taller than me, but he'd filled out some. Fine lines fanned his green eyes. A few days' worth of stubble covered his jaw. His dark hair was longer than I remembered, tousled. He wore faded jeans and a green military-style jacket.

"I'm sorry to hear about your dad," I said. "He's sick?"

"Yeah. End-stage cancer. I'm staying at his house until . . ." Jacob shook his head, his Adam's apple bobbing as he swallowed hard. "I'm sorry about Kat. Like, what the fuck happened? Do the police have any leads?"

"I don't know. Andrew seems to think they . . . suspect me."

Jacob stared, incredulous. Then he threw his head back and laughed. It was inappropriate and ill-timed, but something about it made me feel a tiny bit better. Like, yes, maybe this was all a horrible joke. Of course nobody really thought I could kill my mother.

"Is he insane? Why would he even think that?"

"I was struck by lightning a few blocks

from here. The problem is, I can't remember anything. The lightning wiped out my memory."

"Struck by lightning? Christ, are you okay?"

"I'm fine."

"Sorry for laughing. Just, the thought of you as some murdering badass . . ." He made a scoffing sound. "You cried after getting stung by a bee because you knew it would die. Anyone who knows you would never think you could hurt your mom."

I handed him Mom's letter. "Apparently she wasn't actually my mom."

He read the letter, then blew out a shocked breath. "She must've been involved in something. Do you have any idea what it was?"

"No. She never said anything. All I have is this stupid, cryptic letter!"

"Maybe she meant to tell you the full story in person."

A shout came from down the street. I stood and peered out the wooden blinds. Detective Jackson and a cop I didn't recognize stood next to my car, watching as an impound truck hitched it to the tow.

"Oh my God!" I backed away from the window and turned the light off, plunging the room into shades of sepia. The streetlight threw yellow strips of light onto the carpet through the blinds.

"That's the detective!" I hissed. "He must really suspect me! He's impounding my car!"

Suddenly I knew it wasn't Mom's death that would haunt me, but the blank space where my last memories of her should've been.

I'm sick of not trusting myself, I realized.

"I have to find out what happened that night," I whispered to Jacob. "I need to know if someone else killed my mom, or if I did it."

THIRTEEN: KAT

25 Years Before

My hand hovered over Rose's front door. I rapped sharply, practicing what I would say.

This is our last day, Rose. Our last day.

The thought of not seeing her every day was truly ghastly. In the few short months I'd known her, Rose had become my closest confidante, my dearest friend. In all honesty, my only friend. But Seb was right. I needed to focus on Eva, especially this last month before she started school. I was certain Rose would understand.

"Looks like it'll be another scorcher," Rose said as we followed her into the sticky belly of the house. She wore a long, flowing skirt with a bright flower pattern and a tight rust-colored tank top, her cleavage on display. Her hair hung in glossy red waves to her shoulder blades. She looked cool and fresh. I, on the other hand, was baking in my brown trousers and collared shirt. I pressed my arms against my sides to hide the sweat stains.

I opened my mouth to tell her then. But Rose clapped her hands and announced that it was too hot to paint so she would take the day off.

"Shall we make lemonade?" she asked.

Laura and Eva jumped up and down, shrieking, "Yes, yes, yes!"

I smiled. "Very well, then, girls, settle down."

Rose and I gathered the lemons from the pantry. She sliced the shiny yellow orbs in half, and we all took turns squeezing them. Eventually the girls tired of the task and began coloring. Sweat beaded on my hair-line and my palms itched as Rose and I continued squeezing, the tart scent heavy in the air.

"Blimey! What a rubbish idea this was!" Rose moaned. "I'm boiling!"

I swiped at a bead of sweat sliding down my nose as I poured a cup of sugar into the pitcher with the lemon juice. Rose rinsed her hands in the sink and fanned herself with one of Laura's books. It gave me a good idea.

"Perhaps you have some fans?" I said. "I reckon we could set them in the windows."

"That's a brilliant idea!"

I followed Rose to a cupboard under the stairs and helped her drag out several fans clouded with dust.

"I forgot we even had these — you're a genius, Katherine." She grabbed a cloth to wipe them clean.

We bustled around the house opening windows and balancing fans in them, drawing the curtains on either side to keep it as shady as possible. Outside, the sun was already high in the sky, a smear of milk-white glistening against the blue. The sweltering heat made it difficult to breathe.

Rose had just settled the last fan in the kitchen window and was pouring lemonade into glasses with ice when I entered. Her skin was glistening at the nape of her neck, damp curls sticking to her forehead.

I noticed she had put the fan in the window the wrong way, blowing in rather than out. As it was the sunny side of the house, the fan should have been blowing the hot air out, whilst the shady side of the house should have the fans blowing in. I was certain I had told her that, but I was too hot and frazzled to correct her mistake.

"Here." She pressed a glass of lemonade into my hand and sighed as she lifted the cool liquid to her lips.

"Mummy, can we watch a movie?" Laura

asked. Her face was pink and shiny from the heat.

"What a splendid idea! *All Dogs Go to Heaven* is still in the VCR. You remember how to press Play?"

Laura nodded and grabbed Eva's hand, tugging her toward the stairs.

"Mummy, can I have Barnaby?" Eva asked.

"Certainly, darling."

I retrieved Barnaby from my handbag, and she headed up the stairs, her thumb already heading for her mouth. The heat was making all of us drowsy.

Rose and I took our lemonades into the living room and collapsed on the couch, our damp skin making soft *thwucking* noises as it stuck to the leather. The sheer, silvery curtains billowed in the breeze of the open windows. The scent of lavender from the garden hung in the air, tangling with the delicate floral scent of the street's many mimosa trees.

"I have an excellent idea." Rose jumped up, her gray eyes gleaming. She disappeared, reappearing after a moment with a bottle of Jameson. She grinned. "Let's make these bad boys Irish."

She poured a large glug into her glass and moved toward mine.

"Oh no — not for me." I covered my glass, but she shushed me.

"Don't be silly. You need to learn to let go, relax a little!" She put a finger over her upper lip like a mustache and lowered her voice to the timbre of a man's. "You're far too responsible."

"Be that as it may —"

"It's only one drink, Katherine!"

I hesitated. It *was* a Friday, after all.

"Very well, then," I relented. "But only a splash."

Rose's idea of a splash was rather a lot more than mine, and soon we were both giggling, the alcohol making us loose-limbed and giddy. It felt glorious.

"Do you reckon the girls are asleep?" Rose asked.

"Almost certainly."

"Oh, good!"

She set her drink on the glass coffee table and slipped out of her skirt. She kicked it onto the floor, her black knickers just hinting at the creamy curve of her arse cheeks.

"There." She slumped next to me on the couch. "That's better!"

She lifted her hair off her neck, the scent of lemons and happiness curling around her body, an intoxicating aroma.

A hot flush crawled up my throat and

cheeks. "Rose. Honestly!"

Rose laughed. "You're so uptight, Katherine! Don't you ever want to let go? Just do something for yourself?"

I kicked my shoes off and peeled the sweaty socks from my feet. "There." I wiggled my toes at her. "I have 'let go.' Happy?"

She laughed and drained her glass. "Delighted. But seriously. Don't you ever want to truly let go? Like, get absolutely pissed, or go skinny-dipping in the middle of the day. Just not have a care in the world?"

I pondered her question. "Frankly, it seems quite impossible. Like imagining going faster than the speed of light, or that I can breathe liquid rather than air, or that Jupiter is more habitable than Earth."

"But why?" Rose pressed.

I took a giant gulp of my drink, wincing as it burned my throat.

"My mother left when I was fifteen. Packed her clothes and disappeared. I was left to take care of my father, the village drunk. I suppose I had to learn at a very young age to be responsible, to squirrel money away, to rely on the kindness of neighbors to eat, to clean up vomit and . . ." I looked away, shame burning with the alcohol in my stomach. ". . . dodge drunken fists. So when I fell pregnant with Eva, I was determined to do whatever was necessary to ensure she had a real childhood. I never want to skip out on my responsibilities like my mother did."

"Bloody hell." Rose shook her head and slopped more Jameson into our glasses. The rims of her eyes were red. "You're like a real-life saint. Keep calm and carry on, right?"

I laughed. "Well, I also grew up Catholic, so there's that. Perhaps I inherited some of the guilt my mother never had."

She threw back half her drink. When she spoke, her voice had tilted into a slur: "There was this woman at the park who said it was a relief becoming a mum because suddenly there was someone more important than her. I thought it was a stupid thing to say. Perhaps I craved domestic bliss and rushed into marriage to ensure that I would have a family, but now I'd almost give it all up."

Her eyes glittered, and for a second she looked rather mad. But she was drunk. She didn't mean it, so I smiled and tried to lighten the mood. "Surely *domestic* and *bliss* don't belong in the same sentence. *Domestic* is a euphemism for a servant, and the idea of blissful servitude is an oxymoron."

Rose threw her head back and laughed for a long time. I laughed with her, the booze loosening my limbs. She looked so comfortable sitting there half-naked, so utterly certain of herself.

She flopped onto her side so she was facing me. "I wish we could drink Irish lemonade every day."

I opened my mouth to reply — but just then the shrill sound of a child's scream sliced through my body.

"What was that?" Rose jumped up.

"Eva." I raced for the stairs, Rose stumbling behind as she yanked her skirt on, and we burst into the playroom.

Laura was sitting on top of a chest-high bookcase next to the open window. The pale drapes fell over her shoulder like a shawl. Her eyes were wide, face pale. One knee hung over the edge of the bookcase, the other over the window ledge.

"What are you doing?" I shouted, yanking her to the floor. "Where's Eva?"

Laura's cheeks hollowed as she sucked in deep breaths.

I gave her a small shake of the shoulders. "Where's Eva?"

She pointed at the open window. I lunged toward it, looked left, then right. I only saw row after row of Regency houses, pale stone and red brick, shiny cars glinting in the white sun. Up and down the street, trees were drooping, their leaves flaccid as day-old lettuce in the heat.

Rose stuck her head out the window and looked down.

"Oh my God," she whispered.

She backed away. Her fingers clawed at her hair, tearing at it. Her eyes were wide, the whites stark and haunting, her voice turning into one long, mournful keen. "OhmyGodohmyGodohmyGod!"

Finally my eyes latched on to what she had seen: the broken figure of a little girl crumpled on the ground. Her long blond hair was fanned around her face, her back and neck twisted at an impossible angle. She looked like a porcelain doll, so still, her blue eyes wide and staring, sightless, at the blue sky above, a puddle of something dark expanding around her head like a halo.

And then I saw Barnaby, Eva's teddy, lying next to the girl's tiny, unfurled fist. A few feet away lay the trumpet-shaped hat, now torn from his head.

And I knew.

I knew.

Eva.

I threw myself down the stairs, bursting out the front door, across the gravel to where my daughter lay in a crumpled heap.

My knees buckled and I collapsed, a howl launching from deep inside me. A widening pool of blood crept from my baby's head. It soaked into the fabric of my trousers as I reached out to touch her, to hold her and beg her to come back to me.

But she didn't. She wouldn't move. She lay limp and lifeless in my arms.

And I screamed and screamed and screamed.

Fourteen: Eva

The impound truck beeped loudly from outside Mom's house. I looked at Jacob through the shades of sepia cast by the yellow street lighting.

"I have to find out what happened the night Mom was killed," I said again. "Maybe this letter has something to do with it."

"And how do you plan on doing that?" Jacob asked.

"I'll go to London. Tonight. I'm going to talk to this David Ashford guy myself."

Jacob looked uncertain. "Really? Don't you think leaving the country's a little extreme? You said you're a suspect."

"My mom's been murdered, Jake! And, oh, it turns out she wasn't actually my mom. I need to find out what 'dangerous' thing she was involved in and if it led to her murder. If anything, I'm not being extreme enough! And they haven't arrested me yet."

"Well, why don't you tell that detective

about the letter?"

Jackson's words echoed in my head: *Don't go too far, Eva. We might need you for further questioning.*

"I can't."

"Why?"

"This is motive!" I shook the letter at him. "They'll think I killed her!" I covered my face with my hands. "What if they don't believe me? I could end up in jail!" The thought winded me. I shook my head hard. "I'll be back before the detective even finds out I've left."

For a second Jacob looked conflicted, but then he shoved his hands in his jeans pockets and lifted his shoulders. "Okay. What can I do to help?"

I handed Jacob my credit card, and he booked me a seat on the next flight to London while I grabbed a backpack and filled it with a handful of the clothes I'd left at Mom's when I moved out. Fortunately, my passport was still in the bedside drawer in my old room, so I grabbed it, too.

I didn't stop to think. I didn't have a plan. I just made it up as I went.

"Come on, I'll drive you to the airport," Jacob said when I was ready. "My dad's sleeping. He won't even know I'm gone."

I locked the door behind us and followed

him in the direction of his house. Jacob still moved in that familiar way — long strides, lazy gait. Like he didn't have a care in the world. He didn't take anything seriously. With a dad like his, how could he? He was the kind of guy who dumped bubble liquid into the city's water fountain one night and randomly drove up to Canada to use his fake ID the next. He was a classic Peter Pan. But Peter Pan was a lot more adorable as a teenager than he was at thirty.

Jacob beeped the alarm to unlock his car while I texted Melissa, letting her know I was going out of town and would get her car back in a few days.

"You still have the Trans Am?" I asked, incredulous.

"I don't really drive it much." He shrugged. "Only when I'm back here between photography assignments. She's had a few new engines, a lot of new tires. I keep her in good shape."

"It must be, like, twenty years old now. You bought it with money from your first photography sale, right?"

"Yep. Best purchase I ever made." He patted the roof of the car, smiling. A navy-blue paint chip crumbled onto the ground.

"I'll never forget when you brought it home. It was the night before the homecoming game, and we were just driving around and you —"

"— decided to dig up a tree and plant it on the football field." He laughed as he opened my door.

"No-o." I buckled up while Jacob started the car and pulled onto the quiet street. "You didn't 'plant' the tree. You cemented it into the middle of the field!"

We burst out laughing, but I stopped abruptly, feeling guilty. How could I laugh right now? I bit my lip and stared out the window. The rain made grimy tracks down the passenger window as Jacob drove.

"What do you think you'll find in London?" Jacob asked.

"I don't know. Maybe this David Ashford guy will know why we were in danger and if that had anything to do with her murder." I pushed my fingers into my aching eyeballs and shook my head. It was all so much to take in. "I wish I could just remember that night."

Why should the detective trust me when I couldn't even trust myself?

"Why don't I go with you?" Jacob said. "Maybe I can help."

I almost agreed. It would be nice to have him there, someone to help me figure out what to do. But I knew I couldn't say yes. I had a fiancé now. And Jacob never stuck around for long. I should know.

The night we slept together flickered briefly through my mind. There'd always been an unspoken rule that we would keep it platonic. And mostly we did. Except once, when I was in college. I'd just gotten home from my weekend job waitressing downtown. My roommate, Holly, was out for the evening. Jacob dropped by and we ended up drinking a bottle of red wine, and then another, and watching *Monty Python.* We were laughing uproariously and then we weren't; we were kissing, tearing each other's clothes off.

The next morning I woke with a mother of a hangover. A note from Jake was propped against the clock on my nightstand saying he'd be in touch when he returned from Peru. I tried not to take it personally, but the rejection had stung. Shortly after, I was attacked and lost my youth, my future, my confidence, the person I was supposed to become.

I glanced at Jacob, his still-familiar profile lit by the intermittent glow of streetlights as he drove, turning to look back at me. "I've missed you, Eva."

"Jake . . ." I said, my voice a warning. There was so much Jacob didn't know, so much I hadn't told him. The girl he used to know was not the same woman sitting next to him now.

"No, I don't mean like that. I miss my friend."

I looked at my hands. "I miss you too," I admitted.

My phone rang then, Liam's name flashing on the screen. I stabbed End.

"Sorry. My boyfriend. Fiancé . . ."

Jacob held my gaze for a long moment before his mouth quirked with amusement. "Aren't you glad thought bubbles can't appear over your head?"

I laughed, relieved, and just like that the moment passed.

Jacob threaded his way through traffic and pulled into the drop-off area at Sea-Tac Airport. The airport was crowded, a Ferris wheel of cars constantly zipping in and out.

"There, right there!" I pointed at a free space.

"I can't fit there."

"There's another one!"

"Would you just let me drive?"

I rolled my eyes and flopped back in my seat. Jacob flawlessly parallel-parked between two hulking Land Rovers, letting the car idle.

"There, see?" He turned to me with a

smug grin. "*I* know how to park. I think it was you who failed parallel parking in driver's ed, right?"

"Only 'cause you lied about how big eight inches was," I shot back.

His eyebrows shot up, and he laughed. "I don't remember you complaining!"

"You didn't give me a chance," I replied sweetly. I grabbed my backpack, keeping a smile fixed on my face, even though the hurt was still sharp despite four years apart.

The smile fell off Jacob's face. "Eva, about that night, I'm really sorry. . . ."

"Don't be —"

"I should've called sooner. I did try as soon as I got back from Peru. Did Holly tell you?"

I looked at my hands, clasped like iron around my backpack. Holly had told me every time Jacob called. Eight times before he accepted that I didn't want to talk.

"Yeah, she did. I was so busy and . . ." I lifted my eyes to his. "It was just too late, Jake. You know?"

He looked at me for a long minute. "Yeah. Yeah, I know."

An aggressive honk sounded behind us.

"I gotta go." I shoved the door open. "Thanks for the ride."

"Wait." Jacob pulled a set of keys from his

pocket and handed them to me. "I have a flat in London. Stay there as long as you want. I'll text you the address."

I lifted my eyebrows, surprised. Jacob had never wanted a house, a mortgage, even a credit card.

He rolled his eyes. "Yeah, I know. But I'm there a lot for work, so it made sense. Just promise me two things."

"Oka-ay."

"Call Andrew and tell him where you're going."

"And two?"

"Tell the detective about that letter from your mom."

I made a face. "All right."

He reached across the console and hugged me. I leaned into him, catching his scent: summer grass and evergreen trees. It reminded me of childhood, of my mom, and that I was suddenly very, very alone.

I got out of the car, a peculiar tightness in my throat as I watched Jacob drive away.

I could do this on my own.

I could.

I waited by my gate for the plane to board, knees jittering, eyes sweeping the terminal. Crossing to a window overlooking the runway, I dialed Liam's number. I felt a little guilty I hadn't called him earlier, but there just hadn't been time. And now the police were investigating me, questioning people I knew, impounding my car.

"Eva." Liam sounded relieved when he answered. "I'm glad you called. I'm so sorry. I should've told you the detective might come by."

"No, I'm sorry. I shouldn't have left the way I did. I don't know why I got so mad."

"It's okay. You were just struck by lightning." I could hear the smile on his lips and a thread of yearning spiraled through me. I wanted nothing more than to go home, feel Liam's arms around me, reassuring me that everything would be okay.

"Look, I was thinking maybe I'd postpone our appointment tomorrow," he said. "And I've canceled all my meetings so I can take care of you. I know you're under a lot of stress and your brain's a little rattled. After we meet the detective, we can just take the day off and relax. Maybe pack a picnic and go to the beach if the weather's nice."

"What appointment?" I asked, confused.

"Remember, we're meeting with Father Byrne at St. Mary's to discuss the wedding?"

"Isn't that next week?"

"No, tomorrow. Wednesday. Don't you

remember? It's been in our shared calendar for over a month. And there's a note hanging on the refrigerator."

The raw force of something messy and unrefined frothed up inside of me: shame that I didn't remember, and then anger, a black, rising fury, unnatural, unfamiliar. I pushed it away.

"My mom has been murdered, Liam," I said tightly. "The police think I might have had something to do with it. And you want to talk about our *wedding*?"

"I just . . ." He paused. "I thought you might want to think about something happy too."

A marble column of guilt landed on me. What was wrong with me?

"I'm sorry." I felt like a broken record.

An announcement came over the airport loudspeaker.

"Where are you?"

"Babe, listen." I told him about Mom's letter and the torn paper with an address for David Ashford on it. "She said she wasn't my real mother and we were in danger. It might have something to do with why she was murdered. So I'm getting a flight to London to talk to this guy."

"This is unbelievable!"

"I know! Obviously there were a lot of

things she never —"

"No, Eva, I mean, it's unbelievable that you're thinking about going to London in the middle of a murder investigation! Are you crazy?"

"It's where all the pieces are! Mom's letter said she took me to protect me, but I don't know who or what from. Maybe David Ashford knows something."

"Why don't you just call him?"

"I couldn't find his number. Besides, this way he can't hang up. He *has* to talk to me."

"Eva, if the police are suspicious of you, leaving the country is going to make you look even more guilty!"

"Then I better find the truth quick."

"The detective is probably already monitoring our credit cards. He'll know if you leave."

I ran a hand over my face.

"We'll talk to my lawyer and sort this out. I know you're scared right now. Your memory loss, mood swings, paranoia, these are all the symptoms Dr. Simm warned us about. But I promise, everything's going to be okay. Just wait there. I'll come get you."

I shook my head. If I stayed, I would always be filled with doubt, a gnawing fear that I was a horrible, broken person capable of murdering someone I loved.

I closed my eyes, fending off the guilt and the longing for him.

"I'll be back," I said. "I promise."

And I hung up.

Fifteen: Eva

"Final call for BA flight 520 to London."

I quickly e-mailed a picture of Mom's letter and the scrap of paper with the address to Detective Jackson, then sent a brief text to Andrew explaining where I was going before boarding the plane.

I stared outside as the airport's squat buildings raced by and we rose into the night sky, rubbing my fingers over the lightning marks on my arm. The electric pulses had faded to a faint tingle, but the skin was still raised. The feel of it under my fingertips was strangely comforting.

I pulled my coat over my head and tucked the airline blanket around my legs, blocking out the cabin light and the man with a hyperactive leg next to me, hoping to catch a few hours' sleep. The ripples of a dream reached for me. Images twisted and shifted like a snake slithering against bare skin.

Mom's living room. Lightning flashes. The

silhouette of a man on the other side of the room. Mom slumped in a chair. My hands splattered with blood. Lightning flashed again. The man turned, his face caught in the light. He was older, much older than me. A mocking smile twisted his mouth. He stepped toward me.

My eyes flipped open, and I battled briefly with the coat over my head. The man in the seat next to me woke with a snort and shot me an annoyed look.

"Sorry," I whispered.

I felt around at my feet for my purse, pulling out a pen, a scrap of paper. My fingers flew over the paper, an image slowly emerging, revealing the shape of the man's face. Wide forehead. Dark, bristly hair. A shadowed jaw. Long, bent nose, like it had a history of being broken.

I closed my eyes, trying to erase the image of the blood on my hands. But it was there, splattered across the backs of my eyelids like paintballs.

When I opened my eyes, the face of the mystery man stared back at me from my sketch. This man had been at Mom's house the night she died.

And I knew, finally, with absolute certainty, that I had been there too.

■ ■ ■ ■

Exhaustion and jet lag made me dazed and disoriented. Day and night had merged into a weird gray color, making it impossible to tell if it was twilight or morning when the plane landed at London's Heathrow Airport. My phone said noon, but my body said midnight.

Heathrow was a dizzying labyrinth of corridors and yellow signs pointing in all directions. The hallways were a crush of travelers jostling for space, people bustling up the escalators and pushing past stragglers while snapping clipped *pardon me*'s. I'd only ever flown to Cancun for spring break when I was in college, but that trip wasn't anything like this one.

I followed a series of signs for taxis, finally finding a line of them, black and shiny as a beetle's shell, in front of the terminal. I opened the back door of one and climbed in, but the driver scowled at me.

"You gotta go to the front of the queue," he barked.

"Oh, sorry!" My skin crisped with embarrassment.

I did a bizarre tourist's walk of shame to the front of the line and opened the back door of the front taxi.

" 'Ow ya doin', love?" The driver turned to grin at me. He was older, powerful-looking, with wide shoulders, a white beard, and a receding hairline. "Bag in the boot for ya?"

"Uh . . ." I looked at my backpack. "No, thanks."

"Where ya off to, then?"

"Shoreditch." I showed him the address Jacob had texted me, and he nodded and pulled into traffic. A sports game played on the radio and he listened intently as he turned onto a highway. Cheers erupted from the speakers and the driver groaned.

"He's a right geezer, innit? Want to gi' him a dry slap." He shook his head, tutting.

I leaned my head against the backseat, my brain too jet-lagged to figure out what he was talking about.

The taxi driver glanced at me in the rearview window. "Name's Graham." He pronounced it *gray-um.* "Right tippin' it down, innit?"

"Excuse me?"

He laughed, revealing long, crooked teeth. "It's raining hard out right now."

"Oh." I looked out the window. "Yes, it is."

"First time here?" he asked.

"Is it that obvious?"

He laughed again. "Little bit."

I scrolled through my e-mail and Instagram messages, all variations of the same thing: OMG, just heard about your mom. What happened? Are you ok? I was relieved that nobody knew the police were suspicious of me but wasn't stupid enough to think it would last. I swiped past texts from my dad and Lily, but hesitated when I read Andrew's.

> The detective is asking where you are. Please tell me you haven't seriously gone to London.

I thought of my brother at eleven, fists on hips, saying, "Uh muh muh muh mum!" when he caught me smoking pot in the backyard with a boy I was trying to impress. Even as an adult he was that type: relentlessly perfect, aggressively good. He organized his socks according to color, studied French in his spare time. When I went through my wild phase — sex, drinking, drugs — he'd been wholly repulsed. Just like my mom. Peas in a pod, those two.

The taxi accelerated onto a highway, droplets of rain slicing diagonally across my window. I rubbed my tired eyes, wishing instantly, intensely for my bed.

Graham caught my eye in the rearview mirror and smiled sympathetically.

"Rough night last night?" he asked.

I stared at him, my throat suddenly dry. He meant on the plane, of course, but his words caused the barbed ends of a memory to snag at the edges of my brain. I squeezed my eyes shut and nodded, trying desperately to block it out. But it was too late. My mind was already tunneling backward to the morning after I was attacked.

I woke next to a pool of vomit on the floor of my bedroom. My head felt like it had been flayed open and doused in chemicals.

"Eva! Eva?" My roommate, Holly, was hovering anxiously over me, her short, pink-streaked hair standing on end.

I tried to sit up, but a wave of nausea washed over me. I bent at the waist and vomited again.

"Sorry," I mumbled.

"Come on, let's get you washed off."

Holly helped me into the shower and sprayed the vomit off me. "Where'd you go last night?" she asked.

I stared at her, horrified as brief flashes came back to me.

"Holly," I whispered, "I think I was raped."

She drove me straight to the police station after that. We were whisked into an interview room, given a hot cup of tea. After about ten minutes a detective came in. He was old, with sagging jowls and a permanent frown between his eyebrows. His badge read DETECTIVE ANDERSON.

"Rough night last night?" he asked, leaning against the edge of the table.

Holly jumped up, her face blotchy with fury. "Are you fucking kidding? A rough night is finding out your car's been towed or that your friend threw up on your couch. Not realizing you've been raped!"

Anderson put his hands up. "Of course. Sorry." He turned to me. "Why don't you tell me what happened?"

I swallowed hard, feeling like a fish bone was stuck in my throat. "We were out last night. At a club."

He jotted something in a notepad.

"I got really dizzy really fast and everything started spinning, so I went outside. I threw up in the alley. I don't remember much after that. Someone was talking to me. A man. He said he'd help me get home. And then we were in his apartment. . . ."

I closed my eyes, trying to remember.

"Did you know him?"

"I don't think so. I can't remember."

"Do you remember anything about him? Hair color, facial hair, did he speak with an accent?"

"I can't remember."

"But you remember having sex?"

"Sort of. I couldn't move. It was like I was paralyzed."

"What about his address? Where he lived?"

I shook my head, tears burning. "No."

"Maybe the neighborhood?"

"She was obviously drugged!" Holly jumped in. "That's why she can't remember."

"Look. We can run a rape kit, do blood tests. But you said you've showered, right? And any drugs will be long gone from your system. So evidence will be . . ." He shrugged. I could tell by his face he didn't believe me.

I stood and moved toward the door, stumbling over Holly's purse. "Never mind."

I decided never to speak of it again. Not talking about it became a protective measure. Maybe he was right. I didn't know what had really happened. I couldn't remember. Besides, I wanted to block it off, box it up, bury it.

Until the day I saw that little pink line on the pregnancy test.

Graham pulled off the highway and veered around a massive roundabout, picking his way through thickening traffic. A sign fixed to a flight of stairs labeled the station below: OLD STREET STATION.

The street throbbed with traffic, people walking urgently on the sidewalks as they spoke into their phones. Ethnic restaurants, vintage clothing stores, and hipster cafés lined the streets. A kaleidoscope of bright murals and street art adorned nearly every wall. The vibe was both dingy and hip, a buzzy urban feel like Seattle's Pioneer Square, only grittier.

Graham pulled up outside a pale, sand-blasted brick building. Downstairs was a trendy-looking coffee shop with a neon sign flashing BEAN GRINDER above the door. He pointed to a series of sash windows above it. "You're in them flats up there."

I paid and signed the receipt. Graham pointed at my hand. "Hey, I'm a lefty too."

"Yeah?"

"You know, most kangaroos are lefties."

"Really?" I asked.

"Yep. I read it in my son's *National Geographic* magazine."

"Huh." I handed him his pen. "Maybe it's because they're on the other side of the world."

Graham laughed and held out a business card. "You need a taxi, give me a call, love."

I waved good-bye, then circled the building until I found the entrance at the side. I used Jacob's keys to let myself in and climbed the stairs to the top floor.

Jacob's flat was large and open-planned with high ceilings and exposed blond-brick walls soaring over pale hardwood floors. To my left a bank of windows overlooked the busy street below, and a cream leather sofa sat in front of a flat-screen TV. To my right was a small white-and-steel kitchen. The walls were filled with pale, rather abstract art. It was all very modern and beautiful, but not at all what I would've pictured Jacob buying.

I threw my backpack on the sofa. Fatigue dragged at my body. My eyelids felt like they were made of glue. I took a quick shower to wake myself up, turning the water up to scalding. There was a bottle of Tesco lemongrass all-in-one soap and a razor in the metal shower tray. I almost laughed, thinking of the expensive handmade soap Liam had imported from Paris.

After I dressed, I heard the sound of my

phone ringing from the living room.

"Hello, Eva." Detective Jackson's voice was smooth and unreadable when I answered. "Thanks for sending that copy of your mom's letter."

"Sure."

"Do you know what she was referring to? The danger you were in?"

"No, I don't. She never said anything, and I never felt in any danger when I was growing up."

"It must be difficult," he said, "finding out your mother wasn't biologically yours. How did that make you feel?"

"What, are you a shrink now?" I snapped. I gritted my teeth, trying to fold my irritation away. I felt like little pieces of me were leaking out.

"Hmm," he said, as if he were placating a testy toddler. "Listen, there are a few things I wanted to ask you about your mother."

"Like what?"

"Our crime scene investigators found a gun in her house. Do you know why she bought a gun?"

"A gun?" I shook my head. "That's not possible. Mom was very antigun. She never understood America's obsession with firearms."

Even as I said it, I was thinking that it was

totally possible Mom had a gun. She was very private — or maybe *secretive* was a better word. She'd kept a million secrets, big ones and small ones. Or maybe you couldn't even call them secrets. Maybe they were just straight-up lies.

"It's a nine-millimeter purchased and registered to Katherine Hansen in May 2017. Did she have a reason to buy a gun?"

"I don't think so."

"We've done some digging into Katherine's background. Do you know much about her life before she moved to America?"

"I guess as much as any kid does about their parents. My father died in London when I was a baby. Mom's parents died when she was young, so we moved to America to start over. She met Mike in Chicago, and when they got married, he adopted me. Why? Is there something I don't know?"

"We're still trying to establish some details. Have you been able to remember anything else?"

I pulled the sketch of the man I remembered at Mom's house out of my purse. "No," I lied. "Nothing."

A beat of silence.

"Have you heard of Interpol?" Jackson asked. His voice had chilled noticeably. "It's an international policing agency, so no matter where you go, Seattle, Whidbey Island, or London, we can still arrest you."

I licked my lips, trying to moisten my mouth. He knew. He *knew* I was here.

"I know you know something about your mother's murder, Eva. And I'm going to find out what it is."

His words at the gallery floated back to me. *I never would've stopped until I found the guy who did that to you.*

I realized now he'd been warning me.

"You have nothing on me," I whispered.

"Not yet, but I will," he growled. "Maybe tomorrow, maybe the next day, maybe the day after, my CSIs will give me their results — your fingerprints, DNA, your car on the ferry to Seattle the night she was killed — and I'll have proof. And when that happens, I'll issue an arrest warrant to Interpol. And no lawyer will be able to save you from a murder charge."

"I have to go, Detective." I was proud to hear that my voice didn't quiver, even though my hands did. "Thank you for your call."

I hung up. Liam was right. Jackson was tracking my credit card, maybe my bank account, my passport. Could he track my cell phone? I turned my phone off and slid the

SIM card out. I stared at the tiny chip in my hand, then squeezed my fingers tight around it.

Maybe I didn't remember the night Mom was murdered, like I didn't remember the night I was attacked. But I wasn't going to slink away and take the blame for something that wasn't my fault. Not again.

SIXTEEN: KAT

25 Years Before

"Katherine?" Seb cracked the bedroom door and peered into the murkiness. Light from the hallway spilled inside, along with the faint, ashy smell of smoke still left from when I burnt the ironing board. I tried to focus, narrowing my eyes against the sudden on-slaught. My body was thick and heavy with the weight of the drugs in my system.

I reached for the bottle of pills on the bedside table, dry-swallowing two. This was my routine when I woke. Pills. Swallow. Sleep. Wake. Pills. Swallow. Sleep. I found anything else quite beyond me.

Seb slid a plate of toast and a steaming mug of tea onto the bedside table and sat next to me, his weight dipping the bed as I lay back, clutching Barnaby to my chest. On some level I recognized his gesture of kindness. But he smelled of stale sweat and cooking oil, and it took everything in me not to retch.

"You have to get up." Seb's voice was wooden. "You haven't come out of here in almost a week. We have to pick a casket."

I rolled away from him and didn't reply. My daughter was dead. What did it matter what casket she had? Cell and tissue, skin and bone, we were all just particles of matter, obeying the laws of physics as we grew and lived and breathed and died and turned to nothingness in our graves.

A good mother would have taken her responsibilities seriously.

A good mother would have been watching her child.

A good mother would have kept her child safe.

I was not a good mother.

"We have to do this together," Seb insisted. "Eva deserves to have both of her parents pick out her casket."

The sound of her name triggered a visceral reaction in me. A stab of white-hot pain sliced through my core, a sharp blow to my solar plexus. It was like being caught in the gravity of a black hole. Once you were within its grasp, there was no escape. All you could do was wait for it to suck you in, to crush you.

I pulled my knees to my chest and pressed Barnaby to my face. My tears seeped into his bloodstained ear, smearing red across my palms. Seb dropped his face into his hands, ragged, guttural sobs wrenching from his chest, a howl of pain so deep it reached into my soul and touched me. I knew his pain, I felt it ravaging me every conscious moment.

"They let Rose go," he said after a while.

I vaguely remembered Seb saying Rose had been arrested.

"Why?" I whispered. The familiar, cottony numbness of the drugs had started to wind its way through my blood.

I meant why had they arrested her, but perhaps he misunderstood.

"Her husband got his fancy lawyer involved. It didn't matter how much I paid my contact in the police department, it obviously wasn't as much as he did. They said they had no evidence to charge Rose with anything." Seb slammed a fist into the bed, making me flinch. "But it was *her* house, *her* window, and *she* opened it! She's the reason our daughter is dead! And I swear to you, *I swear to you,* if it's the last thing I do, she will pay. I will make Rose pay."

■ ■ ■ ■

I woke abruptly later that afternoon, as if I had been shaken. I bolted upright, gasping for breath and drenched in sweat. The sound of Eva's scream echoed in my ears. I unplucked my rigid fingers from the tangled duvet, pain shooting from my knuckles to my elbows.

The rays of the late-afternoon sun were bleeding through the pulled shades. The sound of voices came from inside the house. I crept down the stairs, my bare feet silent on the cold hardwood floor. Cool air swirled up my nightgown, licking at my legs.

The familiar voice of Seb's dodgiest business partner, Paddy, wormed through the crack in his office door. "Oi, mate, I was down the local with this fit bird —"

"I don't give two fucks about that, Paddy!" Seb's fist hit something, the desk or perhaps the wall. "What did you find? Did you follow her?"

Paddy sighed, and I heard creaking as he sat in one of Seb's leather chairs.

"Yeah, mate, I did like you asked. Rose goes for a walk every evening. It would be the perfect chance. The only problem is she's always with the girl. Never goes out without her."

My heart was slamming in my chest, my breath rattling, fast and loose like a container of Pop Rocks.

It was silent for a long moment; then Seb spoke, his voice low and dark. "An eye for an eye." The sound of a drawer opening. A hard, metallic clunk. "Take this. . . ."

Another long pause. "All right."

I didn't listen for anything else. I turned and fled back upstairs to my room, diving under the covers and pressing Barnaby tight to my chest. After a while, Seb came in. He stood over me for a long time. I kept my eyes closed, my breathing steady and even.

And finally, he turned and left.

I dressed quickly and grabbed the car keys from the hook by the front door. Fortunately, the car was still outside, which meant Seb had left with Paddy. I was uncertain how long I had.

I drove along Hyde Park, passing expensively coiffed Kensington mums and aggressive Rollerbladers. The orange-gold sun hovered just over the horizon, the color of a tangerine.

I turned onto one of Mayfair's quiet back streets and parked just down from Rose's house.

It wouldn't be long, I knew. Rose took Laura for a walk every evening to tire her out before bed. The street was quiet, empty. A gentle, summer breeze set the mimosa trees stirring. I clutched Barnaby tight, feeling dizzy and disoriented. When was the last time I'd eaten? The last time I'd spoken to another human besides Seb? I couldn't remember. I had been demented with grief and despair and anguish since Eva died.

I fiddled with the radio to fill the silence as I waited. Somewhere through the fog of my mind, I heard the newscaster reporting on the fire in North London last week.

"Cooking oil was detected on the outside of the Gardener, at the spot where investigators believe the fire started. . . ."

Cooking oil.

I thought of the tin of cooking oil Seb had thrown at me. And the policeman who had questioned me.

I felt like such a fool. How had I not put it together sooner? Seb started the fire at the Gardener. I was certain of it.

I gazed at the pink-streaked horizon, a soft blush as twilight draped itself around the city. Big Ben chimed the evening hour in the distance. The sky was darkening, turning the deep, satiny blue of a ball gown. There wasn't a cloud in the sky, just a few peekaboo stars twinkling in the distance.

A wave of dizziness rushed over me. I shook my head to dislodge it.

What a bloody wretched night to kill a child. I couldn't let him do it. I had to stop this.

Finally Rose and Laura emerged. They were wearing matching green cardigans, the last strands of late-evening light winding through their red hair. They held hands as they turned up a cobbled street, heading in the direction of the private garden the neighborhood residents had access to.

I felt quite faint as I watched them, my palms slimy with sweat. I rubbed furiously at Barnaby's bloodstained ear. After a moment, I put the car in gear and crept slowly after them. Nobody could see me. If word got back to Seb that I had warned Rose, my punishment would be severe.

Twilight pressed in, the pink bleeding into the darkness. Rose withdrew a key from her coat and slid it into the park's locked gate. My heart twanged painfully in my chest. She was going to disappear and I would miss my chance.

I threw the car in park and staggered out. "Rose!"

Rose jumped at the sound of her name, darting a furtive look around. When she saw me she grabbed Laura's hand and tugged her through the gate, shutting it as fast as she could behind her.

I stared at the blank space where they had just stood as the final rays of the sun slipped beneath the horizon.

Seventeen: Eva

I grabbed a cup of strong tea and a cheese croissant from the café beneath Jacob's flat. On Old Street, I found a stall selling pay-as-you-go phones and bought the cheapest one. The first thing I did was google David Ashford.

Clicking on David's gallery's website, I saw that it sold everything from antique to contemporary pieces of Asian art, including ceramics, ancient Japanese armor, and an entire display of items that had been repaired using kintsugi. When I clicked on History, I read that the gallery had originally opened in 1972, but had relocated to the bottom floor of Selwyn House in Mayfair about ten years ago. The address was the same as the one written on the torn piece of paper from my mom's.

That's where I needed to go.

"Excuse me," I asked the shopkeeper. "Do you know how to get to Mayfair?"

He handed me a Tube map. "Take the Tube to Bond Street."

It sounded so simple. It wasn't. Even the ticket machine was a ridiculous puzzle to navigate. I somehow managed to buy a day ticket before a helpful businessman informed me that an Oyster card would've saved me money.

I made my way to the platform and boarded the next train, getting off at Bank Station to change to another line. Bank Station was a cramped maze of tunnels with escalators leading in every direction. I promptly got lost and spent the next twenty minutes shuffling, bewildered, through underground passageways to nowhere.

I finally managed to find the right Tube line and made my way to Bond Street, my eyes gritty, nose itching from subway dust. Outside, the sun had broken through the clouds, leaving the sky a dazzling blue with puffy, cotton-ball clouds skidding by. October leaves glowed like golden embers.

I plugged David Ashford's address into Google Maps and followed my phone past eighteenth-century Georgian mansions, swanky redbrick Edwardian buildings, sophisticated wine bars, and exclusive designer shops.

Selwyn House was a beautiful three-story

house with a symmetrical white-stucco façade, white bow windows, and fluted pillars that rose on either side of the entryway. It was set a little way back from the road behind a gold-tipped fence. A plaque above the door read SELWYN HOUSE ART GALLERY.

Inside, the open-plan space was painted a stark white with elegant mahogany cornices. Oriental rugs were scattered artfully across the dark hardwood floors. Wooden room separators with birds in flight carved into the panels sectioned off each area: sculptures, armor, ceramics, silk screens, paintings.

I walked through the gallery almost reverently. It was, I realized, exactly how I would've decorated my own gallery, if I had one. It practically murmured with the voices of the past, ancient and true.

A group of college kids chatted in front of the East Asian ceramics, talking loudly and jotting notes into their notebooks. I stopped in front of a mahogany-and-glass case filled with items repaired using kintsugi. There were bowls and plates, teapots, urns, vases, even lamp bases that had been repaired using gold to mend the broken pieces.

One bowl in particular caught my eye. It was plain, the gray-green of old clay, spidered with threads of gold. But where one chunk was missing, the artist had used a large opal to fill the hole. The end result was stunning.

I pressed my fingers to the glass, wishing I could hold it in my hands and see how the artist had mended it. My own clay plates and bowls seemed so amateur in comparison.

"It's a beautiful piece, isn't it?"

I whirled around to see a very young woman beside me. She was thin, her shoulders protruding from her black sheath dress like tiny fists. She had a sharp nose and chin, angular cheekbones, and strawberry-blond hair pulled into a sleek bun. "Yes, they're gorgeous."

"You know about kintsugi?"

"Not much," I admitted. "It's funny, I only heard about it for the first time the other day, and suddenly I'm seeing it everywhere."

She laughed. "Yes, I often find it's like that. Like when you buy a car and then you realize there are so many more of that model on the road than you ever noticed."

"Exactly." We smiled at each other.

"That piece there, the one you were looking at, the artist repaired it using a kintsugi technique called yobitsugi. That's when a completely new piece is used to fill in the missing area. This artist used opal to fill the hole. I think it was a rather good choice." She clasped her hands behind her back and smiled at me. "This is my favorite display. I think there's something rather magical about how kintsugi transforms the broken, isn't there?"

"I think so too. You work here?"

"Yes. I'm Charlotte. This is my father's art gallery."

Her father?

A child's cry filled the gallery. Charlotte bustled over to a stroller next to the cash register and lifted out a baby who looked about a year old. She cradled the girl's head as she bounced in slow, rhythmic moves. After a moment the baby stopped crying, blinking at me with wide doll-blue eyes and pink-stained cheeks.

"Apologies." Charlotte returned to me still bouncing the child. "I'm helping my father for a bit. Is there a particular piece you're interested in?"

Up close, I realized that Charlotte looked very tired. Her mascara was smudged a little under her eyes. She had a smile taped on, the kind I knew was fake because I'd done it so many times.

The little girl grinned and reached out

her chubby hands for me. I smiled and extended a finger for her to grasp. "She's adorable."

Charlotte kissed the child's cheek. "And she knows it!"

I swallowed hard, my throat raw as a wound, and the all-too-familiar spiral of regret and anguish coursed through me.

After I found out I was pregnant, I'd decided to have an abortion. But the day I went to the clinic, my mom had unexpectedly shown up. It was fall, the golden afternoon light dripping over the abortion clinic like butter. I still remembered looking at the light, the way it oozed over the buildings, dribbling over the metal and concrete, and thinking, *I would kill for some pancakes.* It was a crazy thought. I didn't even like pancakes, and my every waking minute was spent throwing up, so why would I want pancakes?

"Having an abortion won't change what happened to you," Mom had said. "It will just damage you more."

"I didn't choose this!" I'd exclaimed. "Somebody did it *to* me, and I can't even remember who. I can't have a baby I hate."

"Sacrifice is hard, but it is part of being a good person. You hold a child's life in your hands. What happened before is done, it is entirely out of your control. But what happens now is your responsibility."

The baby squealed, straining against her mother's arms to get down.

Charlotte rolled her eyes and laughed. "She's getting to the age where she wants to explore, but I can't have her wandering around an art gallery."

She strapped the baby back into the stroller and gave her a cracker to gnaw on, then kissed her forehead. Her eyes were washed with a love so intense it physically hurt me.

"So, was there something I could help you with?"

"I was actually looking for David Ashford," I said.

"I'm sorry. My father isn't seeing visitors right now." Her smile had frozen, revealing one front tooth that was slightly crooked.

"It doesn't have to be right now," I assured her. "I can come back later. I don't mind."

"No, I'm afraid you don't understand. My father's in the hospital. He's been taken ill, you see. I'm running the gallery in his absence."

My heart sank. "I'm so sorry to hear that. I hope he's okay. It's actually really important that I speak to him. Is he okay to see visitors at the hospital?"

Her gaze turned a shade cooler. "I'm not certain that's a good idea. What did you say you wanted from him?"

"I . . . I . . ." I stuttered, taken aback by her tone.

"What was your name again?"

"I'm . . ." I reached into my purse and withdrew the birth certificate I'd found in the folder at my mom's, unfolding it to show her. "I'm Eva. Eva . . . Clarke. I think he knew my mother a long time ago."

For a second, Charlotte looked lost, her eyes darting back and forth between me and the paper. Slowly the puzzle pieces clicked into place, her mouth twisting as she took a step away from me. Her elbow caught the edge of a stapler on the desk, and it clattered to the floor. I knelt, fumbling for the stapler.

"Here." I held it out to her, but she ignored it.

"How dare you!" Charlotte clenched her fists, her voice low. "Are you another reporter? My father is sick! Don't you get that? He's *sick*! Why won't you leave us alone?" The college students across the room turned to watch us, tittering behind their hands.

I gaped at her, embarrassed and confused,

helpless in the face of her anger. "What are you talking about? I'm not a reporter. I'm Eva Clarke."

"You can't be Eva Clarke!" she cried. "Eva Clarke is dead!"

I stumbled back, her words striking me like blows.

Dead? But it wasn't possible. I'd seen my birth certificate.

I shook my head as I backed away from her, the walls pressing in on me. And then I turned and ran outside, into the cool, bright day.

I leaned against the brick entrance to the Tube station, the air like sludge in my chest. Cold sweat beaded on my face, slid down my back. I felt like I'd been shredded into a million tiny pieces; that a small gust of wind could blow me apart.

Eva Clarke is dead.

The words ricocheted inside my head. Trying to control my spinning thoughts, I watched red city buses, black cabs, and delivery vans lumbering past.

If Eva Clarke is dead, who the hell am I?

My chest squeezed like someone was crushing it in an iron grip.

"Fuck," I muttered.

A woman walking into the Tube station

clutching a young child's hand glared at me. *Sorry!* I mouthed.

"You all right, missus?" a voice interrupted my thoughts.

I whirled around. A dreadlocked man sitting on a damp piece of cardboard was staring up at me. He shook a Styrofoam cup hopefully. I dug in my purse and pulled out a two-pound coin.

"Thanks, lady." He grinned, revealing a mouth of missing and jumbled teeth, like toppled little headstones. "You gonna go talk to 'im?"

"Who?" I asked.

He jerked his chin across the street. "That man over there been starin' at you."

I followed where he was pointing and saw the outline of a man across the road — dark hair, tall build, dark coat — then a bus whizzed by, obscuring his face. The skin at the back of my neck prickled.

A feeling of déjà vu crawled over my skin, cold and sticky as pudding.

I was on the floor of Mom's living room. A leaden weight was crushing me. And then the weight was gone. A man crashed to the floor next to me. Mom's voice cried out.

"Run, Eva!"

Run, Eva!

I launched myself into the Tube station,

slammed my travel card into the ticket reader, and lunged for the escalator. I flew past the tiled walls, along the corridor, and onto the first train that approached, not caring where it went, as long as it was away from here. The doors slid shut, and the train rumbled into the dark tunnel, shifting under my feet as I gripped a metal pole, trying desperately to steady myself.

The lightning marks on my arm pulsed, a scalding trail of fear zipping through my body, adrenaline and panic fighting for space.

Because I knew.

Whoever was at Mom's house that night had found me.

EIGHTEEN: EVA

The carriage was packed. I wedged myself into a corner, my thighs touching someone's knees, swaying along with the sea of humanity as the train rumbled down the line. It smelled like someone had burped after eating a burrito, the greasy scent hanging thick and heavy in the air. I covered my nose, my stomach roiling dangerously.

But I didn't get off.

Someone exited at the next stop, and I slid into their seat. I closed my eyes and let myself relax for just a moment as the train clattered along, feeling safe among the press of other humans. Nobody here knew me. Nobody was following me.

Most people — normal people — hated crowds. They hated rush-hour traffic and shopping malls at Christmastime and the crush of a mob after a baseball game. But I'd always liked them. There was something reassuring about being one of many who acted the same, cheered at the same time, groaned at the same time. I knew how to act in a crowd, which way to turn and what expression to put on. I loved the vibe and energy of a crowd. I could be anyone or no one. It was when I was alone that the sharp fangs of fear and insecurity sank into my brain.

For the first time I realized that maybe that was why I'd felt a little . . . off since moving into Liam's house. It was so isolated.

A metallic shriek filled the carriage as the train jerked to a stop at the next station. I felt calmer now, so I got off, checking over my shoulder and along the platform to make sure no one was following me. I stepped onto an escalator that seemed to continue for miles, only to be elbowed in the back as someone plowed into me.

"Stand to the right," he barked.

I squeezed to the right as a parade of people marched up the left. When I finally emerged at street level I started walking, wandering the cobblestone streets in a daze. The fall sun was warmer than I would've expected, absorbing into my hair and heating my skin as I walked.

Eventually I ended up in a place called Covent Garden, which was packed with tourists and street entertainers performing magic shows, miming, juggling, unicycling, and breathing fire. Music from the buskers filled the air. I wandered into a soaring glass atrium and through a bustling market filled with designer fashion stores, cafés, and crafts stalls.

In one of the stalls, a piece of grayish-green jade caught my eye. It was smooth, roughly shaped like a heart. I picked it up, thinking of the kintsugi art I'd seen at David Ashford's gallery and of Fiona Hudson's urn, which I still needed to repair.

It was kismet. It had to be.

After buying the jade, I stopped at an old Victorian pub to grab something to eat and to call Liam. Mahogany-red banquettes, ornate woodwork, and elegant chandeliers decorated the interior. The place was packed, and I instantly relaxed.

I approached the bar and grabbed a menu.

"What can I get you?" The bartender was small and very young, with dark hair and bright-blue eyes, her bangs cut severely across her forehead. She was wearing all black, a trend I was noticing among Londoners.

"What's a toad-in-the-hole?" I asked, pointing at the menu.

She smiled. "You American?"

I nodded.

"It's sausage."

I made a face. "I'm a vegetarian. What's black pudding?"

She laughed out loud at this. "You won't like that if you're a vegetarian. It's blood sausage."

Just the thing to serve a family of vampires, I thought, trying not to gag.

"We have a baked potato."

"Oh, that sounds good!" I said, relieved to find something normal. "And a cup of tea, please."

I sat at a table near the back where I could watch the crowd. Young professionals in sharp suits drank elaborately mixed cocktails. Middle-aged businessmen laughed loudly, sloshing amber liquid all over the floor.

In America, you needed a reason to drink in the middle of the day. Celebrating something? Fine. Drowning your sorrows? Okay. Watching a sports game? Absolutely. But in England, apparently all you needed was £4 and a spare hour.

I pulled out my new phone and dialed Liam's number. I was worried he might be in a meeting with that building inspector who was giving him so much grief, but he answered immediately.

"Hello?" Liam's voice was brisk, the impatient tone of a busy businessman.

"Liam, it's me."

"Eva! Oh my God! I've been calling and calling! Do you have any idea how worried I've been?"

"I'm sorry, I had to turn my phone off. I bought a new one. Detective Jackson knows I've left the country, and I was afraid he could trace me."

"Babe." His voice softened with pity. "Don't you hear how crazy that sounds? Please come home."

"I can't, Liam. I'm close to finding the truth." I was about to tell him about the man following me, but he cut me off.

"Eva, you need to listen to me. I'm worried about you. You're in a different country with a major head injury. You're forgetting things, little things like our appointment with the priest and big things like the night your mom was killed. And now you're being paranoid. This is insane!"

I was suddenly glad I hadn't told Liam about the man I thought had been following me. Had I imagined it?

The bartender set my baked potato and tea in front of me. I mouthed, *Thank you.*

Maybe Liam was right. I couldn't trust

the things I remembered, David Ashford wasn't available to talk to, and I was running around in circles. *What the hell am I doing here?*

"I just want to know what it all means," I said, frustrated. "My mom, David Ashford, me. If only there was a place to look up —" I stopped, my fork halfway to my mouth. "Oh my God! I can't believe I didn't think of it before. The library! They'll have news archives."

"Remember what the doctor —"

"No."

"Eva! You —"

"The doctor's wrong!" I cut him off.

There was a long silence. I could imagine Liam's face, the pinch of his mouth, the crumpled brow. Liam hated when I argued with him. It was a relic from his childhood, his arguments with his father, which he never won.

I took a deep breath. "I'll come home soon," I said, softer now. "I just have to figure this out first, okay?"

"Fine," he finally said. "Just . . . take care of yourself, and stay safe. You'll call me if there's anything you need, right? Even if you just want me to hop on a plane?"

"Of course. I love you."

"Love you most."

I said good-bye, guilt thick in my throat. But what was I supposed to do? I couldn't leave now. I couldn't.

As I picked at my food, a busboy started collecting empty glasses from the table next to mine, young, oily hair hanging limp against a pimply face.

"Excuse me?" I tapped his arm. "Do you know where the nearest big library is?"

"I reckon it'd be the British Library in King's Cross."

"How do I get there?"

"Hop the Piccadilly line. It's straight up from here."

"Thanks."

I grabbed my phone and purse and headed outside.

It took me longer than I thought it would to get to the British Library, thanks to boarding the Tube going the wrong direction. I transferred to the right train and got off at King's Cross, but instantly got lost amid the puzzling array of entrances, exits, and shops.

Finally I made it back to street level. Cyclists and joggers rushed past. Cars and taxis and buses honked, competing for space. Schoolchildren and businesspeople and policemen in bright-yellow jackets hurried along the sidewalks.

Forgetting that traffic was coming from the opposite side, I stepped onto the road, only to leap back when a motorcycle blasted its horn as it barreled toward me. The driver shook his fist, shouting angrily as he zoomed past.

The British Library was set in an unassuming redbrick building that looked like a school. Inside, I wound my way through the multilevel atrium to the escalators, which swept up each floor like a wave. I followed the instructions to receive a Reader Pass and headed to the news reading room. A tiny mouse of a woman with large tortoiseshell glasses and a poof of curly brown hair showed me how to use the news archives.

"What are you looking for?" she asked. "Our archives go back to the seventeen hundreds."

"To be honest, I don't have a lot of information to go on," I admitted. "I wanted to find any news articles about a man named David Ashford. He owns the Selwyn House Art Gallery. It's for a research project for art school," I rushed to add.

"Certainly." She clicked the mouse efficiently, navigating to a page and using the advanced search tool to narrow the parameters. "Let's try this."

A dozen articles popped up, all featuring

David Ashford's name. Judging by the headlines, David was prominently known in the art industry, actively involved in his community, and a generous donor to a number of charities.

"What about older articles?" I said. "Maybe twenty, thirty years ago?"

The librarian filtered the articles from oldest to newest. I scanned the first few, which were mostly media releases about his art gallery. And then I saw it.

Woman Held for Murder after Tot Dies in Tragic Fall

"Thank you," I said, reaching for the mouse.

"Just click each one when you want to view it. When you're done, hit Back."

I nodded, waiting until she'd moved away before I clicked into the story.

Woman Held for Murder after Tot Dies in Tragic Fall

A woman has been arrested on suspicion of murder after three-year-old Eva Clarke died at the Mayfair home of David Ashford, owner of a local art gallery.

Officers were called to the property at 3.45pm on Friday following a call that the girl had fallen from a third-storey window, sustaining fatal head injuries.

Police said they were not looking for anyone else in connection with the incident.

A police spokesman said: "A report is currently being prepared for the coroner and a woman has been arrested in connection with the death."

I put a hand to my mouth. *Murder.* I actually felt sick. Charlotte Ashford was right — Eva Clarke was dead. Was Mom the woman arrested for murdering her? It didn't seem possible. Just a few weeks ago, she'd been awarded for *saving* a little girl's life.

I clicked Back and went on to the next article.

Wife of Gallery Owner Kills Self and Daughter in Thames Suicide Jump

The watery grave of the Thames has claimed two more lives this year after Rose Ashford, wife of art gallery owner David Ashford, jumped into the river with their young daughter.

Mrs Ashford was arrested last month after her nanny's daughter, Eva Clarke, was found dead following a three-storey fall at the Ashford property. The fall was subsequently ruled an accident and all charges were dropped, but Eva Clarke's parents issued a statement to the media condemning the police's investigation as insignificant, calling for an inquiry to be held. Sources close to the family say Mrs Ashford's suicide note apologizes for her role in the toddler's death.

There are no other suspects in the murder-suicide.

I sat back in my chair, stunned. Mom wasn't the murderer; it was David's wife. And she'd gone on to kill herself and their child out of guilt. A wad of bile filled my mouth, bitter as a chewed-up aspirin.

I zoomed in on the grainy black-and-white photo next to the article. Eva Clarke's parents had been captured leaving their house. The mother had her hand up, as if her eyes couldn't adjust to the light.

I leaned in, squinting. There was no denying it. Eva Clarke's mother, Katherine Clarke, was younger, blonder, thinner, but definitely the woman who'd raised me: Katherine Hansen.

My mind went dull with shock.

Once when I was about six or seven, I ran away in a huff because Mom had forgotten to take me to a friend's birthday party.

Andrew had been a baby, and Mom was exhausted caring for us both, but at the time I didn't care. I was furious I'd missed the unicorn party I'd been looking forward to for weeks. So I ran away to the backyard and climbed the gnarled limbs of our old oak tree.

Mom knew where I was — she was in the kitchen watching me the whole time. At some point I dozed off and fell maybe ten feet to the ground, landing, arms splayed, on my back. Mom shrieked my name as she ran out of the house and collapsed at my side. The impact knocked the breath from my lungs, and I lay there, suddenly awake but not sure if I really was.

That was how I felt now, like I had fallen and landed with a rude jolt and all I could do was lie there wondering if this was really happening. The truth was here in front of me, but only partially. I still didn't know what to believe.

I squinted and looked at the picture again. There was something familiar about Sebastian Clarke, Katherine's husband. I rifled through my purse, pulled out the sketch I'd drawn earlier, and compared it to Sebastian Clarke.

The man in my drawing was much older, his nose larger and more crooked. He had facial hair and his forehead was a little wider, but there was something between the eyes, maybe the shape of his jaw too.

I covered my mouth to stifle a gasp.

Was Sebastian Clarke the man I remembered at Mom's house the night she was murdered, the man following me earlier?

NINETEEN:
EVA

Back at Jacob's flat that evening, I changed into a *Bendy AF* T-shirt and yoga pants and made myself a cup of tea. I feverishly called Andrew over and over, wanting to ask if he'd known anything about this. But he didn't pick up. I then tried Liam, but he didn't pick up either.

I took my tea to the living room window and looked outside. I could barely process that I wasn't me, and that my mom, who wasn't my mom, had been murdered, and that maybe I had murdered her, but maybe I hadn't. Maybe somebody else had, and now they were after me.

What did it all mean?

I felt like I'd been trapped in a bubble where all sound had been muted, only the vibrations reaching me, thrumming inside my chest. What I really needed was time to grieve, to mourn, but I couldn't even have that. I had to keep going, keep moving, keep running so I could unravel this mystery.

If I didn't, I could end up in jail.

Outside, the sky was clear and velvet black. A smattering of the brightest, most determined stars pierced the night. I was surprised by how clear they were. I traced the blaze of the North Star down to the hard lip of the Big Dipper, hovering low in the evening sky.

Once when I was five, maybe six, my mom came into my room and woke me in the middle of a hot summer night. She slipped my coat on and wrapped a light blanket around my shoulders.

"I have something to show you," she'd whispered.

She buckled me in the car. I fell back asleep as she drove, but then she was lifting me out and we were in a field surrounded by nothing but stars as far as the eye could see.

"Mommy," I breathed. "The stars are dancing!"

Mom smiled. She laid the blanket on the ground, and we sat down.

"That there is the North Star," she said, pointing to the brightest star. "A long time ago people used it to guide themselves home when they were lost. And that" — she moved her finger to a collection of stars —

"is Ursa Major. At school you'll probably call it the Big Dipper. It has seven stars, but five of them move together, like a family."

She tilted her chin up, her elbows bent behind her, and stared up at the stars. "It's extraordinary. They all originated from a single cloud of gas and dust, became individual stars, and yet still move as one."

I looked at my mom, her eyes wide, her profile bathed in the creamy light. At that moment she was the most beautiful person I had ever seen.

She turned her head, trapping my gaze in hers. "There are millions of stars in the sky, Eva. They're all different, completely unique. Just like you. Don't ever doubt that, all right?"

The memory tugged softly at the corners of my mouth, but then despair washed over me, filling me with the heavy, liquid feeling of being seasick. She'd known I wasn't Eva. But who the hell was I, then, and how did I fit into Mom's murder? If I didn't know who I really was, how did I know if I could trust myself? Maybe I really was the type who could randomly freak out and hurt someone, *murder* someone she loved.

I spent the next half hour doing yoga poses — Warrior, Lotus, Half-Moon — until my mind was relaxed. I wiped away beads of perspiration and flopped on the bed. I tried to distract myself on Instagram, then opened Gmail.

There was an e-mail from Detective Jackson. I clicked into it but it was empty except for an attachment. When I clicked it, a pdf of a toxicology report opened.

I tried to read it, but it was a jumble of scientific words and numbers I couldn't make sense of.

"Jerk," I muttered out loud. I nibbled a fingernail, trying to decide what to do. I dialed Andrew's number again, relieved when he picked up.

"Andrew, I've been trying to call you. Where've you been?"

"Eva? What do you mean, where have I been?" he exclaimed. I heard the clacking of a keyboard and papers shuffling. He was at work, as usual. "I've been busy. There are things — procedures for events like this. Mom prepared for it, so I'm taking care of the arrangements."

For a second I was too stunned to speak. "She . . . prepared for her death?"

"Of course she did. She wrote her will years ago. She paid for her cremation and memorial too."

"Right."

"Where are you?" he asked.

"I told you already. I'm in London."

Andrew sighed. I could imagine him shaking his head at me, his disapproval blistering me even here. "I can't believe you left the country."

"I can't believe you're still at *work* in the middle of our mother's murder investigation," I shot back, even though it wasn't actually true. Finding something predictable during a crisis was comforting for Andrew. But I didn't like whatever he was insinuating.

"You have no idea what I'm going through right now!"

"I'm not a suspect! I'm not under arrest. I didn't *have* to stay," I snapped at my brother.

My brother.

Andrew had always been my brother, never my half brother, even though we had different dads. But now we had different moms too. Was he still my brother with no blood shared between us?

"No, but it doesn't look good."

"Whatever. Listen, Detective Jackson sent me Mom's toxicology report, but I don't understand it."

"What's it say?" Andrew asked with a sigh.

"The drug screen result says there were elevated levels of digoxin in her blood."

"Digoxin? That's a drug for heart disease, I think." I heard clacking as his fingers flew over a keyboard. "Yeah. It's prescribed to treat cardiac disease and chronic atrial fibrillation."

"Mom had heart problems?" This was the first I'd heard of it.

"Not that I knew of. Hold on, it says here it comes from the plant *Digitalis purpurea,* also known as foxglove, a toxic flower that's become prevalent in the last few years around Seattle. Too much of it causes fast heartbeat, nausea, loss of appetite. Sometimes it seems the victim is just tired or suffering from the flu."

I flashed back to dinner with my mom, how she'd clutched her chest after a vicious coughing fit. "So maybe she ate a flower?"

"Yeah, but . . . she was stabbed too." He was quiet for a minute. "You know, the police have footage of you on the ferry back to Seattle. They have security video from one of Mom's neighbors showing you running down the street. You were there that night."

"I know. At least, I think I know. But someone was with me. I've been having these memories . . . there was a man there. I was able to sketch his face. I don't know who he is, but maybe he poisoned Mom."

"Did he stab her?"

I tried to clutch at the fragments I did remember — the knife, the man, the blood — but they disappeared, like evaporating drops of water.

"I can't remember," I said, frustrated.

"Can you remember anything else?"

He meant did I remember killing Mom, but I didn't have an answer. "I've told you everything I know."

Silence.

"Andrew?" I bit my lip. "Don't you believe me?"

It sounded like he was crying. The tears that had been ever-present at the back of my throat were suddenly hot on my cheeks.

"What happened that night?" Andrew's voice was rough.

"I swear," I whispered, "I don't know."

He took a deep breath in, and then let it out, like he was deciding something. "That detective, Jackson, he isn't going to stop until he finds out what happened to Mom."

"Good," I said. "I hope he finds out the truth."

I heard someone call Andrew's name and more shuffling as Andrew covered the phone and replied.

"I've gotta go," he said. "Send Detective Jackson that sketch. Maybe he can run it through some profiling software."

"If I tell him about it, I'll have to admit I was at Mom's house."

"He already knows you were there!"

"Fine." I relented. "But I have more to tell you —"

"Can you catch me up later? I have to be in court in twenty minutes. And don't be a jerk. Call Dad. He's worried about you."

"Yeah, but —" I started to reply, but he'd already hung up.

I stared at my phone, then opened Gmail to send Andrew the phone number to my new phone. There was one new e-mail: Andrew had sent through a link with information about Detective Kent Jackson. I opened it and learned that a few years back Jackson had been working on a high-profile case with the Boston PD when his wife was killed by a gang member he'd been investigating. Shortly after, the man suspected of murdering his wife was found shot in the head. Although no evidence was ever found linking Jackson to the murder, he'd quit the Boston PD and moved to Seattle.

I blew out a breath I didn't know I was holding. Shit. Andrew was right. This was not a guy who would let things go easily.

I closed the website and e-mailed a picture of my sketch to Jackson, then downloaded the Skype app so he wouldn't be able to track my location and used it to dial the number on his business card.

"Detective Jackson? This is Eva Hansen."

"Hello, Eva." The sound of a door, then the creak of a chair came through the phone. "You received the toxicology report?"

"Yes, did you get the sketch I e-mailed you?"

"I'll check it now."

"I don't understand. My mom didn't have heart disease."

"You're right, she didn't. We found no prescription bottles containing digoxin, and when I checked her medical records, there was no history of it."

"So why was it in her blood?"

"We think your mom was poisoned. Likely over the course of a week, possibly longer. Somebody switched the leaves in her tea canister with dried foxglove. The official cause of death is digoxin toxicity compounded by a sudden loss of blood, which produced a massive heart attack."

I put my hand on my head and sank back against the couch. I stared at the dark TV, gripping the phone so hard my fingers ached. The scab from the cut on my palm pulsed viciously.

I felt like Alice in Wonderland, stumbling and falling down a hole in the ground. I tried to map everything out like a jigsaw puzzle, but nothing made sense. None of the important pieces were there.

"Poisoned." My voice sounded very far away. Stabbed *and* poisoned. Somebody had slowly and deliberately killed her.

Who would do that? She didn't have any enemies. At least, that I knew of. She was loyal, steadfast. She always did the right thing in that stoic, practical English way. It had to be someone who had access to her house, to something as ordinary as her tea canister.

"You know," Jackson's voice elbowed into my thoughts, "women are seven times more likely than men to choose poison as their murder weapon. Daughters are most likely to die from being poisoned, but obviously Kat's mother didn't murder her. I mean, you said you've never even met her, right?"

"Yes. I mean, no, I never met her." The thundering in my head made my voice sound hollow.

"The thing is, Eva, the fingerprints on the mug Kat drank from, the one that poisoned her? Those fingerprints are yours."

Twenty: Eva

Dread oozed over me like black ink across a white cloth.

"You think *I* poisoned her?" I exclaimed. "I didn't even know what digoxin was until Andrew told me!"

"What medications do you take, Eva?" Jackson asked.

"E-excuse me?" I stuttered, trying to keep up with his sudden change of direction.

"Your fiancé mentioned you went to bed with a migraine the night your mother was murdered, that you'd taken your 'meds.' Plural. What other medication do you take?"

I shook my head, confused. "None."

"I saw on your chart at the hospital you'd been prescribed pills for anxiety in the past. Are they the same ones you took after you were assaulted?"

I frowned. I vaguely remembered Liam mentioning getting my medication, but I hadn't taken any. Had I? I had no idea if they were the same pills I took two years ago.

"Did you take anxiety pills at the same time as the migraine pills?"

"I don't . . ." I was so confused, doubt thumping in my chest. I didn't know what was true, what to say, what to believe.

"Are you aware that taking migraine and anxiety pills together increases the risk of serotonin syndrome? That's a potentially serious negative drug reaction. You could have hallucinations, agitation, and even — listen closely to this one — memory loss."

The white walls of Jacob's flat pressed around me, fear contracting around my chest.

"Are you suggesting I combined a bunch of pills and then murdered someone while I was blacked out?" A sudden, surprising anger coiled between my ribs. "Or maybe I just faked getting struck by lightning so I wouldn't remember what happened? How did I do that exactly? Did I stand directly in the path of the lightning holding up a metal hanger to make sure it hit me?"

A memory flashed like a fish's fin, an image of my mom falling to the ground, blood smeared across her throat.

I had that feeling you get when you're a kid and you're chasing a squirrel, the wind of its tail dancing across your palm, and you're sure, so absolutely certain you're going to catch it any second. I closed my eyes, straining to pull aside the veil and see the rest of the memory. But it was gone, leaving my head feeling hot, tingly.

Jackson's voice cut through my thoughts. "Eva, you are now a person of interest in what is a very serious murder investigation. I suggest you get home before I issue an arrest warrant to Interpol."

"No, wait!" I exclaimed. "There's something — I remembered something. I think you're right, I was there, but I wasn't alone. Check the sketch I e-mailed you. The guy's name is Sebastian Clarke, and I think he was there too. You must've found other fingerprints at Mom's house, not just mine. They're his. He was my mom's husband before she moved to America. He must've done it."

"Why would this Sebastian want to kill your mom?" Jackson sounded irritated.

"I have no idea, I swear!"

Jackson sighed.

"Listen, I'll come in to the police station, and you can ask me anything you want. I just need two or three more days."

"That isn't how this works," he warned.

"I know this looks bad, Detective, but I'm

sure Sebastian Clarke has something to do with this. He killed my mom. You need to find him!"

"No, what I need to do is formally question you, Eva. You need to come back right now, today, or I'm going to issue that arrest warrant with Interpol."

"Two days," I replied. Then I hung up.

I awoke with a start as morning dawned over London in soft shades of misty gray. Rain ticked against the windows, sent down from a cotton-wool sky. Crumpled leaves twisted in the wind, falling past the windows like teardrops.

My eyes roamed Jacob's bedroom, a masculine space with white-painted brick walls and a small IKEA desk. Travel photos he'd taken filled the walls. The bedside table was a cluttered mess of phone chargers, electrical converters, and loose change. A Dan Brown book had been left facedown on the dresser. This room felt more like the Jacob I'd grown up with than the rest of the flat.

I was too awake to go back to sleep, so I dinked around on my phone, checking my e-mail and Instagram. I knew social media was like standing in front of a crowd screaming into a microphone: "Look at me! See how great I am! Be jealous of my life!" We had twenty-four-hour access to the worst things happening in the world, and twenty-four-hour access to other people's apparently perfect lives. It was simultaneously disturbing and confusing, and yet I continued using it. Maybe something inside me needed to feel worthy of others' approval. But weren't we all like that?

The story of my mom's death was obviously making the rounds now — I had twelve messages on Instagram, including three from my college roommate, Holly: one congratulating me on my engagement, one asking if I was okay, and another asking me to call her.

Fortunately nobody seemed to know the police were questioning me. I replied to each message, then scrolled through my feed. Jacob had posted a picture of his travel backpack perched against his pillow like a lover. "Hanging this bad boy up for a while!" he'd commented.

I summoned Jacob's number from a long-locked vault in my mind and reached for my phone.

"Jake, it's me."

"Eva. Hi." He sounded pleased to hear from me. "How's it going? Did you talk to David Ashford?"

I told him about finding out that David Ashford was in the hospital and what I'd learned at the British Library.

"Mom's real daughter was a little girl called Eva Clarke, who died in a tragic accident," I said. "Mom raised me as Eva Clarke, but I have no idea why, or who I really am, and if I can't find David Ashford, I won't be able to find out."

I got up, peering through the wooden blinds. On the street below, a garbage truck cruised along, stopping every once in a while for the trash collector to toss black bags into the back.

"Why don't you just visit him in the hospital?" Jacob suggested.

"I don't know which one he's at."

"There aren't that many in central London. Just call them and ask to be transferred to David Ashford's room. You'll eventually find the one he's at."

"I don't know. Maybe I should just come home. I'm not finding anything, and the detective is probably going to issue an arrest warrant soon. Even my fiancé thinks I'm acting like a lunatic."

"Don't be ridiculous. You're so close to finding out the truth about Kat's past. *Your* past." His voice softened. "You can't run away from this, Eva."

"I'm not running away," I said defensively. "*I* don't run away."

Jacob didn't reply, and a long silence stretched between us. I tried to twist my ring, forgetting that nothing was there.

I hadn't meant to sound so bitter. I didn't want him to know that being left with just a note after our night together had hurt. Time had only calcified my resentment the way a kiln hardens clay. Now it was chipping off, fragments scattering, spilling out and slicing those who loved me.

"Is that what you thought?" Jacob finally said. "That I ran away?"

"No . . ."

"I wasn't running away, Eva. I just needed some time to figure things out. I was scared shitless, okay? We went from best friends to sleeping together, and I didn't want to fuck it up. You were worth more to me than that. But when I came back, you wouldn't answer my calls. I had to find out what happened to you from Holly."

Horror and shame slid through me. "She *told* you?" I whispered, aghast. I didn't think he knew.

"She was worried about you. You moved back into your mom's house and you wouldn't talk to anybody."

The hurt in his voice wrenched my heart

tight with guilt. I didn't want to think about it, to remember it, but there it was. The night I was attacked, my identity as a valuable, thinking person had been crushed because I couldn't even remember it. I didn't want anybody to know, because who would possibly want to step into that new world with me?

"I'm sorry I didn't tell you." Tears sprang to my eyes, but I blinked them away. "I was scared and ashamed. I was afraid it was my fault, like maybe I was flirting with him or I drank too much. I don't know what happened, really, because I don't remember."

"Don't you know?" Jacob said gently. "You don't have to remember it to know you weren't to blame for it."

For so long I'd been trying to move past it, around it. I'd moved all the way to Whidbey Island to get away from it. But it hadn't worked. It was always there, tearing me up, breaking me to pieces.

Only now did I see — it didn't matter how far I went; I couldn't outrun myself.

Twenty-One: Kat

25 Years Before

"Rose!" Adrenaline pulsed wildly in my chest as I lunged for the gate Rose and Laura had disappeared behind. I rattled the locked handle. "Rose, please! Listen to me! Seb's hired someone to kill you!"

I pressed my forehead to the gate, breathing heavily.

After a second the gate clicked open. I stepped back as Rose peered out at me uncertainly, Laura half hidden behind her legs. I tried to see myself through her eyes: a wild woman, dirty and disheveled hair, glazed eyes.

"You must be mistaken."

"I'm not."

"Then change his mind!"

I snorted in a distinctly unladylike fashion. Changing Seb's mind when it was made up was a bit like negotiating one's way up a cow's arse. He would never stop until he got revenge.

"I truly wish I could. But he already has a man working on it. There's a hit on you and Laura."

Rose looked stricken, her face the color of damp chalk. In fact, she looked quite ill. Her eyes glittered madly, her cheekbones sharp and skeletal. The skin under her eyes sagged, her lips cracked in angry, raw patches.

She looked down at Laura, wrapped like a barnacle around her leg. "The police —"

"— are in Seb's pocket," I cut her off. "Look." I lifted my top to show her the kidney-shaped bruise under my ribs. "Seb hits me, and I can't go to the police because they won't do anything about it. They know he's involved in drugs, extortion, money laundering. They don't do anything about it because he pays them not to." I glanced over my shoulder. "Where is David? You mustn't stay. Leave London for a while. I'll send word when it's safe to return."

"David's out of town!" Rose's eyes filled with tears. "He had to get a piece for a client. He won't be home until next week."

"Take Laura and go without him. This is important, Rose. You must listen to me."

"Go where? How?" Rose was panicking, dragging in tiny sips of air too fast.

I handed her an envelope. "It's Eva's birth certificate. Use it for Laura. Nobody will ever question it. My passport is in there too, for you to use. They won't look if you go to France. Just get out of the country. You can send word to David later."

Rose stroked a hand down Laura's hair, a burst of color against her pale, bony fingers. A streetlight shimmered on, casting a golden glow onto the street. I looked around, expecting to see someone, anyone, but the street was quiet, empty as a wish.

"David's never around," she said. "He can't keep her safe!" Then she reached for my hand, her eyes aglow. "Come with us."

"Don't be daft." I snatched my hand away. "I can't leave."

"Come with us," she repeated, more forcefully this time. "Did you think I hadn't seen your bruises, Katherine? Of course I know your husband beats you. You will suffer horribly if he learns you warned me. Do you really want that for the rest of your life? Would Eva want that for you?"

I inhaled sharply at the sound of her name. My memories of my daughter were already slipping away. When I pressed my face to her sheets, I no longer smelled the mango scent of her hair. The exact sound of her laughter, too, was already fading. Her laughter was contagious, and now I couldn't even remember it. But her name, the daughter I'd loved and lived for, she was still here, in my heart.

Rose wrapped her arms around me and pulled me tight to her. I dropped my face to the soft skin at her throat, the familiar scent of lemons coiling around me.

"We'll start over together," she whispered. "Without David or Sebastian. We'll live the way *we* want. Come with us."

I teetered there on the brink of a momentous decision that I knew would take my life in one of two polar-opposite directions. Stay or escape. I was like Schrödinger's cat, sealed in a box of my own making, both alive and dead. Until I decided, both realities were equally possible.

My daughter was dead. There was nothing tying me to Seb except fear and lies. I let myself imagine what it would be like to be free.

"Yes," I breathed. "Yes, I'll go with you."

"Oh, thank God." Rose closed her eyes in relief. "What do we do now?"

I racked my mind, trying to form an escape plan. "We need money. Clothes. Your passport."

She nodded and handed me back the envelope I'd brought. "Take Laura with you," she said. "I'll get my passport. I have to wait for the bank to open tomorrow, but I'll meet you after. Where should we meet?"

I thought fast. "Ibis Hotel near Heathrow Airport. After you arrive, we'll fly to America."

"Mummy?" Laura tugged on Rose's hand. "Where are we going? Is Eva coming?"

"Not today, Laura-loo." Rose knelt and tucked a lock of hair behind Laura's ear. "I need you to go with Katherine now."

"I don't want to." She scowled. "I want to stay with you."

Rose pushed her gently toward me, and I grabbed her arm.

"Mummy!" Laura tried to squirm out of my grasp, her fingers clutching onto Rose's coat.

I threw the envelope with my passport into the car and used both hands to tug her off Rose. She screamed, a sound that ripped through the quiet street like a banshee's cry.

"Laura, stop it!" I said sharply. "We will see Mummy soon."

"Muu-mmy!"

Rose took a step away, her hand over her mouth, tears streaming down her face.

"Katherine, I'm so sorry," she sobbed.

I covered Laura's mouth as she opened it to scream again and hoisted her into the car. She flailed against me, her tiny fists hitting me like little hammers. I strapped her into the backseat, then got in and started the car. I rolled my window down, and Rose reached in through the open window and hugged me hard, her face wet and hot.

"Keep our girl safe," she said.

We waited for Rose at the hotel for two days. I fretted constantly, growing increasingly worried when Rose didn't arrive as planned. On the second day, the hotel receptionist flagged me down and handed me a letter that had arrived in the post. Inside was a slip of paper with a series of numbers. A bank account number and sort code.

We took the lift to our room, and I settled Laura with a coloring book and crayons while I called the bank. The account was in Eva's name, matching the birth certificate I had, with me as the co–account holder. It held enough money to get the three of us to America and settled somewhere new.

I sat on the bed next to Laura and leaned against the headboard. There was nothing to do but keep waiting.

I flicked the telly on. The BBC was reporting on a breaking news story.

". . . that Rose Ashford and her daughter,

Laura, have died in a murder-suicide after finding a note taped to the young girl's buggy. The note indicated Mrs. Ashford jumped into the Thames with the girl because of guilt over the death of Eva Clarke, her nanny's young daughter. Mrs. Ashford's note reportedly admits full responsibility for opening the window the child . . ."

I stood slowly, utterly stunned. I glanced at Laura, who seemed blissfully ignorant of the news story.

Rose was dead. And somehow she'd made it look like Laura was too.

The reporter's voice faded in and out. I stared out the window. An airplane roared overhead, the jet stream a haze in the pale afternoon sky.

I cast my mind back to her last words, an apology. *Katherine, I'm so sorry.*

The clouds shifted, a shaft of light pouring into the room, shining directly on Laura, her dark-red hair alight. I wanted to reach for that light, grasp it in my hand, bend it the way a wave of light is bent by gravity. If I could loop it back on itself and redo that day, none of this would be happening. Eva would be alive. So would Rose.

I could no longer contain it. I ran to the washroom and slammed the door shut as vomit burst up my throat. When I was empty, I sank to the floor and pushed my hands hard into my temples, rocking as I cried. The pain in my chest was dreadful, an excruciating throb of self-blame and re-crimination.

Nobody would come looking for Laura now. Seb would think she and Rose were dead. Had that been Rose's plan all along? To give Laura a fighting chance?

But then the truth hit me like a brick wall. Seb would come looking for me. How long before he realized my passport was gone? Before he sent one of his men after me or notified the police I was missing?

If he found me, he would find Laura. What had he said? *An eye for an eye.* I could not be certain he wouldn't hurt her, and yet I had promised Rose I would keep her safe.

Gradually numbness seeped, like a drug, into my veins.

"Miss Katherine!" Laura's voice brought me back to earth with a jolt. "Miss Katherine, I finished my picture!"

I wiped my eyes. I had to deal with this as I'd dealt with everything in life that came snapping at my back. Laura's safety was my responsibility, my only priority, now.

Pulling the bathroom door open, I dropped to one knee in front of Laura, my eyes landing briefly on the envelope with my passport and Eva's birth certificate sitting on the bedside table.

"Laura, today we are going on an airplane," I said. "And we're going to play a game. I shall call you Eva, and you must call me Mummy."

Twenty-Two: Eva

After Jacob and I got off the phone, I called all the hospitals in central London. I found David Ashford at St. Thomas' near Westminster. It was too early to visit, so I decided to take a bath.

I turned the water on to fill the bathtub and peeled my clothes off to inspect my body. The bruises on my chest, my shoulders, my hips were fading, losing their defined edges. Even the fern-shaped edges of the Lichtenberg figures on my arm had blurred, the new skin a bubblegum pink, the electric vibrations muted.

When the tub was full I climbed in, tentatively lowering myself until I was covered to my chest. I stared at the ceiling; a cobweb with a fly trapped in the middle hung in the corner of the bathroom. Outside, the outline of a small bird hopped along the frosted-glass window.

The quiet flat folded around me, the water

occasionally sloshing against the tub, intermittent drops from the faucet splashing into the water. Suddenly a sharp crack came from outside the bathroom door, then the thud of footsteps. I jumped, my eyes flipping open. I held my breath, straining to hear.

There. The unmistakable *thud-thud* of boots stuttered across the hardwood floor.

Someone was inside the flat.

A drawer scraped open, the silverware inside rattling. More drawers opened and closed. A floorboard groaned as footsteps came closer.

I leapt out of the bath, water cascading onto the linoleum. I flung the lock across the door. My heart thundered in my ears as I tried to squash rising panic. The walls loomed around me, a prison I couldn't run from. Adrenaline surged through my blood so fast I felt dizzy. The horror of being confined, completely naked, overwhelmed me, sent me back to the night I was attacked.

There was nowhere to run. The bathroom window was a tiny slit at the top of the room, four or five inches tall at best. I was trapped.

Fear prickled along my skin. I gulped at the air, trying to think clearly. I pulled a towel from a hook on the back of the door and wrapped it around my body, scanning the bathroom for something to use as a weapon. The shower rod would make too much noise to get down; the toilet scrubber wasn't lethal enough.

I dropped to my hands and knees and peered under the door. There was no sound. Everything had gone quiet. Too quiet. My pulse hammered in my ears.

Suddenly heavy black boots drew level with my nose, just on the other side of the bathroom door. I rocked back on my heels as the door handle rattled abruptly, a sudden image flashing in my mind.

A different apartment.

A different door handle.

A long corridor flashing as I ran past.

"Wait. Eva, don't go!" A man's voice.

And then I was outside racing past a sign for Vista Square Condos.

The bathroom door handle rattled again. The sound yanked me back to the present. I jumped to my feet, looking around wildly. My eyes fell on a bottle of bleach tucked neatly behind the toilet. I lunged for it.

In the bathroom mirror, my wet hair was slick against my skull, my face pale with terror. But there was something else there too: the glint of determination. Maybe I was trapped, but I wasn't completely defenseless. I could move. I could fight.

I unscrewed the cap off the bleach, ready. But then the footsteps trailed away from the bathroom. A long moment of silence passed.

I waited, unsure what to do. Had the intruder left?

Finally I unlocked the door as soundlessly as possible. I edged it open, the bleach ready. A woman was standing in the living room, reading something on her phone. I must've made a noise, because her head jerked up, and she screamed.

"What do you want?" I shrieked. I held the bleach up threateningly, but the towel started to slip. I grabbed for it while still trying to hold the bleach.

Shockingly, bizarrely, she laughed. "Your towel . . ."

She had a thick accent, Eastern European, maybe Russian. She was stunning, tall and slim, her body encased completely in black, like a panther. She wore a pair of chunky black Doc Martens. White-blond hair cascaded nearly to her waist. She had high, Slavic cheekbones, full lips, and dark-brown eyes framed by thickly mascaraed eyelashes.

I clutched at my towel, breathing hard.

"Why are you in Jacob's apartment?" she asked.

"Jacob's my friend," I replied, defensive. "He said I could stay."

"He did not tell me this. I will call him."

She tapped at her phone, then spoke in a low murmur. I slipped into the bedroom and pulled on my clothes from yesterday.

The rush of adrenaline was fading now, leaving me nauseated and trembly, fear clutching at me like a fist. The blond woman appeared in the doorway.

"It is okay for you to stay," she said stiffly. Her jaw, sharp as an arrow, was set in a way that said she didn't approve. "I am Anastasiya. I am also Jacob's friend," she said. "I check on his flat when he is away. And sometimes I stay here."

My face flushed hot with mortification, followed by an unexpected coil of jealousy. It was stupid. I was going to marry Liam. Jacob could date whomever he wanted. It was just our history, I guessed.

"I see." I pulled on my shoes and socks and stood.

"Jacob said to help you if you need it. Do you need help?"

I slid into my jacket and pulled the collar up. "No."

"It is very cold today. You won't be warm enough in that." She pointed at my quilted coat. "Have this. . . ." She pulled a chunky, knit scarf from a large leather handbag sitting near the door and held it out to me.

"Thank you, but no." I was touched by her kindness, but I never wore scarves. I couldn't stand anything around my throat. Not since the night I was attacked. It was why I'd cut my hair. "I'll be gone tomorrow. Do you need the flat before then?"

"No." She shook her head. "Jacob said you must stay as long as you need."

"My flight leaves tomorrow."

She stared solemnly down at me. "Jacob said to tell you . . ." She paused, as if she was trying to recall the message. "He said, 'Be careful, Eva. You don't know what you'll find.' "

Maybe Jacob's real words had gotten lost in translation, but on her lips it sounded like a threat.

I hunched in my coat as I walked to Old Street Station. Anastasiya had been right — it *was* too cold for this coat. I tucked my chin low into my collar. I was jittery, agitated, like I was standing on the razor edge of a mountain, waiting for an avalanche to crash down on me, knowing it would crush me beneath its weight.

I ached to call Liam. I missed him, the way his smile soothed my fears, how confidently he took charge of things. His calm, doggedly persistent way of fixing all the messes I made. Like when I forgot to pay my taxes last year, or when I missed an important appointment, or that time I overdrew my bank account and he'd patiently taught me how to use Excel to track my money, then opened a joint account so we could share our finances.

But it was the middle of the night in Seattle.

I was on my own.

I checked my Tube map and plotted a route to the hospital. I miraculously found the right train and felt a little spurt of pleasure at my newfound independence.

As the train swayed down the tracks to Westminster, I tried to untangle the memory I'd had of my hand on a doorknob, seeing the apartment complex name, a man shouting, "Wait. Eva, don't go!" Was it real, or was I mixing it up with another night, a dormant memory fragment only emerging now? I had no way of knowing, and my memory was the least trustworthy thing I had right now.

I exited the station just outside the Houses of Parliament, the Victorian Gothic structure of Big Ben right across the road from me. I stared up at it openmouthed, people bumping and jostling as they pushed by.

The clouds were clearing, the sky the color of washed denim marbled with lacy white clouds. Puddles glinted in the morning sun. Gulls wheeled through the air, shrieking above the din of black cabs and red buses thundering past.

I consulted Google Maps and headed toward the bridge. Across the river, the London Eye twirled slowly. I leaned over the bridge's stone balustrade and watched the river's sludgy brown waters slip by. According to the article I'd read at the British Library, this was the bridge Rose had jumped off.

Or had she been pushed?

The thought hit me out of nowhere. If you knew how to swim, you could probably make it, but not if you had a child with you.

The sound of giggling interrupted my thoughts. A handful of Japanese tourists were gathered next to me, all pointing and laughing while taking photos of the ground. Finally I got what they were seeing. The clover-shaped holes in the walls of the bridge had cast a neat row of penis-shaped patches of light at our feet.

A woman in a severe black business suit smirked as she slowed to watch them.

"The Ponte Vecchio and the Golden Gate

Bridge are all fine and good, but only in London do you get to stomp on willies," she said to me.

Hysterical laughter bubbled up my throat, wave after wave of it until tears glossed my eyes. For the first time in days, the sharp-toothed fear that had been hot against my neck lessened.

The woman looked at me like I'd completely lost it.

"Sorry!" I waved my hand, a white flag of apology. "Sorry."

She rolled her eyes and walked away.

The laughter finally tapered off. I took a deep breath and headed across the bridge. I needed to talk to David Ashford and get the hell out of here.

Before I became Sebastian Clarke's next victim.

Twenty-Three: Eva

St. Thomas' Hospital was an expansive network of stone buildings and glass-encased wings. I wandered around bewildering loops and abrupt turns before finally finding the hospital's main reception hall. A chubby woman with a neat brown bob, thick glasses, and a string of heavy pearls greeted me.

"Hi," I said. "I'm looking for one of your patients. His name's David Ashford."

"David Ashford." She typed it into her computer. "I'm afraid Mr. Ashford is on St. Ann's Ward, and he is only accepting family." She peered up at me, her eyes huge behind her glasses. "Are you family?"

I stared at her. Was I family? He was, possibly, my biological father. Did that make him family?

She took my silence as a no. "You're welcome to put in a visitor's request, and we'll pass it along to his family for you."

"Oh. Okay," I replied, but she'd already moved on to another customer.

I turned around, disappointed, and slammed hard into someone. Papers and folders flew everywhere, blown by a gust of wind puffing through the open front door.

"Oh my God, I'm so sorry!" I dropped to my knees, scooping papers into a pile.

"It was my fault, honestly." The doctor I'd hurtled into knelt next to me. She was in her early to mid-thirties with smooth, olive-toned skin and shoulder-length dark hair, straight and glossy as a shampoo ad.

"My father always tells me not to rush everywhere, and yet I persist," she said. I handed her the last folder, and she stood, smiling cheerfully.

"Can you tell me how I'd get to St. Ann's Ward?" I asked.

"It's on the fifth floor." She pointed in the direction I needed to go. "Just take the lift and turn right."

The elevator deposited me onto a quiet floor decorated entirely in white and blue: white walls, white ceiling, blue-tiled floor, blue signs. To my right was a pair of doors, a sign above them blaring ST. ANN'S CANCER WARD.

David Ashford really was sick.

I pushed through the doors. There was an

unmanned reception desk to my left. I strolled down the corridor as if I knew where I was going, trying to look confident. But there was no need. None of the doctors or nurses paid any attention to me. I peered inside each room, but I couldn't see much because the curtains were all pulled. I was working out a lie to tell a doctor in order to find David Ashford when I heard a familiar voice.

"Lie down, Dad. Save your strength. The chemo will wipe you out before you know it."

A bed creaked as a weight settled on it. I followed the voice and peered around the corner. It was that girl from the art gallery, Charlotte, tucking a sheet around a man's waist. He was small for a man, thin as paper. His skin was patchy and dry, the ashen gray of the very ill.

Charlotte looked even more exhausted than yesterday, older and harder too. The harsh fluorescent light cast stark shadows on her face. She was wearing jogging bottoms and an oversize gray sweater — clothes you pull on when you're too tired to care.

She looked up, catching my stricken gaze, and her eyes widened.

"You!" She strode angrily toward me. "What are you doing here? I told you no interviews!"

I ignored her and walked toward the hospital bed. It was him. The man from the articles at the British Library. Older, balder, sicker, for sure, but this was David Ashford.

Once when I was little, Mom and Dad took Andrew and me on a road trip to Pismo Beach. I stood where the sea meets the sand and let the waves crash against my ankles. As the water sucked back out to the Pacific, the sand shifted under my feet, my heels hovering over nothingness. That was what it felt like now. Like there was nothing holding me up, nothing to catch me if I fell.

David blinked up at me from behind round glasses. His jaw hinged open. He stood slowly, the sheet dropping to the floor, exposing thin, bony knees beneath his blue hospital gown.

He opened his mouth and said one word: "Laura."

Goose bumps skittered up my arms as a memory unfolded over me. A woman with red hair, the same straight nose and milk-pale skin as me, bent to lift me in her arms. She nuzzled my neck, and I giggled as her hair tickled my nose.

"Mummy, that tickles!"

"I love you, Laura-loo!" she exclaimed, blowing a raspberry on my cheek. . . .

"Laura," David Ashford said again.

That one word splintered everything inside of me.

Laura.

David and Rose Ashford's daughter.

The child who'd died in the articles.

But she wasn't dead at all. Laura Ashford was very much alive.

I'm Laura Ashford.

Twenty-Four: Kat

25 Years Earlier

I locked all three locks to our apartment and hurried after Eva. Even though we'd been in Chicago for three months, I wasn't used to so many locks. At least they kept us safe, at any rate.

"Blimey, Eva! Would you ever wait up?"

Her short four-year-old legs pumped as she barreled down the corridor, shooting a cheeky smile over one shoulder. Just then a tall, balding bloke exited his apartment and Eva smashed into him, the air bursting from her mouth.

"Oh! I do apologize!" I exclaimed, hurrying to them and pulling Eva out of his way.

"That's all right." The man smiled, his hazel eyes crinkling, and patted his belly. "I have some extra cushioning."

He *was* a rather large man, broad, with a significant paunch on him. Yet he had an air of gentleness, and his smile was so warm I couldn't help returning it. I'd seen him around the apartment complex a few times, checking his post box and washing clothes every Sunday in the communal laundry room downstairs.

Eva giggled. "Like Santa Claus!"

"Exactly like Santa Claus." He laughed and held out a hand to shake Eva's. "I'm Mike. And who are you?"

I held my breath, awaiting her reply.

"I'm Eva," she exclaimed.

It was rather extraordinary how easy it had been to start a new life in America. Children didn't need their own passports in the UK, and anyhow, she was Eva now, and Eva was listed on my passport.

What surprised me more was how quickly she adapted to *being* Eva. She occasionally asked for Rose, especially at first, but her entire life in London was quickly melting away as she adjusted to being Eva. Her British accent had already flattened, and she now called me Mommy, even when I insisted on Mummy.

Mike knelt so he was close to Eva and stage-whispered, "And what's your mom's name?"

"I'm Kath— Kat. Just Kat."

"Kat. A lovely name for a lovely woman."

His smile revealed a row of very white,

very straight teeth. Why did Americans always have such perfect teeth? I did not return his smile a second time. He was talking rubbish. I wasn't the type that men ever referred to as "lovely."

Eva tugged on my hand. "Can we go?"

"Very well, then." I nodded politely at Mike. "It was nice meeting you."

"And you. Hopefully I'll see more of you both."

Outside, a brisk wind slapped us in the face, causing me to shiver. Although we had bundled into the thick winter clothes I'd bought, the wind still nipped at every exposed bit of skin. We'd flown to Chicago simply because it was the next flight leaving after we arrived at Heathrow. But as winter descended on the Windy City, I regretted not waiting for the next flight to Florida. It was utterly frigid here.

We walked to the nearby lake, the ghostly outline of downtown Chicago sketched in charcoal against the pale, distant sky. The beach was a tree-lined affair with a boat launch and an abandoned stall for kayak and sailboat rentals. Dirty snow clumped in giant gray patches. The lake itself was a desolate beauty, ice waves making a quiet shushing sound. Closer to shore, ice had crusted in giant blocks along the sand.

I trailed behind as Eva clambered over the ice and snow, my mind a million miles away. On Rose. Sebastian. Eva. Even David. I had contemplated contacting him many times, but each time I remembered Seb's words: *An eye for an eye.* And then I thought of what Rose had told me: *David can't keep her safe.*

Eva's voice interrupted my thoughts. "Mommy! Mommy!"

I looked around, heart stalling as I realized I could not see her. Suddenly a snowball thumped me in the middle of my forehead.

I gasped and took my glasses off, watching the snow slide to the ground. "What the . . . ?"

Eva jumped out from behind a tree, her gray eyes gleaming with mischief. Her red hair poked out of her green snow hat.

"I'm gonna get you!" She scooped up another handful of snow and launched it at me, but this time I ducked.

"You cheeky little monkey!" I gasped. A smile, new as a baby's skin, tugged at my mouth.

I rolled a small snowball and ran after Eva, enjoying her whoops of delight.

A strange feeling unfurled deep in my chest then. Later, when I took it out and examined it, measured its peaks and troughs and let it truly sink in, I recognized it: love. At least the potential for it.

After a few moments we both collapsed, breathing heavily, onto a picnic bench. Eva threw her arms around me, her sweet, childish voice rising over the wind. "I love you, Mommy!"

I opened my mouth to say it, but it felt like a betrayal. It was too soon. I couldn't force the words past my charley-horsed throat.

Instead I squeezed her hand three times: *I. Love. You.*

The winter sun was dwindling as we trudged toward home, leaving everything a smudged shade of dirty gray. Giant flakes of snow had started to fall. After spending the morning at the lake, we'd walked to the grocery store to stock up on food. A car horn sounded, and Mike leaned his head out of a rusted Ford Escort.

"Hey, Kat! Get in, I'll give you a ride home."

I hesitated, but I was more practical than paranoid. "Thank you."

"My pleasure. I was just on my way home from work. Glad I saw you."

I carefully set the bags of groceries in the backseat, then got in front and maneuvered

Eva awkwardly onto my lap and pulled the seat belt over us. She slumped against my shoulder, her eyelids drooping.

Mike glanced at her as he pulled into traffic. "Looks like she's all tuckered out."

"Yes. Finally." I forced a polite laugh, wiping my glasses on the inside of my sleeve. "Are you just now returning home from work?"

"Yep."

"That's a terribly long day, isn't it?"

He shrugged and chuckled. "I'm a car parts salesman after a promotion. I work all the hours they want me to."

Mike nosed the car into a parking space in front of the apartment complex. I lifted Eva onto my shoulder, and Mike opened the front door, following behind as we climbed the stairs.

"Thank you for the lift," I said.

"Anytime. Bye."

He waved and headed into his apartment, then paused.

"I'm single," he said, turning to me. He ran a hand over thinning brown hair, his skin reddening under my gaze. "In case you were wondering. I mean . . . what I mean is . . . I'd love to take you to dinner. Sometime."

"I have Eva," I said stupidly.

"Okay. Well." He raised a hand. "Night."

I jostled Eva on my hip, flustered, trying to get my keys out of my pocket.

"Evening, Kat! Need any help?" Nancy Mitchell, our next-door neighbor, called. She was peering out her front door, her cotton-ball hair a poof around her face.

"No, thank you, Mrs. Mitchell." I turned the key, hustling inside before she could say anything else. I deposited Eva in the darkened bedroom we shared and flexed my bloodless fingers. A muscle twinged in my lower back.

I turned the heater up, relieved when I heard the telltale clunk. The apartment was dingy and old, the carpet stained, the curtains the dull yellow of old pee. But it was the best I could afford on our limited funds. I had withdrawn some money from the account Rose set up before we left London, but it didn't feel right spending money Rose had given her life for. I endeavored to keep it for Eva for university when she was older.

In the kitchen I got a glass of water from the tap and drank it thirstily.

That's when I saw it. My passport was on the kitchen counter. Open.

Ice trickled down my spine.

I had not left it there.

I looked around. The curtain in front of the balcony swayed, a cold draft swirling around my ankles. The door was open just a fraction. I slid a knife from the block next to the refrigerator and held it behind me, moving slowly toward the balcony.

I felt it then, like an electrical charge in the air. Someone was behind me.

I turned as a shadow fell into my peripheral vision. But I wasn't quick enough. Something hit me from behind, the force throwing me to my knees. The knife clattered to the floor, skittering across the carpet and disappearing under the couch.

I lashed out with my leg as I scrambled away on all fours, catching the man in the shin.

"Oomph . . ." He made a muffled sound but kept coming.

He grabbed my hair. I felt the roots rip from my skull, pain radiating throughout my entire head. My eyes filled instantly with tears. I twisted away and scrambled to my feet, trying to run, to move, to just not die, but he was on me again.

I opened my mouth to scream. Too late. The weight of his body drove me backward so my head cracked into the wall. Stunned, I went limp in his arms, every wisp of breath gone from my body. He cradled my face in his massive palm almost tenderly, and smashed my head against the wall.

Once. Twice. Three times.

Stars exploded in front of my eyes. I gagged and slid to the floor next to the couch, boneless, landing on my back, arms splayed. He straddled me, his thick fingers wrapped around my throat. I was floating, I was flying, I was —

"Mummy?"

It was Eva's voice.

The man's grip loosened, his eyes widening in surprise. He clearly hadn't known a child was here. In my peripheral vision, the knife glinted under the couch. As he hesitated, I reached for it, felt the smooth, cold weight of it in my hand, and pressed just the tip of it against his belly.

"I have money," I gasped. "I can pay you to leave us alone. Or I can stab you right now."

The man froze. His gaze darted between me and the blade, then over his shoulder at Eva, then back to me again.

Slowly he got off me and we both stood. Eva ran to me, throwing her small body against my legs. I almost fell then, the crushing pain in my head simultaneously overwhelming and unbalancing. I worried, momentarily, that I might actually be sick.

I dropped my hand onto the back of her neck to ground me, to hold me up, and looked at the man. He was very young, early twenties at a guess, with longish, oily dark hair and broad shoulders, a strawberry-shaped birthmark on his left temple.

I forced a smile onto my numb lips.

"Eva. Darling. We were just . . . looking for this cooking knife." I held up the knife in my hand, knowing it was a stupid excuse, the flimsiest lie possible. "This is . . ." I turned to the man, making sure the knife was within striking distance at all times. "Sorry, I didn't catch your name."

"Colin," he said, a lazy grin creasing his mouth. "Colin Wilson. Pleased to make your acquaintance, little lass. Your mum here was just about to pay me rent, and then I'll be off."

He had a British accent.

I closed my eyes for a brief second. Bollocks. I felt like such a fool. I'd rather thought I had gotten away with it. And there I'd just gone and used Eva's name.

"I need your account details," I said. "There's a pad of paper on the kitchen counter."

He walked slowly, almost languorously, to the kitchen, his gaze on Eva. He wasn't afraid of me in the least. If he wanted to, he could kill us, he was far stronger than I. But the offer of money was too much for him to refuse.

I swayed on my feet like I was drunk, and put a hand against the wall to steady myself. Sweat dripped down my back as I analyzed my options. I could scream, but then my neighbors would come and they would want to know why he was here. I could kill him, stab him in the throat when he was distracted, perhaps while he was writing down his bank account number. But I did not want to kill a man in front of Eva. And how would I eliminate the body? I was strong, but small. I could not do it on my own.

"I shall phone my bank and transfer it as soon as you leave. I'll pay you double what your other . . . tenant paid you. Write it down."

He did as he was told, the pen scratching across the paper.

"Don't forget to pay that *rent,*" he said, his eyes dark and malicious on mine. "I know where you live if you don't."

I glared at him. "It will be there tomorrow."

He strolled to the door, throwing a nonchalant wink at Eva. Eva turned her face into my stomach. A second later his footsteps thumped down the corridor, followed by the ricochet of the downstairs door slamming shut.

Weak with relief, I threw the dead bolt shut and collapsed shaking onto the couch.

We were safe. For now.

TWENTY-FIVE: EVA

I rolled the name around in my mouth, trying it on for size.

Laura.

Laura Ashford.

A nurse came into the hospital room and took David's blood pressure. Nobody spoke. I stared outside where hard drops of rain clattered against the window, coloring the room in shadows. I felt detached and disconnected. As if getting struck by lightning had split me from myself: Eva on one side and Laura on the other.

After a moment, the nurse bustled out.

"How did you find me?" David asked. His accent was cultured, upper-class. Straight out of *Downton Abbey.*

"Dad, this is mental!" Charlotte protested, her face red and blotchy. "You've just had a round of chemo. Would you just lie down?"

"Darling, this is Laura." He turned to me. "I mean, Eva. I believe you're called

Eva now?"

I nodded mutely. Charlotte crossed her arms over her chest and pressed her back against the wall, scowling.

"How do you know I'm Laura?" I asked David. Like a contrary child, I wanted desperately to deny what he was saying.

"You look very like my sister did at your age. But you want proof, yes?" He thought for a second. "You have a scar on your right shoulder. You fell out of your pram when you were a year old."

I tugged the collar of my T-shirt down to expose the silver half-moon scar I'd had on my shoulder my whole life.

"It's you," he breathed.

He held a veined, liver-spotted hand out to me. I stared at it, unable to move, to step over the threshold into that new world. Everything in me was screaming to run, get away, but I wanted to know the truth.

I looked up, catching the stunned disbelief on Charlotte's face, the relief on David's. Emotion overwhelmed me. My eyes filled with hot tears. The sterile hospital room blurred in front of me, a mirage of movement and light as another piece of the puzzle clicked into place.

"So the prodigal daughter returns," Charlotte said bitterly. She shook her head, her unwashed strawberry-blond hair swinging limply around her face. "Where were you months ago when he first got sick? Why are you here now?"

"I didn't know about . . . any of this." I turned to David. "I swear."

He nodded. "I know. Katherine insisted it was better that way."

"Why would she do that? And how did you know my name is Eva now?"

"Katherine wrote me when you were twelve. She told me what happened. We've kept in touch ever since."

"You knew I was alive?" I whispered, horrified. Shouldn't he have looked for me? Shouldn't he have taken me back? "You abandoned me."

David flinched as if I'd physically hit him. "Certainly not! But I understand why you feel that way, and I'm ever so sorry. I wanted to keep you safe, but please understand, I argued with her about it. I wanted you home with me. Those first months after I thought you and your mother had died were excruciating. But Kat told me this was the only way to keep you safe. That's all I ever wanted."

The muffled cry of a baby came from the corner of the room. Charlotte rushed to the stroller there and scooped her daughter out.

"Ma-ma," the girl said, rubbing tiny fists into tired eyes.

"Yes, my love." Charlotte kissed her chubby neck, clutching her to her chest like a shield.

"Rose. Is she really dead?" I asked David.

"Yes. I'll never forgive myself for it. She jumped into the river while I was away for work. I didn't realize she was missing until I returned."

"Did they find her body?"

For a moment David looked like he'd be sick. "In central London the width of the river, the strength of the current make underwater searches nearly impossible. It was weeks before we found her, and when we did she was . . . unrecognizable."

He rubbed a thin hand over his eyes. "I always wondered what would have happened if I hadn't gone away at such a difficult time, if I'd put her first."

"But she didn't jump with me. Where was I?"

"With Katherine. Rose asked her to take you."

"Why?"

"Because Katherine's husband, Sebastian, had put a hit on Rose. He blamed her for Eva's death. Katherine told me most of the cops were in Sebastian's pocket. She said you would never be safe in London."

Questions twisted through me, followed by anger. The anger that had been tucked up in little black corners inside me was now escaping. I felt like I had a dragon inside of me that was slowly waking, the fire of its breath burning my insides. So many lies. It seemed that was what my life had been built on.

I shook my head. "Suicide seems pretty extreme."

David smiled sadly, his eyes pinched and tired. "I agree. Rose was always rather impulsive. She was fun and passionate and magnetic, but she rarely thought about the consequences of her actions. Perhaps she simply caved in to the guilt. She was tormented after Eva died. And given her medical history, it didn't seem such a surprise."

"What medical history?"

"She'd been medicated before. After you were born. I believe now they call it postnatal depression. There were no services for that sort of thing back then, you just got on with it. Keep calm and carry on, you know. I thought it would pass, and it mostly did. But she was terribly unhappy sometimes. She struggled with being home all day with a small child. It's why I suggested hiring a nanny."

David leaned against the bed. The pain of speaking about the past was visible on his face.

Charlotte sighed loudly, exasperated. She shifted her baby to her hip and went to David, tugging him toward the bed. "Dad, please get in bed! You're about to fall over."

David nodded. He slipped his feet under the sheet, his back propped against the upraised bed. He stared into empty space for a long minute, his breathing shallow and fast. The sharp angles of his ribs tented the sheet.

"Rose must've thought that faking your death would throw Sebastian off your track," he finally said. "What I never understood is why she sent you with Kat instead of me. Some days, I hate her for that. I never got over losing you both."

Charlotte looked like she'd been slapped, her cheeks hollowing as she inhaled sharply. She whirled and strapped the baby into her stroller.

"I'll be back later, Dad," she said, refusing to meet his eyes. A few seconds later, I heard the elevator ding as she got on.

I dropped my head into my hands, my breath coming in short, shallow bursts. The lightning marks on my arm had gone all prickly, the way a limb feels when it's fallen asleep.

"This must be rather shocking to you," David said.

He looked like he was going to get off the hospital bed to come to me, but that was the last thing I wanted. I put a hand out, to stop him, and to steady myself, and he stayed where he was.

"I'll be okay," I said roughly.

Blood whooshed around my brain. I felt like I was rising out of my body, up to the ceiling. The air was too thin. Sweat prickled under my armpits. I took my coat off, trying to get some cool air against my skin. David's eyes widened as they landed on the lightning marks on my arm.

"What happened?" he asked.

"I actually got struck by lightning."

"Lightning? Oh my God! Are you okay?"

"I'm fine. The doctor said they're called Lichtenberg figures." I twisted my arm to look at the marks, which had faded to a dull pink. "They'll go away."

"It's actually very beautiful." He smiled at me.

I snorted. "Ha! I look broken."

He shrugged. "In Japan, they believe in the ethos of wabi-sabi, which says there's beauty in the broken."

"Like kintsugi," I said, thinking of the pottery I'd seen at his art gallery yesterday.

He looked pleased. "Exactly. The cracks are essential to our history, rather than something to disguise."

David leaned his head against the bed, seeming to have suddenly lost all energy. "I wasn't sure if Kat would tell you about my condition. Please extend my gratitude to her."

"She didn't," I said. "Mom was murdered four days ago. I found your address in her office."

"Murdered!" David's hand fluttered to his chest. He turned an even more sickly shade of gray. "Sebastian."

My stomach clenched as I thought about the man following me yesterday. "I think so. And now he's looking for me."

Twenty-Six: Eva

David didn't want me to leave the hospital. He was terrified for my safety, afraid Sebastian would find me. I was scared of that too, but I was more afraid of going to jail.

"I'll call you as soon as I get back to Seattle," I promised. "I'll tell the police everything I've learned. They'll protect me. I'm sure they'll be in touch."

"Don't forget Charlotte," he murmured as I left, his eyes already drooping shut.

I looked at him blankly.

"Charlotte. Your sister. Half sister. She'll be across the street at the café with Eloise. She grew up in your shadow, so, yes, maybe she hates you a little right now. But you're family."

Outside, the cold wind bit at my fingers. A heavy drizzle quickly saturated my coat. People had started to put up umbrellas, the rain splattering against building windows and plummeting to the ground. It slapped into my hair, cold but oddly refreshing.

My mom had loved the rain. "Rain washes the world clean, Eva," she always said. "It makes everything fresh and new again."

I was quickly getting soaked and didn't have an umbrella, so I jogged across the street and pushed open the door to the Tea and Sympathy café.

I could use lunch about now anyway.

Steamy air smacked me in the face, the competing aromas of coffee and fresh baked goods greeting me. The décor was somewhere between douchey hipster and slick Manhattan — exposed brickwork, pale hardwood floors, reclaimed wood tables.

Charlotte was hunched at the back of the café, her back to me. She was trying to get Eloise to eat a spoonful of something green.

I ordered a sandwich and a pot of tea and plopped my tray on the table next to her. She glared at me, baby spoon hovering in the air. Eloise smacked it, spraying sludgy green food all over Charlotte's face. She gasped and froze. I expected her to be mad, but instead her eyes softened and she laughed.

"You cheeky little monkey." She grabbed a napkin and wiped her face, then unbuckled Eloise from her stroller and wiped her clean too.

She was so young. Far too young to be responsible for both her child and her parent. I scanned her face, devoid of a scrap of makeup, blue smudges underneath her eyes. She must've caught the pity on my face because her smile dropped, her jaw jutting out defensively. "I know what you're thinking. Silly cow should've remembered her birth control."

"What? No!" I was shocked by her acerbity.

"Eloise is the best choice I ever made. And believe me, there have been days when it's been hard. Especially now that Dad's sick."

She jiggled Eloise on her knee. Eloise held her fingers and laughed, a sound that squeezed my heart.

"You're right, I was judging you," I admitted. "I'm sorry. We all make the choices we can live with, and you've clearly made a good one. Eloise is beautiful."

She turned away and took a sip of her coffee. "Listen, Eva, or Laura, or — I don't know what to call you."

"I'm . . ." I stared at her, unsure what to say. Was I Laura now?

"Whatever. You can go home. I don't want you here. My mum will be here to collect me in a minute anyhow."

Hurt cracked through me. I doctored my

tea with sugar and milk, trying not to be so sensitive. This girl was my sister. All of this was new for her too. I folded my hands together and leaned forward.

"Tell me about her."

"My mum?"

"Yes."

"She's lovely. She's an academic. She teaches art history at Oxford."

"She doesn't live here?"

Charlotte shook her head. "No. She and Dad divorced when I was two. I think what he said is true — he never got over your mum, and my mum didn't want to be second-best. After they divorced, she took a job at Oxford and I stayed with Dad."

Seeing the look on my face, she rolled her eyes. "People don't give men enough credit. Dads can be amazing too."

I laughed. "Yeah, sorry. That was a little sexist of me."

She laughed drily. "I know I chose to have Eloise and stay home with her, but some women don't want or can't have that. Mum has a fantastic career and I'm really proud of her."

"She sounds really great."

"The best." Charlotte agreed. "It must be crazy, right? Finding out you aren't who you thought you were your whole life?"

"I'm not sure I've wrapped my head around it, to be honest."

Eloise bashed both hands against the table, rattling the saucers and mugs. Intrigued by the vibrations, she reached for my mug. I moved it out of her reach, sloshing tea onto my jeans. Eloise laughed, holding a hand out to me. Charlotte sighed and stood up.

"I'll grab you a few napkins," Charlotte said. She thrust Eloise at me and hurried to the front of the café.

I held Eloise like I would a football, cautiously, with my fingertips, afraid to drop her. I stared into her wide blue eyes, thinking of the massive, breath-stealing pain I'd carried under my heart ever since giving up my own child.

In the end, I'd decided on adoption. I knew I couldn't keep my baby, because how could you be a good mother to a child you didn't even want? A child you hated and blamed, whose every glance would remind you of what you wanted to forget?

Even now, I could picture Mom in the hospital room with me, the baby nestled in her arms. "Hold her just for a minute, Eva."

"No." I'd turned my face away. I couldn't even look at the baby without thinking of that night. How could I possibly care for her, love her the way a mother should?

"Eva —"

"Get her out of here!"

I had wanted to protect my daughter from my past, not make her a part of it. I wanted her life to be fresh and innocent and pure.

Maybe Rose had wanted the same for me.

Twenty-Seven: Eva

The next morning, my plane set down at Sea-Tac Airport. A bank of clouds was just disappearing, a pink smear of light touching the horizon. The tarmac still glistened from the rain, drops of moisture dribbling down the plane's windows.

I'd slept in random bursts most of the flight from London, the stress of the last few days wearing on me. My eyes were gritty. My mouth tasted like a badger had crawled into it and died. I could feel my body inching toward total collapse, so after frog-marching through passport control, I headed to Starbucks.

Even though it'd only been three days, it felt like a lifetime had passed since Jacob had dropped me off at this airport. Time was relentlessly ticking by, each second dissolving like a mirage across the desert. I'd found out so many things in London, but none of them answered my one burning question: Had Sebastian killed my mom?

Or had I?

Instead of taking the taxi to Mom's house, where Melissa's car was still parked, I gave the driver my dad's address. He pulled up to a small rambler perched on a neatly manicured lot a few blocks behind Angle Lake. Dad had moved here after the divorce. Even though they'd tried to split custody of us, like most things in life, the break wasn't even. I was mostly at Mom's while Andrew was mostly at Dad's because it was closer to his school. Gradually I visited less and less. It was too hard seeing how their lives had moved on, as if our family had never existed.

"Eva!" Dad looked exactly the same when he opened the door: large potbelly, kind hazel eyes, a hooked nose, bald except for a thin ring of hair at the bottom, stretching from ear to ear. He grabbed me in a tight bear hug.

"Hey, Dad." I wrapped my arms around him, my voice muffled against his wool sweater.

Ever since he'd remarried, there had been a shift in our relationship. But he was my dad, the only father I'd ever known, and it felt good to be in his arms.

"I've been calling you. Are you okay?"

I nodded.

"Come in, come in." He moved aside and I followed him into the living room. "I was just finishing breakfast."

I smiled. "Two eggs and toast?"

Dad was a predictable man, wrapped in his routines. It was probably what had attracted Mom to him in the first place.

The living room had been updated since I was last here. Donna, his new wife, had painted the walls a warm magnolia and hung sheer lemon drapes from the windows. A cream wool rug offset the brown carpet.

I caught sight of myself in a wooden-framed mirror hanging over the fireplace. My roots were growing out, the mahogany red stark against the bottled toffee color I carefully applied every month. I looked haggard, almost unrecognizable, like I needed about four years of uninterrupted sleep.

We sat next to each other on the corduroy couch. Tux, Dad's ancient black-and-white cat, ran across the room and jumped onto my lap. I nuzzled his neck as his purr kicked in.

"This is crazy." Dad shook his head. "I mean . . . I just can't believe it. This sort of thing doesn't happen to normal people. I feel like I'm watchin' a movie or somethin'."

I snorted. "Tell me about it."

"Do you know what happened? The police aren't saying much, and Andrew's too broken up to talk about it."

"Mom was poisoned."

Dad slumped against the couch in shock, blowing out a stunned breath. His cheeks jiggled with the movement. "But . . . she's a high school teacher! Why would someone poison her? Do they know who did it?"

I hesitated, stroking Tux's silky fur. "No, but I think I might be a suspect."

"You! Why?"

I tried to process that question.

What if I did what the detective thinks I've done?

Had I, in a moment's fury, lashed out, foolish and impulsive, an action bitterly regretted but impossible to undo? Maybe Mom had told me about our past. Maybe I'd meant to punish her for lying to me. I'd lashed out before. How could I trust that I hadn't done it again?

"Do you remember when I left Seattle and moved to Whidbey Island?" I asked.

"Yeah."

"I left because Mom and I got in a massive fight. I was living with her after . . . what happened to me. I'd given the baby up for adoption, and Mom came into my room one day. We started shouting at each other."

"You made the choice to give the baby up, Eva. Now it's time to stop being a victim and start being a survivor."

Only now did I realize I'd never forgiven her for those words. My bitterness and unforgiveness had burrowed inside me, folding into the fabric of my identity and creating the distance that had grown between us.

"The cops didn't even believe me when I told them what happened, and then I found out I was pregnant and I had to give the baby up. I was so *angry* that she could think everything would just go back to normal. I totally freaked out."

"Move on? I can't just move on. This isn't some science experiment where the answers are black and white! What happened will never be over for me!"

I had started crying, tears hot and sticky on my face. Dad wrapped his arms around me. I laid my head against his chest, the way I used to when I was a little girl.

"We shouted at each other. We said some horrible things."

"Maybe it's fine for robots like you!"

"You're acting like a weak-willed little child!"

"Mom stormed out of the house and didn't come back all afternoon. That night I woke up to a scraping sound outside. When I looked out the window, I saw someone was jimmying the lock on the front door. You can't imagine how scared I was. Mom was still gone, and my phone was downstairs. I know it was totally irrational, but I thought the guy who attacked me had returned. I'd been so scared. I picked up this really heavy vase Mom had and, when the door opened, I smashed it into the burglar's head."

Understanding dawned on Dad's face. "Ah. It was your mom."

I nodded. "Yeah. There was no burglar. It was all in my head. Mom had forgotten her keys and didn't want to wake me. One of the neighbors called the cops when they heard me screaming. They arrested me and I spent the night in jail for assault. Mom told the police it was all a misunderstanding, and eventually they decided not to press charges, but I left Seattle after that. That's why the detective thinks I killed her. Because I've assaulted her before."

Dad rubbed a hand over his balding head. "You didn't mean to do it, though."

"No, but they don't care about that. They just care about what I did before." I laughed, a dry, bitter sound. "Plus, I can't remember a single thing about the night she was killed."

"There's no way you did it, Eva."

I shook my head, and Tux hopped off my lap, tossing a disdainful look over his shoulder. "Did you know my real name is Laura, not Eva? Or that Mom wasn't even my biological mother?"

"Honey, what are you talking about? Your name is Eva."

I pulled Mom's letter and the copies of the newspaper clippings I'd taken from the British Library from my purse.

"Mom lied about who we were my whole life."

Dad read the articles. His face reddened, his breath coming in short little puffs. He stood and strode across the room. He stared out the living room window, a hurt sort of anger radiating off his back.

"She never . . . I never . . ."

"I know." I folded the articles and the letter into small, neat squares and slid them back into the envelope.

"I have to go in to the detective's office," I said. "I have to let him question me."

"No, don't do that." Dad shook his head vigorously. "Don't talk to that detective."

"I have to, Dad. What if I did it? Maybe I'm dangerous. Maybe there's something wrong with me."

Maybe I'm losing my mind.

Dad knelt in front of me. "I've known you since you were four years old. From when you were a rambunctious little girl to when you got your driver's license to now, this beautiful, kind-hearted, sensitive woman here in front of me. There is *nothing* wrong with you." He touched my cheek. "You hear me? Nothing. This is all gonna get sorted out. They'll find evidence of whatever really happened, and it won't point at you. But if it will make you feel better to talk to that detective, do it. Just make sure you take a lawyer with you, okay? Promise me."

I nodded, my heart swelling with love. "Thanks, Dad. Liam organized a lawyer for me back in Langley. Maybe I'll go back there first and have the lawyer come with me to the detective's office."

"I think that's a good idea." Dad put a hand to his lower back and moved to sit next to me again. "I just can't see why anybody would kill her. Kat was a good person. Don't get me wrong, she could be hard to live with. She was . . . dry. Suspicious. Had that streak in her, you know, like you had to prove you weren't up to something. I guess now I understand why."

"I didn't know Mom was paranoid."

"Yeah. It was one of the reasons we divorced. She wanted to know where I was, who I was with every second. For a long time I thought she was jealous. I sold car parts for a living! I spent my days on the lot and was home by dinnertime. There was nothing crazy about it. And then, you know the rest. . . ." He shrugged.

I frowned. "No. I don't think I do. I only remember your last fight."

Dad winced. "Jesus, Eva. You remember that?"

"Of course. I was, like, eleven, not a baby. We came home from hiking, and you were in the shower. You shouted at each other and you slipped when you were getting out. You smashed your head against the countertop."

I remembered the blood seeping between Dad's fingers, splattering onto the carpet. He packed a bag and left that night.

It wasn't like I never saw him again. He picked me up from school all the time. But it was never really the same after that. The happy bubble I'd lived in until then had been burst.

He shook his head. "I didn't slip. She pushed me. Hard."

"Mom did?" I exclaimed. I couldn't imagine my stoic, quiet mother lashing out violently. But I guess I was finding out there was a lot I didn't know about her.

Dad nodded. "Did you know what we fought about?"

"No, I guess I don't."

"Kat was cheating on me. She had an affair with a woman."

Twenty-Eight: Kat

25 Years Before

I might have been rather a lot of terrible things by then — a thief, a fraud, a kidnapper — but I was certainly no liar. So I transferred the money to Colin Wilson as promised.

I tucked Eva back into bed and lay on the couch with a package of frozen peas pressed to my sore head. I stayed awake deep into the night watching the door through blurry eyes and trying to figure out what to do. Paying Colin Wilson had only bought us time, but I'd use that time wisely. We had a few months, perhaps, if I was lucky. I had known men like him before.

The terrifying thing was that he knew where we lived, and he knew I had Eva. At some point, Seb would likely find out.

We had to leave. But first I needed money. Money besides what Rose had given Laura. I needed to save that to buy off anybody else who came looking for us.

I needed a job.

The next morning, the pain in my head was vicious and debilitating but I dressed Eva and myself with shaky fingers and we took the bus to the center of Evanston.

Eva peppered me with questions the entire way. *Why is poop brown when you eat orange carrots? How does snow get on top of mountains if they're above the clouds? When I get to heaven, can I be a hot dog? I think your boobs look down 'cause they're grumpy, Mommy. What's inside a rainbow?*

By the time we got off the bus, the pain was so intense I was ready to throw her against a wall. I kept my jaw firmly locked in place, wishing I had some painkillers to ease the pounding in my head. I couldn't seem to shake the pain.

I first went to the public library. Although I hadn't finished university, I did have some education and felt I would fit well there temperamentally.

But they had no positions for an unemployed person without a degree.

Next I went to an upscale hotel, thinking it would be easy enough to answer phones and greet customers. The sleek, blond, pencil-thin girl at the front desk looked me up and down and smirked.

"Honey, do you even own a pair of heels?" she asked. Her nasal American accent made her sound as if she were stretching her mouth around all the letters simultaneously. I wanted to slap the cruel smile off her face.

I tried in a series of shops with no success. Just as I was about to take Eva home for lunch, I saw a NOW HIRING sign in a small Chinese restaurant. Inside, the Asian owner thrust an application form at me, barely even looking at me.

Eva was hungry and grumpy and wandered to the other side of the restaurant to look at the goldfish tank while I filled in the application form.

"Here. I've finished." I handed the form to the owner. He had small, round glasses and a thin, unkempt mustache. He scowled and snatched the application, adjusting his glasses as he read.

"You know how to drive?" he asked. "We need a delivery driver."

I didn't even have my license in America. The thought of driving on the opposite side of the road, the opposite side of the car, with all those large vehicles rushing around, filled me with abject terror.

I swallowed hard and smiled. "Yes, certainly. I can do anything, I just —"

Suddenly I realized that Eva was not there.

I spun around. "Eva?" I called.

I raced to the fish tank, but she wasn't there. "Where's Eva? Where's my daughter?"

He shrugged.

I pushed past him to look in the kitchen. A chef looked up from chopping celery, his face a mask of surprise.

My heart thudded, making the pounding in my head swell to an unbearable crescendo. I felt cold and hot all over, my hands shaking with terror. Had Seb found us already? Had he taken her?

An intense, all-consuming panic crashed into me, unfamiliar and strange. I had always sat on my emotions. As a child I'd learned no one would listen, and as an adult I knew emotions were simply a chemical reaction in the limbic system, fleeting and unreliable. My ability to remain impassive had suited me well in my adult life. But now, after everything that had happened, to lose Eva a second time . . .

I slammed the front door open and stumbled into the street. A bus whizzed by, forcing me to stagger backward.

"Eva!"

I crashed into a man dressed in a business suit and smoking a cigarette.

"Hey, watch it!" he shouted angrily.

"My little girl —" I clutched his forearm, my fingers like claws. I must've looked like a madwoman, but I didn't care. "Have you seen my little girl?"

"Get off me!" He shook himself free, straightened his sleeve, and strode briskly away, throwing a disgusted glance back at me.

I saw her then. She was a ways up from the Chinese restaurant, looking in the front window of a pet shop. She saw me and waved exuberantly.

"Mommy, look!" she called. "Puppies!"

I staggered to her, clutching my chest as if it would burst out of my coat. I wanted to slap her and hold her all at once. I fell to my knees and shook her, just once, hard and sharp. I touched her cheek with my fingertips, stroked a hand down her silken hair, and clasped her to my chest.

She looked surprised, unused to my touch other than a firmly clasped hand as we walked. She was absolutely fine. Not a scratch on her.

But at that moment I knew.

I wouldn't be getting a job.

I could not survive on my own with a small child.

I tried to think what Rose would do, and

suddenly the solution seemed so obvious. I bought red lipstick and mascara, a low-cut dress from the charity shop, a cheap bottle of red wine.

That evening I stared at myself in the bedroom mirror. I looked rather good, if I did say so myself. It was a shame I had not found high heels that fit — the girl in the hotel had been correct, I didn't even own a pair. But it could not be helped. I was as sexy and unlike myself as I could possibly muster.

When I knew Mike would be home from work, I went to Mrs. Mitchell's apartment next door and rang her doorbell. She opened the door, peering at me through thick glasses that enlarged her rheumy blue eyes.

"Oh, hello, Kat! Would you like to come in?" She pulled the door open, the sound of her telly wafting out to me.

"Thank you, but no. I've left Eva inside. I'm meant to have a date, and my babysitter didn't arrive. I was just wondering, could you watch Eva for a bit? Two hours, tops. I know it's last-minute, I'm truly sorry. I feel dreadful."

She grinned, her eyes lighting up. "A date, huh?"

"Yes."

"Well, sure, honey. I don't mind at all. I was a single mom myself. I know how hard it is. You go enjoy yourself."

"Brilliant! Thank you so much!"

She followed me back to my apartment.

"Eva, darling, Mrs. Mitchell is going to watch you for a bit this evening."

For a moment Eva looked frightened, like she would protest, but Mrs. Mitchell opened her arms, her smile wide and friendly.

"Come here, honey," she said. "We can watch some cartoons together. Would you like that?"

Eva nodded and climbed onto Mrs. Mitchell's lap. She popped her thumb in her mouth, her gaze on the telly. I hesitated. I knew I should hug her good-bye. That's what a good mum would do. But I could not seem to get my body to do so. She wasn't the little girl I wanted to hold.

I shut the door gently and walked away. There were more pressing matters at hand right now, like how we were going to survive. I continued down the corridor to Mike's apartment, wiping my damp hands on my dress.

This had to work.

Mike's eyes widened when he opened the door, sweeping from my face to my low-cut dress. I thrust the wine at him. "I brought some wine."

"Uhhmmm . . ." His cheeks flushed, his Adam's apple bobbing up and down. "Come in."

Mike's apartment had the same layout as ours, filled with much the same things: cheap, saggy furniture; crooked, generic photos on the walls; a tattered brown rug in the entryway. His sink was overflowing with unwashed dishes. The air smelled of grease and TV dinners.

I tried to ignore the mess and faced him. "I have a daughter."

Mike smiled, long and slow, and reached for my hand. I hesitated for the barest of moments, fear churning in my belly. I had been burned before, and I feared Mike treating me as Seb had. The fists I could almost endure, but not being controlled and oppressed. I'd had a taste of freedom from a man's tyranny these last months and I'd rather grown to like it.

And yet I knew somehow that Mike was not like that. He was a good man, a kind man, I was certain.

And so I let him take my hand and pull me against his chest.

"That's okay," he said. "I have a lot of knock-knock jokes."

■ ■ ■ ■

We had sex that night and nearly every night afterward when Eva was in bed, until I awoke one morning and knew I was pregnant. Was it wrong to trick Mike when I did not love him? Perhaps. But it was the only way. Rose was dead; David could not protect Eva. Her safety, *our* safety was in my hands. Sexual attraction was simply the release of pheromones in the brain. Androstenone, androstadienone, and androstenol in the right quantity could make you attracted to anybody. It was just biology, after all.

I could forge a good life out of this situation.

Mike and I married in a simple ceremony at City Hall with Mrs. Mitchell as our witness, and he adopted Eva soon after. When he told me he was being transferred to Seattle for a management position at a car dealership there, I was utterly thrilled. My plan couldn't have gone any better.

In Seattle, with new names, we would finally be safe from Seb.

Twenty-Nine: Eva

Dad drove me to Mom's house to get Melissa's car. I put the SIM card back in my phone and turned it on. It immediately sprang to life, vibrating and pinging with app notifications and alerts, missed calls, texts, e-mails.

Dad glanced at me and smiled. "Popular much?"

"I turned my phone off for a few days," I explained.

I scrolled through the notifications. More condolences on Instagram, a few e-mails from news reporters requesting interviews, a link from Holly to an obituary for my mom, missed calls from Liam, Andrew, and Detective Jackson. I scrolled through texts from Melissa and a few other friends, stopping when I came to a blocked number.

I stared at the text message. It had been sent two days ago.

It took a long time for her to die after her throat was slit. Go home or you'll die the same way.

My fingers went numb with fear. I scrolled to the next message. It had been sent from a different blocked number.

Go home now, Eva. Or go home in a body bag.

"Everything all right?" Dad asked.

"What? Oh. Yeah." I forced a laugh. Dad was worried enough about me as it was. I couldn't tell him about this too. "Just letting Liam know when I'll be home."

Dad pulled up behind Melissa's car. I leaned across the console and hugged him good-bye, but he grabbed my arm as I turned to go.

"Eva, promise me you'll speak to that lawyer. You have to take him in with you when you talk to the detective. I'm serious now, okay? Promise me."

I nodded. "I promise, Dad."

I hugged him again. An extra one for luck.

The evergreen trees and steel-gray waters of Puget Sound were shrouded in an uneasy fog as I drove off the ferry a little later. I couldn't get my mind off those texts. Who were they from?

As I drove through Langley, I decided to swing by the gallery and get Fiona's broken urn. I had the piece of jade, and I knew exactly how it should be repaired now. I would fix it tonight before I went in to see the detective tomorrow morning.

Melissa was out to lunch, so I grabbed the things I needed and ran back to the car. I drove home too fast, an invisible urgency pushing at my back. The house was painted in stark bands of light and shadow that fell between the evergreen trees. Dirty-gray clouds lumbered through the sky. The air smelled earthy and damp, like pine and rainwater and rotting leaves and death.

Shadows danced across the gravel at my feet as I got out of the car. The house looked quiet, almost abandoned in the shifting light. I shivered, that familiar tingling feeling zipping like electricity down my arms and up my spine. I looked around, expecting the weight of someone's eyes to be boring into me.

But there was no one there.

It's just because it's so empty out here, I reminded myself.

Mr. Ayyad appeared around the curve of the lake in the distance, out for a run with his husky faithfully keeping pace. He waved, his lined face creasing into a huge smile. I waved and forced a smile, turning quickly to hurry toward the front door.

"Liam?" I called as I entered.

I dropped my backpack on the floor. The gunshot sound of my shoes striking the hardwood floor reminded me to take them off. I was just kicking them into a corner when Liam appeared at the top of the stairs.

"Eva!"

He jogged down the stairs and swept me into a hug. He was wearing a charcoal-gray business suit with a crisp white shirt and a navy tie. I pressed myself against him, savoring the feel of his body, his smell, the warmth of his skin.

"I've been so worried about you!" he murmured into my hair. "How's your head? How are you feeling?" He held me at arm's length, his eyes caressing my face, checking to make sure I was okay.

"Fine. Look." I shrugged my coat off, dropped it to the ground, and lifted my shirtsleeve to show him my arm. "The marks are almost gone."

Liam hung my coat and backpack on the coatrack and tugged me over to the couch. I sat next to him, letting myself relax into him, his presence like a warm cup of tea after coming in from the rain.

For the first time in days, I felt safe.

I leaned my head back against the couch. "It is *so* good to be home," I said.

"Err . . . not to bring you down, but that detective was here again yesterday," Liam said. "He wants you to call him."

I stiffened. "Why was he here?"

"He had more questions. I think he wants to formally question me, and I'm sure he'll want the same from you. I told him we wouldn't answer his questions without our lawyer."

"What sort of questions was he asking?"

"The same ones, really. Where were you that night? What time did you leave? He mentioned . . ." Liam hesitated.

"What, Liam? What did he mention?"

He froze, his face blank. Too blank. He pulled a blanket from the side of the couch and tucked it tight across my lap, like I was a child.

"Just . . . that night, the night your mom was killed. You had a migraine and said you were going to take some medicine and go to bed. Did you take anxiety medication with the migraine meds?"

"I don't remember," I said finally.

Liam looked disappointed, like I'd failed a particularly important question, so I rushed to add, "But I did learn some things while I was in London. Apparently my mom kidnapped me when I was three years old. My name isn't Eva. . . ." I hesitated, unsure I wanted to say it out loud, to make it real. I took a deep breath. "My name is really Laura Ashford."

Liam stared at me, his face slack, the color of old putty. His mouth moved, but no sound came out. It was the first time I'd ever seen him completely speechless.

I laughed drily. "Imagine what you're feeling now and multiply it by a thousand. That was me a couple days ago."

"I don't understand," he finally said. "You were kidnapped?"

"Sort of. . . ."

I told him everything I'd learned about Mom's past, excluding everything about my own. Call it pride, call it shame, I still didn't want Liam to know what happened to me. Maybe I should've told him in the beginning, but how could I when I doubted my own memories? I couldn't risk losing him, then or now. Besides, it was too late to sit around stroking my Freudian beard and pondering all the things I should've done instead.

"I think it was Sebastian who killed her," I told Liam. He stared at me, horrified.

"Someone was following me while I was in London."

"Have you told the detective?"

"No, I haven't spoken to him yet. I'll tell him when I go in to his office tomorrow. I just need to make sure that lawyer you spoke to can come in with me."

Liam stood and started pacing. He clasped his hands behind his back, the corners of his mouth tugging down the way they did when he was thinking. Relief swelled in my chest. Liam would fix this. After days of dealing with it on my own, I was glad to let him take control.

"Are you absolutely sure someone was following you?" he asked.

I hesitated, suddenly unsure. *Had* somebody been following me? That prickly feeling of someone watching me wasn't new. But no one was ever there.

"We can't tell the detective somebody maybe, possibly followed you. Especially after you got struck by lightning. They'll think you're . . ." I knew he was about to say *crazy.* "Unreliable."

"Well, I definitely got these texts." I handed him my phone, and he scanned the sinister texts. "I think they're from him."

Liam's eyes widened. "Oh my God." For a second, he looked a little unhinged. He pulled me against his chest, cupping my head in his hand. "We need to get out of here, get you someplace safe, away from whoever this lunatic is. I have a property over on Orcas Island. It's totally secluded and the security system is state of the art. We'll be safe there."

"Wait. What?" I shook my head. If there was one thing I'd learned lately, it was that running away from a problem didn't make it go away.

"Just for a little while," he reassured me, "until all of this dies down."

"I have to talk to the detective tomorrow. I can't leave now."

He pressed his mouth together, his lips turning white. "You certainly didn't have a problem leaving last time!"

"That isn't fair," I protested. "I *had* to go to London! I needed to find out if my mom's past had anything to do with her murder. Don't you get it? If I can't prove someone else did it, they're going to put me in jail!"

"So sue me for being worried!"

"Stop. Worrying. Then," I said between clenched teeth. "I didn't ask you to."

"I can't even believe you just said that. I'm trying to help you!"

"I'm sorry. . . ." I couldn't believe I'd said

it either. Where had it come from? This was why nobody trusted me, why I couldn't trust myself.

He snatched his keys from the entry table and grabbed my coat. "Let's go. I'm taking you to the hospital."

"What?" I leaped to my feet. "No. I'm not going!"

"This is not you, Eva! You aren't acting like yourself. You were struck by lightning only a week ago, or had you forgotten that too?"

I gasped, shocked he'd throw my memory problems in my face. "I'm sorry, Liam . . ."

His shoulders relaxed, his handsome features dragging downward in relief.

". . . no."

His mouth hinged open. Of *course* he was surprised. Because I never said no to him. I never argued with him. I did what he wanted. Was that how our relationship had always worked? How pathetic was I, if that was true?

"Listen to me." He was using his calm, grown-up voice, his *be reasonable* voice. For a second, I fucking hated him. "You were *struck by lightning.* You ripped an IV out of your arm and ran away from the hospital, then you flew to London on a whim. You're exhibiting every single one of those psychological symptoms the doctor warned us about. You can't even remember things right. What about that cut on your hand? You thought it happened at your mom's house, but you cut it here, with me."

I looked at the cut on my palm, now scabbing over.

"The knife," I whispered. "If Sebastian killed Mom, why do I remember holding it? And those texts from my mom I remember but aren't even on my phone . . ."

I sank back onto the couch, pressing the heels of my hands into my temples. Nothing made sense. My brain felt like it was full of loose marbles, scattered and confused. I choked back a wave of terror rising in my throat. I didn't know what to think, what to believe.

"Do you see what I mean?" Liam was pleading with me now. "Let's get the doctor to check you out."

"Fine," I relented. "You're right, I need to go in. They still have my ring anyway." I showed him my bare hand. "They must've forgotten to give it to me after the CAT scan."

"Don't worry about the ring. I'll get you a new one."

"I'll go to the hospital tomorrow," I promised. "I have to go in to speak to the detective anyway, and I can't go tonight. I don't want him to have any more reason to think I'm a crazy person."

In the garage, I poured dried cat food into Ginger's bowl and let her inside to eat. I tuned the radio to my favorite dance station and slipped on a work apron, then slid the heart-shaped piece of jade out of my backpack and shook the broken pieces of the urn onto my work desk.

My hands were shaking, from fatigue or fear, I wasn't sure, but I felt a sense of impending doom curling around me like smoke. I closed my eyes and took a few deep yoga breaths. Then I mixed a batch of epoxy with fine gold dust and meticulously applied the mixture to each of the broken pieces, reconstructing the urn like a jigsaw puzzle.

After an hour the urn was back to its former shape, with just one large piece missing. I slid the heart-shaped jade into the hole and smiled. It was a perfect fit. I filled the cracks with more epoxy and gold dust and held the jade in place until it had set, then carefully painted a lacquer–gold dust mix along each crack.

When I'd finished, I traced my fingers over the urn's surface. It was beautiful. A thick line of gold outlined the heart-shaped jade. Fine webs of gold expanded outward across the curls of pinks and browns. Gold dust sparkled in the air, making the urn shimmer, like a mirage. I blinked as it landed on my eyelashes and distorted my vision, a memory suddenly swirling with the gold dust.

I was reading in bed, Liam sleeping beside me. My phone chimed a text from my mom.

Eva, can you come over? I realize it's late, but it's urgent.

I sat up abruptly, the bedcovers falling to my waist. Mom wasn't one for exaggeration. She must really need me. I checked the time. The ferry was still running for a few more hours. I could probably get to her house and back before the last one returned at 2 a.m.

Ok, but I'll have to wait for the ferry. Can prob get next one but will still be an hour or so.

I'll be waiting. Love you.

I sneezed, the gold dust tickling my nose and snapping me back to the present. I stared at the labyrinth of gold on the urn's surface. My brain jolted, and I inhaled sharply. There was something wrong with the texts. Not just that they were missing.

I closed my eyes, letting the memory replay. I could see the screen hot white in the dim light of my bedroom, the text conversation parading before my mind.

And suddenly I knew what was wrong.

The words. The terminology. It was all wrong.

Mom never signed her texts *Love you.* She'd never even said it out loud, as far as I could remember. Not that she didn't love me, just that her love had always been implied instead of explicitly said. Talking about emotions, *feeling* emotions, was completely off the table for her.

So who'd really texted me?

Because if there was one thing I was suddenly certain of, it was that Mom hadn't sent those texts.

THIRTY: EVA

After I'd finished the last coat of gold lacquer paint, I set the urn aside to dry. Ginger wound around my leg, her familiar purr filling the room. I scooped her up and set her outside. I didn't want Liam to see her inside. He wasn't exactly a cat person.

My phone rang. It was Andrew.

"Are you back from London?" he asked when I answered.

"Just back a few hours ago."

"Good. We need to meet Mom's lawyer to go over her will. Are you free next Thursday?" I heard a police siren in the background and the brisk clip of shoes on pavement.

"I think so. Why?"

He didn't reply.

"What is it, Andrew?"

"It isn't my place to say," Andrew said finally. "We have to address everything together at the lawyer's office."

I wanted to reach through the phone and throttle my brother. "God, Andrew! You could at least tell me what's going on before I get there."

"I can't," he said stiffly. "The will stipulates that we read it together."

"Fine," I huffed. "Send me the details, I guess, and I'll try to meet you there."

"Okay. See you then."

"Wait! Andrew, I actually wanted to ask you something. Did Mom ever say 'I love you' to you? Like out loud or in a text?" I stroked my fingers over the marks on my arm. The electric tingling was gone now. Instead the feeling running over my skin was dread.

"Hmmm." Andrew paused to think about it. "I guess not that I can remember, no. She wasn't great at expressing emotions. She was raised in a different era, a different country. You know."

I nodded. He was right, I did know.

"Why?" he asked.

"I just have this weird memory of reading a text from her that said, *Love you,* but it isn't something I can remember her ever saying. I'm probably just imagining the text anyway. I can't even find it on my phone."

"No offense, but I wouldn't trust any of your memories right now. You probably just imagined it." Andrew's voice was strangely high-pitched.

I leaned back in my chair and looked outside. Ginger had jumped onto the window ledge and was bathing herself, one hind leg thrown up in the air, looking at me with half-closed eyes. Night was drawing around the house, dark and dreary. Small drops of rain gathered into silver rivers that snaked down the windows.

"Have you remembered anything else?" he asked.

I hesitated. "Not really." A telephone conversation was not the right time to explain everything to my brother, I decided. I would tell him next time I saw him.

There was silence on Andrew's end of the phone.

"I miss her," I said softly.

"Yeah, me too. Remember when we had that garage sale, and Mom made you and me, Jacob and Lily write price tags to stick on every single item we were selling? She even filled out a spreadsheet so she could compare what we'd sold against how much we'd intended to sell it for. But then that kid from your school, his house had burned down and his family was renting an empty apartment —"

"— and Mom hired a moving van and Lily

got all the guys in the neighborhood to pack it full of things that they would need instead of doing the garage sale." I smiled at the memory. It felt nice connecting with my brother.

I picked at a splotch of gold lacquer on my desk, but my stubby nails were too short to get it off.

"Are you just getting off work?" I asked.

"No, I was at the police station. Detective Jackson brought me in for questioning." Andrew enunciated each word sharply, the way he did when he was pissed off.

"Why? They don't suspect you too, do they?"

He sighed. "They suspect everybody. It's part of their job." I could tell when Andrew put our call on the hands-free system, the sound becoming a tinny echo. "Did you know the police found your DNA and fingerprints at Mom's house?"

I didn't reply.

"Eva —" He stopped abruptly, like he was debating what his next words should be. "It's strange that you can't remember anything. And you didn't remember the night you were . . . you know. You didn't remember that either. . . ."

What was he really trying to ask me? I thought of the knife in my hand, the blinding, all-consuming rage, so intense it hijacked the logical part of my brain. But then I thought of our camping trips on Whidbey Island when I was a kid. Dad always stayed behind to work, but Mom would pack up our camping stuff, and she and Andrew and I would squish into one tiny tent and it would be cold and rainy, even in June, but we'd all be laughing as we set up another game of Uno.

I loved my mother. I did. That was real.

"Did you hurt Mom?" Andrew asked.

"I can't believe you would even ask me that," I whispered. My eyes burned. Was I really capable of doing this thing they all thought I did? "It's just circumstantial evidence. It doesn't mean I did anything wrong! What about you? Weren't your DNA and fingerprints there?"

"Yes, but I was at her house last week."

"Why?"

The sound of shifting gears reverberated over the hands-free.

"I was meeting her for dinner. She didn't answer my knock, so I let myself in and waited. Anyway, I was always visiting her. I mowed her lawn, took her to dinner, changed her fucking lightbulbs. What did you do? You were never around! Even now, you're off in your own world! So explain to me, Eva, why are your fingerprints on the mug? What did you do to Mom?"

He'd raised his voice so he was almost shouting. I gasped, stunned by the vitriol from my stoic brother.

"Did you know Mom had a gun?" Andrew bit out. "Did you ever stop to think, maybe she bought a gun because she was afraid of you?"

"Eva."

The sound of my name made me jump. I lifted my head from where it was resting on the surface of my desk. Liam was standing in the garage doorway holding a glass of red wine. His eyes were circled with purplish rings, his features dragged down by exhaustion. He held the glass out to me like a peace offering.

"Thank you." I took a giant gulp, relishing the acidic burn of the wine sliding down my throat. I rarely drank since that night four years ago, but I needed something to soothe the venom of Andrew's words.

"You okay?"

I sighed. "Yeah."

"I'm sorry." Liam knelt next to me, his gaze earnest. "About earlier. I shouldn't have tried to force you to go to the hospital."

I pressed a finger to his lips and kissed

him, long and slow. His arms tightened around me, his body solid and steady against mine.

"You have nothing to apologize for," I said. "You're just worried about me, and I appreciate it. And you're right, I do need to go. Maybe the lightning *has* changed me. I feel like I've landed in the wrong country, a million miles from the person I used to be."

"Well, I'm here to take care of you. I'll help you fill in the gaps."

I pressed my face into the crook of his neck, my body softening against his. Liam's heartbeat thrummed against my forehead, steady as a drum. He lifted my chin and kissed me again, a kiss that told me I was his world.

When he pulled away, he was smiling. "I'm not going anywhere. We're in this together, okay? Forever."

I nodded, and Liam pulled me to my feet.

"Come on," he said. "You're too pale. You need a proper meal, something with lots of protein. Go wash your hands and clean yourself up. I'll get dinner started. I have a salmon in the fridge. It's wild and sustainable so we don't destroy the oceans."

He smiled, a teasing glint in his eye. Liam thought it was charming — his word — that I'd spent most of my adult life trying to reduce my carbon footprint. I wore second-hand clothes. I had been a vegetarian since I was a teenager. I recycled everything. These things were completely foreign to a man like Liam.

Fish was, strictly speaking, against my rules as a vegetarian. But right now I didn't want to argue. I wanted Liam to be happy, and he was happiest when he was taking charge.

"Fine." I followed him into the kitchen. "But after we eat, I need the number for that lawyer. I want to make sure he'll come with me to the detective's office in the morning."

"No problem." He gave me a wry little smile. "I'll even go with you if you want."

I washed my hands with soap and hot water, using the dish scrubber to scrape at the epoxy on my fingertips. When I'd finished, my hands were raw and bright red.

Liam grabbed the salmon out of the fridge.

I sat at the island, watching him bustle about the kitchen as I sipped my wine. The tannins tingled delicately at the back of my throat. The wine hitting my empty stomach created a glorious sense of floating inside a feather pillow.

I couldn't stop thinking about what Andrew had said. Had Mom really bought a gun because she was scared of me? I wasn't in my right mind after the rape, and I was even more messed up after I gave the baby up. But the thought that she'd bought a gun because I scared her made me feel physically sick to my stomach.

More proof that I couldn't trust myself.

Liam washed the salmon and set it on a wooden cutting board. He pulled a gleaming black boning knife from the knife block, pressed the knife into a point behind the fish's head, and sliced through the ribs to the tail, then backward, from tail to head, until he had two glistening pink fillets. Then he slipped the knife between the rib bones and flesh, grasped the bones, and ripped them out in one swift movement.

My stomach turned, nausea shimmering in my gut. The knife glinted under the kitchen can lights, sparking the memory again, now sharply etched, demanding to be seen.

I look down at my hands. A knife is resting in my outstretched palm. One of my mom's wooden-handled knives. It's covered in blood. I fold my fingers over the blade, squeezing until the blade digs into the soft skin of my palm, slicing deeply, crimson blood running free.

I got up and crossed the kitchen to grab the open bottle of wine from the countertop. As I refilled my glass, my eyes fell on the knife block, sitting innocuously next to the microwave. I reached for the other boning knife. Despite being small and narrow, it was surprisingly heavy. I turned it over in my hand, the blade flashing black against my pale skin. The handle scraped against the crusted scab on my left hand and I winced.

I curled my fingers around the handle. My brain was light as a feather, a cluster of bubbles floating and twisting in the breeze.

This knife was totally different than the one I remembered from Mom's, a pale wood handle with black Japanese steel compared to Mom's dark-wood handle and silver-steel blade. And yet . . .

It felt familiar. I could imagine the blade slippery with blood, the weight of it in my hand, the sharp, narrow blade hot and slick as it sliced into my palm.

I was there.

I remember.

Don't I?

I closed my eyes as an unexpected anger hissed through my body like poison, screeching a demand to be released. I gritted my teeth, pain shooting from my molars to my temples.

The problem was, I *liked* it.

"Eva?" Liam's voice snapped me back to reality.

I whirled around unsteadily. My body weaved as I blinked at him, the walls swaying behind him. He had a strange look on his face. A *worried* look.

How long had he been talking to me?

Liam walked slowly toward me, his hands outstretched. He reached for the knife. I yanked it away from him, rage coursing through me deliciously.

"Eva." His voice was firm, authoritative.

I fucking hated it when he used that stupid boomy voice on me. Like I was one of his minions. Like I was just someone to —

"Give me the knife, Eva."

I looked into his clear blue eyes and the strange black cloak that had descended on me tumbled to the floor.

"Sorry. Here." I thrust the knife toward him, blade down. I felt dizzy and lightheaded.

Liam plucked it from my outstretched hand and slid it back into the block. He put his hands on my shoulders and led me back to my seat at the island.

"Here. Sit back and relax." He set my wineglass in front of me and returned to preparing dinner in that efficient, single-minded way he had, as if I hadn't just acted like a completely insane person.

He babbled on and on about a vacation to Vancouver and his plans for extending the greenhouse, and then I lost the thread of what he was saying. I couldn't concentrate on his words.

I tried to remember the psychological symptoms Dr. Simm had told me I might experience. Was trouble concentrating one of them? Why was Liam talking about Vancouver? I seriously couldn't give any less of a fuck what he did with the greenhouse.

I staggered to the bathroom to pee. I flushed and turned the faucet on, letting the cool water run over my wrists and splashing it on my pink cheeks. I used my damp fingers to smooth my disheveled hair.

The feel of my fingers on my hair called up a memory so powerful it twisted something in my stomach. I was sitting on the floor at Mom's feet in a bedroom I didn't recognize. Mom was sitting on the bed as she slowly, steadily pulled a brush through my long hair. Delightful chills chased up my neck as the brush scraped over my scalp. When she finished, I asked if I could brush her hair. We switched places, her on the floor, me on the bed, the brush in my hands.

I could hear my child voice in my head: "Why's your hair yellow and mine's red?"

"Red hair is caused by an MC1R mutation found on chromosome sixteen," she'd replied.

"What's a moo-tation?" I asked.

She'd blinked at me like she'd suddenly realized where she was. Her face softened. "It means when you were a baby, a fairy kissed you right here." She tapped me on my nose. "She knew that redheads are the warriors of the world, and it would make you brave and brilliant and bold. Her kiss turned your hair red."

It was such a trivial memory, but it opened a floodgate. White pain sliced into my heart, tears blurring my vision, turning the bathroom to a pastel watercolor. I cried and cried and cried.

When I was finished, I stared in the mirror at my puffy face, my eyes glossy with moisture, my lips twisted and bloodless. Who was that woman in the mirror? Was *that* Laura? Because this other woman, Eva, didn't recognize her at all.

I splashed cool water on my throbbing eyes and took a few deep breaths to calm myself. Back in the kitchen, Liam was checking his phone, his forehead furrowed. When I came in, he set it on the island, sweetly not commenting on my bloated face and puffy eyes.

I staggered to my chair at the island and sat heavily. My glass was nearly empty, so I refilled it and took another glug of wine.

"What's that sound?" Liam asked, tilting his head as he listened. I didn't hear anything.

Liam left the kitchen, but returned a second later. "Did you leave the bathroom faucet on?"

I tried to say I didn't think so, but couldn't get the words out right. "Don thshso."

Liam threw me a strange look. "It's fine, I've turned it off now. Do you want to go to bed? You look pretty wiped out."

What I really wanted was to gather everything I felt and bury it somewhere I never had to think about again.

Liam's phone buzzed, and he checked it again. I wanted to ask if everything was okay, but the adrenaline that had carried me through the past few days had seeped away, leaving me empty and drained. The walls seemed to slip and slide around me, an odd shuffling of images stacking and shifting.

I couldn't face another moment awake. I lowered my head to the cool island surface, a shadowy blackness stealing across my vision.

"Eva?" I heard Liam's voice from very far away. "Babe, are you okay?"

My head was thudding, a thickening, soupy mess. My mouth tasted like the smell of freshly poured asphalt. My fingers felt detached from my body, floating light as a feather. And then Liam's strong arms were lifting me, carrying me like a child up the stairs, to our bedroom.

I closed my eyes, falling toward sleep the way a stone sinks into water, hard and fast. My last thought before darkness folded around me was the realization that my brother had the key to Mom's house.

Andrew would've easily had access to her tea canister.

THIRTY-ONE: EVA

My dreams were dark and terrifying. I was running toward a frozen lake edged by a black winter forest. Someone's breath was on my shoulder. I stepped onto the ice, skidding across the surface. Footsteps slapped behind me.

Suddenly a crack cut the air, sharp as a whip. The ground beneath me disappeared and I slid into the lake, icy water filling my nose and mouth.

"Help!" I screamed, thrashing to stay afloat.

Somebody was there, the faceless man from my nightmares. He grabbed one of my arms and pulled. Hard.

POP!

My arm snapped out of its socket, and he reached for the other one.

"No!" I gurgled, water filling my mouth.

He grabbed the other arm and tugged until it popped off too.

I was sinking, fear and outrage filling me. Fingers tangled in my hair, and for a second I thought he'd save me. But then I realized he was trying to yank my head off.

I woke with a start, my heart pounding like a winged beast.

I sat up too fast, the dream tumbling from my shoulders. A tsunami of pain stormed into my head.

"Ohhh . . ." I pressed my hand to my temples, my stomach roiling.

I peeled my eyelids open. The blankets on Liam's side of the bed were already pulled up, tucked in. The pillow was straightened in his efficient, organized way.

What the actual fuck had happened to me? I felt like I'd been poisoned. A blurry memory of finishing off a bottle of wine, then the floating sensation of being carried upstairs crashed into me.

I'm never drinking again.

Like I hadn't said *that* before.

The bedroom curtains had been pulled open, shadows tangling along the dove-gray walls. I had that prickly, itchy feeling that someone was there, watching me, standing just outside my window perched in a tree, maybe, or on the drainpipe. I knew it was stupid, totally insane, but I couldn't shake the feeling that something was wrong.

There's no one there, I told myself.

Fear eventually beat nausea, and I pulled myself out of bed and over to the window, peering out, just to make sure. The balcony was empty. The tree just beyond the bedroom empty. So was the drainpipe, the yard, the lake beyond. A handful of dead leaves shivered in the breeze. The sun was already high in the sky, white clouds skittering by.

How long had I been asleep? I had to call the lawyer, and then Detective Jackson. I guzzled a glass of water and some painkillers and made my way down the stairs.

I stopped abruptly when I reached the landing.

The living room had been demolished. Couch cushions were on the floor, torn and vomiting cotton fluff. The crystal vase where Liam kept his black roses was smashed, slivers of glass glinting in the sunlight. Crushed purple-black petals were scattered across the floor. A wall clock had been ripped from its mounting above the stone fireplace and shattered against the hardwood. The books in the built-in shelves had been torn from their positions by the fireplace and scattered.

Liam came out of the kitchen, a mug of tea in his hands. He was dressed in a navy suit, his tie draped around his neck, but he hadn't shaved, his jaw dark with growth. Liam rarely went a day without shaving. He was very particular about his appearance. He visited a fancy barber in Seattle every second and fourth Friday of the month. He wore designer clothing and ordered expensive cologne direct from France.

But now he looked gray and haggard.

He didn't smile when he saw me. His expression hovered somewhere between uneasy and upset.

"What happened?" I gasped.

Liam's mouth flapped open, then closed. He lifted his shoulders, casting his eyes over the mess. He blew out a long breath while shaking his head. "*You* happened."

"What do you mean?"

"You went crazy last night, Eva."

"*I* did this?" Guilt surged as what I'd done hit me full in the throat. "I-I don't remember. Last thing I knew I was in the kitchen watching you cook. And then you carried me upstairs."

Liam nodded, his blue eyes shadowed. The fine lines around his eyes were more pronounced than usual. "But you woke up. You came downstairs and said you had to go see the detective. You were obviously exhausted and pretty drunk so I tried to stop you. You went absolutely ballistic."

His words bolted down my spine.

"I'm sorry," I whispered.

"You were pretty pissed at me. And you said you were scared of this Sebastian guy. I swear, Eva, I didn't even recognize you."

I sank onto the steps and pulled my knees to my chest, remembering how I'd started to pass out in the kitchen, my mind drifting in and out like the tide. I dug my fingers into the thick pile, gripping it to keep me in place.

"I don't know what to say. I'm so, so sorry."

His forehead was creased with that intense look of concern that'd become familiar lately. He handed me the mug of tea and knelt in front of me. He tugged the zipper of my hoodie up, pushing the hair from my forehead.

"How do you feel?"

"Not the greatest," I admitted.

"Well, I've organized some things that might help. Come look." He helped me to my feet and tugged me around the broken glass to the front door. He pulled it open. The sunlight sliced through my retinas, too bright for my fragile brain. I shaded my eyes and squinted in the direction he was pointing.

"Motion detector floodlights. I've installed

them at the front and the back of the house so if anybody approaches, we'll see them. I've also changed the locks and put in a dead bolt and a chain on all the doors: front, back, and the one in the garage. And, best of all, I've called an alarm installation company. They'll be here tomorrow. I got the premium package: video monitoring, two-way intercom, panic buttons. Everything you need to feel safe. And it'll all be hooked up to their central monitoring system." He smiled, looking proud of all the manly things he'd accomplished. "What do you think?"

"Wo-wow," I stuttered. I took a giant sip of scalding tea, trying to give myself time to answer.

Liam threw his arms up in the air and pulled away from me. I'd offended him. "What's wrong? You said you were scared. You said you were afraid someone's been following you. I wanted to help. I just want you to feel safe."

"You're right." I rushed to fill the space widening between us. "This is great. Thank you."

He pulled me inside and threw the new dead bolt shut, slid the chain into place.

I should've been grateful he'd gone to all this trouble to make me feel safe. Liam was a nurturer. He liked taking care of me, and I'd never minded before. In fact, maybe — no, definitely — I'd encouraged it. He made me feel safe and cared for; it was one of the things I loved about him. Paying the bills, organizing life insurance, planning our meals, getting my kiln and pottery wheel set up in the garage, and driving me to and from work — he was so much better at these tasks than I was.

So why did this bother me so much?

Standing in the middle of the overly bright living room, all secured with locks and bolts and alarms, the sickening heat chugging out of the fireplace, I didn't feel grateful. I just felt *unsettled.*

I stared outside at the lake. It was a peculiar shade of gray, reflecting the ominous clouds hovering in the sky. No matter how hard I tried, I couldn't remember what I'd done last night. A shutter had fallen over my mind.

"I can't remember." Nausea churned in my stomach, my breath coming in shallow bursts. Panic narrowed my vision to pinpricks. I stumbled backward, away from him. "Liam, I can't remember any of it!"

He reached for me, his face a mask of pity. "It's okay."

I shook my head. "No, you don't understand! Maybe this is what happened at my mom's! Maybe I snapped. Maybe I went crazy and accidentally . . ."

My legs went weak and I collapsed onto my knees, my eyes squeezed shut. I was shaking so hard my teeth were chattering. When I opened my eyes, my distorted reflection shimmered in the shards of the crystal vase shattered across the hardwood floor.

Thirty-Two: Kat

17 Years Before

Over the next eight years, I learned that time is an intractable thing, barreling on no matter how broken our hearts or minds. At times I wanted to curl up and die. To just give up. But my children demanded I live, and so I did. I could not allow bitterness to wear me down.

Mike and I settled in Seattle with Eva and our son, Andrew. I went to university and became a high school physics teacher. We were mostly happy, I certainly cannot lie about that.

Eva easily forgot about her life before America. Only now is research about childhood memories becoming clearer: children can remember events before the age of three when they're small, but by the time they turn seven, those memories are lost, sometimes forever, in the neurons of their developing minds.

No, I did not worry about Eva. I, on the other hand, would never forget.

"Eva, stop faffing about!" I shouted up the stairs. "You mustn't dally or we'll be late for school!"

Eva slunk down the stairs, the hallway light glinting off her hair. She'd dyed it a horrific black after we'd moved out of Mike's house last month, as if she were in mourning.

"What is this?" I waved at her outfit: a form-fitting T-shirt and a short blue skirt with long fringes that swayed when she moved. On her feet were shiny black lace-up ankle boots. "We just bought you new trousers and that lovely pink sweater-vest."

"*You* chose it, Mom. I didn't. I don't want to dress like I'm fifty."

I scowled. I didn't dress like I was fifty. I punched my arms into my coat sleeves, trying not to feel foolish.

"Brilliant," I muttered. It was too late for her to change. "You look like a bloody lampshade."

Her hand moved to her mouth, her teeth worrying at her nails. I grabbed her hand and examined the ragged nails.

"Look at this! You mustn't bite your nails,

Eva! Do I need to make you wear gloves again?"

I tried to be understanding, but honestly, it was such a filthy habit! Last year she'd chewed her nails so badly one became infected. Nothing I did got her to stop — foul-tasting polish, cutting them short, manicures, gloves. She hated the gloves the most.

"No!" She folded her hands under her armpits. "I'll try harder, Mom, I swear. Do you have gum?"

I rummaged in my handbag and handed her a new pack of Trident.

"Thank you." She slid her coat on, grabbed her backpack, and headed for the door.

"And it's Mum, not Mom!" I called after her. I grabbed my keys from the hallway key rack. "Don't forget Dad's picking you up from school today. You're staying at his house this weekend."

Her eyes darkened. At twelve years old, she was in the fever of prepubescence, her emotions a wild bevy of ups and downs. Or perhaps it was simply our divorce at the root of these flashes of petulance. Either way, Eva was no longer as eager to please as she'd been when she was small. We rowed frequently, and sometimes it felt as if we would draw blood. It rather seemed like a familiar text had turned into hieroglyphics without warning.

"Can't I stay here?" she whined.

"Certainly. If you want to help me paint and unpack."

She looked at the boxes still stacked in haphazard groups around the house. After years of not touching the money Rose had given us, I had withdrawn the funds necessary to purchase our new home. I had no other choice, really. I hadn't saved enough during my marriage to Mike to afford a house, and now I was on my own again.

Quite a lot of work was needed on the three-bedroom Queen Anne–style house. But I loved it: the homey shutters on the windows, the sloping front yard and white picket fence, the decorative wainscoting and carved crown moldings. Mostly I loved that it was mine and mine alone. I no longer depended on a man for my security, and I swore I never would again.

"Fine," she huffed. "I'll suffer through Dad's for the weekend."

I rolled my eyes. Eva was a champion sulker.

"You might have fun. He's chuffed to bits you're staying the whole weekend."

Eva slid her backpack over her coat, and

we headed outside. Water was coming down in sheets from the sky, standing pools gathering on the pavement. We both groaned.

"Shall I drive you to the bus stop?" I offered.

"Yes, please!"

We got in the car and I pulled onto the suburban street, glancing in my rearview mirror every few minutes, an old habit I could not shake, even though I had never seen any sign of Seb in Seattle. Eva fiddled with the radio, landing on a rather appalling electro beat.

I winced. "It sounds like a record skipping."

"What's a record?" she asked. I looked at her, horrified. Was she serious? I opened my mouth to ask, but she turned the music up, blocking me out.

"Why isn't Andrew coming over to our house this weekend?" she asked after a minute.

I turned the music down. "You were both here last weekend. You know it's every other weekend."

"Andrew's almost always at Dad's," she pointed out.

"He's still in school near there. It's just easier."

"Is it because I'm not his real daughter?" she asked quietly, teeth at her nails again.

I gave her a stern look. "Eva, that's absurd." I swiped her hand away from her mouth. "Your dad loves you and Andrew equally and you know it. It doesn't matter if you're biologically his or not. You're his daughter in every way that's important."

I had told Eva from the time she was small that her own father had died in a fire when she was a baby. But since the divorce, she'd been questioning Mike's love more and more.

"Hey, look, there's Jacob!" Eva brightened, pointing at a lanky, dark-haired youth in a jean jacket walking on the sidewalk. "Mom, pull over. Let's give him a ride."

I recognized the boy as one of our neighbors and did as she asked. Eva was already rolling the window down and calling out to him. The boy had one of those utterly ridiculous bowl haircuts, the ends tatty and uneven, as if he had cut it himself.

He climbed in, dripping water all over the backseat.

"Thanks, Mrs. Hansen!" he said, a smile stretched ear to ear.

I couldn't help returning the smile. What a lovely boy. So polite. But, dear Lord, he was too thin. I glanced at him in the rearview mirror. His clothes were threadbare, his jeans torn at the knees. His jacket was faded, a stain that looked like ketchup or maybe barbecue sauce on the collar.

Jacob and Eva chatted the rest of the way to the bus stop about a photography club they had joined and how to use a long exposure to capture the stars in the Milky Way. When we pulled up to the bus stop, she jumped out without giving me a backward glance. She seemed to have utterly and completely forgotten what she had said just a few minutes before. But I hadn't.

Did she really think she was less loved just because she wasn't Mike's biological daughter? She must never find out about me. I couldn't bear for her to feel unloved by both of us. The science of how she came into existence was unimportant. She was mine as surely as if I had borne her myself. While my heart would always ache for the Eva I lost, I loved the daughter I had now. Her big feelings and big opinions. Her creativity and sensitivity and insight.

I imagined the sweet weight of her in my arms when she was young, the soft pad of toddler's feet coming down the hall, then the warmth of her little body as she climbed into my bed. How she used to press her head into the crook of my arm while we read stories together, and the sound of her tinkly laugh floating through the house when she played with her dolls.

I rolled my window down. "Eva!"

She said something to Jacob and he jogged across the street, disappearing amidst a crowd of youths. Eva hefted her backpack higher on her shoulder and came back to the car.

"Yeah?"

I wanted to tell her that Mike and I both loved her, despite our divorce. That the blood in her veins did not change that and never would. I wanted to reassure her that she wasn't responsible for the breakup of our family or the dissolution of our marriage. In fact, she was the reason I even *had* a family. Honestly, I should be *thanking* her!

But I could not seem to speak.

I am not a stupid woman. I could tell you how many sunspots were on the sun (up to two hundred at any one time) or which planet rained glass (HD 189733b) or which dwarf planet had volcanoes that spewed ice (Ceres). But the instant I needed to speak honestly about feelings, I became utterly useless.

I had a sudden memory of my own mother driving me to school shortly before she disappeared. I was thinking about the girl who had stolen my bra during PE and hung it over the school's front door. I wanted my mum's reassurance and love, but she was staring out the window, unbearably vacant. I knew better than to complain. There would be no motherly hugs, no comforting words. She was not interested in how I felt or what I had to say.

Perhaps, I realized now, it was a coping mechanism for a life she didn't choose.

Had I done that to Eva? I certainly hadn't meant to, but perhaps that was always the way with parenting. You tried so hard to be different than your own parents. To be better, listen more, get frustrated less, but in the end you just got stuck in the same damn loop. Perhaps all parents felt that their choices were a barrier to the life they dreamt of when they were young. Only when you became a parent yourself could you fully understand that they did the best they could.

I reached for Eva's hand, gave it a kiss, then squeezed it three times, hoping she knew what I meant.

I. Love. You.

The morning flew by, and I quickly fell into the familiar pattern of teaching. Routine comforted me more than ever these days. It was marvelous to know that across the planet and, indeed, the universe, the rhythms of our lives were governed by our journey through space, from the pull of the tide to the time we woke in the morning.

When my classroom emptied at lunch, I headed to the park across the street to enjoy what had turned into a fine autumn day. An unseasonably warm breeze ruffled the lacy boughs of the blood-red Japanese maples. A swirl of clouds as white as a turning page meandered toward Puget Sound. Crunchy yellow leaves whirled through the air like birds.

Autumn had always been my favorite season. Something about the light and the air — like breathing in hope and new beginnings. I loved hiking through the forest as orange and red leaves crackled under my feet; curling up under a blanket with a book; the gentle patter of rain on the roof.

I sat on a bench, my hair partially obscuring my peripheral vision, which was why I only just caught the outline of the woman emerging from beyond a tree in the distance. I squinted and adjusted my glasses. A cold shiver slid down my spine, and my mind turned to liquid.

I stood, unable to comprehend what I was seeing.

Her hair was a duller shade than it used to be, her mouth thin and pale, her skin now creased at the edges of her gray eyes. Her clothes were modest and shabby, the type that came from a charity shop, although she wore them with pride.

But it was her, without a doubt.

She was back from the dead.

Her name burst in my mouth like a radish, sharp and bitter.

"Rose."

Thirty-Three: Eva

Liam cleaned up the mess I'd made, sweeping up the broken glass, throwing the torn cushions away, and washing the things that could be salvaged. He insisted I lie down on the couch, but it felt wrong watching him clean up my mess. What was happening to me?

Once we'd finished, Liam made me a fresh cup of tea and a plate of toast, setting them on the coffee table in front of me.

"You feeling better?" He sat next to me on the couch. I nodded, leaning my head against his chest. He wrapped an arm around me and stroked a hand down my hair. I was lucky he was here to take care of me.

"I'm sorry." My voice was muffled against his suit blazer.

"It's okay," he assured me. But for the first time I wasn't sure if he meant it.

Liam's phone buzzed. He pulled it out of

his pocket and read a text. His face went slack with shock.

"What's wrong?"

He looked up at me. "The building inspector rejected my building permit."

He sat for a moment, paralyzed, then lurched for the stairs, taking them two at a time. Anybody else would cut their losses and walk away. I certainly would. But not Liam. Backing down was too close to rejection, and Liam would never allow that. He wouldn't allow *no* to stop him from getting that building permit.

I trailed up the stairs after him, but he was already coming back down, his briefcase bulging with files. He brushed past me and grabbed his coat and keys.

"Keep all the doors and windows locked," he ordered. "I'm really sorry I have to go. I need to talk to this building inspector in person. I'll call the lawyer and take you to the detective's office when I get back, okay? And after that, we'll get you to the doctor." He brushed a quick kiss across my forehead. He'd returned to his old self, his jaw set, his eyes flashing with determination. "I can't let this fall through."

The door shut behind him, the chain lock swinging dizzyingly against the wood.

Can't? I thought. *Or won't?*

I lay on the couch for a little bit feeling sorry for myself, my head thumping horribly. Finally I managed to drag myself into the kitchen to make another cup of tea. While the kettle boiled, I looked at the calendar on the refrigerator. The appointment we'd scheduled with Father Byrne was there, written in clean block letters on Wednesday. I could've sworn it was for next week, on Tuesday, because I'd scheduled to get off work early that day.

I got my phone from my bedside table and opened the calendar to Tuesday. *Off work early* was written at 2 p.m. on Tuesday. But when I scrolled back to last Wednesday, our meeting with Father Byrne was clearly scheduled. I clicked into the appointment and it told me: *Created by Eva Hansen.*

God, I was *useless.*

I took my tea back to the couch and stared at the dead bolt on the front door, the shiny polished gold of new metal. The house felt oppressive. It was all those locks, the bolts slid shut, the chains fastened tight. Claustrophobia, thick as a sea mist, closed around me.

I pulled my yoga mat from the hallway closet and tried a few poses, but I couldn't relax my mind. My body was filled with a restless, electric energy. I dressed in clean jeans and a blue sweater Liam had left out for me on the dresser and went outside for a walk.

Ginger saw me and bounded across the grass. She headbutted her nose against my jeans and fell into step behind me as I strolled along the dirt path that hugged the lake. Damp, cold air seeped through my coat. The wet soil released an unnatural fog that swirled over the brackish water. The air smelled like a storm was brewing. My left arm prickled in reply, electric pulses crawling up my skin.

Maybe it was the acid left from the wine, or the fear that had hounded me for the last week, or the knowledge that I was Laura and not Eva, and I didn't even know what that meant, but something was . . . off. I felt disoriented and unsettled, restless. I couldn't quite put my finger on it, but it was there, just out of reach.

I sat on the edge of a damp, rotting log and dialed Detective Jackson's number. Ginger twined around my legs, purring and blinking at me with huge green eyes.

"Detective Jackson. It's Eva."

"Eva. Good to hear from you."

"I'm back from London. Actually, I got back yesterday, but I was just so tired. . . . I mean — what I mean to say is, I can come in to you today. I have a lot to tell you."

"Okay, great. That's really great, Eva. Thanks for letting me know." He sounded distracted. The jabber of voices filtered through the phone, punctuated by the whistle of the wind. "Sorry, I'm in the middle of something. Hold on a sec."

There was a long pause, then a muffled directive as he called something to someone.

After a minute, he returned. "Have you spoken to your brother today?" Jackson asked.

"No. I haven't. Not since yesterday. Why?"

Somebody spoke to Jackson. The rustle of fabric covering the mouthpiece crackled in my ear. I couldn't quite make out Jackson's reply. The cold started seeping through my jeans into my thighs. My fingers were going numb. I wished I'd worn gloves.

Jackson came back on the line sounding rushed. "Really sorry, Eva, but I hafta go." A gust of wind whooshed in the phone. From somewhere far away somebody called his name. "Just stay where you are, and I'll call you back a little later, okay?"

"Wai—"

But the line had already gone dead.

What the hell? I stared at my phone, confused. Clearly going in to his office wasn't urgent. Now I was glad I hadn't rushed there this morning.

I tried Andrew, remembering what had seemed so urgent before I passed out last night: he had the key to Mom's house.

Andrew's phone rang and rang, finally kicking to voice mail.

"Andrew, I just got off the phone with Detective Jackson. He was being weird. Is something going on? Call me."

I pulled my hat lower on my head and lifted the collar of my coat, letting the warmth of my breath heat my chilled face. On the horizon, dark, bruised-looking clouds raced closer.

What was it Mom always said? *Not all storms cause chaos. Some just clear the air.*

Ginger had disappeared, so I headed home alone, my boots squelching in the mud. I picked my way over the rocky incline that sloped steeply into the water and rounded the last bend to home.

I froze.

Someone was there, moving just beyond the garage. He threw a glance over his shoulder, then walked behind the house. I dropped down behind a large bush and peered into the thickening shadows. Was it Sebastian? Or the man who'd been following me in London? My heart thumped painfully in my chest.

A second later, the man reappeared. He was very tall, with a grizzled face and colorful tattoos crawling up his throat. He wore black steel-toed boots, a black raincoat, and a black beanie pressed tight against his skull.

"Hello, Eva!" a voice boomed behind me.

I jumped to my feet, heart thudding. Mr. Ayyad stood grinning at me. He was clad in full Lycra running gear. His dog gazed at me with bemused blue eyes. *You are so ridiculous,* his expression said.

"This is Jung," Mr. Ayyad said, waving at the dog. "After Carl Jung. It is ironic, no? Because I was a psychologist in my former life." He grinned and stroked a hand down his beard, which hung past his collarbone.

I held out a hand for Jung to smell. "You nearly scared the life out of me!" I laughed, but it sounded a little strangled in my throat.

Mr. Ayyad's smile dropped. "I am terribly sorry!" He followed my gaze to the person creeping around my house. "Oh, I see."

He tugged Jung's leash, and together they strode across the gravel drive.

I was too far away to hear the conversation, but Mr. Ayyad said something to the man, who walked up the driveway to an unmarked van I hadn't noticed. He pulled a small box out of the back, handed it to Mr. Ayyad, then got in the van and drove away.

"Here you are." Mr. Ayyad handed me the box. The bank of clouds had started to release a fine drizzle, the moisture glistening on his lined skin. "He was one of those freelance delivery guys."

I took the box and read the packaging: ISLAND ALARMS. Liam's house alarm had arrived early.

"Thank you. I-I thought he was a burglar or something." I felt ridiculous saying it out loud.

He nodded, his dark eyes serious as he stroked his beard. "No need to apologize. We must trust our instincts, no? Certainty can only arise through doubt, after all."

"Thank you."

"You will reach out if you need me, yes?"

I nodded.

"I am an old man, but I am good for some things." He smiled one of his full-face smiles, and tapped his ear. "Listening is one of them."

My face flushed and I looked at my feet.

Jung tugged at his leash, ready to return to running. Mr. Ayyad raised a hand as he started jogging in place. "I must run now. I'm practicing for the Ninety-Five to One Hundred World Championship race in November."

I gaped at him.

He laughed at my obvious surprise. "We aren't dead until we're dead, my dear."

He waved good-bye and jogged away, Jung following close behind.

I dug my keys out and unlocked the front door. In the bedroom, I stripped my damp jeans off but couldn't find a clean pair, so I headed into the walk-in closet and emptied the dirty clothes basket onto the floor. Grabbing the cleanest jeans I could find, I pulled them on, but as I turned to go I caught sight of something that had been stuffed in the very corner of the closet, behind the dirty clothes basket.

My missing green corduroy coat.

I picked it up. And then I saw something that made me freeze. Large rust-colored blotches stained the collar.

Blood.

My hand went limp and the coat dropped, lead-like, to the floor. Horror slid like heated metal through my insides.

Whose blood was on it? And why had I hidden it at the back of the closet?

Something scratched at my brain. A memory? A shadow? It felt tantalizingly close. I thumped my forehead with the heel of my hand, something flickering there. But nothing came.

My phone started ringing from downstairs, cutting through the blankness. I shoved the coat back behind the laundry basket and hurried to answer it.

THIRTY-FOUR: KAT

17 Years Before

Seeing Rose had numbed my brain. Eight years. I'd thought she was dead for eight years!

Finally I managed to open my mouth. "Rose?" My voice was hoarse with shock.

She threw her arms around me, laughing and crying at the same time.

"Katherine! I found you!" She pulled back to look at me, her hands caressing my face, running over my shoulders, my arms, as if to ensure I was real. "It's you! It's really you!"

"Where . . . what . . . ? I thought . . ." I had so many questions I had no idea where to start. All that came out was a statement: "You aren't dead."

Rose shook her head. "No."

"But you killed yourself!"

"No! I faked my death to throw Sebastian off our trail."

"I . . . how?"

"I was crossing the bridge on my way to meet you at the hotel and I realized: if Sebastian thought Laura and I were dead, he wouldn't look for us. So I got Laura's old buggy and wrote a suicide note and left them on the bridge. I knew David would tell the police I had been medicated for depression before. But by the time I got to the hotel, you and Laura were gone."

"I was afraid Seb would find my passport gone and come looking for me." I could barely get the words past my constricted throat. "As soon as I found out you were dead, we went to the airport. Where have you been all this time?"

"Obviously I couldn't stay in London, so I went to New York. I thought I'd be able to track you when you withdrew money from that bank account I set up. I got a job as a waitress, and I started painting. My work started selling. And then one day I checked the bank account and saw you'd withdrawn money from a bank in Chicago. I got a flight there and looked for you, but never found you." Rose grasped my hands. "I checked the account every day for years, but you never withdrew anything until last month."

"I bought a house." My voice sounded hollow. I wanted to cry, but the tears had been incinerated somewhere between my belly and my eyeballs.

"I saw that the money had been paid to a mortgage company for a person named Kat Hansen in Seattle. I googled that name and found the school you work at. There's a picture of you on the staff pages."

A chill wind kicked up, sending the Japanese maple leaves shivering. My vision went momentarily blurry, and I realized it had been a rather long time since I had blinked.

"Let me make sure I understand this correctly," I said slowly. "You have been living the carefree, child-free life of an artist you always wanted in New York, whilst I have been raising your daughter for eight years and thinking you were dead, and that it was my fault?"

Rose's face closed, tight as a fist. She dropped my hands and stepped away from me. "Don't make it sound like that. I tried to find you! I *missed* Laura! I was utterly bereft without her."

Anger, too much anger, flared in me. "What do you expect to happen now, Rose? She thinks *I'm* her mum."

"We'll tell her the truth. It'll be fine."

I snorted and shook my head. Her temerity was truly unbelievable.

Rose straightened, her gray eyes hot as

just-poured asphalt. "I'm her mother. I did what I had to in order to keep her safe."

"No, *I* had to keep her safe! You don't even know her name now!" Rose looked confused. "It's Eva. Surely you don't actually think you can just waltz in here and be her mother and expect her to accept you?"

Rose stared at me, mouth agape. Clearly this was not going the way she had expected. "You never told her about me?"

"No, of course not!" I threw my hands in the air. "I couldn't risk her telling anybody who we really were."

"You could've told her she was adopted."

"I would've had to make up a whole story —"

She cut me off. "You made up a story anyway!"

I gritted my teeth together. "I was trying to balance the things she didn't need to know with what would keep her safe. And I have, Rose. *I* have kept her safe. *Me!*"

"You aren't better than me just because you got to stay and pretend to be her mother."

I drew myself up to my full height and glared at her. "Perhaps not. But I *deserve* to be her mother more than you."

"Don't you think I would've *chosen* that? I couldn't find you! It isn't my fault, and

Laura, Eva, whatever she's called now, she needs to know that!"

"What do you think she will say when she finds out the truth? That we lied about who she is and our entire past? That I'm not her mother, you are, but you've been living a bohemian, child-free life this entire time, just like you always wanted?"

Rose paled and did not reply for a long time. Eventually she pulled a pack of cigarettes from her brown leather bag. She lit one and sucked deeply, pursing her lips as smoke gathered in her mouth. When she parted her lips, O-shaped clouds rolled out.

She smoked like that in silence for a few minutes, then stubbed the cigarette out and flicked it to the ground. She was too close, smelling of nicotine, ashy and dry. I stepped away, glancing at my watch.

"I must return to work." I brushed away the crumbs that clung to the fibers of my wool coat.

"Oh, Katherine." Her voice was thick, tears glistening in her eyes. "Do you hate me so much? That you would take my daughter from me?"

"I don't hate you." It was true. Never, not once in all these years, had I hated her. Quite the opposite, in fact. I had loved few more. But things were very, very different now.

"You must. It's written across your face. I would hate you too, if you caused my daughter's death."

"What are you talking about?"

She sat on the bench, covering her face with her hands. "You must blame me for opening the window Eva fell out!"

My stomach dropped, leaving my knees weak, my hands shaking.

"Rose." I puffed my cheeks out and exhaled, long and loud, then sat next to her. I pinched the skin between my eyes. "You didn't open that window. I did. It was my fault Eva died."

It was the first time I had admitted it to anybody but myself, and the pain was a sharp skewering in my chest. What sort of mother opens a third-story window when her child is inside?

My mind darted back to Eva's tiny, broken body sprawled on the ground. I squeezed my eyes shut, trying to suppress the memory, the way I always did. I would never, ever forgive myself.

Rose's brow furrowed. "What are you talking about?"

"I opened the windows and put the fans upstairs."

"But I remember . . ." Her voice trailed off.

"I did it. I know because the playroom was on the shady side of the house, so I opened the window and pointed the fan inward. I remember thinking you did it wrong downstairs, in the kitchen."

"The detective said it was me —"

"Memories can be distorted when trauma is involved," I said. "Whoever questioned you could have easily planted an initial memory of you opening the window. They do that, you know. They look for vulnerable points where they can manipulate you. But I can promise you this: You did not open that window. I did."

Rose wrapped both arms around herself, tears spilling over her cheeks, making them shine like glass. She cried quietly for a moment, her eyes closed, an enormous weight lifting from her shoulders.

"You were right," she said after a moment. "I didn't look for you hard enough at first. Part of me enjoyed working and being successful." She lifted her gaze to mine. "But I'm her mother and I love her. I've spent the last eight years trying to find her. Please. We must tell her everything."

My stomach sank, an inky horror spiraling through me. Rose would take Eva from me. My stomach churned with the familiarity of it, the potential to lose my daughter. I could not allow it. Eva was already afraid Mike didn't love her because they didn't share the same DNA. I could not allow her to find out I wasn't her real mother. It was my job to protect her, even if that meant protecting her from Rose's selfish impulses.

I forced a smile, brain ticking rapidly as I formulated a new plan. "Eva is rather fragile right now. Let's give her some time." I took a crumpled receipt from my bag and wrote my phone number on it. "Phone me in a few weeks. We will tell her together then."

That night I composed a long letter to David Ashford telling him the truth — that I had taken Laura, but explaining why I had to. I knew David would be the ace Rose thought she had up her sleeve. She would threaten to tell him I'd kidnapped Laura, and if she did that, he would involve the police, and the police would inform Seb. My letter would protect us against that.

David needed to hear my version of events first, and then I had to repeat it to validate it. If you repeat something enough, it becomes the truth. When people hear the same story again and again — especially when they *want* to believe that story — a new type of reality can be created.

In the end, David wanted to protect Eva as much as I did, and he agreed she should stay with me. Rose, however, was far less agreeable.

"You bitch!" she spluttered, her pale skin mottled with fury. She had arrived with an unexpected snow flurry just after Thanksgiving, bringing the cold along with her. "You went to David? You devious fucking cow!"

I glanced anxiously at the door. I expected Eva home from studying at the library with Jacob at any moment.

"Calm yourself, Rose. I didn't tell him you were still alive, just why I took Eva. He knows Sebastian is still a threat. He's agreed I should keep her safe."

"I can't believe you went behind my back like that!"

"That wasn't my intention. All I've ever wanted was to keep Eva safe. Surely by now you realize that. If you went to David without him understanding the full story, he would go to the police, and they would tell Seb. You know what that could mean."

Rose stilled, the fire in her eyes slowly receding. She slumped onto the couch, pulling a cushion to her midsection. She sat very still for a long time, as if one wrong move might incinerate her, turn her to ash. As if all I had to do was blow one quick puff, and she would disappear.

"I used to hide in the bathroom crying," she finally said, staring across the living room with tear-glazed eyes. Did she see the photos of Eva framed proudly on the walls? The Mother's Day card still propped on the fireplace mantel? "I didn't know what was wrong with me. Cooking and serving and getting meals on the table, at the time it all made me so angry. I suppose I wanted to find myself, but I didn't think I'd lose her along the way." She lifted her eyes to mine. "I don't know what to do."

I sat next to her. "Sometimes the right choice is the one that feels the worst. And sometimes the wrong choice brings us to the right path. Being a mother comes from making the best decisions one can in the best interests of her child. That's why being a mum is the hardest job in the world. We have to do what's right for Eva."

She nodded and swiped at her wet face. "Yes, you're right. Of course you're right. She must stay with you. It's safest."

Keys jangled in the front door, and Eva came in, snow clinging to her eyelashes. I wondered what she looked like to Rose after all these years. She was still fine-boned, her skin the milk-pale of a redhead, but her hair was now dyed that shocking black, her eyes thickly lined, her clothes a weird mix of deliberately ripped black jeans and an oversize green-velvet top. *Artsy,* I believe she called it.

"Mom? You ho— ?" She stopped, her eyes flicking between Rose and me. "Sorry, I didn't know you had company."

Rose stood, a smile pasted on her face. Only I could see that her hands were shaking.

"You must be Eva," she said. "Lovely to meet you, my dear."

She shot a look at me. I shook my head, a sharp warning.

"I was in the neighborhood looking at purchasing an art gallery up the street. I thought I'd chat to some of the neighbors."

Rose looked at me again. The rims of her eyes were blood red. She smiled a sad little smile. "I was just leaving."

THIRTY-FIVE: EVA

I snatched my phone from the coffee table and answered.

"Hey." Jacob's voice was hollow. I knew instantly something was wrong.

"What's up?"

"My dad passed away last night. I'm having a funeral for him next week, if you're around."

"Oh, Jake." I sat down on the couch. I'd been so wrapped up in my own fears and worries that I'd completely let slip that Jacob's father was dying. "I'm so sorry. Of course I'll be there. You okay?"

"Yeah." He sighed. "I'm . . . sadder than I thought I'd be. It's a lot to process. What about you? You're home from London?"

"Yeah, just back yesterday." I went to the kitchen and made myself a cup of tea, giving him a quick highlight reel of what I'd learned in London, including that my birth name was Laura.

"It's just a name," he said. "Didn't Shakespeare say something about names and roses? Your name doesn't change who you are."

"Maybe. But it scares me to think I'll never be able to go back to who I used to be."

"I guess you don't go back," he said. "You just keep going forward and trust you're doing the right thing."

I sank onto the couch and tucked my feet under me, the tea gripped in one hand, the phone in the other. A million thoughts fluttered through my mind. The corduroy jacket. The gun. The texts. I closed my eyes, projecting Mom's living room onto the chalkboard of my mind. Maybe I'd missed something when I was there last. Some important detail my brain was hiding from me.

My eyelids flipped open. "Jacob, were you home the night Mom was killed? You would've been right across the road! What did you see?"

I wanted to shake myself. I would be a seriously god-awful detective. How had I overlooked asking Jacob what he'd seen?

"I was home, but I didn't see anything useful. I'm sorry." His voice was filled with regret.

"Anything could help."

"I'll tell you what I told the detective. I heard a really brief scream and looked out the front window, but it was dark and I didn't see anything unusual. I gave my dad a dose of pain medicine. When I looked out the front window about fifteen, twenty minutes later, I noticed your mom's front door was open. I called the police then."

Crushing disappointment filled me. He really hadn't seen anything useful.

"There was one thing, though," he said hesitantly. "Not that night, but a few days before. I was up with my dad around four or five in the morning — he wasn't sleeping very well by that stage — and I saw a woman sneaking out of your mom's house."

"What?" I exclaimed. "Sneaking out, like stealing something?"

Jacob laughed. "No, more like doing the walk of shame."

I held my tea under my chin, letting the steam warm my face. "I guess it makes sense. My dad told me yesterday that Mom was gay. I guess it's why they divorced. Mom cheated on him."

"Huh. No kidding." He didn't sound that surprised.

"Did you know?"

"No, not at all. I just wondered after seeing that woman. Plus, you know, Lily and her were always so close. . . ."

"No. . . . Lily and —" I shook my head.

I couldn't see Mom and Lily together. They were close, but close like sisters; they loved each other but they competed with each other too. Christmas was a race to see who would decorate the most elaborate tree; Halloween a ridiculous contest to see whose pumpkin was biggest and who had the scariest spiderwebs strung across the boxwoods in their front yards. Mom wasn't usually a competitive type; Lily just brought it out in her.

I'd never forget when I was fifteen and I lost my photography club's annual photo competition — to Jacob, of course. Mom had brushed it aside and told me not to worry about it. "Winning isn't everything," she said.

After she'd left the room, Lily had caught my eye. "Don't listen to her. Winning *is* everything. You don't have to win today or even tomorrow. Just make sure you win one day."

I said to Jacob, "I can't believe she didn't tell me."

"Does it matter?" he asked.

"No, but why would she hide such an important part of herself?"

"Maybe she was scared. Self-doubt and fear are sort of a buy-one, get-one-free package. They work together to make us feel like shit about ourselves."

His words punched me in the face. Maybe he was right. Maybe it was as simple as believing I was worth trusting.

"My dad was a complete bastard to me my whole life," Jacob said. "For a long time, I thought . . . I don't know, that everybody would reject me because he did. Maybe that's why I ran away. It's definitely why I came back. Like, if I helped him when he was sick, he'd suddenly love me and I'd mean something to him. But he never said it. He never apologized. In a way, it's good, I guess. I can see now it has nothing to do with me. He's fucked up because he's fucked up, you know? At least you know Kat did her best. She tried. You have to remember that."

He was right. One year when I was about fourteen, Mom had taken Andrew and me out to one of those places you chop the tree down yourself to get a Christmas tree. We wanted the biggest tree, and it was ridiculous, dwarfing our small car. But Mom managed to cut it down, wrestle it onto the car, get it into the house. But we were so excited, hopping from foot to foot as we hung the decorations and strung the tinsel in messy clumps. Finally Mom plugged in the lights, her face beaming as she watched our faces light up. She was happy that we were happy.

My memory of decorating that Christmas tree was like a perfect photograph in my mind. I was glad it had stayed with me, fully formed when so much else was broken or gone.

Outside, the evening newspaper thudded against the front door. Phone to my ear, I got up to get it, setting my tea on the entrance table and peering out the peephole. The paper was lying facedown on the welcome mat, wrapped in plastic. I unlocked the door, the bolt, and the chain, and grabbed the paper.

A crunching sound came from my right. I jumped.

But it was just a coyote, caught in the glare of the floodlight. It froze, its eyes glinting like wet coal before it sprang into motion, disappearing into the shadows.

"You know, I used to think Mom was like some sort of god." As I said that, I shut the door, relocked it, and tossed the newspaper onto the entry table next to my art nouveau lamp, the one Liam said was tacky. He'd literally groaned out loud when I told him I got it from a garage sale.

It was one of the rare times I'd ignored him. I needed one thing in this house that was mine.

I pulled the lamp's dangling metal chain to turn the light on. The bright, stained-glass lampshade cast red and yellow lights over the newspaper, highlighting the headline through the damp plastic.

Second Body Found in Queen Anne Murder

Everything in me froze. Jacob was talking, but I tuned him out as I picked up the paper to read.

A second body has been found at the home of Katherine Hansen, the Queen Anne woman murdered in unexplained circumstances last week. The body was discovered in a septic tank in the backyard and identified as British citizen Sebastian Clarke. Police believe Mr. Clarke was Ms. Hansen's ex-husband.

The room tilted around me.

Sebastian was dead.

He'd been dead all along.

I raised a shaking hand to my mouth. If

Sebastian was dead, who had been following me in London?

If Sebastian is dead, who killed Mom?

From far away, I heard Jacob still talking, telling me about the funeral plans for his dad, the people coming to the service.

Think, Eva, think.

I stared at the picture of Sebastian Clarke in the newspaper, trying to remember the face of the man who'd been following me at the Tube station. My brain juddered to a stop, my fingertips going numb from the adrenaline.

I never saw his face, I realized. A bus had driven by before I ran into the station; I'd only caught a glimpse of the man's profile. It could have been anyone. Or no one.

I'd drawn that sketch of Sebastian *before* I realized anybody was following me. Had I transposed Sebastian's face from my sketch onto a stranger's, filling in the blanks with my own assumptions?

I couldn't trust anything. Not what I remembered, not what I thought I saw.

Not myself.

I stumbled, my elbow cracking against my mug sitting on the console table. Tea spilled across the oak surface, the mug hitting the floor with a sickening crack. I stared at the pool of liquid expanding like blood, a memory mushrooming inside me, playing across the backs of my eyelids like a movie.

I was standing in Mom's living room, my breath coming in short, sharp bursts. I looked at my feet, where two bodies lay on the floor. One was my mom.

A few feet away from her was the man from my sketch. The man from the article.

Sebastian Clarke.

The back of his head was split open, blood oozing toward my toes.

And I knew with a horrible certainty.

I killed Sebastian Clarke.

And if I'd killed Sebastian, that meant I was capable of killing Mom.

It was me all along.

THIRTY-SIX: KAT

4 Years Before

I secured a seat at the back of the cocktail bar — always the back, so I could see who entered — and waited for Lily. This waterfront bar was her favorite, overlooking Seattle's lovely seascape: the snow-tipped Olympic Mountains soaring over Puget Sound; the evergreen-cloaked islands in the distance; the setting sun casting a pink and gold glow over the horizon. A Washington ferry chugged into the blue expanse of Elliott Bay, heading in the direction of Bainbridge Island.

Lily entered like an actress sweeping before her adoring crowd, her long, flowing skirt fluttering behind her, her giant gold earrings dancing. She tossed a wave to the bartender, whose face brightened as he waved back. I stood to hug her.

"Happy birthday!" she exclaimed, handing me a card. We'd agreed long ago never to exchange gifts.

"Oh, thank you." I rather hated being reminded of my birthday but dutifully opened the card.

"Sorry I'm late." She dumped her bag on the chair across from me. "I walked up from my studio. I needed the exercise." She patted her stomach. "I can't get fat now that I'm getting old! I have another art exhibit in San Diego next week!"

I didn't respond. Lily sometimes said ridiculous things in an effort to get attention, but I had long since learned to ignore these attempts.

"I'll get us a drink," I said, sliding out of my seat.

Lily waved me away. "No, no, it's your birthday. I'll get the drinks."

She chatted with the bartender for a few minutes longer than was strictly necessary, then returned with a pint of ale for me and a glass of champagne for her. The bartender came up behind her carrying a slice of chocolate cake with a candle pressed into the center.

"Lily! Goodness!" I flushed, mortified, but at least she hadn't insisted on singing — or, worse, that the bartender sing. It was one of the most appalling American traditions, singing "Happy Birthday" in public spaces in front of complete strangers.

"I couldn't let your birthday pass without cake!" She leaned over and swiped a fingerful of icing.

"Thank you." I took a bite. The cake was a little dry, the chocolate frosting rather too sweet, but it was a lovely sentiment, so I forced myself to eat the entire slice.

"How was San Diego?" I asked.

"Good. Very good, in fact! The exhibition was a wild success. Almost every single painting sold!"

"Blimey, that's absolutely brilliant!" I exclaimed, truly happy for her. After a slow start, her paintings had really started selling in the last few years, and she'd built a great name for herself within the Seattle art community.

"So." Lily sipped her wine and slid me a sly look. "I saw a woman leave your house last night. New girlfriend?"

I blushed furiously and busied myself with folding a napkin and placing it under my glass.

Lily laughed and waved a hand in the air. "It's fine. I've always known you like women, Kat. I just wondered when you'd tell me. Why did you keep it secret for so long?"

I polished my glasses on my sleeve, giving

myself a moment to respond.

"I suppose," I said slowly, "I was uncertain of who I was, and what role that played in my identity. It was difficult to trust what I truly wanted."

"I understand that. How can you be true to yourself when you don't trust yourself?" Lily said. "You know it makes no difference to me, right? I love you no matter what."

"I do. Thank you."

"Do you like her?"

"Yes, I rather do. But it's just casual really, nothing serious."

"How did you meet?"

"I was hiking out by Snoqualmie Falls last June. She'd lost her phone, and we got to talking. . . ."

"Hiking." She laughed. "Is that what you kids call it these days?"

I frowned, and Lily laughed again. "All right, all right. I get the hint. No more questions." She looked down at our empty glasses.

"One more drink?"

I smiled. Lily was the devil on my shoulder, always trying to lure me away from being good. "You know I only have one if I'm driving."

"Lucky for me." She grinned and waved a hand to the bartender, signaling for another.

■ ■ ■ ■

It was dark when I pulled up outside my house later that night. Lily stumbled down the street to her place, absolutely pissed. I didn't envy her the headache she would have in the morning.

I was locking the car when someone stepped into the glow of the streetlight. I pressed a hand to my racing heart.

"Eva!" I exclaimed. "Darling, you frightened me. I didn't notice your car there!"

She had been crying, her eyes puffy and rimmed with red.

"Mom, where have you been?"

I gave her a reproachful look. I didn't need to explain my comings and goings to my grown daughter. "I went out for a drink after work."

"Mom . . ." Her voice was high-pitched, scratchy.

"Come inside, darling. We can chat there."

I pushed the door open and turned the downstairs lights on. Under the bright living room lights, I could see that her skin was a very pale, pasty gray, the area around her mouth red and spotted with acne. Her hair was lank and unwashed, dark with oil. She was rather plump too, as if she had been eating too much rich food, her face and fingers bloated.

I felt the first flicker of worry shimmer in me. I paused as I shed my coat, one arm in and one arm out.

"What's the matter?" I asked.

Eva sank onto the couch and looked up at me, her gray eyes suddenly impenetrable. She dropped her head into her hands and started crying.

"I'm sorry! I completely forgot your birthday and now I've ruined it!"

"Don't be daft!" I exclaimed. I hung my coat up and sat next to her, patting her knee. "How could a visit from my daughter ever ruin my birthday? Come now. What's all this about?"

"Mom, I was raped," she said, still crying. "And now I'm pregnant."

The whole horrifying tale tumbled out.

"Oh, Eva. Why didn't you tell me?"

Eva bent over her knees, pressing her face into her hands. "I was ashamed! And . . . I don't exactly remember it!"

"What do you mean, you don't remember?"

"Everything was spinning, so I went outside to get some air. I remember being in the alley, and then a man was there. . . ."

She started sobbing again, her shoulders shaking. "I went to the police, but they didn't believe me and I had no evidence to prove it had happened, so I left. I tried to convince myself I'd just imagined it, but now I know I didn't!"

"You were drugged." My voice sounded flat, unemotional, and I was glad, because inside I felt like I would be sick. All this time I thought I was keeping her safe from Seb, but it was the other dark things in the world I should have been looking out for. Once again I had failed to keep her safe.

"Yeah, I think so. I have to get an abortion."

"You are not serious!" I stiffened, horrified. "What happened to you isn't the baby's fault!"

"Are you fucking kidding me? You think it's *my* fault?"

"There's no need to curse at me," I snapped. "You know that's not what I meant."

"I can't have a rapist's baby! And how would I even support it? I just got fired from the restaurant. I'm too sick and too messed up to even work."

"Move back in here," I said. "I'll help. You are responsible for a child's life. There is nothing more important than that."

"I don't know." She shook her head. "I just don't know. This is so messed up, Mom. No matter what I decide, it's going to break me."

"Then make the best choice for the child."

Eva did move back in with me, and she agreed not to get an abortion, but despite my best arguments, she decided to give the baby up for adoption. All through those long months she stayed with me, her stomach expanding as her cheekbones hollowed out, I hoped she would change her mind. I hoped that as soon as she held her baby's tiny body in her arms, she would forget how it had been made.

But I was mistaken.

After she gave birth, I brought Eva the small, pink bundle of her daughter and begged her to hold her.

"Just for a minute, Eva," I said. "See the miracle you've created."

She turned her head away, refusing to look at the child.

I remembered holding my daughter after I'd given birth, the sound of her cry when the maternity nurse thumped her on the back, the heaviness in my breasts and the weight of responsibility that had pressed on my shoulders.

I would have given anything to have her back. Eva didn't know what she was giving up.

"Get her out of here!" Eva snapped.

I took the baby out to the hallway, where the nurse scooped her out of my arms and handed her to the new parents. I watched them coddle her, stroke her downy forehead, and was mortified to find myself unable to contain my emotions.

I hurried away, thumping down the metal staircase and out the door into the brisk spring air. Everything was bursting into life, cherry blossoms and azaleas and cornflowers bright in bloom. I sat on a bench, trying to gather my thoughts.

There is a point, I recognize, at which a parent must resist being the protector and instead abandon their child to their own choices. The loss shook me, but I could not change it.

After a little while I went inside. I flung the door to the ward open, almost colliding with a well-built man with tidy fair hair. He stepped aside, holding the door open. The cuff of his business suit rode up, exposing a pale slice of white flesh and a silver Rolex.

My heart pulsed as adrenaline charged up my throat. I heard Seb's laugh as he flashed his new Rolex at me. *The face you put on becomes your identity.*

I ran to Eva's bedside, but she was sleeping, blissfully unaware of anything.

He isn't Seb. He isn't that guy from Chicago, I assured myself, my hands shaking. *Anybody could have a Rolex.*

But even though I repeated it to myself over and over, I didn't quite believe it.

Thirty-Seven: Eva

I killed Sebastian Clarke.

The realization made my body go completely boneless. My fingers, my toes, my elbows, everything felt like it was floating, completely separate from my body.

"Eva, you there?" Jacob's voice on the phone startled me back to the present.

"Yeah, sorry. I don't know where my head is." I forced a light laugh. "Hey, I need to get going. I'll call you later, okay?"

I expected him to question me, to ask why, the way Liam did. But Jacob just said, "Sure. Talk to you later."

A sick kind of adrenaline bubbled in me. My phone rang, and when I looked, it was Detective Jackson. I knew I should answer it, but I was too scared. My hand hovered over the phone. Detective Jackson had been so distracted earlier. Had he already gotten the arrest warrant? Was he on his way here now?

The phone stopped ringing and went to voice mail, then started up again.

The walls curled around me, tilted inward. Beads of sweat broke out on my upper lip and beneath my arms. I could feel myself breaking into a million pieces.

Guilt encased me like a sleeve, hot tears tumbling down my cheeks. If I couldn't trust myself, how could anybody else?

The phone went silent, this time for good.

I don't know how long I sat there, trying to figure out what to do. I thought of all the men in my life who controlled me. Detective Jackson, Andrew, even Liam. And I'd let them. Yes, even Liam. For so long, I'd relied on him to fix me. But even he couldn't fix this.

Only I could do that.

I would turn myself in to the police. Tonight. I wouldn't even take the lawyer. I deserved everything I got. Arrest. Prison. My brother's hatred.

I called Liam to let him know, but his phone went straight to voice mail.

"Liam, can you call me back right away? It's important. I'm going to the detective's office now."

Even with my new resolve, I tried to delay leaving until Liam called me back. I wiped up the tea I'd spilled, washed the kitchen counters, and went through the pile of mail gathering on the kitchen island. Liam would like the house neat and tidy when he came home.

I pulled out the bills that were addressed to Liam and climbed the stairs to the third floor to put them in his office. Masculinity dominated the décor: charcoal tile flooring, green-shaded lamps, dark-gray walls hung with local and state business awards. A huge glass desk overlooked the lake outside. Black leather couches were positioned in an L-shape in one corner, an expensive black-on-white rug under a glass coffee table.

I put the envelopes in the inbox on his desk, my eyes falling on a document lying there. It was a letter from the building inspector listing the building code violations Liam had been cited for. Asbestos in the drywall joints. Spliced electrical wires without a junction box. The wrong size circuit in the light fixtures.

I frowned. Those sounded like very serious violations. No wonder the building permit had been turned down. I immediately felt guilty for thinking that. Liam wouldn't cheat and lie and risk people's lives for a building site. Would he?

For Liam, the goal was never as much about developing a property as *winning* at developing it. He liked beating his competitors, proving he could do something better than them. Actually, if I really thought about it, his desire to win was less about winning than it was about *not losing.* To him, losing was the same as being rejected.

But these were actual crimes.

I almost laughed out loud. Who was I to judge? If Liam broke the law, his offenses were tiny in comparison to murder.

I set the letter down and turned to go, but my eyes had already snagged on something else. A spreadsheet of properties Liam owned, with check marks next to the ones that had been sold. Right at the top was a property that rang a distant bell.

Vista Square Condos.

Where did I know that name?

Adrenaline hit me, as if my body remembered what my mind couldn't.

Outside, a murky gray gloaming had rolled in. I turned on the desk lamp and sat in Liam's chair, reading through the spreadsheet details. The condo he'd sold was a one-bedroom, one-bathroom in downtown Seattle. But he bought and sold properties all the time. It was part of what he did as a developer.

I ran my fingertip over the scab on my palm. My brain felt like it was turning to liquid. I couldn't trust where my mind was going.

Suddenly the unmistakable thunk of a chain snapping came from downstairs. Then Liam's voice: "Babe?"

I dropped the spreadsheet back in the inbox, turned the lamp off, and scurried downstairs. The front door was partially open. A slice of Liam's face appeared through the narrow crack allowed by the door chain.

"Could you undo the chain?" he called irritably.

"Sorry!" I slid the chain free and opened the door.

Liam scowled. He was probably still upset that I'd wrecked the living room last night. He dropped a backpack and his briefcase onto the couch and started peeling layers from his body: hat, gloves, windbreaker, fleece jacket, wet spandex.

"Were you rowing? I thought you had a meeting."

He grunted a reply but didn't look at me.

"I was trying to call you."

"I went out on the lake after my meeting. What's up?"

"I . . ." I hesitated. How to tell my fiancé I was a murderer?

I went into the kitchen and grabbed a

tumbler from the cupboard, filled it with water. Liam followed in his boxer shorts, his face pinched.

"Eva." He sighed, exasperated, and took the glass from my hands. "That's a juice glass. It's not for water."

He took two tall, skinny glasses down from the cupboard and filled them both with filtered water. He handed one to me and drank the other in one long gulp. When he'd finished, he rinsed his glass under the tap and put it directly in the dishwasher, then took mine and did the same.

"Are you okay?" He tilted his head at me. "You look strange."

I picked up the newspaper and handed it to him.

"Look." I pointed at the headline. My guts twisted. "Sebastian Clarke is dead! He's been dead this whole time. It wasn't him following me in London. Do you know what that means?"

Liam shook his head.

"It means *I* killed him! I was there. I remember being there. I remember holding a knife. I —" My voice cracked. "I did it."

Liam blew out a long breath and reached for me, wrapping me in his arms and pressing my face to his broad chest. His skin felt cold and clammy, the wiry hairs of his chest tickling my nose. I leaned into him, wanting the warmth of his reassurance, but his skin was so cold it just made me feel empty.

"I'm sure there's an explanation," he said.

"I'm going to turn myself in to the police."

"What? No! Sebastian Clarke is dead."

"Yeah, so?"

"So nobody knows what really happened that night! You can't remember; you just keep saying that. That's what your lawyer will say too."

I hesitated. Doubt crackled like frostbite along my spine. Maybe I'd stabbed Mom — but who poisoned her? That was done over time, not one night, and I definitely didn't do that. And what had cracked Sebastian's head open like that? Not the little knife I remembered holding. And who put Sebastian's body in the septic tank? I wasn't strong enough to do that.

Liam was right. I still didn't know everything.

"Eva, listen to me." He grasped me by the shoulders. "You could go to jail for something you don't even really remember. Trust me, babe. Your mind is all messed up right now. Going in to talk to the detective just opens you up to a lot of legal problems."

I stared at Liam, thinking about all the things I loved about him. How diligent and persistent he was. How confident and loyal. I imagined how our life could be if I gave in to him, pretended I didn't know I had killed two people. Maybe the police would never find out. Maybe there wasn't enough evidence to convict me. We could have our Christmas wedding, go on honeymoon to Barbados, maybe have a baby one day. I could get it right this time.

But getting struck by lightning and everything that had happened since had stripped me bare and exposed who I really was: broken but healing, flawed but strong.

Liam tried to pull me to him again, but I put a hand on his chest and pushed him away.

With Liam, I would never be whole because he would always be the one filling the cracks.

"No." I shook my head. The image I'd painted of our future faded away. "If I killed my mom, I have to pay for that. I have to put myself back together."

Liam's face paled, his hands dropping limply to his sides. "What are you saying?"

"I'm sorry," I whispered. Hot tears slid down my cheeks, splashing into my mouth and tasting of salt and sorrow.

"Eva, don't do this." His pain physically hurt me. If there was one thing Liam couldn't bear, it was rejection.

I couldn't meet his eyes. I grabbed my coat and purse and opened the front door. A rumble of thunder came from a bank of clouds concealed somewhere in the distance. Night tugged at me like a riptide.

And I stepped into the darkness.

THIRTY-EIGHT: KAT

The Day Before

I was just putting the kettle on for tea when the doorbell rang. I pulled the door open and a delivery boy thrust a gorgeous bouquet of daffodils in a round-bottomed vase at me.

"Delivering on a Saturday?" I said with a smile. "That's dedication."

"You're my last one. Hopefully I'll be home before the rain gets here!" The kid peered anxiously at the sly streaks of purple and gray creeping across the horizon.

He waved good-bye as a sudden wind ripped through the trees, buffeting the house.

I shut the door and opened the card.

Congratulations.

Me xx

I cut away the packaging and set the flowers on the island in the kitchen, then picked up the phone and dialed a long-familiar phone number.

"Thank you," I said when she picked up.

"How did you know it was me?"

"Who else knows my favorite flowers are daffodils?" I smiled. *"Rose."*

"I read in the news that you saved a little girl's life. You're an amazing person, Katherine Hansen."

"Blimey! How'd you hear about it all the way over in New York?"

"It's been picked up by national networks."

"Oh dear. I did decline the interviews."

"Are you still worried about Seb?" She tutted. "If he was still looking for you, he'd have found you ages ago. He's either long dead or has moved on. I think you can relax now."

"I shall never be able to relax."

"You always did have an overinflated sense of responsibility," she teased.

"Hmmm . . ." I scooped a teaspoon of loose-leaf tea into a small teapot and poured boiling water over it. "How are the paintings selling?"

"Very well. I have dinner shortly with a gallery owner, in fact."

"Bravo, you." A gust of wind rattled

against the windows. Feeling feverish, I tugged my cardigan off the back of a chair and draped it over my shoulders. A sudden cough swept through me, an agonizing rattle.

"You should get that looked at. You don't sound well."

"It's just a cold. I'm quite certain I shall be fine." I was rarely ill. I rather believed that much of illness was in the mind. But then my vision blurred, a series of strange yellow halos appearing. I shook my head and blinked to dislodge them, feeling quite faint. Perhaps a visit to the doctor was in order. Just this once.

I poured the tea through a mini strainer into my mug, dashed a bit of milk in, and sipped it. It tasted a bit funny. I checked the milk's expiration, but it was still in date.

"How's Eva?" she asked.

"I haven't heard from her much lately," I admitted. Our relationship was rather like dark energy these days, a black force pushing us apart rather than drawing us closer together. "Ever since she moved away, to be perfectly honest. Perhaps I was too brusque with her after what she went through," I said. "I suppose I wanted her to be strong, to learn to trust herself again. But I reckon it backfired in my face."

"Not to worry. I'm sure she'll come around."

But I did worry. I'd realized long ago that when it came to Eva, I always would.

"Do you ever think we should tell her the truth?" she asked. "Perhaps it would help if she knows who she really is, now that she's experienced childbirth and loss."

"I've thought about it." I blew on my tea. "But I reckon after all this time it would confuse her more than help her."

"Perhaps you're right."

I rubbed my chest, which was tight, coiled like a wire. My heart throbbed against my rib cage. I took my tea to my armchair and looked out the living room window at the night sky, a blue-black canvas of stars rippling in the distance.

Out there in the expanse of our solar system, there was a cosmic laboratory, each planet's position, size, atmosphere, and composition creating a world wholly different from its neighbors. Perhaps it was the same with humans — different parents created different children. Perhaps if I had been a different mother, a kinder mother, more sympathetic and compassionate, Eva would have fared better.

"I wasn't very good at it," I said slowly. "Being her mother. You know, I worried when I was pregnant with Andrew that I would love him more than I loved Eva. But I don't. I never did. I discovered that the heart is an ever-expanding organ. Metaphorically, of course. I love them both equally, but in different ways."

"Some relationships flow easier than others. I'm sure she knows you love her, Kat."

"I worry that you would have been better for her. I've always worried that."

A stunned silence came down the phone. "Why did you fight so hard to keep me away, then?" she asked finally.

I shook my head, trying to form the right answer. "I'm afraid it is an utterly selfish reason. I wanted to prove that I was worthy as a mother. I suppose I thought it would make up for failing my Eva. I let Laura slip into Eva's identity, but I couldn't let her take her place in my heart. I'm afraid I failed her, and you as well. Can you ever forgive me?"

"Forgive you?" She laughed. "You kept her *safe*! Mother is a verb, not DNA. The world is quite eager to give women criteria for what makes a good mother, but you said it best all those years ago, Kat. We have to make the best choices for our child. You loved Eva and you kept her safe. One day she'll grow up and understand and forgive our failings and see that we did the best we could."

"Do you ever regret it?" I asked. "Letting me raise her?"

"A million times," she replied honestly. "But she didn't need to suffer for my mistakes. Life is difficult, it's complicated and beyond anyone's total control, but I think it all works out all right in the end."

I heard a muffled knock on the other end of the line.

"Listen, I must dash," she said. "That's my date for dinner tonight."

"Certainly."

"I'll speak with you soon," she said, her voice soft. I imagined, just for a moment, that I could feel her lips brushing my cheek, the faint scent of lemons tangling in the air. My heart crunched, and I stiffened, speechless with a yearning that had never quite disappeared.

"Good-bye," I said, more abruptly than I'd intended.

And a moment later, she was gone.

Thirty-Nine: Kat

That Night

It had been raining off and on since last night, and now it seemed the storm was worsening. The trees were writhing and flailing, the wind churlish and angry. Drops of icy rain tumbled through the night. I hurried from my car to my front door, fumbling with the lock, my fingers oddly thick and clumsy. Inside, I slipped out of my wet coat and changed into a thick cardigan. The cold had seeped into my very bones.

I longed desperately to go to bed with a hot water bottle. The pain in my head was dreadful and I felt quite ill. But I had papers to grade, so instead I headed upstairs to my office.

I sat at my desk and watched as withered leaves tore past the window. A far-off rumble of thunder rolled closer. My head was throbbing dreadfully, my vision still plagued by those odd yellow halos. I stared at the papers, troubled and unable to concentrate.

I thought back to dinner earlier this evening. Andrew, as always, appeared to be doing well in his job as a corporate lawyer, and Eva seemed . . . happy, I supposed. Just quiet. No, *quiet* wasn't the word. Eva used to be so very vibrant and full of life. And now she seemed a shadow of that girl, unbearably uncertain of herself. Perhaps that was the root of my deep sense of unease.

I stood and peered briefly through my telescope. The narrow scope was still focused on Bill's living room. I had been looking at the three largest moons of Jupiter last week when I'd inadvertently seen Jacob administering a dose of medicine to Bill, his hand cupped behind his father's head. The scene had been so unbearably tender I hadn't looked away for a long moment. Now Jacob was slumped on the couch, watching TV as Bill slept.

A sudden scratching sound from the window made me jump — but it was just the branches of a tree scraping against the glass. Opening my filing cabinet, I reached to the back and pulled out Barnaby, Eva's old teddy bear, and rubbed the faded bloodstain on his ear, memories pulsing like a scar.

I sighed.

Eva. My poor girl. Would knowing the truth help or harm her?

Answers, I know, are rarely absolute. We each intend to do the right thing, and yet we are all helpless in the face of fate. We make a choice and must then move forward with the consequences. But perhaps a day would come when she would need to know. And so I began to write.

Dear Eva,

I've written this letter a thousand times and thrown it away each time. The truth is you are not my daughter. I should have told you about your past — our past — many years ago, but I wanted to keep you safe. If anybody knew who we really are, we could all be in very grave danger. Perhaps it is not an excuse, but your safety has always been my priority.

I am so sorry.

Mum xx

I found Eva's birth certificate and the scrap of paper on which I kept David Ashford's address and slid them into an envelope with the letter. At least now I was prepared to tell her, whenever the time might come.

A racking cough launched up my chest. When it had passed, all I could do was slump weakly in the chair. My heart was racing so fast I feared I would have a heart attack.

"Blimey," I muttered.

Pain tugged just beneath my breastbone. I lurched to my feet, throwing a hand out to steady myself. A sound came from somewhere in the house: a click, or perhaps a scratch.

I froze.

I do not feel safe.

It was a fleeting thought, gone as quickly as it had come. I made my way downstairs, glancing around warily, to check the front door, then the back. Everything was locked. I set the alarm, trying to remember if I had armed it when I first got home.

I climbed the stairs to check that the windows were locked, gasping at oxygen that had turned to syrup in my lungs. The bathroom door was closed. I pushed it open slowly. The rusty hinges creaked in protest. My whole body flinched in reaction.

At first I didn't understand what I was seeing, my vision distorting with those strange yellow halos.

But then I saw a tube of lipstick lying uncapped next to the sink.

And written across the mirror in scarlet letters were the words:

I
Found
You

FORTY: EVA

Night was an obsidian fist squeezing me in its grasp as I neared the ferry dock. Five minutes until it left. My thoughts knotted, spinning like tires in mud. I felt so much I almost felt nothing.

I paid the ferry fee and pulled onto the car deck. Headlights bounced up and down as other vehicles drove up the metal ramp. I put my car in park and waited. Nobody got out of their cars. The wind had picked up, the water choppy. The heavy purple clouds from earlier had turned black, releasing icy drops of rain that pummeled the water. I watched as the lights of the dock receded into the distance.

Memories flashed in my mind: the cottony smell of Mom's hand lotion; her guiding hand on my back as she ran alongside me when I first learned to ride a bike; listening to the sound of rain drumming against the roof while we watched *Monty Python;*

the cup of tea she'd made me the morning I came home from the hospital.

The thought that I'd hurt her was unbearable, a shard of glass twisting in my eyeball. I laid my head on the steering wheel and smacked my palm against the dashboard over and over and over. Goddamn it. I didn't want to cry. I didn't deserve to. Not if I'd killed her.

But still, that seed of doubt persisted. What really happened that night?

It had been a long time since I'd trusted myself. I didn't think I was good enough, worthy enough. I'd kept secrets. Secrets from myself and secrets from others. And now here I was, on the edge of something huge, and nothing I said or did would ever be worth anything if I didn't tell the truth now.

The ferry docked with a gentle bump. Workers in orange high-visibility jackets waved their wands. I started the engine and slowly made my way off the ferry, my car bumping over the metal ramp.

There was one last truth I needed to tell — one person I had to speak to.

"Jake!" I pounded on Jacob's front door. "Jacob!"

After a moment, the porch light flicked

on. The metallic sound of a lock sliding open came from inside, and Jacob opened the door.

"Eva?" He blinked in surprise. He was wearing black sweatpants, a dusty black T-shirt, and a leather tool belt, a hammer gripped in his right hand. His hair was tousled, dust clinging to the ends.

"I need to talk to you."

"Come in."

Jacob set the hammer on the hallway table, and I followed him inside.

I gaped at the mess. The house was in complete disarray. The hallway from the front entrance to the living room had been smashed through, a massive hole of crumbling plaster and rotting wood exposing the living room. The wall that had blocked off the kitchen had been demolished, ancient brown appliances, green-and-yellow wallpaper, and dark-veneer cupboards showing through.

"I needed a project," Jacob explained. "I couldn't live here the way it was, so I thought I'd do a bit of remodeling."

I stepped over piles of drywall and crumbled plaster. The house smelled of cooking grease, the stale scent of booze and cigarettes. Jacob and I sat on the sagging corduroy couch that had been in the living room for as long as I could remember. Everything was covered in a fine layer of dust.

We were sitting too close, so I moved a few inches. I noticed a tattoo on his right arm. Grayish-purple clouds curled from under his T-shirt sleeve, streaks of jagged lightning forking down the top of his bicep.

I pointed at the tattoo. "Where . . . ?"

Jacob glanced at his tattoo. "This? I got it in Venezuela. I was photographing the lightning strikes of Lake Maracaibo. It's the most electric place on earth. One of the guys I was working with said that in Venezuela, lightning means strength and illumination."

I shrugged my coat off and showed him the marks left on my skin by the lightning. They were almost the invert of his tattoo. As if someone had laid a sheet of tissue paper over mine and used a coin to emboss them onto him.

Jacob ran a finger over the marks. Goose bumps prickled along my skin at his touch. "We match," he said, so softly I had to lean closer to hear.

Our eyes met, and he withdrew his hand, clearing his throat. "So, what was it you wanted to tell me?"

"Oh, Jake." I stared at a photo on the wall, the only photo Bill had hung of Jacob. He was four, maybe five years old and he was sitting in a swimming pool in the backyard. Bill was lifting the hose over their heads, the water shimmering in the light as it fell onto their faces. They were both smiling. I looked at Jacob, confused and disoriented. Nothing was ever as it seemed. "I had a baby."

"What?" He ran a hand through his hair so it stood on end. "When?"

"After I was raped, I found out I was pregnant. I couldn't keep her. Not after that night. So I gave her up for adoption."

I pressed my fingers into my eyes, trying to stop the tears.

"I felt so . . ." I tried to articulate my emotions, the shame frothing up inside me, hardening like beaten egg whites. ". . . ashamed and mortified. I didn't want to hate her for something that wasn't her fault. Something she had no memory of. So I gave her up."

"Eva —"

I held up a hand. "Please. I need to finish."

Jacob nodded.

"I've thought for a long time that I couldn't trust myself, because if nobody believes you, if the *police* don't believe you, how can you trust yourself?" Only flashes of that night had stayed with me. The crack that ran the length of the ceiling. How hard the bed was. The turning of a door handle. Was my lack of memory a blessing or a curse? "I'm sorry I didn't tell you before."

Jacob looked surprised. "You don't need to apologize to me. You didn't do anything wrong."

I got up and crossed the room, trying to get a bit of space. I wasn't saying it right. I took a long, shaky breath and tried again.

"I think I killed my mom. I don't know if it's possible to fix myself. But I do know I have to make amends for what I've done. So I'm going to turn myself in. I might go to jail for a long time. But before I do, I needed you to know the truth about why I never called you back. The reason I ran away."

Jacob half-stood, a look of alarm on his face. "What is it?"

"The night we slept together was just a week before I was attacked," I said. "The baby I gave up for adoption, Jake. She could be yours."

FORTY-ONE:
KAT

That Night

I stared at the words on the bathroom mirror.

I
Found
You

The adrenaline and fear were too much. I heaved forward and vomited, the tea I'd drunk earlier swirling around the drain. I rinsed my mouth and dabbed it with a wad of toilet paper. I suppose on some elemental level I knew one day Seb would find me. He was not the sort of man to forgive a betrayal.

I felt like such a fool. I had become complacent, and now he was here, ready to ruin the life I had built for myself.

Suddenly angry, I wiped the words off the mirror with a tissue. I would not let him frighten me.

I walked downstairs, my hand slippery against the banister. Outside, wind thrashed against the house and a flurry of rain galloped down the windows. My neighbor's floodlight went on. I entered the living room, and there he was, Sebastian, my husband, sitting on my couch. He held a cup of tea in his hand, as if it were the most natural thing in the world to be here after all these years.

Time had not been kind to him. He looked rather older than I knew him to be. Smaller and more shrunken. His skin was pockmarked, scars nicking his cheeks. His nose was crooked, as if it had been broken many times. Dark stubble sprouted on the lower portion of his face, his blue eyes small and beady. His dark hair was thin and streaked with gray.

My mind flitted to the gun locked in a storage cupboard upstairs. I'd bought it after Eva moved in, hoping to reassure her that she was safe. But then she'd left, and it had sat locked away ever since. It did me no good now. I couldn't even get to it.

He smiled, revealing stained yellow teeth. "Hello, Katherine."

"Sebastian." I hid my shaking hands in

the folds of my trousers. “How did you get in?”

He made a scoffing sound at the back of his throat. “That lock couldn’t keep a teenager out.”

“The alarm —”

“Oh, you mean this alarm?” Seb rose and went to the alarm panel near the door. He typed in a series of numbers and the alarm beeped and disarmed. “You were always so predictable, Katherine. I knew it would be our daughter’s birthday.”

“How did you find me?”

“The good old BBC. ‘British Citizen Wins Prestigious Medal of Courage in Seattle.’ The news report said you were a teacher here. All I had to do was look through the staff pages of local schools.”

The same way Rose had found me. I knew Eva and I should have left then, but I had been so certain I could keep us safe. And I had. Until now.

Seb moved closer to me. I flinched, but all he did was hand me the mug he was holding. He smelled of fried food, grease, and the oily scent of someone who hadn’t washed in a long time.

“Here, I made you some tea. Sit down.”

It was so normal, so domestic, it felt utterly surreal. I took the mug and sat in my armchair, tea sloshing onto my trousers.

"Drink up, Katherine. You look a little pale."

Wordlessly, I sipped the tea. Rain clattered like shards of glass against the windows and thunder boomed. The storm edged closer, the air heavy and dense.

I wiped a bead of sweat from my forehead with the back of my hand. "Are you going to kill me?" I asked quietly.

He raised an eyebrow. "Maybe. But I want something from you. And you're going to give it to me."

He was always a cocky bastard. I was too naïve to see it as a flaw when I was young, and once I did we had a daughter and I couldn't risk losing her. But I saw it now. His arrogance was something I could use. I just had to keep him talking.

"What could I possibly have that you'd want?"

"You know I want Rose. And the girl."

"They're dead."

"We both know that's a lie. I know you were on the run with a little girl, red hair, about three years old. You called her *Eva.*" He shook his head and laughed, but not like it was funny in any way. An angry laugh that bubbled, caustic, like acid reflux, in his throat. "I knew it was Laura. You planned it all with Rose, didn't you! You ran away with her."

I closed my eyes. The bloke who'd attacked me in Chicago. He'd gone back and told Seb about Eva. I knew I shouldn't have let him live.

"How could you?" He reached across the space between us and slapped me, so fast I didn't see it coming. I was out of practice. I used to see it coming.

I gasped, my hand flying to my cheek, stunned as he glared at me, breathing hard.

"How could you run away with our daughter's murderer?"

"Rose didn't murder Eva. It was ruled an accident, remember? The police released her."

"She still opened that window! She may as well have pushed her! Maybe you don't care about justice for our daughter, but I do."

"But why now, Seb? It's been so long!"

"Let's just say I was a little . . . indisposed while I was detained at Her Majesty's pleasure. Otherwise I would've found you much sooner."

"The fire. You were caught starting the fire at that restaurant. The Gardener."

"Guilty. At least according to a jury."

No wonder I hadn't seen or heard from

him all these years.

"So where is she?" he asked. "Where is Rose?"

"I told you, Rose is dead. She really did jump off that bridge."

Seb leaned back against the couch and folded his arms over his chest. His expression grew calculating. "I saw you meet *Eva* at that restaurant. Did our daughter really mean so little to you that you thought you could slot another child in where she used to be? You disgust me."

"She did nothing wrong, Seb. She's never known about any of it."

My neighbor's floodlight went on again. Somebody was outside, so close. I could scream for help, if only I could catch my breath. My vision blurred, hazy yellow clouding everything. My heart felt like spark plugs were pulsing in my chest. My limbs were utterly, utterly useless.

"You have no idea what it feels like!" Sebastian's voice shook. "I lost *everything.*"

"She was my daughter too! I've suffered every single day since she died!"

Pain, physical and emotional, draped itself over me. The guilt and blame I'd carried for so long was a sharp stone boring into my chest.

Seb sucked his upper lip between his

teeth, his face twisted. "I dream about her. Dreams where I'm watching her fall, but our angel has no wings to hold her up. I dream that I'm under the window about to catch her, but somehow I miss. I dream I'm watching her in the window but my legs are made of cement and there's nothing I can do. I couldn't protect my own daughter."

"Oh, Seb," I murmured.

Guilt was eating him up, just as it had me. But he'd swallowed the sweet medicine of revenge to cure his guilt, only to become addicted to it. That addiction was driving him even now, festering and turning into a living, breathing thing.

"Rose opened that window and she has to pay, Katherine. It's the only way to get justice." He grasped my hand, his touch reptilian.

I shook my head.

Seb leaned forward, his nose only inches from mine. "You get her here, or I'll kill your precious *Eva.* I know where she lives. Don't think for a second I won't do it."

A cold wave of sickness rolled through me, coating my skin in a thick, pin-prickly feeling. The armchair cradled my back, the only thing keeping me upright.

I had to keep Seb talking. I was too weak to fight him off.

"It wasn't Rose, Seb." My voice was thready. "It was me. I opened the window."

Forty-Two: Eva

Jacob's elbows were propped on his knees, chin cupped in his hands. He was staring at the green shag carpeting, his forehead crumpled as a tissue. He hadn't moved in a few minutes.

"Jake, please say something," I pleaded.

He shook his head, dazed. "You never said a thing."

"I know. I'm so sorry, Jake. You deserved better than that. I was so messed up and —"

"Where is she?" he cut me off.

I shook my head. "I don't know. It was a closed adoption."

"What?" Jacob stood slowly. "You gave up a baby who might have been mine to a closed adoption?"

"I didn't know whose baby it was! I thought about getting one of those prenatal paternity tests, but they're expensive. Plus I would've needed a swab from your mouth for them to analyze your DNA, and how was I supposed to explain that to you? Besides, you left. You *left,* Jake. I didn't know where to find you!"

"Don't give me that bullshit story, Eva. You know you could've gotten in touch. You should've tried harder!"

"I'm sorry. You're right. But how could I say those words? *I'm pregnant, but I was raped and I don't know if the baby's yours or his.*" I dashed at the tears brimming in my eyes. "I'm not saying I was right, but try to understand what I was going through."

Jacob stared down at his clenched fists, his shoulders heaving. He wouldn't speak now. His reaction to anything uncomfortable was to go into lockdown, retreating into silence.

I straightened my shoulders and lifted my chin. I was done apologizing for things that weren't my fault. "Look, I just wanted to do the right thing here. I thought you should know the truth."

I grabbed my coat and picked my way back over the piles of broken plaster and shattered fragments of wood to the front door and let myself out.

Thunder rumbled in the distance. The trees that lined the road bent and swayed in the increasing wind. Rain mingled with the tears on my cheeks as I ran to my car. I wrenched the door open and threw myself in. Icy rivulets dripped from my hair down the back of my neck, making me shiver.

I turned the key in the ignition. The starter made a raspy clicking sound. I tried a few more times, but no luck. And then I realized what the problem was. I'd left the headlights on.

"No!" I shrieked. I smacked the dashboard with my palm and dropped my forehead to the steering wheel.

What now?

I couldn't call Liam. There was no way I was going back in to Jacob. And I couldn't call the detective to pick me up right here. It would be too mortifying. Maybe Uber or Lyft? I'd never needed to use them on Whidbey Island and had no idea how they worked.

The darkness wrapped around me, pressing on the windows. I shivered as drops slipped off my hair and dove down the collar of my coat. I looked across the road at Mom's house.

I was cold to the bone and soaked when I let myself in the back door. First I went upstairs to Mom's office where I remembered seeing an electric heater. I unplugged it from beneath the desk and straightened.

My gaze fell on her telescope. I smiled, remembering how baffled she'd been when I chose the arts over science.

I peered through the eyepiece and pulled back in surprise. It was looking directly into Jacob's living room. I could see where his lanky frame was slumped like a question mark on the shabby brown couch. I flushed, embarrassed that Mom had been watching Jacob and his dad.

A sudden chill crept into my skin as I thought of the night I found Mom's letter. How Jacob had come into the house without knocking. I remembered thinking it had been a long time since we were kids and could come into each other's houses unannounced. I looked again into the eyepiece. Maybe I should be asking *why* Mom was looking into Jacob's house.

Back downstairs, I tugged on a sweater of my mom's I found draped over the back of a kitchen chair. Her smell gusted off of it. I pulled it tight around my body and surveyed the living room. The bloodstain on the floor near where Mom's armchair had been was still there. Swirls of fingerprinting dust stood out on the fireplace mantel. I picked up a picture of my brother when he was about a year old. No wonder Mom had no pictures of me when I was a baby.

I set the picture down and dialed my brother's number.

"Eva? What's up?" Andrew's voice was low. Voices filtered in the background, the tinkle of piano music, the clatter of silverware against porcelain.

"Andrew, I need help."

A woman's voice floated through the phone. Andrew hushed her; then a door clicked and there was silence. For so long, Andrew had been just my little brother. Then he was my competition for love, time, attention from our parents. Then he was my judge, my number-one critic, and the benchmark I held myself against. But for the first time I thought of him as an adult with an actual life. A girlfriend, maybe children down the road, happy dinners and laughter with good friends.

God, I could be awfully self-involved. No wonder he was angry at me.

"I-I'm so sorry," I stuttered. "I didn't mean to interrupt."

"No, it's fine. Actually, I'm glad you called. I was in court all day and then in the office. I only got your message a little bit ago. I've been worried about you."

"I'm sorry."

"Stop saying you're sorry, Eva," Andrew said, not unkindly. "What do you need?"

"I need a ride to the detective's office. I was on my way there, but I stopped by Jacob's and I left my lights on and now the battery —" My voice cracked. "I need a jump."

"Sure. I have some jumper cables in my car. I'll bring them to you."

"I'm at Mom's now."

He hesitated, but didn't question me. "I'll be there in a few. And remind me when I get there to give you the ID number you need to pick up your ring."

"From the hospital?"

"No, from Detective Jackson. He called me asking where you were yesterday. He's cleared your ring from evidence he found at the scene."

I looked at my bare hand, where my engagement ring should've been. Something jangled at the back of my mind.

A knock came at the door. "Somebody's here, I've gotta go."

"See you in a few."

When I opened the door, Jacob was standing on the porch hunched against the rain. The wind tossed his hair around his face.

"I'm sorry." He looked like he was in physical pain, his face twisted and gray. "I didn't handle that very well."

"It's okay —"

"It's *not* okay. The way I acted — I'm not that guy. I should've done better. And I get why you couldn't tell me. I really do. I should've —"

A brilliant flash of hot white light split the sky behind Jacob. Forks of lightning etched into the inky canvas of night, burning into my retinas. A second later, the horrific crack of thunder boomed across the charcoal sky. It permeated the air, reverberating throughout my body.

My brain lit up, neurons fizzing and crackling in a dizzying swirl of white light, my mind suddenly falling back, back, back.

Jacob was speaking, but I couldn't hear anything because I was back there, the night Mom was killed. The lightning from that night and the lightning from right now fused, illuminating what had been hidden, as if the veil had been pulled aside, and I was seeing it all for the first time.

Forty-Three: Kat

That Night

"I opened the window, Seb," I repeated. "Not Rose. Do you remember how hot it was that day? I set fans in the upstairs windows, but the one in the playroom was too large to put a fan in, so I opened the window and left the fan on the desk. And then I went downstairs."

Tears dripped down my face as the image of my daughter's small, broken body accosted me.

"It was an accident." For so long I'd blamed myself, the self-hatred hulking like a tumor under the skin. Now I felt it soften and dissolve, washed away by the truth.

It was an accident.

Sebastian stared at me, as if unable to comprehend my words. "It's your fault."

He stood slowly, his body bulky with rage. I tried to stand too, but staggered, the tea dropping from my limp fingers and splashing onto my feet. The living room tilted precariously, but Seb grabbed me by the front of my shirt and yanked me upright. His face was twisted with loathing.

"You bitch." Seb pointed something at me then. It glinted in the light, a sharp flash. I blinked, trying to clear my hazy yellow vision. He pressed the object to my cheek. It was a knife. One of my knives.

But he didn't stab me.

The punch sent me flying backward, my cheekbone smashing against the floor. My glasses skittered under the couch. My vision erupted in red stars. Blood exploded inside my mouth, the taste of iron, hot and bitter.

I gasped and gagged, rolling onto my side as I cradled my throbbing cheek in my hand.

A voice inside my head screamed at me. *Fight. Escape. Run.* But I could barely stand, let alone get away. I was trapped. Gutwrenching fear gripped me, my breathing ragged as a dark, rising panic wrapped its bony fingers around my chest.

I was going to die.

I turned and looked into Sebastian's puffy red eyes and made a decision. He could kill me, torture me, maim me, but I wasn't telling him anything.

The words tightened in my stomach, flying up my throat and bursting from my mouth. "Go to hell, Seb."

The next thing I knew, Seb's boot was heading toward my face.

And then everything went black.

I had no idea how long I'd been out — a minute, an hour? The rain was a torrent, the storm settling around the house as if it were under siege. My shattered cheekbone was pressed to the floor. Halos shimmered across my vision. The squeezing knot of my heart thudded like a trapped bird. The tips of my fingers and toes were numb.

Something was very wrong with me.

"Good to see you're awake," Seb said. He grabbed me under my arms and threw me back into the armchair, then sat on the couch and stared at me. "Doesn't look like you're going anywhere."

I moaned and clutched my chest. The pain was dreadful, making me nauseated. I could feel my life seeping away, slowly circling toward the drain.

"I had a little time to think while you were out," he finally said. "I don't need Rose. *You're* to blame for our daughter's death. So I thought about it. What should your punishment be? And then it came to me. Laura. *Eva,* as you call her now. I'll kill her, and you'll know forever it was your fault."

"It won't bring our daughter back," I wheezed, clutching my chest. Blood oozed from my split lip, and I licked it, my tongue sticking to the dry skin.

"Maybe not, but it'll make me feel better. I might even let you live, just so the guilt can eat you up." He smirked when he saw my expression. "You don't believe me?"

I glared at him, but he just shrugged.

"Doesn't matter." He waved my phone at me. "I found Eva's phone number and texted her for you. She should be here soon."

I closed my eyes and thought about Eva. The way her dark mahogany hair shimmered in the sun. How she tilted her head to the right when she laughed. The sound of her calling out for me in the middle of the night when she was small. The feel of her cheek when she pressed it to mine and whispered, "I love you, Mama."

I should have told her how I felt. I should have said the words out loud. *I love you, too.*

In my mind, she was all the ages I had known her: the three-year-old torn, terrified, from her mother's arms; the precocious little girl asking a million questions; the twelve-year-old with knobby knees, unused to her sudden breasts; the sullen fifteen-year-old locking herself in her bedroom, uncertain of who she was or her place in the world; the terrified woman doubting herself after a horrific attack.

Seb was wrong — I didn't just slot her in to fill the space where our daughter should have been. I loved her; I had always loved her. I was just too scared to acknowledge that love because it meant accepting that my daughter was truly gone.

I had held my blame and unforgiveness up like a flag, wrapped my body in it, and heralded it for all to see. It had made me hard and abrupt and distant.

But I had to forgive myself. Maybe then Eva could forgive me too.

A rumble of thunder boomed outside, the living room lights flickering on, then back off. And suddenly the front door creaked and swung open. An outline filled the doorway.

Eva.

Forty-Four: Eva

I shoved my keys and phone into my back pocket and reached for the door handle. I froze. The door was unlatched, open a few inches.

"Mom?" I pushed the door open with my toe and felt around in the dark for the light switch. I'd sneaked in late at night enough times when I was in high school to make it feel instantly familiar.

"Mom, I'm here. Is everything okay?"

The living room light flickered on. I gasped, barely able to comprehend what I was seeing. Mom was slumped in her old armchair, which had been turned to face the front door. She wasn't wearing her glasses. Her lip was split, blood dripping from a gash in her cheekbone. Her arms hung limply on either side. Her skin was waxy and gray.

Suddenly the world lit up, fireworks zipping along the insides of my eyelids as a private bomb exploded somewhere inside my head. My knees loosened, but a thick arm snaked around my neck, holding me up. Something cold and hard pressed against the tender skin at my throat.

"Let her go, Sebastian," Mom rasped. She didn't move from her chair, her eyes drooping, chest heaving. "It's me you want, not her."

The man — stout and grizzled, with dark hair and a misshapen nose — ignored Mom, shoving me into the chair next to her. He ripped off a length of duct tape and bound my wrists together behind the chair.

Blood rolled hot and sticky from my temple, splattering onto my coat collar and pooling in the crevice of my collarbone. Pain rocketed in bands around my head.

"Mom," I whimpered, terrified. "What's going on?"

"I'm so sorry," she whispered. "I tried to keep you safe."

Think, I told myself. *Think!*

My car keys. They were in my back pocket. If I could reach them, maybe I could cut through the tape.

I rolled my shoulders, pretending to stretch my neck as I maneuvered my fingers to slide the keys out. The movement sent off an avalanche of pain. I gritted my teeth and pushed through it. I had to do something. I had to keep going, or Mom and I would both die.

A moan rasped from Mom's throat.

"What have you done to her?" I asked.

"Foxglove." He had an English accent, the word hard and round, as if his mouth were full of rocks. "I mixed the leaves into her tea." He looked pleased with himself.

"The flower?" I shook my head, trying to cover the movement of me sawing at the tape around my wrists. Pain surged from my blood-soaked temple through my entire body.

"Flower. Poison. Whatever. Her heart will stop soon."

"You poisoned me? Really, Seb?" Mom managed a quirk of her lips, a mocking glint in her eye. "How very passive of you."

"Technically, you poisoned yourself," he replied, smirking.

"Why are you doing this?" I whispered. "What do you want from us?"

"Tell me where Rose is."

I glanced at Mom, confused. "Who's Rose?"

Sebastian looked at me for a long time. "Rose Ashford. She's the reason I texted you."

Suddenly the *Love you* in the text made

sense. I knew something had been off.

"We don't even know a Rose!" Anger and relief danced feather-soft in my throat. Maybe this was a mistake. A silly case of mistaken identity. Maybe everything would be okay.

Sebastian threw his head back and laughed. His blue eyes glinted, wet and oily in the overhead light.

"You really don't know? She never told you?"

I shook my head, using the movement to again slash at the tape. I felt a thread loosen and give way.

"Rose is your real mother, not Katherine. And you aren't Eva, my dear. You're Laura. Eva was *my* daughter. She died falling out of a window when she was just three."

I shook my head. "I don't understand."

"Katherine used to nanny for a woman named Rose Ashford. Her daughter, Laura, and my daughter, Eva, were the same age. They became quite the foursome. Did you fuck her, Katherine? You certainly wanted to."

Mom's head slid back against the armchair. Her eyes closed for so long I started to panic. But her chest was moving.

"Katherine opened the window in the room where you girls were playing. Eva, my

Eva, climbed onto the window ledge. She fell out of the window and died. Rose was arrested and released, but a few weeks later she and Katherine disappeared with you. *Laura.*" He turned to Mom. "Why? Why did you run away with them?"

"I heard you talking to Paddy." Tears seeped from between Mom's eyelids. "You were going to have Rose killed. I couldn't have another death on my conscience."

"So you used *our daughter's* birth certificate and let *her* become Eva." He turned to me, shaking his head in disgust. "Like you could slot into her shoes. *You.*" He looked at me, really looked at me then, his eyes hard and cold on mine. "You worthless piece of shit. You were too stupid to even realize she was lying to you all along. You're nothing like my bright Eva."

Anger frothed up inside of me. It felt good boiling in the cauldron of my belly; better than the sadness and doubt that'd been my constant companions for years. I wasn't going to spend my last few minutes on this earth apologizing for something that wasn't my fault.

"You sadistic fuck," I shouted. "I haven't done anything wrong!"

He pressed the tip of the knife into my neck, slowly, with excruciating precision.

The skin broke, a hot bead of blood rolling down to my throat. Sebastian pressed harder. I screamed as pain hit me.

The front door crashed open. A familiar shape stood in the doorway, dripping rain all over the carpet.

Sebastian jumped back, the knife in front of him. I gasped as I recognized the person.

My savior. My hero.

"Liam!"

"Eva!" His eyes darted around the room, landing on the knife in Sebastian's hands.

Liam would save us.

But as my brain tried to adjust to the fact that Liam was here, a secret, insidious voice whispered in my ear.

How did he find me?

Forty-Five: Kat

That Night

Lightning forked outside the house, bright fireworks igniting behind the man as he stumbled inside. Blond. Well-built. A boyish face. He was wearing jogging pants and a shiny Adidas shirt, and on his wrist was a silver watch.

A Rolex.

I looked again at his face. I'd seen him before.

"Liam!" Eva pulled against her restraints. "Help!"

Liam lunged for Sebastian, but Sebastian had the knife. He stabbed it at Liam so he had to jump out of the way, the sharp edge of the blade narrowly missing his belly. Sebastian pressed the knife to Eva's neck.

"You move, and I'll kill her."

Liam froze and raised his hands. "Come on, man. Let's talk about this. Just put it down."

Without looking away, Sebastian grabbed another chair from the dining room table and set it next to Eva's. He waved the knife toward it. "Sit down."

Liam did not budge. "Is it a ransom you want? I'm sure we can come to some arrangement here. Nobody needs to get hurt."

Sebastian thrust the knife toward Eva's neck. She flinched. "I said, sit down!"

"All right, all right!" Liam complied, nostrils flaring.

Sebastian taped Liam's wrists behind his back. I coughed wetly, stomach roiling. Vomiting out the poison earlier was likely the only reason I was still alive.

"I recognize you," I said to Liam. "You visited Eva at the hospital after she gave birth."

Liam's eyes darted between mine and Eva's. He shook his head, a sharp jerk of his chin. "I think you're mistaking me for someone else."

Eva's eyebrows tightened into knots.

"No, I'm certain of it," I insisted. "You held the hallway door open for me. I noticed your watch because it was very like the Rolex Seb used to wear."

I looked at Seb's wrist, but he shrugged. "I sold that years ago."

"Sorry, I really don't know what you're

talking about."

Eva shook her head, wincing. "He couldn't have been at the hospital, Mom. We didn't meet until after I moved to Whidbey Island." She bit her lip and looked at Liam. "Right?"

"No! No. Of course not! I mean, not that I remember. M-maybe we saw each other somewhere along the line, but . . ."

He was talking too much, the lie stamped inadvertently on his face. Even Eva could see it, a dawning realization settling gently across her face.

"How did you find me tonight?"

Liam pressed his lips together.

"Liam! How did you find me?"

He sighed. "I put a tracking device in your purse."

Eva's eyes widened. "Why? When?"

"I guess, I don't know — years ago." He shook his head. "You're just so *stupid* sometimes!" he exploded. "So naïve. There are some bad people in the world, like this guy!" He tilted his head at Sebastian, and Sebastian rolled his eyes. "I wanted to protect you. I've *always* wanted to protect you. Even from yourself."

"What are you talking about?"

"You don't even remember the night we met, do you? We were talking at the bar when my phone rang. I left to answer it, but when I came back you were talking to someone else. You are so beautiful, Eva, so sweet and innocent, but you trust anybody, *everybody* but yourself. I watched as he slipped something in your drink, and you didn't even notice! He followed you outside and I knew what he was going to do. But I got to you first. I *saved* you."

Eva's face paled even further. She looked positively ill, her lips a disturbing shade of blue-white.

"I'm sorry about the tracking device. I know it sounds weird and creepy, but I swear, it isn't like that. I wanted to keep you safe because I love you! That's how I found you!"

Sebastian snorted a laugh. "Fat lot of good you've done here, eh?"

Eva looked down, crying silently. Only I could see the gentle sawing motion as she worked her way through the final threads of tape at her wrists.

"He's right." She looked at Liam, her face hard and cold. "You weren't able to save me, Liam. Then or now. *You're* the one I shouldn't have trusted."

Liam looked like she'd slapped him. He opened his mouth to reply but suddenly Eva exploded out of her seat. She lunged for the mug I'd dropped on the floor earlier, grasped the handle firmly, and smashed it into the side of Sebastian's head. It made a hollow thunk as it ricocheted off his skull. He stumbled to his knees, clutching his head, the knife clattering to the floor.

"Run, Eva!" The words snapped out of my throat. I tried to stand but couldn't, my hands and feet weighted like sandbags. I clutched my chest, my heartbeat suddenly slowing, as if the brakes had been put on. I collapsed into the armchair.

Eva wrenched the front door open, opening her mouth to scream, but Sebastian was already there. He grabbed her shirt and dragged her back inside. The material ripped and he tossed her to the floor. Her head cracked, a sickening *thunk.* She slumped onto the floor, stunned.

Sebastian kicked the door shut and leapt on her. She tried to roll out from under him, but he punched her in the face and she went limp, dazed.

Then the knife was in his hand, raised over his head, moving in slow motion toward her throat.

"Eva!" Liam strained against his restraints. The muscles in his neck were like cords as he tried to free himself.

I summoned every last shred of strength in me and threw myself out of my chair.

The full force of my weight landed on Sebastian. We crashed to the floor, my body thudding hard into the fireplace grate. But he still had the knife, and suddenly he was on top of me, rising above me like a moon. I watched the knife's downward trajectory, felt the steel burning as it slid into the base of my neck, like hot metal through butter.

Sebastian staggered off of me, the knife still in his hand. His face momentarily registered what he had done. He leapt on top of Eva, his eyes crazed, void of all reason.

I pressed my shaking hands to my throat, trying to stop the blood, but it was gushing out too eagerly, hot and sticky on my fingers. I stumbled to my feet, my slick hands fumbling for the fireplace poker. The knife in Seb's hand slashed down, down, down toward Eva.

I lifted the poker above my head and smashed it into the back of Sebastian's skull with all my might. Sebastian's head cleaved in half at the back, making the wet *shluck* of a watermelon splitting. He hung suspended in the air for a split second, eyes wide, as if surprised that I had dared defy him. Then he crumpled on top of Eva, limp as a tissue, the knife in his hand clattering onto the floor.

"Eva!" Liam shouted.

"Oh my God!" Eva screamed, shoving Sebastian's body off her and rolling away, staggering to her feet. "Oh fuck! Oh my God! What have I done?"

Nothing, I wanted to say. *You are innocent. You always were.*

But the words came out an unintelligible gurgle as blood pooled in my throat. I slumped to the floor next to Sebastian's body. How fitting that we would die together after all these years apart. I should've known it would end like this. I should've known how easily things come unraveled when they were stitched together with lies.

"Mom! Mom!" Eva dropped to her knees. She tore her coat off and pressed it to my spurting neck. The pain was extraordinary, gripping me with razor-sharp talons. My pulse stuttered, my lungs crumpling like paper bags. "Oh God. Mom! What do I do? Tell me what to do!"

Our eyes met, and I wanted to tell her how absolutely perfect she was. How much I loved her. That I didn't regret our time together, not one bit.

I wished I had time to say it.

As the blood seeped out of me, I realized there was a terrible sort of symmetry to my death. I had done what I always planned to do — I'd saved Eva. And with that realization, I was able to forgive myself.

"It's . . . okay." Blood dribbled, hot and sticky, out of my mouth.

A huge weight was crushing my chest. I could not catch a breath. Eva thrust the coat away, pressing her hands to my throat. "Mom. Don't try to talk. I'm going to call the police."

I smiled, a universe of sadness filling me at everything we would lose, a solar system mapping planets of pain and sorrow. I wanted more, so much more, but oh, how grateful I was for the time we'd had. Love, a mother's love, is infinitely expanding, like the universe we exist in. Eva taught me that.

"My girl," I whispered, my breath bloody in my throat. "You healed me." I coughed, a wet rattle. "You're stronger than you think. Trust . . . that. Promise."

"I promise, Mom." Eva was crying, tears drawing streaks down her bloodstained cheeks.

There was something important I had to say, that I had wanted to say since that day so long ago, standing on the edge of an icy lake. I grasped her hand, gave it three weak squeezes, and whispered the words: "I. Love. You."

My gaze drifted up, to the painting of daffodils hanging over the fireplace.

"Find her. . . ." I said, my voice failing me. "Your mother. Find . . ."

And then I whispered her name in Eva's ear.

Forty-Six: Eva

What have I done?

The thought charged at me, stark and unrelenting. Blood was everywhere. Under my fingernails. In my mouth. In my hair. It was streaked across my shirt. On the floor, it blackened and congealed, filling the air with its metallic breath. The sickly sweet scent clung to the back of my throat.

My mother was slumped on the floor in the living room, mouth gaping, brown eyes staring at nothing. A dark pool of blood seeped like molasses from a gaping wound at the base of her neck. The urgent beat of her pulse had faded to an unrelenting nothingness.

Both my hands were clamped around her throat. An emotion thudded so viciously in my chest it was painful, like searing.

"Mom!" I tried to scream.

But only a choked sob came out.

I looked at her glassy eyes, and a grief so

fierce I couldn't help but howl cinched around me.

This was my fault. Sebastian had stabbed her because of me, because I tried to run.

I started to shake uncontrollably.

All the memories we shared bore down on me. She was my protector, my guardian, the one who'd held me in her arms when I cried after a bad dream. She'd wiped my tears and tucked me into bed. Her cool hand had brushed the hair from my feverish cheeks when I was sick. She'd taught me to play chess and build a tree house and stick up for myself when boys bullied me.

I'd been so blind, so selfish and self-involved, all the while I'd stupidly ignored her many small gestures of love: leaving the light on when I was out late; waiting up to see I was safely home; double-checking the tire pressure on my car; making sure there was always a fire extinguisher in the house; putting a can of mace in my purse.

She'd showed me she loved me the only way she knew how. She was my safe place, my home, my roots. And then I touched her cold cheek, already gray and slack, and she was none of these things.

She was gone.

And my heart shattered into a million pieces.

I tried to move. I needed to call the police. But an intense wave of dizziness walloped me across the head.

I stood, my legs like rubber bands, but Liam's voice came to me from very far away. "Wait. Eva, don't go!"

His words triggered a memory.

Wait. Eva, don't go!

Flashes of an alley slick with rain.

Someone calling my name.

The words burst in my ears like tiny grenades, sending me tumbling backward in time. Everything froze; time hung suspended, like it was holding its breath. The moisture drained from my mouth.

"No." I shook my head. I was wrong. I was looking for things that didn't exist.

Wasn't I?

But Liam had come to the hospital after I'd given birth. He'd been there at the club the night I was drugged. He'd followed me outside, watched as I threw up. I could feel his hand on my back, hear his soothing voice.

Come with me, we'll get you all cleaned up.

"It was you," I said. My hands were shaking. "You were the man I went home with that night. The man who raped me."

"Don't be ridiculous, Eva!" Liam was giving me that look — scrunched brow, pinched frown — that meant he pitied me, that I couldn't trust myself. But there was something else there, something unfamiliar. A shift to his eyes that scared me.

I stared at him. I knew I could be wrong about what I was thinking, what I remembered and what I didn't.

But then I heard those words echo again in my mind — *Wait. Eva, don't go!* — and I knew I *could* trust myself. More than that, I knew I *had* to trust myself. I couldn't let him control me anymore. Because those words were real, and the voice saying them was Liam's.

"Hurry up. Get this tape off me right now!" Liam was now using his low, authoritative voice, the one I never questioned.

But it no longer had any power over me.

Lightning scrawled across the sky outside the living room window, turning the blood the color of oil. Something else had replaced grief. A curl of white-hot anger sparked in me, scalding my face and arms. It caught fire, turning into a vicious type of fury with a new texture, the consistency warping and changing into something else: hatred.

I wrenched my engagement ring off, my finger so slick with blood it slipped off easily. I threw it at Liam. It glanced off his shoulder, and he flinched.

"You *raped* me!"

"What? No!"

I knelt and picked up the knife, my fingers wrapping around the blade. The hot steel bit into the flesh of my palm, and yet I liked it, that pain.

My brain felt too light, like it was full of air. Like I would float away at any moment, a balloon coming untethered. My breath came in short bursts, and a strange darkness tinged the edges of my vision. Lightning forked from the sky, illuminating Mom's body.

I stared at Liam, this man to whom I'd given my heart, my soul, my life. But not anymore. The knife was heavy in my hand. For a second I was afraid of what I might do.

"You raped me." This time I could only whisper it. Shock slid down my body like ice, making me suddenly numb.

The knife fell from my fingers as I staggered backward, away from him.

Suddenly I was outside, the night sky pressing on my skin.

The burning scent of ozone scorched the fine hairs of my nostrils, mingling with the pungent scent of wet earth. Black and purple clouds roiled in the night sky above. Thunder rumbled ominously. The air crackled with electricity, static lifting the fine hairs along my bare arms. Rain skidded into my scalp, licking at my face.

I was crying so hard I could barely breathe.

All I could do was run.

Forty-Seven: Eva

I blinked back to the present.

I was lying on my back in the entryway of Mom's house, Jacob hunched over me, his face crumpled with concern. Raindrops clattered hard against the porch, galloping down the slick surface of the open front door.

"Are you okay? What happened?" he asked.

The memories assaulted me like blows, making me see stars. I didn't want to remember. It hurt so much.

Jacob grasped my elbows, pulling me to a sitting position.

"I remember the night she died. I didn't kill her. Sebastian did."

Memories poured in. A familiar voice calling my name. Liam standing in the doorway. The knife in my palm, blade cutting into the tender skin as wave after wave of fury rolled over me.

I lifted my bare left hand and showed Jacob. "Look. No burns. If I'd been wearing Liam's ring when I got struck by lightning, the metal would've burned my finger. That means the ring was off my finger *before* I was struck by lightning. Liam —"

And then, as if I'd conjured him out of the shadows, Liam was there, standing wet and dark in the doorway. He was holding something in his hands. A flash of lightning hissed behind him as he slammed it onto Jacob's head. Jacob crumpled silently, his eyes rolling back as he sank to the floor, unconscious.

I screamed and scrambled backward on my butt.

Liam dropped the cement garden gnome onto the porch and leaned down to me, his face flecked with Jacob's blood. "Eva, it's okay. It's me!"

"What have you done?" Blood expanded out from a widening black halo around Jacob's head. But his chest was moving. He was alive. "We need to call an ambulance!" I staggered to my feet and tried to run to him. Cold sweat beaded my face.

Liam blocked my way. "No." His voice was flat, his eyes dark.

He reached for me, but I wrenched away.

"Don't look at me like that, Eva!" He

pulled something out of his back pocket and held it out. It was two passports, one for Dan McIntosh, the other for Sarah McIntosh. They had our pictures. "Look! We can run away together. Wherever you want. Forget any of this ever happened. We'll start new lives. I won't let the police arrest you."

He didn't know I'd remembered everything. I glanced at Jacob. He still hadn't moved. I had to figure out a way to get us both out of here.

Alive.

Hail clattered outside, wind howling through the open door. The burning scent of ozone was strong in my nose, the hair on my arms standing straight up. Lightning flashed behind Liam, hot bolts of yellow roaming through the air.

"You were here the night my mom was killed," I said.

"You don't know what you're talking about. Your memories —"

"You let me think I murdered her!"

"Babe, come on —"

"My coat." My mind was flying, tripping over itself. "You put it in the closet. I wore the coat to Mom's house, but the paramedics took me straight to the hospital after I was struck by lightning. I couldn't have gone home and put it in the closet. *You* did it!"

Liam shook his head sadly. "You're not well, Eva. The lightning scrambled your mind, and you don't remember anything. But I'm here to help you. I'll make this right."

Events from the past week flashed through my mind. He'd worked so hard to make me doubt myself. To make me think getting struck by lightning was making me paranoid and unreliable.

I felt a sense of vertigo sweep over me. Things I might once have chalked up to my own self-doubt and fear, I exhumed and reevaluated. That fateful meeting over dinner; how he just happened to be there when my tire blew; how he eagerly, persistently encouraged me to move in, forget the past, trust in him.

"You switched our dinner date in your calendar to the same day I was having dinner with my mom and Andrew, didn't you? And the date we were supposed to meet the priest. The faucet in the bathroom — I didn't leave it on, but you told me I did. And the living room — oh God! — *you* trashed it, not me! Did you . . . did you drug me so you could make me think I did it? Why? Were you trying to make me think I was fucked up?"

"Don't be so stupid!" Liam snapped. Sweat glistened above his upper lip. "You *are* fucked up! You would be a wreck if it wasn't for me! You should be grateful I've taken care of you all this time. I deleted the texts from your mom and hid your coat so the police wouldn't have any evidence you'd been here. Without me, the police would've already arrested you. But I've got these passports, and we can get away now, together. You don't have to go to jail."

It felt like I was watching the film of my life from a different vantage point, searching for something I'd missed at the time. Stop, rewind. Look again. Oh, there, I see it now: Vista Square Condos, where Liam owned an apartment. For the first time I could see everything as clear as day: Liam loved it when I fell apart so he could put the pieces back together.

"I didn't do anything wrong."

"You killed her, Eva. But I have a plan to get us out of here."

"Stop it, Liam!" I shouted. "I remember everything. I wasn't angry at my mom. I was angry at *you*! You were here the night Sebastian killed her. You said you put a tracking device in my purse. And you — *you* raped me."

"That is *not* what happened!" he roared. "You were sick after that man in the bar drugged you. You went out into the alleyway, and *he* was going to rape you. I brought you home and I took *care* of you. I protected you. And then we started kissing and it was magical. I *made love* to you."

I closed my eyes. "I couldn't move, I'd been drugged! But I said no, I told you to stop!"

He looked down at the floor, sheepish, and I knew I was right.

His silence was all the answer I needed.

Fury boiled inside of me, starting in my bowels, spreading through my veins and infecting my blood. I'd always thought sadness was my default state. Sadness seemed more selfless than anger, like I was holding the pain in rather than making someone else deal with the sharp edges. For years, I'd described myself that way.

I was so many other things: sad, scared, uncertain. I wrapped my emotions in a tiny box, sealed the lid, and buried them so I didn't have to confront the truth of what had happened to me. But I was never angry.

Until suddenly I was.

"You fucking raped me!" I screamed, hoping my voice would wake Jacob. But he lay silently, not moving.

"No!" Liam tried to reach for me but I slapped him, backing away until my legs pressed against the dining room table. "I swear what we shared was beautiful, special. That's why I found you again. I moved to Whidbey Island and I found you so we could be together again!"

"Why didn't you tell me the truth then? Why did you hide it?"

Liam threw his arms up in the air. "Because I was scared of being rejected, okay? But when we met again, it was perfect. You felt it too. We got to have two first times — how many people can say that?"

A rumble of thunder boomed outside, shaking the floor beneath my feet.

Anger zipped through my veins. "I hate you! You raped me, you motherfucker!"

"Stop saying that!" Liam pressed both hands to his ears.

"You raped me, you raped me, *you raped me!*"

I turned to run, but Liam was too quick. He grabbed a handful of my hair, yanking me back. I screamed as the roots tore from my scalp.

"You can't leave me!" he howled, a sweaty voice in my ear.

I fell to the floor, Liam on top of me. His fingers dug into my throat, squeezing. I punched at his chest, clawed fingernails across his hands, his wrists, trying to get away. But it was no use. His fingers were like iron.

I stabbed two fingers into Liam's eyes. He howled and fell to the ground. I kicked hard, my foot landing squarely in his groin. He made a choked *oomph* sound and curled into the fetal position. I ran to the other side of the living room. The couch blocked my way to the front door. I scanned the room frantically for anything to use as a weapon.

Liam staggered to his feet. His face was twisted with pain.

"I can't let you go!" he roared. "I love you too much, Eva!"

He practically vibrated with fear, but that didn't make me feel better; it made me feel worse. He would kill me rather than let me go.

"You don't love me. You just love controlling me, and I won't let you do that anymore!"

Headlights swept the front windows, casting streaks of light against the living room wall.

A car door slammed shut. Andrew's voice filtered in the open front door. "Eva?"

Suddenly there was a gun in Liam's hand.

A gun I never knew he had.

The thump of shoes on stairs.

The taste of blood on my lips.

The air crackling with electricity.

The wind a sharp caress on my cheeks.

My brother's startled face stared at Liam's gun.

"No! Andrew!" I leaped toward Liam, grabbing for the gun.

And then the cold, hard barrel was against my chest, and I was no match for Liam's strength. I was never going to beat him. But Andrew was there, and we were engaged in a three-way tug-of-war. Andrew used his whole body to break Liam's hold, but he stumbled, his knees dropping to the floor, leaving me in control of the gun.

My eyes met Liam's.

I could shoot him, I realized.

I could shoot him and everybody would think it was self-defense. Even Andrew would say so. I'd failed last time. The night my mom died. I had the chance to kill him then, and instead I'd run. But I didn't have to run this time.

Death at my hand was no less than he deserved. I lifted the gun, my finger tightening on the trigger.

Liam's eyes on mine were hot, tortured windows into the broken person inside. The pain of my rejection had made him unrecognizable to me.

"I love you most," he whispered.

And in that split second I realized that getting struck by lightning was more than just a close call I was lucky to survive. It had illuminated the me who'd been buried inside all along. And that woman was not a murderer.

My grasp on the trigger loosened, my arm going limp. Andrew swayed forward, his hands trying vainly to pluck the weapon from my grasp. My fingers tangled around the barrel, then released it as he wrenched it away, causing me to spin and fall forward as my knees collapsed.

The crack of the gun firing roared in my ears, a high, hollow ringing. Pain exploded in me. I was submerged in the fire of a kiln, everything raw and red and hot as the bullet ripped through my shoulder. And then I was on the floor inside a mushroom cloud of blood and bone and stringy gray beads of brain matter, the only sound that high-pitched squeal in my ears.

Something thumped next to me, the reverberations in the floor sending more shock waves of pain ricocheting through my body. I turned and saw it was Liam.

Half his face was gone.

I started screaming, but I couldn't hear a thing. Andrew's mouth was moving, silent, empty words. The world sharpened around me: a cobweb on the ceiling, the shape of the daffodils in the painting above me, the smudge across Andrew's glasses, the scrape of the carpet beneath my cheek.

Andrew ripped his shirt off and pressed it to my shoulder, trying to stop the blood. He was crying, his face splattered with splotches of crimson. His mouth flopped open and closed. Somewhere on some superconscious level, I realized I'd never seen Andrew fall apart like this.

My hearing had started returning, the sound of Andrew shouting for Siri to dial 911 just beyond the horrific whine swirling in dizzying, painful circles around my head.

Sirens pierced the air. Uniformed officers burst into the living room. Two paramedics flanked me. A stretcher was rolled out. The shrieking pain was white-hot fire licking at my very core.

"I shot him," I babbled over and over. "I shot him."

Andrew looked confused but had no time to argue. The paramedics lifted me onto the stretcher. They were carrying me outside, just about to put me in the ambulance when a cop car screeched to a stop, lights flashing. Detective Jackson slammed the door and sprinted to me, his leather jacket flapping open in the wind.

His face was white as an envelope. He touched a hand to my forehead, almost a caress.

"He tried to kill us," I whispered.

"I know," he said. "I know. I believe you."

Darkness was coming fast. Too fast. And then red. Tendrils of red and black swirling over my vision.

And then nothing.

Forty-Eight: Eva

A soft tap came at the hospital door just as Dr. Simm finished examining me.

"Come in," I called.

Detective Jackson poked his head inside. He smiled, fine lines like little half suns crumpling the corners of his blue eyes. It softened the wolfish blueprint of his face, made him seem younger, less severe. He stepped inside the door.

"All done! You officially have a clean bill of health," Dr. Simm said. "Maybe just don't leave home next time there's a lightning storm."

I chuckled. "I'll keep that in mind."

"Okay. You know where to come if you need anything." She turned to go.

"Hey, Dr. Simm?" She turned around. "Thank you."

She smiled and nodded. Detective Jackson approached my bed as she left. He lifted a bunch of white roses clutched in his hand.

"Hey there, Eva. I brought you flowers." His Boston accent came out stronger than usual in the word *flawers.*

"Oh. Wow. That's really sweet of you. Thanks."

I propped myself higher on the narrow hospital bed as he set the flowers on the counter and pulled a chair up to sit next to me.

"So." He looked at my right arm, which was heavily bandaged and resting in a sling. "The doctor said the bullet went through the front of your shoulder?"

"Yes. And out the top."

"You're acquiring quite a collection of scars there. You're lucky the bullet missed any major arteries."

"At least I remember getting this scar," I replied.

Jackson threw his head back and laughed. "Well, they do say you never get struck by lightning twice." He sobered. "So you're being discharged today?"

"Yep. All official with checkout paperwork and everything." I plucked at the blanket on my legs. Slanted rays slid through the blinds, heating the material so it was warm beneath my fingers. "Detective, why didn't you just arrest me after you found my DNA and fingerprints at Mom's house?"

He leaned back in the hard plastic chair, stretching his feet in front of him.

"Your DNA wasn't under your mom's fingernails; Sebastian Clarke's was. Plus you sent me those photos of the articles and the letter from your mom. No guilty person would do that. My gut instinct was to see what you found in London. I saw your credit card activity the minute you bought the ticket. Although I'll admit I got a little concerned when you took your SIM card out of your phone. But I had a PI following you, so it wasn't like you could go far."

The eyes I'd felt on me in London. The man at the Tube station. It made sense now. Between Liam tracking me and the PI, no wonder I'd felt so watched lately.

"I wish I'd answered your calls. I could have avoided everything that happened. Maybe Liam would still be . . ."

I could barely force the words out. I turned to stare out the window, blinking fast. A hard ache of grief pressed on my chest, surprising me. Why did I care? I shouldn't. Liam had stalked me. Oppressed me. Raped me. But I'd loved him once, and the hurt and betrayal were still raw.

"How'd you know Liam was at Mom's house the night she was killed?" I asked.

"We looked through video footage from

the Mukilteo–Whidbey Island ferry. Liam got the ferry to Seattle Sunday night, shortly after you did. Then, a few hours later, he caught the last ferry back to Whidbey Island. Obviously, that made me suspicious. When I came out to question him the other day, I took a DNA sample. I don't have the results back yet, but I'm pretty sure it'll match the DNA we found on the septic tank in your mom's backyard."

I watched the detective as he spoke, all sharp angles and quick eyes, his voice low and intense. He was exactly what I'd needed without even knowing it.

"When you e-mailed me that sketch, I told our CSIs to go back and widen the search area out from the immediate crime scene. That's when they found the trailer. There were obvious signs it had been pulled over the septic tank. And then we found Sebastian Clarke's body."

Jackson's leather jacket creaked as he leaned forward. "We'll be closing your mom's case soon. Sebastian Clarke's wounds match the fireplace poker at her house, and hers are the only fingerprints on it. And Sebastian's fingerprints were the only ones other than your mom's found on the tea canister. It all matches what you remember."

I closed my eyes, relieved. "Thank you."

"Thank *you.* And thanks for giving us permission to search your house. We found passports for Liam in various names and thousands of dollars in cash in the safe. We also found documents with the names of local building inspectors he'd paid off to let building code violations slide."

I wasn't surprised. Liam had been pathologically incapable of hearing *no.* It just wasn't in him to let anything stand in the way of what he wanted.

"There were also a number of photo albums in the safe. Mostly . . ." He cleared his throat. "Mostly long-lens shots of you."

I closed my eyes, struggling to accept the magnitude of Liam's betrayal.

Jackson slid a thick folder onto the bed. Inside were stacks of photos of me: leaving the hospital empty-handed; getting in my car; crying outside my mom's house; walking along the edge of the lake by our house; coming out of work one day; leaving a restaurant one night with Holly. My life since the night I was raped was held in this folder.

"He followed me," I said bitterly.

Jackson nodded. "I'm afraid so."

He pulled an evidence bag out of his jacket pocket and set it on the bed. Inside was an iPhone. "We found this in a locked drawer in Liam's office. The phone has an app on it called Burner. It lets the user have an anonymous number. Those threatening texts you got were from him."

I felt like I'd been elbowed in the throat. I would never be able to explain what it was like knowing my own doubt and fear had blinded me to the biggest threat: my very own fiancé.

"You know . . ." I shook my head. "I kept thinking I wasn't remembering things right. I thought I was losing my mind. And the more I thought I couldn't trust myself, the more I relied on and trusted him. It's probably exactly what he wanted me to do."

"I believe psychologists call it gaslighting." Jackson pulled a card out of his wallet, dropped it on top of the folder. ANNI DAVIDSON it said in bold black letters. "Anni's a good therapist. If you like that sort of thing."

"Thank you."

He shrugged.

"No, seriously. Thank you. For believing me."

He nodded. "Sometimes we're in control of the things that happen to us, and sometimes we're not. But what he did to you, that wasn't your fault. Don't waste any more time blaming yourself. It'll drive you crazy."

I looked him full in the face. "I was sorry to hear about your wife."

"Thank you." Jackson didn't look surprised that I knew his story. He just looked sad.

"Did you kill him?" I asked. "The man who murdered her?"

Jackson didn't blink; his face didn't move, not even a muscle, but I saw something darken his eyes. Then he smiled, a contorted twist of his lips. "I'm not the sort of person who could kill someone in cold blood."

I didn't believe him. I knew now that we were all that sort of person when pushed beyond our limits.

"What happens now?" I asked. "Will I be charged for shooting Liam?"

"Washington State law allows an individual to use reasonable force to defend themselves when they're attacked." Jackson's eyes sharpened. "It was self-defense, right?"

"Of course."

"Well, then." He smiled. "It sounds pretty clear-cut to me. And I hear the district attorney has no desire to press charges."

I closed my eyes in relief as Jackson began gathering his things.

"How's your friend doin'?"

"Jacob? He's stable," I said. "Fortunately, he has a hard head. He'll be out soon."

Jackson gazed at me for a moment. "You going to be okay?"

"Me?" I looked out the window at the mottled sky. Memories flickered before me. My brother hunched over his homework early on a Sunday. Jacob with his grass-stained knees flying down the street on his bike. Mom driving me to school on a cold, rainy morning. The squeeze of her hand as she said some of her last words, *I love you.*

"Yeah, I think I will be." I smiled and held Jackson's gaze. "In fact, I'm sure of it."

Forty-Nine: Eva

A few weeks after I got out of the hospital I was at Mom's house — home for now — slicking the last bit of gold lacquer onto a piece of pottery I was repairing. The radio was on, an old dance track by Sandra Collins playing in the background. A car pulled up outside and I peered out the wooden slats. Andrew slammed the car door shut. He walked around the side of the house, returning with a rake, and started scraping leaves into a pile.

I watched my brother move the rake in precise parallel lines. He looked older than I remembered. Lines bracketed his blue eyes, worry and grief chiseling his face. I awkwardly pulled a heavy sweater over my sling and went to greet him. The November day was crisp and clear, the sky a strip of brilliant blue.

I hugged Andrew with one arm. His brown knitted sweater smelled of rain and freshly cut apples. He straightened his glasses and returned the hug, a rare but much appreciated gift.

Andrew resumed raking the leaves, and I used my feet to drag smaller piles into Andrew's larger one. When the yard was clear, Andrew and I stood in front of the pile of leaves. With a sort of silent acknowledgment only known between siblings, we fell backward onto the pile.

We stared up as a plane bisected the sky, leaving puffy white trails in its wake. Fall leaves shivered and spun in the air, a gust of wind causing a riot of burnt orange and scarlet and sienna to sprinkle onto the lawn.

Andrew and I laughed. "Well. That was a little bit pointless!" he said.

"No. Not pointless," I replied. "Sometimes you have to clear up the mess before you can start over fresh." I elbowed him in the ribs. "So. When do I get to meet your new girlfriend?"

Andrew blushed. "Soon," he promised.

I dropped it. He'd tell me more when he was ready.

After a moment, he asked. "Are you glad he's dead?"

I thought about it. Liam had lied to me every day I knew him. He'd violated my trust, betrayed me, controlled me. But he had loved me too. That was real. Wasn't it?

I tried not to question myself or doubt myself too much these days. Most days I failed. Maybe doubt never really went entirely away. Maybe all you had to do to silence it was ignore it long enough.

"I'm . . . relieved. I don't think Liam was evil, just broken. Maybe we all are a little bit."

"I'm glad I sh—"

"*I* shot him," I cut him off. "*Me.* Remember? It was self-defense."

Now Andrew rolled onto his elbow; his eyes behind his glasses were a battleground I'd never seen before. My brother had spent his life playing by the rules, coloring inside the lines. But he was learning there were an awful lot of shades of gray in there.

"You can't blame yourself," I said. I stood and brushed the bits of dead leaves from my jeans. "Trust me. It's a waste of time."

Andrew glanced at his watch. "You ready to go? We don't want to miss the ferry."

The tires of Andrew's car crackled on the gravel as we pulled up to Liam's house. He turned the ignition off, and for a moment we sat in silence. The red Douglas fir timbers of the house were brightly lit by the afternoon sun, the lake a perfect mirror for the jean-blue sky. A sharp breeze skimmed the rippled surface. The muddy shoreline was a twisted mass of reeds and roots writhing down into the water.

"What's going to happen to this house?" Andrew asked.

"Liam named me next of kin in his will. I'll sell it once everything is finalized. All the money from his estate will go to a charity for those who've been sexually assaulted."

"Do you really need to go back in there?" he asked.

I nodded. "I need to get my cat. Melissa's been driving out here to feed her for long enough."

He sighed. "All right, come on, then."

He pushed the car door open, but I laid a hand on his arm. "I think I need to do this on my own," I said.

He nodded. I stepped out of the car and my shoes crunched across the gravel to the front door; I was trying not to think about the last time I was here. I was glad it was daytime, the sunlight making everything shimmer.

Inside, I stood in the middle of the living room, letting memory after memory assault me. Liam's hands gently massaging my feet. The tender caress of his fingers on my cheek. We could sit and talk for hours and it felt like minutes. I had loved him, and I knew he'd loved me too. Just not in the right way.

"Why did I love him, and trust him?" I'd asked my therapist in our last session. "Shouldn't I have known on some level he was my rapist?"

She'd leaned forward so I was forced to look her fully in the eye. "Trust involves a unique juxtaposition of a person's loftiest hopes and deepest fears. You were deeply, deeply hurt, but you still wanted to be loved. You just needed to learn to love and trust yourself first. Don't be afraid to give yourself permission to accept both the love and the betrayal. You're allowed to trust all your emotions, not just the easy ones."

I went to the garage and lifted Fiona Hudson's urn from my work desk. Using kintsugi to mend it had taught me so much: that true repair requires transformation, that our full potential is impossible to see until a crack opens us up.

Ginger came running when I opened the door and called for her. I tucked her into a cat carrier, grabbed my art nouveau lamp, and left. I didn't look back.

On the way to the ferry, Andrew stopped by the Crafted Artisan so I could say good-bye to Melissa. She'd just returned from the lunchtime yoga class, her legs lean, arms sinewy under her *I Am a Warrior* T-shirt.

"It's so good to see you!" she said, hugging me warmly. "And your hair, oh my God, it's gorgeous!"

I'd dyed it back to its natural mahogany red. It had grown out a little, the waves flicking along the collar of my shirt.

"Thanks. How've you been?"

"Oh, you know!" Melissa rolled her eyes. "Claire wanted lessons on the tuba. I think she likes a boy in band class or something. So I got her a private tutor, but every time he's over she suddenly needs to poo. Like, blowing makes her need to have a shit! Last week she was in the bathroom for half an hour. That's half her lesson, for Christ's sake!"

I laughed. Melissa never changed. It was refreshing.

"And, big news, I've reinstated Claire's weekend visits at her dad's house."

"That is big news!"

She shrugged. "She's been asking, and so has he. He's still her dad and he loves her. I have to make the best choice for her, right? I guess I'll see how it goes. What about you? Are you staying in Seattle, then?"

"For now," I said. "I have so much work

coming in lately."

The truth was, I didn't have to work right now. There was enough in the savings account Mom had for me in London. That was what Andrew hadn't wanted to tell me about the will without the lawyer being there to explain. But I found kintsugi therapeutic, the pottery I repaired a canvas for my scars. And I was busy. It turned out people loved the art of kintsugi as much as I did.

"I called that gallery in Seattle about their spring art exhibit," I said. "I asked if they'd be interested in displaying a few of the pieces I've repaired with kintsugi, and they said yes."

"That's fantastic! I'm so proud of you. Oh! Before I forget — !" Melissa dug in her purse and pulled out a blue ribbon. "Mr. Ayyad wanted you to have this. He won that race last weekend. He dedicated his win to you."

I grinned and took the ribbon. "That's so sweet! I'll visit him next time I'm back."

"So . . . Eva Hansen." She gave me a hesitant smile. "Or is it Laura?"

I hesitated. "I used to be Laura."

"Are you going to change it?"

I think having two childhoods, two identities at such a young age gave me a warped sense of identity. I didn't know who I was supposed to be for a really long time.

But I did now.

"No. I'm Eva."

FIFTY: EVA

Andrew and I released Mom's ashes into Puget Sound on the ferry home. It was hard to describe how painful saying good-bye was. Like she'd slipped through my fingers.

I wanted more time, just a little bit, to tell her I loved her. To say thank you for everything.

Afterward, Andrew dropped me off at home and I drove myself down to the beach to build a bonfire.

It wasn't easy. The pain in my shoulder was still pretty bad, but a crapload of kerosene and some dry kindling got the fire going fine.

It had been a beautiful day. One of those November days that makes you feel like winter will never come. A child's moon dangled low in the sky, floating against a strip of blue that hung opposite the sinking sun, two personas inhabiting one body. I sat in front of the flames and opened the folder

Detective Jackson had given me.

I fed the pictures into the flames. And in that moment, I was fine. Everything was fine. And sometimes that's all you can ask for. Fine.

The heat from the fire warmed my face and I leaned back to stare at the sky. The moon lit the world in ethereal shades of pale yellow, the velvet-black tapestry littered with pinprick stars.

In my head I drew the lines connecting the five stars of the Big Dipper, remembering that they came from just one cloud of gas and dust, yet formed one perfect constellation. Just like me. There were so many parts to me. Scared. Brave. Insecure. Worthy. But that was okay.

I looked down at the empty space where Liam's engagement ring used to be. Maybe he'd buried me, but I was a seed. My shell was cracked, but that meant I could grow.

I stared at the creamy glow of moonlight on the horizon, and Mom's words that last night at the restaurant floated down to me.

We can be strong and brave and broken and whole all at the same time.

Later that night, Jacob knocked on the front door. He was wearing a green windbreaker and ripped black jeans. He smelled clean, like freshly laundered clothes and peppermint gum. His dark hair was shorn close to his skull, a ragged scar visible at the back.

"Hey," I greeted him.

"You ready?" he asked.

"Yep."

Jacob raised an eyebrow.

"Okay, I'm a little nervous," I admitted.

He shrugged as I locked the front door. "It'll pass. Just like a kidney stone."

I laughed, the feeling a glorious relief, like when you get all the lights green on your way to work. A string of good luck.

A light breeze from Puget Sound kicked up, the air fresh, like it had been washed clean. We walked slowly to Lily's house. He moved this way now, a little stiffly. He was in physical therapy to regain full use of his right arm, but the remnants of his loose-limbed walk were still there.

"So you're going to London this Christmas?" he asked.

"Yeah. David's chemo went really well, and he's invited me to stay. I thought it might be a good chance to get to know him."

We'd reached Lily's house, but as I stepped up the stairs, Jacob tugged on my hand. His face was earnest and open, a sailor looking to the night sky.

"I'm not going anywhere this time," he said. "Whatever happens, I'm here."

"I know. Thanks." I hugged him, and for a moment we just stood there in front of each other, breathing. One day maybe we'd explore these feelings more. But for now, I was learning to be strong on my own.

Lily opened the door wearing a floaty pink skirt and a fuzzy, white cardigan. Her hair was immaculately cut into a precise silver-platinum bob. Her eyes were red-raw, the skin around them swollen and puffy.

"Eva!" She started crying and pulled me into a tight embrace. "Oh, you poor thing. And poor Kat. I miss her terribly." Lily pulled away and sniffed. "Come in, love. Come in."

Lily sat on one of the couches. Jacob and I sat across from her. I looked around the living room. It was exactly the same, the décor fresh, a clean white, with cream-colored couches, wicker chairs, and splashes of teal highlights. Like being near the ocean.

"Aunt Lily . . ." I began. *"Rose."*

Lily's hand fluttered to her throat, her eyes darting between Jacob and me.

"How do you know?" she whispered.

"Mom told me before she died. It just took me a while to remember."

A range of emotions stormed across her face.

"Why didn't you tell me?" I asked. "You lied. Both of you. About my whole life!"

"They say that behind every lie is a person and a reason. Please understand." Her voice was thin, tremulous. "We wanted to keep you safe. And later, when you grew up, it seemed too late, and we thought we'd lose you if you knew the truth."

She looked down, but left her hand on my arm. The hot skin of her fingertips was warm through the fabric of my shirt. There were more words in her fingertips than she ever could have said out loud. She revealed the depth of everything in that one touch.

"I wish I'd known. Maybe I would've understood." Tears clogged my throat. "She always seemed so . . . cold. I thought Andrew was her favorite, that I had done something wrong. And now . . ."

A tear slid down my cheek into the crevice of my chin.

"Now you're worried your relationship will be frozen the way it was. But you mustn't think that way. She loved you *so much.*" Lily leaned forward. "I'm so sorry."

"Why didn't you want me?" I asked quietly.

Lily's face blanched. "I did! More than

anything. I *never* wanted to stop being your mum. I would never have chosen that, I swear!"

"Then why didn't you come for me?"

"I did. But by the time I found you, you already had a life without me. Kat was your mum. I didn't want to upset that. I had been so selfish, made so many wrong choices, but I wanted to do what was best for you. Kat gave you structure, and I gave you laughter and fun. You got the best of both of us." She reached out to touch my cheek. "Sometimes things happen and you can't go back and do them over. You can't change them. All you can do is keep moving forward."

I met Jacob's eyes. He had said the same words not too long ago. He gave me a sad little smile.

"You turned into a wonderful, resilient young woman. Watching you grow up, being your friend instead of your mum, it's been hard, but it worked out. Right?" She was pleading with me, her eyes hot on mine.

For a moment I didn't know what to say. My words now would dictate our future relationship.

I thought of Mom taking me from London to keep me safe, and me running away from my past, giving up my daughter to a better life. I thought of David, who'd decided to let me go, and Charlotte, who'd kept her baby.

All we could do was keep trying, keep going, keep doing our best no matter the circumstances.

"It's okay," I said. "I get it."

Lily blew out a long, shaky breath. She slapped her hands onto her knees and stood. "I have something for you."

She took a small, square envelope from the mantel over the fireplace and handed it to me. I lifted the flap. Inside was a piece of paper clipped to a picture. The paper had an address in Oregon jotted on it.

I tugged the paper clip off and looked at the picture. It was of a little girl about three years old. She was sitting on a carpet of foamy puzzle pieces. The bedroom behind her was decorated in pink and gray, with white wooden floorboards, and pictures of bunny ballerinas on the wall. Her red hair hung in tangled waves down her back. She was looking up at the person taking the picture, smiling, her charcoal-gray eyes bursting with happiness.

Tears welled in my eyes as I imagined all I'd given up. The dewy softness of her head in my palm. The weight of her body against my chest, her hair like silk against my face, her breath on my cheek smelling of honey. I imagined her as a toddler, learning to pull herself up; watching her as a child flying through the park on her bike; and then later, holding her veil as she prepared to walk down the aisle.

"Kat said you regretted giving her up," Lily said. "I'm very good at finding people. Lots of experience, you see. I tracked down her adoptive parents. If you want . . ."

I traced my daughter's face, the beam of her smile, the light in her eyes. I didn't see Jacob or Liam in her. I just saw myself.

She was so happy. Who was I to take that away?

I looked at Jacob. His eyes were rimmed with red, hot with an ache I understood acutely. But something else was there, too. Forgiveness. Acceptance. Love. I realized something then. We aren't defined by our tragedies, by our history, by our mistakes, but by pieces of love and sadness and happiness, and the whole range of human emotions we feel.

Despite the trauma, or perhaps because of it, I had become who I was supposed to be. The moment sprinkled down on me like warm rain, filling my cracks. In a world of bad breaks — broken hearts, broken promises, broken dreams — I'd somehow managed to create the most beautiful future out of my very broken body.

I slid the photo and the address back into the envelope and laid it on Rose's fireplace mantel.

In my mind, I held my little girl in my arms, hugged her close to my chest. And then I let her go.

Finally, I was whole.

ACKNOWLEDGMENTS

This book took me on an interesting journey, but there are two people who really made *Behind Every Lie* possible: my agent, Carly Watters, and my editor, Kate Dresser. Carly, thank you for your perfect blend of patient guidance and cheerful honesty. And Kate, thank you for taking my story and making it a book. Your insight and vision has taught me so much and I am incredibly grateful.

Thank you to the phenomenal team at Simon & Schuster and Gallery Books for giving my book babies wings. And to Crystal, Taylor, and the team at BookSparks, thank you for your enthusiasm and for giving my books the reach I hoped for.

Thank you to my son Adam, who is such a massive cheerleader and takes a huge interest in my writing and my career. It inspires me to know that I inspire you, Adam. And thank you to Aidan, my littlest, most charming little man, who constantly gives me funny things to add to my books. I love you both.

I'm eternally grateful to my husband, Richard, who is always my first reader and biggest champion. From making dinner to doing laundry to keeping the kids occupied so I can write, you've worked as hard as I have to complete this book. Thank you for pushing me to achieve this dream, and for supporting me as I reach to achieve more.

Authors are nothing without the other authors who've supported them. Thank you to Heather Gudenkauf, Mary Kubica, Kimberly Belle, David Bell, Claire Douglas, Alice Feeney, and Jenny Blackhurst, and so many other writers who've kindly read and championed my books and just been such a wealth of information throughout this crazy writer journey I love so much.

Thank you to Lisa and Michael, who've patiently answered so many bizarre police and detective questions without even flinching a single time.

And most of all, thank you to all my readers, reviewers, and book bloggers. I wouldn't be here without you and I am forever grateful to every one of you who has bought a copy, shared a review, or posted a picture of *Behind Every Lie.*

■ ■ ■ ■

Behind Every Lie

CHRISTINA MCDONALD

■ ■ ■ ■

This reading group guide for *Behind Every Lie* includes an introduction, discussion questions, and ideas for enhancing your book club. The suggested questions are intended to help your reading group find new and interesting angles and topics for your discussion. We hope that these ideas will enrich your conversation and increase your enjoyment of the book.

INTRODUCTION

Eva Hansen wakes in the hospital after being struck by lightning and discovers that her mother, Kat, has been murdered. Eva was found unconscious down the street. She can't remember what happened, but the police are highly suspicious of her.

Determined to clear her name, Eva heads from Seattle to London — Kat's former home — for answers. But as she unravels her mother's carefully held secrets, Eva soon realizes that someone doesn't want her to know the truth. And with violent memories beginning to emerge, Eva doesn't know whom to trust. Least of all herself.

Told in alternating perspectives from Eva's search for answers and Kat's mysterious past, Christina McDonald's *Behind Every Lie* is a "complex, emotionally intense" (*Publishers Weekly*) domestic thriller that explores the complicated nature of mother-daughter relationships, family trauma, and the danger behind long-held secrets.

TOPICS & QUESTIONS FOR DISCUSSION

1. We know from the outset that Eva's mother, Kat, is dead, but the author chooses to open the book with Eva and Kat at a celebratory dinner together. How would you describe their relationship based on this single interaction?

2. Detective Jackson appears fixated on Eva from the start as the prime suspect in her mother's murder. What do you think of his investigation tactics? Do you think he is being insensitive to Eva's recent and past trauma, or is he simply doing his job?

3. Eva describes Liam as the perfect man. Discuss the way he treats Eva after she is struck by lightning. What is your initial impression of Liam? Do you find him kind and protective or overbearing?

4. Kat and Rose's friendship has an unorth-

odox beginning. Describe their different parenting styles as seen in chapter six. Are the friends similar in any respects? With such differences, how does their relationship work?

5. We learn about Kat's husband, Eva's father, in one of Kat's flashbacks. Discuss Sebastian and Eva's relationship. Why did Kat stay with him? How is his behavior different around Eva? Why can't Kat discuss their relationship with Rose?

6. Eva goes to dramatic lengths to remember the night her mother was murdered and to learn the truth about Kat's past. With her innocence in question and relationships on the line, why do you think she took such huge risks? She has accepted losing memories before; what is different about this experience? Why fight so hard to get these memories back and not the others?

7. In chapter fifteen we learn more about why Eva doesn't trust the police. How would you feel if you reported a crime and were treated as Eva was? Despite her past experience, she still tries to share what she learns with Detective Jackson. Why is she

so forthcoming? Would you trust the police to get it right in this instance?

8. Everyone seems to doubt Eva's memory loss, and with her own brother questioning her role in their mother's death and memories gradually returning, even Eva begins to suspect herself. Before you finished the novel, how involved did you think she was in Kat's death? Would you still want to know the truth if you were responsible?

9. Since Eva was struck by lightning, it appears that she has experienced some psychological side effects. She has been moody, aggressive, and paranoid. How does her reaction when Liam tells her she's trashed their living room fit in with these behaviors? Do you believe Liam's version of events, since Eva can't remember anything?

10. When Rose returns from the dead, Kat decides it is still best to keep the truth from Eva. What do you think the right thing to do is? Does Kat make this decision for Eva or for herself?

11. Discuss the differences between Eva's

relationship with Liam and her relationship with Jacob. Why does Eva finally walk away from Liam? What inspires her to tell Jacob the truth about the baby?

12. Upon Rose's return, we learn the truth about the day the first Eva fell from the window. How might things have been different if Kat had told Sebastian this twenty years ago? Why does she choose to tell him when he finds her?

13. When Eva's memories finally return, she learns the truth about more than just the night her mother died. What aspects of her memories shocked you most? Were you able to predict any of what unfolds by the novel's end?

14. Discuss the new relationships Eva forms with David and Rose. Do you think her relationships with them will change the way she views the people who raised her? How will the truth about her past change her relationship with Andrew?

15. The Japanese art of kintsugi is a recurring theme in Eva's life. How does it tie back into her discovery of the truth? Do you think understanding kintsugi will

influence Eva's healing and how she moves forward?

ENHANCE YOUR BOOK CLUB

1. Eva's whole life is turned upside down after her mother is murdered. The more she learns, the more lies she uncovers. Discuss how you would deal with these kinds of life-changing revelations. How would you process them?

2. Both Eva and Kat dealt with serious trauma in their lives. They are survivors. Discuss the way each of them handled these experiences. Describe their personalities. What does Eva learn from her mother? What have your parents taught you about surviving hardships? What have you picked up from them subconsciously?

3. Imagine that you, like Eva, have lost your memories from a critical moment in your life. Discuss what that would be like. How far would you go to recover those memories? If you knew that a traumatic experi-

ence had robbed you of those memories, would you still want to get them back?

ABOUT THE AUTHOR

Christina McDonald is the author of *The Night Olivia Fell,* which has been optioned for TV by a major Hollywood studio. She has worked for companies such as *USA TODAY, The Sunday Times* (Dublin), and Expedia. Originally from Seattle, Washington, she has an MA in journalism from the National University of Ireland Galway, and now lives in London, England.

The employees of Thorndike Press hope you have enjoyed this Large Print book. All our Thorndike, Wheeler, and Kennebec Large Print titles are designed for easy reading, and all our books are made to last. Other Thorndike Press Large Print books are available at your library, through selected bookstores, or directly from us.

For information about titles, please call:
(800) 223-1244

or visit our website at:
gale.com/thorndike

To share your comments, please write:
Publisher
Thorndike Press
10 Water St., Suite 310
Waterville, ME 04901